NEXUS

D1077953

The Androma Saga

Zenith

Nexus

SASHA ALSBERG & LINDSAY CUMMINGS

NEXUS

THE ANDROMA SAGA

HQ

This novel is entirely a work of fiction. The names, characters
and incidents portrayed in it are the work of the author's
imagination. Any resemblance to actual persons, living or
dead, events or localities is entirely coincidental.

HQ
An imprint of HarperCollins*Publishers* Ltd
1 London Bridge Street
London SE1 9GF

This edition 2019

1
First published in Great Britain by
HQ, an imprint of HarperCollins*Publishers* Ltd 2019

Copyright © Sasha Alsberg & Lindsay Cummings 2019

Sasha Alsberg & Lindsay Cummings asserts the moral right to be
identified as the author of this work.
A catalogue record for this book is
available from the British Library.

ISBN: 978-0-00-822837-8

MIX
Paper from
responsible sources
FSC
www.fsc.org
FSC™ C007454

This book is produced from independently certified FSC™ paper
to ensure responsible forest management.

For more information visit: www.harpercollins.co.uk/green

Printed and bound by CPI Group (UK) Ltd, Croydon CR0 4YY

All rights reserved. No part of this publication may be reproduced,
stored in a retrieval system, or transmitted, in any form or by any means,
electronic, mechanical, photocopying, recording or otherwise,
without the prior permission of the publishers.

This book is sold subject to the condition that it shall not, by way of trade
or otherwise, be lent, re-sold, hired out or otherwise circulated without
the publisher's prior consent in any form of binding or cover other than
that in which it is published and without a similar condition including this
condition being imposed on the subsequent purchaser.

From Sasha:

To my mother,
who I know is watching from the stars.

From Lindsay:

To my dad, Don Cummings.
Thank you for being the ultimate bookworm in my life.

Waltham Forest Libraries

904 000 00648285	
Askews & Holts	21-Jun-2019
TEE	£7.99
6066998	

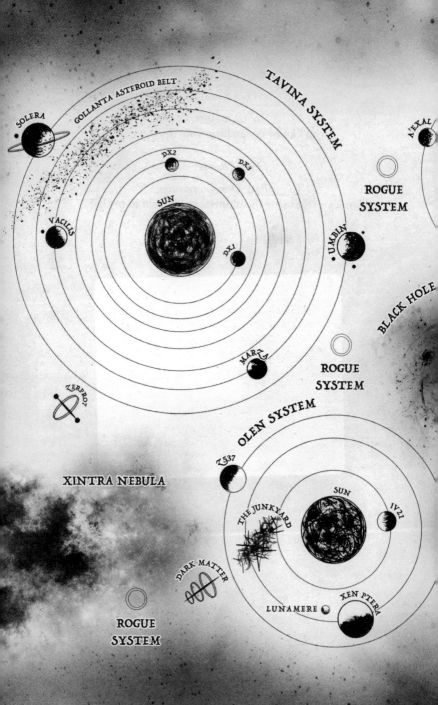

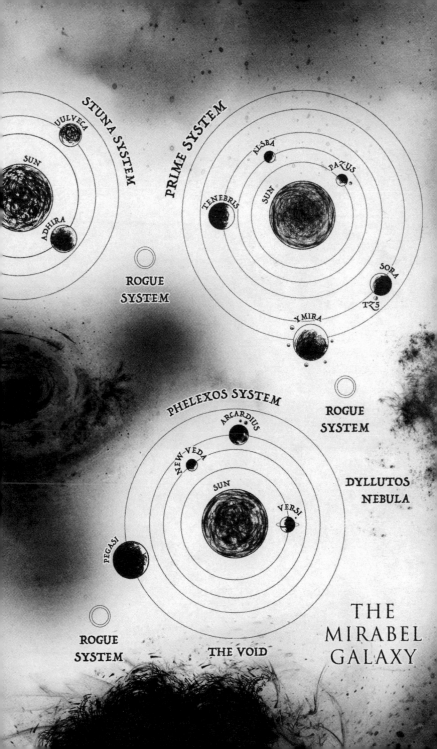

CHAPTER 1

DEX

Dextro Arez had never truly believed that the Godstars were tangible beings.

They were soul-felt, a comforting presence inside your heart, an idea that filled your mind as if soldered on with iron and fire. Always nearby, yet as far away as the stars in the night sky.

Dex's body was tattooed with the Godstars' white constellations; a living shrine to their power and strength. Here, on his left arm, were the twisting, intertwining patterns that symbolized the twin Godstars of life and light. And on the back of his right shoulder, stretching up toward his neck—the angular constellation that marked the godstar of hope.

But tonight, as Dex slumped forward in his chair, the thick, rigid lines of the godstar of death stared up at him from his left hand. The tattoo stretched out like a narrowing eye as he clenched his fist. Dex looked away from it, swallowing hard. He felt as if death were truly here—a beast breathing down his neck as he turned his gaze to Androma's pale, still form.

Andi had been unconscious for nearly a week now. Dex knew that it was due at least in part to the painkillers they'd given her for the wound on her chest—a parting gift from the traitorous Valen Cortas, who'd turned his blade on her after stabbing his own father during Queen Nor's attack on Andi's home planet, Arcardius.

But Dex also wondered if Andi's mind just wasn't ready to return her to this world yet, too terrified by what had transpired in the moments before Valen tried to kill her. And if that were true, how long would it be before she came back to them?

Wake up, he pleaded silently as he watched her. *We can't do this without you, Andi.*

Whatever *this* was, Dex wasn't quite sure. The fate of the entire galaxy had changed, the hopes and dreams of so many melting away into the shadows the moment Nor Solis took control. They'd all assumed that the Cataclysm had destroyed the threat of Xen Ptera forever; that the final battle had drained the planet's resources and broken the will of its people and their queen. No one had ever imagined that Queen Nor would someday rise again, or that she'd somehow have the ability to bring all of Mirabel under her dominion.

There was only one person who might have the power to free the galaxy from Nor's rule—and yet completely unaware that the lives of millions now rested in her hands.

Wake up, Andi, he thought again.

She looked so frail as she lay on the soft white medical bed now, lost in sleep. Dex winced as he imagined what she likely saw there.

Nightmares.

Never dreams, not anymore.

The harsh lights of the med bay bounced off of the silver plates implanted across Andi's cheekbones as Dex leaned back, stretching his aching muscles. He'd hardly moved from this spot since they'd fled Arcardius, determined to be by her side when she finally awoke. Determined to be the one to tell her all that had happened...even though he couldn't yet find the words to do so.

Dex closed his eyes, remembering that fateful night. Remembering the desperate words of Cyprian Cortas, the former General of Arcardius, as he lay dying in this very med bay.

The fate of the galaxy is at stake. The leaders are dead, and I'm sure their successors soon will be, as well... Androma is the only Arcardian on this ship once I die. If she survives... Androma Racella will be the rightful General of Arcardius.

General of Arcardius. Leader of the planet that had once wanted her dead. Godstars, how she would hate the very idea of it.

Dex sighed heavily and shifted his chair closer to Andi, tentatively grazing a hand against hers. The warmth of her skin was soothing, that small sign of life the only thing that made the knot of tension inside him loosen in the slightest. He studied the thick white bandage on her chest, just below her collarbone. Hidden beneath were the dark stitches that held her skin together. Mending the flesh that Valen's knife had torn apart. Dex had seen and inflicted plenty of wounds, some far more gruesome than this. But seeing Andi in such a state brought back a wave of memories that sent his head spinning out of control.

Valen Cortas stood before Andi at the Ucatoria Ball, blood dripping from the knife that he'd just plunged into her chest. Andi fell to her knees, grasping for the hilt with shaking hands, wrenching the blade free. Then she swayed, and the knife tumbled to the ground as Andi collapsed, surrounded by a growing pool of her own blood.

He was too late. For a heartbeat, Dex thought she was dead. All around him, the room was growing quieter, the screams dying down. A few more shots here. A few more there. The thump of a body hitting the floor. The click of another silver bullet sliding into a rifle's chamber.

Dex finally reached the stage. The system leaders were huddled together in their chairs, bodies of Patrolmen littering the ground around them. But Andi was the only person he had eyes for.

"Hang on," Dex said to Andi. His fingers found her throat. A tiny heartbeat beneath her skin. "You just hang on."

Dex blinked at the sound of Andi's sudden groan.

He realized he'd been squeezing her hand too hard. The ends of his fingernails, ragged from chewing the past few sleepless nights, were biting into her palm. He let go at once, but leaned forward all the same, unable to look away from her face.

"Andi?"

Her eyelids fluttered.

For a moment, Dex feared she was dying. That her stitches had become infected, or the blood that Lon had donated in the few precious moments after their escape had mixed wrongly with hers, universal donor or not. Perhaps even the godstar of death, still so hauntingly present in this room, was laughing as he raised a shadowy scythe and readied himself to bring Andi to the other side.

But then her eyes opened.

Gray as a storming sea.

Dex let out a whooshing breath that he hadn't even realized he'd been holding.

"Hey," he said, feeling the tightness flood from him, gone in an instant. "How are you feeling?"

"Dex?" For a moment, Andi simply looked around, as if trying to make sense of her surroundings. She seemed calm, just a person waking from a sound night of sleep.

Then her eyes slowly moved to lock onto Dex's, and confusion seemed to sweep through her as her forehead wrinkled.

"What…happened?" Andi asked. Her voice was raw from disuse, a whisper trying to break free into something more.

"You're alive," Dex said, unable to stop a smile of relief from spreading across his face. "You're safe."

"Safe?" Andi asked. She tried to sit up and groaned, a hand flying up toward the white bandages covering the knife wound in her chest.

This was the most awake she'd been in days. Dex took a deep breath, reaching for her hand, still unsure of how to explain it all to her. She may have been gravely injured, but she wasn't a child. She wasn't weak in her heart or her soul. She could handle this, though it might come close to breaking her.

"There was an attack on Arcardius," Dex said. "During Ucatoria. Do you remember?"

Andi's eyes hardened.

"Nor Solis…she came, and…" Dex's words trailed off. How could he explain what had happened? How could he tell her that an entire ballroom of people he'd thought dead had suddenly risen and pledged allegiance to the very woman who'd attacked them? The very woman they'd all feared, *hated*, for nearly ten years?

Worst of all, how could he tell Andi that her crew was among the dead-then-risen who had joined Nor's side?

"Where is Lira?" Andi asked suddenly. "Breck and Gilly?"

Dex's heart nearly stopped beating. He opened his mouth, but no words came out.

And then he saw Andi's expression change as she remembered, the memories slamming into her, making her recoil away from him.

"My crew," Andi croaked out, voice still raw. He handed her a cup of water. She gulped it down greedily.

"Androma," Dex pleaded. "I tried. I tried to get to them, but…there was so much chaos. So many enemies. And you were *dying*."

Her eyes were wide with fear and rage. Her entire body had begun to shake. "Where. Is. My. Crew?"

She sat up so suddenly he couldn't stop her, the lurching movement so rough that she cried out in pain. The cup clattered to the floor. Her hand became a vise over Dex's, his fingers crushed beneath hers. She gritted her teeth and swung her legs over the edge of the bed, facing him head-on, and pain flared in her eyes as red began to blossom against the white of her bandages.

"Where are they?" Andi asked. "*Please*, Dex. Tell me where they are."

"They're…" How could he be the one to break her with such news? He'd only just earned back her forgiveness mere days ago, after years spent hoping to find a place in her heart once more, and now he'd betrayed her again. He was a coward. A failure, for not being able to save her crew before Nor had overtaken them. "Godstars, Andi. I'm so sorry. We left them behind."

He hated the words the second they fell from his lips, but what was he to do? He couldn't hide a damned thing from her. She'd already seen the answer in his traitorous eyes, and that the moment she left this med bay, she'd find the ship cold and empty, Lon the only other soul aboard.

"No," Andi mouthed. So silent, Dex could hardly hear the word. She shook her head, disbelief flooding her features, darkening the half circles beneath her eyes. *"No."*

"There was no way for me to get to them in the aftermath of the attack," Dex said, his voice choked. "The last I saw, they were alive. But they were… Andi, they joined with Nor."

Everyone in that Arcardian ballroom had. Everyone but Dex and Andi and a few others, but Xen Pterran soldiers had slaughtered those other people at once.

He'd never forget the way that Andi's fierce crew had fallen. How they'd risen again, and hailed Nor as their queen. Leaving them behind had pained him, still haunted him.

He would relive that day forever in his heart and in his mind.

"We have to go to them," she insisted. Before he could open his mouth to respond, Andi was on her feet, the loose gray pants she wore swishing as she whirled and stumbled for the door.

NEXUS

"Andi!" Dex lunged toward her. "Stop!"

She slammed the red exit button beside the door, then wobbled and nearly dropped to a knee, gasping in pain. But she recovered as the door opened, the silver hallways of the *Marauder* waiting beyond. Dex leaped in front of her, arms outspread.

"You have to *rest*," he said. "You're going to rip open your stitches even more. Valen almost reached your heart."

Andi looked down at her chest, as if just noticing the wound for the first time.

"I wish he *had* reached it," she said, eyes wide and reddening with tears that Dex knew she wouldn't shed. "I don't want to live without them."

Already, her blood had soaked through the bandage. Andi wobbled, leaning against the door frame. She had too many pain meds in her system. She hadn't eaten in days. Dex didn't even know how she was still standing.

"Move," she growled. "Please, Dextro. Before I move you myself."

"Don't you think I want to?" Dex asked. "Andi, I've hardly slept since we left them behind. I've hardly eaten, hardly done *anything* but sit by your bedside and relive that night in my mind."

Gilly. Lira. Breck.

They'd become important to Dex, too. And he'd betrayed them, betrayed Andi, by leaving them behind. Even Lon, normally so gentle and calm, had looked as if he'd wanted to kill him when Dex arrived on the *Marauder* with Andi and the general in tow, but without Lon's twin sister, Lira.

Why had it all fallen to Dex? He couldn't change the tide of this war alone.

He swallowed hard. "There's nothing we can do. *Nothing.* You weren't conscious. You didn't see what happened to them. You didn't see how they *changed*."

Dex reached out to grab her shoulders, to guide her gently

back to the bed, but Andi screamed in fury, slamming the wall with her fist as she stumbled away from him.

"Damn you, Dextro. Get the hell out of my way!"

"Please," Dex begged. Already he could feel the weakness inside of him, that hideous fear of losing her again when he'd only just gotten her back. "Please, just let me help you. There's nothing you can do for them, Andi. Not before you rest and *heal*."

"You can't do this to me," she whispered. Her voice shook. "Please, Dex. You can't hurt me like this."

"I'm trying to protect you." *Because I love you*, Dex thought. But the words failed him, and his hands fell to his sides.

"I don't want to be protected," Andi said. "Not now." She turned around, shoulders slumping as she pressed one hand to her chest and shuffled back toward her bed, breathing heavily.

Dex ached, seeing her this way. He ached because he was a traitor to her, a traitor to her crew. But there was no way to save them. Not now, at least. Maybe not ever. He still didn't know how Nor and the Xen Pterrans had taken control, or what was in those silver bullets, or if there was any way to reverse what had been done to everyone's minds.

And he had no idea how far and how wide Nor's reign had spread in the days since they'd fled Arcardius. For all Dex knew, Nor now had control of the entire galaxy.

"I swear to you," Dex said, trailing Andi across the room. "I swear on my life, Andi, we'll figure out what Nor did to your crew. We'll figure out a way to get to them. We just have to—"

Andi whirled around, her face a mask of pain as she swung her fist at him.

Dex ducked reflexively, but the hit connected at the last moment. He gasped at the pinch of pain in his neck. Then a languorous warmth flowed through him, as if he was sinking into the hot springs of Adhira.

Dex reached up slowly, dreamily, his fingers clumsily removing the empty syringe buried in his skin. The same syringe that had just been sitting on the bedside table, left there by Lon, should Andi wake in too much pain. The syringe full of *soduum*, a potent pain medication.

"Why?" Dex gasped. But he should have expected something like this. The syringe fell with a soft *clink* to the floor, and Dex followed, hardly aware as his knees hit the ground. He knew he only had moments before the *soduum* would steal him away. Warmth swam through his veins, too fast for him to ignore, already beckoning him to enter the folds of deep sleep.

He heard gentle footsteps and ragged breathing as Andi stepped closer. When he looked up, her features were already melding together, fuzzy at the edges as she stood over him, her chest bleeding bright red in the stark med bay lights. A trickle of blood seeped out from the wrappings, staining her shirt as it slid down her abdomen.

"I'm sorry, Dex," Andi said, her voice like a funeral dirge as his head hit the floor. "There is no *me* without *them*."

When she left the med bay, she was no longer Androma Racella.

The Bloody Baroness stepped into the halls of the *Marauder*, a captain who would tear apart the skies to rescue her crew.

CHAPTER 2
ANDI

Everything hurt.

Andi's bones ached, her muscles screamed, and the wound in her chest pleaded for her to stop moving. But images of her crew flashed within her mind, propelling her endlessly forward through the silver halls of the ship.

If she could just get back to Arcardius...she knew she would find a way to save them.

Lira. Breck. Gilly.

Dex's words echoed in her mind as she stumbled into the small hallway leading toward the bridge, reverberating through her skull as she held her palm up against the blue access panel to the right of the door.

They joined with Nor.

Andi shook her head, willing away the treacherous notion.

Her crew would *never* join with the queen of Xen Ptera, no matter how threatened. But what had Dex said about them... *changing*?

Then the door slid open, and all thoughts were driven from her mind as Andi darted inside, quickly scanning her palm on the interior access panel and entering a command to seal off the bridge. She exhaled, for what seemed to be the first time since she woke up, as the door slid shut behind her. It wouldn't keep Dex out forever—after all, the ship *had* been his for years—but he'd still have a hell of a time getting in here once he came to.

For a moment, Andi rested her forehead against the cool metal of the door, which was at such odds with her flaming flesh. She closed her eyes and took a slow, deep breath, then turned to look at the row of seats where her crew had once sat.

Seats that were now so terribly empty.

Her vision, once murky from the drugs, slowly started to clear as Andi made her way toward the front of the bridge. A groan slipped its way past her lips when she finally sat down in the pilot's seat. It felt so wrong sitting there, as if she were taking the space that had always belonged to Lira. A space that she had no right to claim, after what had happened to Kalee. But Andi pushed her discomfort aside, replacing it with the fierce need to get her girls back. How she felt about piloting didn't matter—not when their lives were at risk.

That was, if Queen Nor hadn't killed them already.

Even as the thought crossed her mind, she vanquished it immediately. They were alive. They *had* to be. She couldn't afford to think otherwise; couldn't deal with that pain. It would hurt more than being skinned alive and slowly burned until her bloody flesh crisped over.

She had to save them, even if she got herself killed in the process.

Trying and dying was better than not trying at all.

With every second counting against her, Andi willed her aching arms up onto the console and slowly, painstakingly entered the coordinates for Arcardius. The navigation holoscreen began to flicker before her eyes, highlighted by the swirling, shimmering clouds outside the varillium walls of the ship.

The dense fog of color obscured Andi's view of the stars, and the sight of it sent a shiver of dread down her spine. "Memory?" she asked breathlessly.

The soothing female voice of the *Marauder*'s control system came to life around her. *"How may I assist you, Captain?"*

"Where exactly are we?"

There was a long pause before Memory responded. *"The navigation system is currently off-line. I am unable to determine our precise location at this time."*

Andi stared at the dancing whorls of pink and gold mist, a sudden suspicion dawning. "Memory, what was the destination of the last hyperspace jump?"

"The last coordinates entered were for a location just outside the Xintra Nebula."

Andi's hands began to shake with rage. Her ship was inside a damned nebula. A massive pocket of space filled with gases and debris that rendered the *Marauder*'s tracking and navigation systems utterly useless. A place only the most skilled pilots could hope to fly through without losing their way.

And not just any nebula—the Xintra Nebula. Clear across the galaxy from the Phelexos System, and Arcardius. As far away as she could possibly be from her girls.

Andi choked out a humorless laugh. She was going to murder Dex when he woke up.

The sound of a pounding fist on the bridge's door made her jump, sending a wave of pain crashing through her body. A muffled shout echoed from the other side. "Andi, please, let me in!"

The unfamiliar voice had Andi rising from her seat and instinctively reaching for her twin swords. She cursed softly when she realized that they were likely still in the med bay, and began scanning the room for another weapon. Surely Gilly or Breck had stashed a gun in here somewhere.

The person outside hammered on the door again, more urgently this time. "Andi, it's Lon. Open the door! We need to talk."

Andi's knees went weak with relief. *Lon*. She'd forgotten that Lira had arranged for him to be moved onto the *Marauder* during the Ucatoria Ball, to speed the crew's departure from Arcardius after they finished their guard duties for General Cortas. He must have already been on the ship when Dex brought her on board after the attack.

And, most important, he was an ally. Surely Lon wanted to rescue his sister just as much as she did. Together, the two of them could convince Dex to pilot them out of here and back to Arcardius.

The anger and adrenaline that had carried her thus far was quickly dissipating, though, and the distance to the access panel suddenly seemed a lot farther than it had earlier. Andi sank back into the pilot's seat, cursing under her breath at the state her body was in, and said, "Memory, unseal the damn door before Lon pummels it to death."

The bridge door slid open with a *hiss*, and Lon entered cautiously, a wary expression on his blue face. Andi raised an eyebrow at him and turned back to the holoscreen, which was flashing with an error message. She swiped it away and brought up a diagram of the Mirabel Galaxy, projecting it into the air around them.

"We're in the Xintra Nebula," Lon said, pointing to the dusty pink cloud that hovered in space between the Olen and Tavina systems.

"Yes, I'd gathered that already," Andi remarked dryly. "And why, exactly, are we *here*, when my crew—when your *sister*—is on the other side of the galaxy?"

Lon looked weary as he sank down into the seat that was usually Breck's. "We're here because Queen Nor is *also* on the other side of the galaxy. Along with her army of mind-controlled minions."

She blinked. "Excuse me? *Mind control?*" Even saying those two words sounded ridiculous. "What the hell are you talking about?"

He sighed in exasperation. "Seriously, Andi? Didn't you let Dex explain *anything* before you knocked him out?"

Andi felt her temper rising as heat flooded her cheeks. "He left my girls behind, Lon. I wasn't exactly in the mood to listen to anything he had to say."

"He didn't have much of a choice. If he'd tried to rescue them, too, we'd probably all be dead or under Nor's control now." Lon shook his head and rose to his feet, holding a hand out to Andi. "Come on. Let's head back to the med bay. You're bleeding all over the place, and we can try to wake Dex up. He was there—he can tell you what happened much better than I can."

For years, Andi hadn't allowed herself to rely on anyone but herself and her crew. No one else had proved worthy of her trust, and even when it came to Lira, Breck and Gilly, Andi vastly preferred being the one guarding their backs.

So as she and Lon made their slow trek to the med bay, Andi was mortified to find herself leaning on him more and more, unable to stand upright on her own. She gritted her teeth in frustration and tried to will some strength into her legs, but the effort was useless.

"There's no shame in accepting help, Andi," Lon said gently. "You nearly died, and you've been heavily sedated for almost a week now. I'm surprised you were even able to make it to the bridge in the first place."

Andi stumbled to a halt as a wave of shock washed over her. She could feel the blood draining from her face as she turned to look up at Lon. "I've been out for a *week*?"

He caught her as she swayed, then guided her the last few steps toward the med bay. "Andi, I don't think you realize how badly you were hurt, how much blood you lost before Dex managed to get you and General Cortas onto the ship."

"Wait," Andi said, her mind reeling with confusion as Lon raised a hand to the access panel beside the med bay door. "The general is here? Cyprian Cortas is on *my* ship?"

The mere thought of that man here, aboard her ship when her girls were not, made Andi's blood boil.

"Was," Lon said. The door slid open, revealing Dex's muscular frame sprawled out on the floor. Lon entered the med bay swiftly, kneeling down and shaking his shoulder roughly. "He died shortly after we left Arcardius."

Andi braced herself on the door frame, trying to gauge how she felt about the general's passing. Cyprian Cortas had been a cruel, ambitious man, but he'd also been one of the greatest generals in the history of Arcardius. And he was the father of the girl she'd once loved like a sister—the girl she'd failed to protect.

Kalee.

The sound of Dex's groan pulled her away from her dark thoughts. She watched, feeling slightly guilty, as he stirred and raised a hand to his neck, wincing when he touched the spot where she'd stabbed him with the syringe.

As Lon helped him sit up, Dex's dazed brown eyes slowly rose to meet Andi's. She held his gaze for a moment, hesitating, wondering what he was thinking. Then his lips quirked up into a half smile, and he said, "I know I needed the sleep, Baroness, but you could have just suggested I take a nap."

His tone was teasing, but Andi could see the underlying sadness and worry in his eyes. She tried to keep her voice light as she asked, "And would you have actually listened?"

Dex ducked his head, but not quickly enough to mask his pained expression. "Probably not. You know I've never been very good at that."

A pang of remorse filled her chest, adding to the gradually worsening ache from her wound. "Me neither," Andi admitted.

He looked up at her incredulously, hope filling his face. Andi tried to smile at him, but it turned into a grimace as a stabbing pain coursed through her. She sucked in a breath through her teeth as Lon stood and hurried to her side.

"You *both* need to rest," he said sternly, steering her back toward the bed she'd woken up in. "And you likely need some new stitches. But I think you might try to stab us with something worse than a dose of *soduum* if you don't get some answers soon."

"You're not wrong," Andi replied weakly, easing herself onto the mattress with Lon's help. Dex clambered to his feet and made his way to her bedside while Lon peeled away the blood-soaked bandage on her chest. Andi glanced down and hissed at the sight of the angry-looking gash.

"Another scar to add to my collection, courtesy of that bastard Valen Cortas," she said darkly.

"That description of him is truer than you might imagine," Dex said, settling into a chair next to Andi's bed as Lon hurried to fetch the supplies he needed to tend her wound. "Considering he's not the son of Merella and Cyprian Cortas."

Andi stared at him, certain she'd misunderstood. "Come again?"

"Well, Cyprian *is*—or rather, was—his father," Dex clarified. "But his mother...his mother was Klaren Solis."

Andi's jaw dropped. *"What?"* she yelped. "But...that means..."

Dex nodded. "That he's Queen Nor's half brother, yes."

Before she could fully process the horror of that thought, Lon returned with a needle, some surgical thread and bandages. He coaxed Andi back onto the pillows and began repairing the damage she'd done to her wound as Dex filled in the rest of the story, telling her what the general had revealed during his dying moments.

How Klaren had somehow bewitched him during the years

she'd lived on the Cortas estate as his prisoner. How she'd become pregnant with his child—a son he'd always feared would someday inherit his mother's strange abilities. A son he could never trust, could never name as his heir.

A son who was half–Xen Pterran—or perhaps something else entirely.

"So Valen and Nor have some kind of compulsion ability?" Andi asked as Lon finished smoothing the new bandage into place.

"Judging from what happened during the Ucatoria Ball, I'd say definitely," Dex said, his expression darkening. "All those people who were shot... I thought they were dead. But they weren't bleeding. The room should have been full of blood, but there was hardly a drop. And then..." He shuddered, as if he were reliving the memory in his mind. "They started to rise. And when Valen told them to bow to their queen, they just... did. Without question."

"The girls, too?" Andi whispered.

Dex nodded jerkily, and Andi looked away, her eyes welling. She breathed in deep, once, twice, holding back the tears that threatened to fall.

Tears wouldn't save her crew. Tears were a weakness she couldn't afford.

"We have to go back," she said. "We have to free them."

"It's not that simple," Lon interjected, shaking his head. "We have no idea how Nor and Valen are controlling them. How they're controlling *everyone*. We can't just go flying back to Arcardius and hope for the best. We need more information. We need a plan."

"They *want* to be there, Andi," Dex added, taking one of her hands in his. "Or at least they think they do. They'll likely fight us if we try to take them away from Nor."

She didn't want to believe their stories of that night. But their faces were haunted, as if, even though they wished it weren't true, they could not escape the reality of it.

The thought of leaving the girls in Nor's clutches broke her heart. Valen and the Xen Pterran queen could be torturing them right now, or forcing them to do the most horrific things. But Dex and Lon were right—they'd never be able to rescue her crew if they got themselves killed in the process.

Andi squeezed Dex's hand and nodded decisively. "So we find a way to free their minds and come up with a plan to get them out."

"And then?" Lon asked.

Andi allowed an icy smile to spread across her face. "And then the Bloody Baroness will go hunting."

CHAPTER 3

VALEN – *THREE WEEKS LATER*

Valen's fingers twitched as he paced the floating garden that had once been the favorite haunt of his younger sister, Kalee.

Half sister, he reminded himself. Now that he was back on Arcardius, Valen found it all too easy to get lost in the memories of his past. A past in which Kalee had been the only bright spot; the only person he'd truly cared about. Merella, the woman he'd once believed to be his mother, had always been distant with him, never quite embracing him with the same warmth she'd given Kalee in abundance. And his father…

Well, now he knew the truth. Now he knew why Merella had never loved him, and why his father had always hated him.

The air was crisp today, a reminder that the cold season was approaching. With the first frost, the verdant plants and jewel-like flowers of this garden would turn a frothy blue, a sign of hibernation. They would spend the five months of the cold season frozen between life and death—held in limbo, just like Valen had felt for his entire existence.

Until Nor.

The only reason Valen stayed on Averia was because he loved his other half sister. The floating mountain that was home to the Cortas estate had always felt like a prison to him, and even now, with the Cortas family gone, his memories of them continued to hold him captive. But Nor had rescued him from his false life. She had saved him by giving him a name.

Not Cortas, but Solis.

He owed her everything, for the way she'd allowed him to see the truth of who he really was: a man with compulsion in his blood, with a rightful claim to a life that was so much richer than the one he'd always known, but never truly felt part of. And even though *he* held control of the minds across Mirabel... Nor was his true queen.

With every moment that passed, with every new soldier that set out across Mirabel to spread the Zenith virus, more minds were added to Valen's nexus of connections. At first, he'd felt the exact moment when each silver bullet hit its target. The bullets contained a serum that Nor's two-headed scientist, Aclisia, had perfected back on Xen Ptera. She'd somehow replicated strands of Valen's DNA and used them to create a virus that forever linked the minds of its victims to his own, leaving them vulnerable to his compulsions.

The noise had been too much to bear at first.

The first few connections during Valen's training on Xen Ptera had nearly overcome him. Nor had supplied traitors and criminals for him to practice on, and he'd often lost himself to their dark thoughts in those early days. Darai, the ancient adviser who'd served Nor all her life, had assisted with Valen's training in the beginning, but Valen hadn't been able to tolerate his condescending nature for long. Nor had taken over then, and eventually, Valen had learned how to control his power.

Over time, he discovered a way to quiet the minds, to lock them away in their very own realm, so that when a new mind was added, it was simply background noise. He'd strengthened the mental boundaries around that realm, building walls around those other minds, until they were contained in an impenetrable fortress that rivaled the obsidinite prison he'd once been trapped in on Lunamere.

And then, finally, there was silence.

Now he need only hear the minds when he pleased. And with the help of the Zenith virus, Valen could reach them from anywhere in the galaxy. He compelled them to serve Nor, their true queen—no matter the cost.

Hiding away again, little brother?

His sister's teasing voice cut through the birdsong in the garden. It entered his mind like a warm, comforting blanket, soothing Valen in a way nothing else ever had. He'd come to love their connection, his power feeding off it every time they spoke into each other's minds.

On Xen Ptera, they'd shared a life together—two years spent honing Valen's powers. And all the while, his heartless father never came looking for him. Valen had once cared about pleasing the general, but now he knew that hope had been futile. Foolish, and utterly pointless. His father had never been capable of loving him, of feeling pride in his son.

Now all he cared about was pleasing Nor, and making up for the time they'd each lost to their tainted childhoods—Valen a prisoner to his father, Nor a prisoner to her pain and grief.

Now they could delight in their shared freedom.

I'm not hiding, Valen thought back to Nor, a smile spreading across his face. *I'm simply avoiding a certain adviser who gets on my nerves. Whenever Darai calls a meeting, you can guess what my next move will be.*

Valen could practically see his sister rolling her golden eyes on the other side of their link. She knew he felt a strong dislike for the old man. Darai reminded Valen of his father—something about his face, or perhaps the darkness in his eyes. He always felt like Darai didn't think he was good enough, *worthy* enough, to be so closely linked to his precious Nor.

Valen suspected that part of his distaste was due to the history Darai and Nor shared. The old adviser had practically raised Nor, and she saw him as an uncle, albeit one who frequently irritated her. And during all their years together since Nor's birth, they'd never had to pretend that Mirabel was all that mattered. They'd always known the truth, while Valen was still playing catch-up.

With a scowl, he tossed a rock into the pond across from him, startling a purple-eyed creature lazing at the water's edge. It scampered away, fading into the overgrown foliage, and Valen followed its path until his eyes landed on the massive silver ring floating beyond the garden, just visible through the trees.

Nexus.

The monstrous satellite had become Nor's new obsession in the wake of their takeover during the Ucatoria Ball. Engineers, scientists and workers had been laboring around the clock these past few weeks, perfecting every angle and plane of the device that would amplify Valen's compulsion ability, sending his message to every corner of the galaxy.

The True Queen of Mirabel is Nor Solis. Protect her, honor her, worship her cause.

It was a massive undertaking, but Valen had every faith that his sister would see it done. Nor was a woman on a mission, and when she set her mind to something, she was unstoppable.

Her voice in his mind drew Valen's focus back to the present. *Avoiding is the same thing as hiding, brother. Shouldn't you want to be here for this? It'll be fun!*

Define fun, Valen thought, sending the message through their mental doorway. A muscle at his temple twitched, the twinge of a headache coming on. Valen sighed and rubbed his forehead with paint-stained fingers.

Another headache? Nor asked. Even through their mental link, he could sense her concern. For ever since Nor took control, and the galaxy was swept up in Valen's compulsion…he'd changed in so many ways.

He was more powerful than he'd ever been, but he was also *tired*. The kind of bone-weary exhaustion he couldn't quite shake.

It's just stress, Valen thought back to his sister. *Probably brought on by the medical droid you've had following me for two days now. Which, if you haven't noticed, has mysteriously disappeared.*

Her silence told him that she knew she'd been caught. He sighed as Nor backed away from the door between their minds, sending him a final image of the scene before her. A makeup artist with deep blue eyebrows was dabbing something colorful onto her cheeks, helping her prepare for the speech she'd be making in a short while.

You look beautiful, sister, he thought. *The people will fall in love with you all over again when they see you on the feeds today.*

Valen felt Nor smile just before the link faded. He knew she was worried about him, but there were so many other things Nor needed to focus on right now.

Like the Unaffected attacks.

It was something Valen had feared from the beginning, after he'd learned that some wouldn't be affected by his compulsion. Their numbers were slim, if Aclisia's extensive testing of the Zenith virus was anything to judge by. For every hundred that fell to Valen's compulsion, bowing to Nor despite their original feelings toward her, only one resisted. So despite his unease, he'd never truly thought they'd be able to *fight back*.

But barely a week into Nor's reign, a group of Unaffecteds had banded together and destroyed the military barracks on

Tenebris that housed many of the newest recruits to the cause. Valen had felt the moment those minds beneath his compulsion had died. As if they were matches snuffed out. There one moment, gone the next.

It happened again, mere days later, on Adhira. A small but organized group of Unaffecteds had emerged from the jungle sector of the terraformed planet and struck down the communication towers. Nor's video feed, which was on a constant loop across the galaxy, had been cut off for half a day's time.

Though news of more attacks continued to trickle back to Arcardius from every corner of Mirabel, it wasn't enough to strike terror in Valen's heart. No, it would take a lot more than that to break him. But he saw the way Nor's hands were often curled into fists. How her lips, normally smooth and polished, had crusted over with small scabs, from biting at them in her sleep. The last thing she needed was to spend even a single moment worrying about him.

Valen needed to stay strong for her. The Unaffecteds would fall eventually, when they ran out of steam. When they realized that the galaxy was beyond saving. And sending Nexus into the sky was the best way to achieve that, to ensure that Valen's compulsion would be sent out across the galaxy forevermore, even long after he was gone.

Sometimes, Valen could scarcely believe what they had already accomplished; how quickly the galaxy had fallen beneath their joined hands. Having a scientist of Aclisia's caliber on their side had been vital to their success in that regard. It had been her idea to send out the orbs full of tainted rain as soon as they'd seized control of Arcardius.

A war does not always require soldiers, she'd said, showing Nor and Valen how the weapon would work. Thousands of silver droplets falling from the skies across the galaxy, unleashing the Zenith virus upon all nearby.

So quickly, the Solis reign began.

So easily, the weak-minded Mirabellians had fallen beneath Valen's compulsion.

Valen shivered a little as the wind blew through the treetops now, drawing the leaves down from the canopy overhead. They were a beautiful shade of purple and blue at their edges, the colors swirling together as they tumbled in the wind.

This garden, once a place he'd used to escape the darkness of his past, had grown brighter under the light of Nexus being built nearby. Even with the chill of winter soon to come, Valen felt almost cozy, safe in his own skin as he lay down by the water's edge, his head on a thick pillow of moss imported from one of the garden satellites outside the Prime system.

Nor would do well with her speech today. The Unaffecteds would see her, and they would tremble in their hiding places. Nexus would be finished on schedule, and all would be resolved soon enough.

Of that, Valen was certain.

He yawned, his headache pulsing a little harder as he closed his eyes and let his consciousness slip deep into the confines of his mind, seeking the one place that was safe and sound and entirely his own.

Dark clouds.

A fortress made of night.

Iron bars that ensured no one else could enter. Only he belonged.

The velvety moss a cushion against his head, Valen allowed himself to relax, to remember the first time they met—a moment of hope and light after the twisted darkness of Lunamere. And as he fell deeper and deeper into his mind, losing himself in the memories, he hardly noticed the twin droplets of blood that slipped from his nostrils, a deep crimson against his pale skin.

CHAPTER 4
NOR

Power. She had always had it, but now she *was* it.

The Mirabel Galaxy bowed to Queen Nor Solis. Its inhabitants worshipped her, and there wasn't anything that could disrupt what she and her brother had created.

Or so she'd thought.

"What do you mean the Unaffecteds are *winning*?" Nor hissed at Darai as he stood in front of her in his gray robes. He winced at the venom in her voice. "There's no war for them to win. Their numbers are few and scattered. Their attacks on us have been pathetic at best."

Still, the mere mention of the Unaffecteds had her bristling, an unwelcome blight on her morning. No reign was meant to be perfect, if history was told true. But Nor could still imagine it: a galaxy that did not dare, not even a single person, to defy her.

"Look left, please, Majesty," the makeup artist whispered. Nor tilted her head slightly, and the man brushed a shimmering dust across her cheekbones. "Lovely," he said, smiling as he dabbed his brush back into the palette. The effect, she knew, looked heavenly, but it did nothing to ease her frustrations.

Nor tried to reach Valen again, but the doorway between their minds was empty, as if he'd backed away from it. He had likely withdrawn to his mind castle, where even she could not travel, exhausted as she was from the past several days.

Valen's compulsion abilities were far more powerful than Nor's. She'd known it from the moment she met him in Lunamere. But the constant strain of compelling so many minds at once was taking its toll on him. She saw it in his thinning arms and his emaciated frame, as if he hadn't eaten in weeks. Dark circles bruised the skin beneath his eyes, and though he smiled often in her presence, it wasn't quite the same as it had been before.

He's strong, she reminded herself. *He will continue to be strong, because he knows what's at stake.*

And because Nor couldn't do what Valen did. It was why she'd needed him for this mission of theirs. Nor's compulsion worked in small, subtle ways. She could get someone to lend her an ear longer than they would have liked. She could ease the tension in a room. But when it came to controlling, to truly holding someone's mind hostage...only Valen had inherited that strength from their mother's bloodline. Somehow, Nor had been passed over in that sense.

It had given her a reason to hate her mother for many years—until she'd discovered that Valen existed. Until that moment, in his cell in Lunamere, after so many years of anticipation and training with Darai, when Nor was able to compel Valen not to fear her. To listen to her, and eventually, to understand the truth of his lineage.

She prodded at the mental doorway again, seeking his presence. But she knew he was likely working, as he always was, on continuing their reign. So much for listening to her speech.

It's worth it, Nor told herself, pushing aside the protective tendencies she felt toward her younger half brother. *You must give Valen his space, so he can better serve your cause.*

"Are we nearly done?" the producer asked. He stood across the room, his four arms crossed over each other with impatience, and Nor almost commanded Darai to remove him from her presence. But he was good at what he did, having filmed her himself before they'd even left Xen Ptera. He'd created the loops that were even now broadcasting on the feeds across the galaxy, a constant reminder of her presence.

They'd had to prepare much ahead of time, knowing how swiftly the Solis reign was to sweep across the galaxy. Valen's compulsion did what it needed to do, ensuring that the people obeyed her. But Nor wanted them to *love* her. To be obsessed with her, incapable of escaping her voice, her name, her image.

So from the moment she'd taken charge, the video loops had begun. Even now, one of them was being displayed down in Veronus, the capital city of Arcardius, far below the estate Nor now called home. The feed was in every glittering shop window, every home and every warm, packed bar where she knew the Arcardian citizens, now her loyal soldiers, proudly proclaimed their adoration for her.

"My art takes time," the artist said, raising a blue brow as he chose another shade. "You would be wise not to press me."

Nor smirked at that, and decided she'd keep the artist as her personal attendant from here on out. Not only for his skill in enhancing her beauty, but also for an attitude worthy of her court.

Behind the artist's intricate pile of braids, another face could be seen.

Zahn.

He stood in the corner of the room, conferring with several of the personal guards he commanded on her behalf. His gaze flickered in her direction for a moment, and he smiled lovingly when his warm, brown eyes met hers. They glowed against his dark skin, familiar and inviting. Nor gave him a small smile in return, her heart warming at the reminder of his presence. Zahn was always there to support her when she needed him the most.

With a sigh, Nor turned her attention back to Darai. Her adviser and honorary uncle wore the trademark frown she'd seen so often of late, further accentuating the scars marking his wise, ancient face. Sweat beaded on his upper lip as he scanned the speech documents he'd prepared for Nor just this morning.

"It's unfortunate news about the Unaffecteds, Majesty," Darai said. "But Zahn and I had a meeting with Aclisia just this morning, and she assured us that we are still on course for Phase Two. Construction of Nexus is continuing on schedule, and Aclisia is making considerable progress on her efforts to adapt the Zenith virus for use in the satellite transmission system." He paused for a moment, then added, "And I feel inclined to remind you that we expected there to be some…" Darai waved a hand, as if searching for an explanation just out of reach. "…some *flaws* when we unleashed the virus on the galaxy."

"Yes, yes," Nor snapped impatiently. "But we never expected these Unaffecteds to have banded together so quickly. It's been less than a month, and they've already shown considerable coordination and strength."

"Laughable strength, Majesty," the producer said. When Nor turned to glare at him, he seemed to realize he'd spoken out of turn, and shrank back into the shadows of the room.

Nor looked back to Darai. "We never anticipated that they would have such finesse in the *way* they're attacking. It's as if they're being led."

Zahn interjected before Darai could respond. "By whom?" he asked. "A shivering child? Their attacks are pathetic." He moved to stand behind Nor, resting his hands on her shoulders. "Their attempts are merely a fear tactic, and one that has already been dismissed. We've imprisoned all the Unaffecteds we've been able to find, and we've heightened our security measures at every military base on the capital planets. They won't find it so easy to resist for much longer."

Zahn's touch and reassuring words soothed her somewhat, but not enough to dispel the anxiety Nor found herself feeling more and more every day.

"You look like you're in pain," Darai said. "Smile, Nor. This problem will be solved soon."

"And the problem of Valen?" Nor asked suddenly, thinking again of her brother's health.

Darai gave a curt nod. "The boy is pushing himself to his limits. But I have seen power like his before. He will endure."

Nor met her uncle's gaze. They both knew where Darai had seen such things before. Abilities like Valen's, like their mother's, weren't found among any of the many races that populated Mirabel. No—that power hailed from somewhere else, a place that was as yet out of their reach.

But not for much longer. Not if their plans came to fruition, as Nor hoped.

"What if he doesn't?" she asked. "We cannot push him so far that we lose him. I won't do that to my brother, and our mission will fail without him."

Darai frowned, then turned away to busy himself with something across the room.

Nor sighed and ran her golden prosthetic hand across the dark wood of Cyprian Cortas's old desk as the makeup artist resumed his work. The old General of Arcardius had been dead for weeks now, thanks to Valen. It was the greatest gift she could have offered her brother, allowing him the honor of murdering the man who'd caused them both so much pain.

As soon as they'd risen to power, Nor and Valen had ordered the servants to clear away the old photographs and family paintings. They'd burned them out on the lawn, the tower of smoke rising high in the sky above the floating mountain estate. All traces of Cyprian Cortas were now gone from Averia—except for the late general's desk.

That, she'd kept as a reminder to herself. A reminder that she'd made this galaxy hers.

She planned to expand upon that dream, and the Unaffecteds would not stand in her way.

"There is also the matter of the Unaffecteds being incapable of coming out of hiding," Nor's uncle said smugly. He signaled the producer to come forward. The man stepped from the shadows, and Darai snatched at one of the man's four arms, holding it out into the light.

Silver veins spiderwebbed their way across his skin. They were beautiful; like artwork in their own right.

And a perfectly executed side effect of the Zenith virus, generally appearing a few days after the infection fully settled in. Any who were affected practically glowed with it, like moonlight swimming just beneath the surface of their skin.

"That *was* a clever trick of Aclisia's," Nor said, admiring the man's veins.

She herself did not bear them, nor did Valen or Darai. Their minds were still free, rooted to the cause since the beginning of their time in Mirabel.

Nor looked down at Zahn's hands, still resting on her shoulders. He, too, lacked the silver veins, for she knew beyond the shadow of a doubt that he was utterly committed to her reign.

And to her happiness.

"The Unaffecteds will have to come out of hiding eventually— to gather supplies, to recruit," Darai said. "And when they do, they'll be discovered, captured and made ours."

Nor nodded, smiling at that.

"Just a bit more, Majesty," the makeup artist said as he uncapped a tiny pot of Nor's classic crimson lip stain. Behind him, camera drones bobbed in the air, while attendants perfected the lighting.

It was no wonder Valen wished to hide away from such things. He was content to work in the shadows. But Nor lived for her time to shine beneath the bright lights.

"All done now, Majesty," the makeup artist said, standing back to admire his work. "You're a vision, as always."

He held up a small mirror for Nor, earning another good mark for himself. She scrutinized her reflection carefully. The artist *was* talented, but even he couldn't conceal the stress that added a certain darkness to Nor's expression. Her lips, rouged as always, were beautiful, but she held them in a frown, and she could still faintly see the bite marks she'd created in her sleep. Her eyes, normally vibrant as the stars, looked dimmer than they had in months past. But her hair, thank the Godstars, hadn't been affected by the stress. It was perfectly curled beneath a crown made of deepest crimson, bits of gold embedded below its sharp points.

"Beautiful," Nor said, tilting her head this way and that. "Thank you, Tober."

The man bowed and backed away behind the bright lights. Zahn stepped back as well, allowing Nor to stand from her chair.

"Beautiful indeed," he murmured, leaning in to kiss her cheek. Nor felt herself glowing in the light of the appreciative look in his eyes as he smiled at her once more before joining Tober.

Nor busied herself with sweeping the wrinkles from the front of her gown as Darai joined her. "The Unaffecteds will bow in fear soon enough," he said. "Just say the lines we practiced."

Nor felt a flash of irritation. "I have done this before, Uncle."

"Back on Xen Ptera, yes. But not like this. Not as the True Queen, wearing her rightful crown," Darai replied.

Nor smiled with satisfaction, turning toward the screen the newscaster droids had erected so that she could watch herself in real time. That rightful crown glinted atop her head in the bright spotlights, shining like a beacon that would inspire every mind across the galaxy.

"Ready, my dear?" Darai asked. He shuffled away at her nod of dismissal, joining the others behind the lights.

Nor took a deep breath and clasped her hands together in front of her. She stood tall, the crown heavy atop her curls, the weight of it like a promise.

She would not bow to anyone. But *everyone* would bow to her.

"Cameras rolling in 3…2…1…"

Nor looked ahead at the camera drones bobbing in front of her and began her speech.

"People of Mirabel." Her voice was steady. Hypnotic, in the way she'd learned to speak to draw their attention. The way her mother had spoken, years ago. It was one of the few memories Nor still had of her—Klaren's voice carrying out like a melody, beckoning all to join her tune.

Nor saw herself on the screen now, just as the rest of Mirabel surely saw her. Regal. Terrifying. All because of Valen's compulsion, far stronger than Nor's ever could be. "I come to you as your queen, asking you to join me in working even harder to build the future we all wish to attain. We must be vigilant in our efforts to complete Nexus, and to root out all those who wish to defy our cause." She paused momentarily for effect. "With your help, by moon's end, we will finish the construction of Nexus, and a new era will rise."

Nexus. It held all of her hopes and dreams for the future.

A massive satellite being built on this very floating mountain, large enough in diameter to rival a small planet. When it was launched into space, it would be the key to everything, sealing her claim on every mind across Mirabel.

And giving her access to the weapons systems on every planet in the galaxy.

It was awe-inspiring, a tremendous creation that would take

weeks, still, to build. Resources and ships and workers from all over Mirabel had come together to construct it, and when it was completed…

Nor could already taste her victory.

She could almost see Nexus working already, channeling Valen's compulsion to the farthest corners of the galaxy. Transmitting the command for all the other capital planets to launch their missiles toward the Void that hovered in space just beyond the outer reaches of the Phelexos System.

To everyone else in Mirabel, the Void was just a swath of darkness, a place where the light of the stars couldn't reach. But Nor knew better. She knew what lay beyond that Void, just waiting for her to open the door. To blast a hole through that darkness to reveal what was hidden on the other side; the very thing Nor's mother had spent her entire life failing to reach.

Exonia, Nor thought, the word like a balm to her soul. The galaxy Klaren truly hailed from, a galaxy of people who had spent years suffering the same fate as those on Xen Ptera, trapped in a dying world with no hope of escape.

She would follow in Klaren's footsteps, but she would not fail like her mother had. With Valen at her side, no matter the cost…they would succeed.

Nor took a deep breath and continued her speech. "I urge you not to falter—"

The screen across from her flickered, then filled with a static so thick that for a moment, Nor lost sight of herself. She paused, waiting impatiently as the newscaster droids scrambled to fix the connection, the producer commanding them about. But the static only worsened. It had never been an issue before, even when they were filming aboard Nor's ship, hurtling through hyperspace toward Arcardius.

"A momentary lapse in the connection," the producer said, his four hands worrying at each other. "I'm certain we'll resolve it shortly, Majesty."

Annoyance flickered to life in Nor's chest, a little flash of heat she forced herself to ignore. Then, almost as suddenly as it had begun, the static faded. Nor rolled back her shoulders and smiled once more, ready to continue her speech.

But as the image sharpened, Nor realized it wasn't *her* on the screen any longer. Her blood went cold at the sight of a massive, shadowed figure emerging from a cloud of darkness.

"What in the hell is that?" The producer's voice squeaked from behind the bright lights. Nor could hear a commotion, the sound of stomping feet as he shuffled around to get a better look at the main screen, but Nor remained frozen, fixated by the image before her.

Someone had hacked into the live feed.

It should have been impossible, with all the firewalls and security measures they'd put into place just this morning, in light of the Unaffected attacks. Nor's skin prickled, her body rooted to the spot as she stared at the screen, wishing she could release the command to shut it all down, to banish the beastly figure from her sight.

But when a single blue light illuminated the massive figure's suit of armor, the words failed her, as if she'd swallowed them whole, along with the lump in her throat.

Nor knew that bloodred armor well.

She'd seen it in her nightmares for years. The spikes protruding from the shoulders, the crimson electric shield covering the soldier's body. A shield that sent out impassable currents, melting bullets in their tracks and preventing enemy blades from piercing a fatal vein.

This armor had been crafted for the soldiers from New Veda, the fierce giants who'd taken up arms with the Unified Systems against Xen Ptera so many years ago. An ancient and dented red helmet, with smoke stains marring the metal, concealed the soldier's face from view. Black designs were etched into the armor, a network of lines that looked like a spider's web.

"What is this?" Darai hissed. All around him, droids scrambled to regain control of the live feed. "Contain this situation, right now, before I…"

His voice trailed off as the soldier spoke.

"This message is for those whose minds still belong to them."

Sweat moistened Nor's palms as fear wrapped itself around her throat. *Valen,* she thought. *Valen, where are you?*

But the doorway was still empty, her brother beyond her reach.

The soldier's words sounded robotic. Horrific. They were spoken in a deep male voice that came not from Arachnid himself, but from a spiderlike droid perched upon his shoulder. The droid's twelve legs, silver and jagged as knives, dug into Arachnid's armor. Four red lights shone on the center of its body like unblinking eyes.

"You are not alone," Arachnid said. With each word, the droid's red eyes flashed and the video feed flickered. Arachnid and the droid turned to pixels, then formed fully again. *"Much of the galaxy has fallen to a false queen, but there are still many who have not. To the strong, to those who continue to fight for freedom—I am Arachnid. And I stand as leader for all those who refuse to bow to anyone's will but our own."*

The droid's knifelike legs clicked as it flexed and dug deeper into the armor. The entire time, Arachnid stood still. A broad-shouldered demon hidden beneath the color of blood.

"Find me. Together, we will build an army. Together, we will destroy the false queen."

Arachnid took a step toward the camera, red armor clanking like a battle ax hitting bone, and Nor felt the weight of his invisible stare land on her.

"You cannot compel me, Nor Solis. I know what you plan to do. I

know the horrors you will unleash, and I will stop you before it's too late. Even if I have to drive the killing blade into your chest myself."

The screen flickered a final time.

Then it faded to black.

CHAPTER 5
ANDI

"You know, carrying out this mission seemed a whole lot easier when we first started planning it," Andi commented, staring at the holograms of various rescue plans that hovered above the varillium coffee table. They lit up the main deck of the *Marauder*, casting shadows against the walls adorned with Gilly's drawings.

Morbid as the drawings were—most of them were made up of stick figures missing limbs or, Gilly's favorite artistic choice, stick figures missing their heads—looking at them made Andi's chest ache.

And not just because of the still-healing wound from Valen.

She missed her crew more than ever before. She missed seeing Breck in the kitchen with Alfie, talking about the latest and greatest recipes from around Mirabel. She longed to see Lira seated at the table in the corner of the main deck, working on homemade Sparks. Gilly would have been peering over her shoulder, eager to learn any way to wreak havoc on the world.

And speaking of Havoc…

Andi's gaze fell on a pair of jagged orange claws that just barely poked out from beneath the sofa, ready to ensnare an ankle. Gilly's bloodthirsty puffball of a feline had grown increasingly problematic in the weeks without its owner, destroying cables, gnawing through the foot of Dex's cot and leaving piles of stinking waste all over the engine room.

She was beginning to wish that the Fellibrag had been left behind on Arcardius, but naturally, Gilly had made sure Havoc was safely tucked aboard the ship before assuming her guard duties at the Ucatoria Ball. And now it was up to Andi to make sure Gilly's beloved pet somehow survived the next few weeks, until they could come up with a plan to rescue her and the other girls.

"Getting the mission done is always the hard part," Lon said, drawing Andi back into the conversation at hand, smiling morosely as their eyes met. His fingertips trailed dangerously close to the edge of the Adhiran cowhide couch, where Havoc swatted and missed.

Andi leaned back into the cushions, sighing deeply. The wound on her chest no longer hurt when she breathed, which was the only positive progress she seemed to have made in the three weeks since she'd awoken.

Andi knew she was being overly dramatic, and that they weren't completely at a dead end. A few days ago, they'd finally had their first breakthrough. Dex had managed to secure a connection to the galactic feed, which was essential to their plans.

Unfortunately, that connection had only confirmed their worst fears.

The world they once knew was far gone. Endless propaganda now littered the feeds, Nor Solis the figurehead of this new world. Her reign of compulsive power had spread to every system, from Phelexos to the farthest reaches of Tavina. Hiding out in the nebula may have kept them safe from the virus, but that protection also made Andi feel incredibly alone.

Isolated. Hopeless.

But she would not accept defeat. Not when the lives of her girls were at risk.

"Okay, let's lay out what we know already," Andi said, needing everything clarified once more before they did…*who knows what*, she thought. They couldn't move forward with any of the plans they'd concocted thus far without more information.

Lon tapped a command into the holoscreen on the coffee table and pulled up a picture of a young man with green hair and dark skin. He would have looked like any other person she might pass on the streets of any city in the galaxy—if it weren't for the network of silver veins glowing beneath the surface of his skin.

Andi had seen this photo before. They all had. The first time she saw it, the sight had puzzled her to the core. She was very familiar with body modification, but had never seen anything like this in all her travels across Mirabel.

"People infected with the virus are left with a visible marker of the compulsion—those silver veins," Dex said wearily, as Lon pulled up other photos of people with a similar mod. "Which makes things more than a bit difficult for us. We can't just waltz into Arcardius and get the girls back. It would be obvious that we're not under Nor's mind control."

"We would be captured and infected, too," Andi said, understanding his point.

"Not *we*," Lon said, eyeing them both. Andi and Dex had both been shot with the virus during the Ucatoria Ball. They hadn't been affected the way the others were, which they all hoped meant Dex and Andi were somehow immune. Lon, on the other hand, had never been exposed to it, and Andi wasn't willing to risk his freedom on the vague hope that he might be resistant to the virus, as well.

Besides, since Lira wasn't immune, then it was unlikely Lon

was, either. He was Lira's twin, her counterpart, half of Lira's heart.

And if Andi saw him fall, some part of her knew it would be like losing Lira all over again. He was part of her crew now—and he was the only one who could feed Havoc without risking dismemberment. The hideous creature had grown to love Lon, in its own demented way, and didn't claw Lon's arms to ribbons *nearly* as much as it did her and Dex.

Andi could hear Havoc purring from beneath the couch, ready to strike again.

It was a cunning move, those silver veins—something Andi had to grudgingly admire, as much as it complicated things for them. Still, there had to be some holes in Nor's master plan, and Andi relished the thought of blasting them wide open.

Dex rubbed his chin thoughtfully. Stubble had started to shadow his face, and Andi tried not to dwell on how attractive she found it. He'd had a beard during the year they'd spent together, after she fled Arcardius the first time, and Andi couldn't help being reminded of the happier times in their relationship when she looked at him now.

He pulled up their brainstorming sheet with a tap of two fingers. "Well, I think out of these three ideas…none of them will work in the current climate."

Then Dex wiped the screen clean, erasing the mission plans they'd so carefully drafted together during countless hours of work over the past three weeks.

"Dex, you're as bad as Alfie sometimes!" Andi snapped, all feelings of nostalgia disappearing in the wake of her aggravation at him.

"Well, seeing as he's not here," Dex said, eyeing the silver holoband encircling his wrist, "someone has to fill in for the time being."

The AI had been dismembered during their short stay at Averia, where General Cortas and his family had once lived.

Andi had managed to save his memory chip, knowing that Alfie had gathered vital information about Valen's blood and DNA when he'd tested him on their ship after leaving Luna-mere.

And though Alfie's chip was now tucked away in Dex's holo-band, they hadn't yet been able to resurrect the AI by connecting him to the galactic feeds. He'd remained as useless as ever, and likely would until they left the nebula, when he was able to get a real connection.

Andi snatched the holoscreen away and undid Dex's action, saving the document. But even as she did so, Andi couldn't help feeling that Dex was right—the more she looked at their ideas, the more she wondered if any of them could actually work.

1. Dress up as Xen Pterran soldiers, sneak onto Arcardius and kid-nap the girls.

Andi thought this plan of Dex's could potentially work—*if* they had clearance, which they did not. Plus, she had a faint in-kling that he just wanted to don a disguise, like the top shows on the social feeds. Those were all gone now, Nor having erased the social aspects of the feeds, replacing them with her propaganda.

Dex was always one for theatrics. But she knew better than ever now that theatrics rarely worked in real life.

After all, playing the part of the Bloody Baroness only ever got people killed.

Then there was Lon's all too reasonable idea.

2. Negotiate

If they had something to bargain with, it could work…but all they had were a few guns and her ship, which was *not* up for negotiation. She would even go as far as to offer Nor her life for those of her crew, but she doubted Nor wanted her dead that badly. Andi was no one. Just a ghost lost to the stars, as far as the galaxy was concerned. Valen, on the other hand…

Andi didn't think the method she'd proposed was too bad. It had always worked for her in the past.

3. Go in guns blazing

Then again, they were just three people against the whole galaxy. Maybe shooting their way onto Arcardius was a bit too unrealistic, especially without her crew. Lon wasn't exactly one for violence, either. She doubted he'd be of much help.

Havoc, though... Perhaps she could use the creature as a weapon.

Even Nor would run from those claws.

Andi looked down, but Havoc had mysteriously disappeared. She made a mental note to make sure she stuck close to Dex for the time being—he was usually Havoc's favorite target, which meant she might be able to avoid becoming his next scratching post.

"We're only three people, with a ship on the verge of collapse," Dex said, uncannily echoing her earlier thoughts. It was true—the *Marauder* needed fuel and supplies, and the thrusters desperately needed a tune-up. With the way things were going, they wouldn't be able to hide out in this nebula much longer.

Andi looked out the window to the dusty expanse beyond. She missed seeing the stars.

Dex continued. "We all want a solid plan that will allow us to rescue the girls without dying or becoming enslaved to Queen Nor in the process. But before we even think about going back to Arcardius, we need to figure out a way to refuel and gather supplies. We're no good to anyone stranded in a nebula."

"Or dead," Lon added.

Dex nodded. "Exactly. We need to get the ship back into shape first. Then we can tackle the rest."

"As much as I hate admitting this, you're right," Andi said with a sigh, glancing at Gilly's drawings again.

Dex's jaw dropped. He grabbed the holoscreen and aimed its camera at her. "Can you say that again? I want to document this moment."

Andi pushed the screen away, rolling her eyes. "Is your brain so addled that you have to document things externally because you can't store the information up there?" She flicked his forehead.

"If you want to know what I'm thinking, just ask." He winked. "Just try not to combust when I describe the dirty—"

Andi was saved from hearing the details of Dex's explicit thoughts when Havoc pounced over the back of the couch, landing on his shoulders with claws extended.

Dex cursed, fighting the creature off and handing it to Lon instead, who allowed Havoc to curl into his arms, its horns poking out from beneath Lon's thin black shirt.

"I swear to the stars, I'm going to skin you and use you for a pair of boots," Dex said with a growl as Havoc yawned innocently.

"Fuzzy orange boots?" Andi said, brows raised. "That *does* sound like just your style."

Dex was about to backpedal when the holoscreen dinged and the feed projected a new video stream into the room. The face of Nor Solis filled the space, and Andi groaned at the thought of yet another propaganda vid.

The queen smiled down at them, looking every bit like the benevolent ruler she definitely wasn't. "I hate her," Andi mumbled.

Memory's voice cut through the room, pausing the video before it could start. *"Fuel supply at thirty percent."*

"Damn," Dex whispered as Andi's eyes bulged.

"Preserve energy use wherever you can, Memory," Andi commanded.

"Command confirmed."

The room went dark, the only light coming from the holoscreen. Andi tapped on the holoscreen to resume the feed. She might hate listening to Nor address her mindless followers, but they needed all the intel they could get.

"People of Mirabel," Nor said in greeting. "I come to you as your queen, asking you to join me in working even harder to build the future we all wish to attain. We must be vigilant in our efforts to complete Nexus, and to root out all those who wish to defy our cause. With your help, by moon's end, we will finish the construction of Nexus, and a new era will rise."

"Talking about that damned Nexus again," Andi complained, but before the boys could answer, the feed started to glitch and Nor's face disappeared, soon replaced by another's. Andi jolted upright, transfixed by the image before them.

The newcomer on the feed was a veritable giant, clad in bloodred armor marred with battle scars and strange black markings. "This message is for those whose minds still belong to them," the figure said, its voice sounding distant and strangely mechanical. "You are not alone."

Andi heard Dex inhale sharply as the feed filled with static for a moment. Then the holo flickered again, and the massive soldier came back into view. Andi leaned forward, utterly transfixed by his words. "Much of the galaxy has fallen to a false queen, but there are still many who have not. To the strong, to those who continue to fight for freedom—I am Arachnid. And I stand as leader for all those who refuse to bow to anyone's will but our own.

"Find me," Arachnid urged. "Together, we will build an army. Together, we will destroy the false queen." He paused, and though he didn't move, Andi could almost feel the threat of violence emanating from him as he spoke once more. "You cannot compel me, Nor Solis. I know what you plan to do. I know the horrors you will unleash, and I will stop you before it's too late. Even if I have to drive the killing blade into your chest myself."

Then the feed went black.

"We aren't alone," Lon whispered, but it came out more like a question. The only sound was Havoc's rhythmic purring as he stroked the fuzzball's horned head.

Dex slowly shook his head. "By the looks of it, no."

"Could it be a trick?" Andi asked, wondering if this was all just a ploy to draw the Unaffecteds—as the news feeds called them—out of hiding. Nor wasn't a fool. She'd managed to outsmart the entire galaxy, Andi and her crew included. Surely she'd do anything to bring others like Andi out into the open, where she could ensnare them once and for all.

"Why would Nor allow uncertainty into the feeds when she's been pumping them full of propaganda all this time?" Dex said.

He had a good point. Which was almost as shocking as what they'd just witnessed.

"If there *is* a resistance group of some kind," Lon mused, looking thoughtful, "then we need to get to them. We have to try, at least. They could help us rescue Lirana and the others."

"Agreed," Andi said slowly. "There are two things standing in our way, though."

"I think there are more than two things," Dex interjected, but Andi shot him a look that shut him up.

"Two *major* things," she clarified. "One is that we are low on everything, and we can't actually get to the resistance without getting supplies. Which means we have to leave the nebula."

"But Nor's forces are out there," Lon said, blue eyes full of worry.

He'd expressed many times before that he felt like it was only a matter of time before their theory of being Unaffected was tested on him, if and when Nor's soldiers found them.

"Which brings me to my second issue," Andi replied. "Nor has control over the galaxy, and we don't actually know *where* the resistance is hiding out. Any attempts to find them will probably be riddled with obstacles, so… We need to be smart about what we do. No acting rashly, no arguing on missions. And nobody gets left behind."

Both Lon and Dex nodded in agreement. They'd all been affected, in their own ways, by the loss of Andi's crew.

"We can't hide in here forever," Lon admitted. "The last month has already depleted us more than I care to admit."

"So, Captain, what do you propose we do?" Dex asked, arms crossed, as if the answer were obvious.

Hell if I know, Andi was about to say. But then her eyes fell on the holoscreen before them. She pulled up the map of Mirabel, scanning it for what felt like the thousandth time in the past few weeks.

"We go to Solera," she answered suddenly, tapping the ringed, frozen planet.

Dex's brow creased. "Why Solera?"

"It's the closest planet to us, for one," Andi said, pointing out where they were on the map. "And it has a fairly small population, but since Solera's a capital planet, we have a good chance of finding the supplies we need."

"It's also the farthest away from Arcardius," Lon added, moving forward to study the map for himself. "Far from Lirana and the crew."

"True. But it's probably the worst possible planet for us to land on with a battered ship and limited food reserves," Dex pointed out. "We'd have to land pretty damn close to a populated area if we want to survive the tundra long enough to stock the ship and then track down this so-called resistance."

"Not great odds," Andi agreed. "Look, I'm not saying it's going to be easy…but we have a lead now, and we should follow it. Or else we'll just wind up becoming space junk."

It was something Breck would have said. Andi frowned, thinking of her head gunner, so far away from her now.

"And if it's a trap?" Dex asked. It was so strange to hear him, of all people, being the voice of reason for once.

Andi glanced between him and Lon, her gaze falling once more on the subtle reminders that the girls were gone. The empty seats, the absence of Breck and Gilly's laughter, the untouched stack of Casino cards that Lira used to love betting on.

It *could* be a trap, but if they didn't make some kind of move, the girls wouldn't ever fill these empty spaces again.

"Then are you boys ready to be on the opposite side of the law again?" Andi asked.

"If we're going to infiltrate Arcardius, we *do* need to take some risks," Lon reasoned.

Dex's eyes twinkled with mischief. "Risk *and* reward."

"I'm beginning to see what my sister enjoyed about this life," Lon said with a grin, setting Havoc down. The creature yowled before scurrying away, almost as if it were in agreement with the plan.

Andi smirked. "Okay, boys. Let's go get our girls."

CHAPTER 6
LIRA

Lock. Load. Aim.

 Fire.

 Lirana Mette stood with her arms crossed over her chest, listening to the sound of organized destruction. A beautiful melody, really, for Lira had always loved chaos.

 A firing squad stood around her, their synchronized motions a cadence in perfect time.

 Lock.

Fifty soldiers slammed their mags into place.

Load.

Fifty rounds, swiftly chambered.

Aim.

Each soldier steadied their breath, squared their shoulders.

Fire.

Lira had never been particularly adept with a gun, always inclined to raise her fists above anything else. But when Queen Nor's reign began, she'd quickly discovered that her accuracy as a pilot served her well when aiming for a target. A deep breath, a rush of air from her lungs, and she imagined her hands were not holding a rifle, but delicately aiming a ship toward its destination as she squeezed the trigger. Her bullet shot straight through the center of the target across the warehouse in a single, glorious explosion.

Their mission was simple: keep the planet under control while recruiting new followers to Queen Nor's rule. Any Unaffecteds they rooted out—their presence like a choking weed that dared to defy Mirabel's rightful monarch—were to be shot with the silver bullets supplied by Aclisia, the queen's head scientist.

"Again!" the soldier in charge commanded.

Lira chambered another practice bullet, remembering when she herself had been shot with the real thing. It was terrifying, at first. A moment of pain, then darkness as absolute as anything she'd ever felt before. She hadn't wanted to go there, to be surrounded by nothingness. But in that dark place, she'd felt herself calming as another presence washed over her, almost ancient in its power. Otherworldly.

It commanded her to understand the truth. To believe it, with every fiber of her being.

Nor Solis is the one true queen.

Lira had spent her entire life running from truths. In Adhira, she'd run from the truth that her mother had abandoned her. She'd run from the reality that her brother, Lon, and her aunt Alara wanted her to stay and rule from a cold, spiraling mountain that hardly saw the light. And when she'd joined a starship full of lady pirates…she'd run even then, flying the *Marauder* as far and as fast as she could away from Adhira.

But in that moment after she was shot, when she heard that

command and was cast back out into the land of the living again…

Lira rose to her feet in the ballroom on Averia and looked up at the brightest light she'd ever seen. Queen Nor stood upon the stage, a pile of dead Mirabellian leaders at her feet, their blood drying in colorful rivers down the ballroom steps.

She'd smiled at Lira, at *all* the people standing around her.

And in that moment, Lira knew that she worshipped the queen. That the silver bullet had been not a curse, but a blessing meant to save her, to show her that when she followed Queen Nor, all would be as it should. For the first time in her life, she was at peace.

"You alright, Lir?" A voice drew Lira from her thoughts. She looked to her right, where one of her oldest friends stood, rifle clutched in her large hands.

"Fine," Lira said, a small smile on her lips as she thought of the queen. "Perfectly fine."

Breck was a giantess from New Veda, a natural warrior who'd spent her entire life behind the sights of a gun. She was the perfect soldier for Nor's army, one who would give her life to serve the queen if she was asked.

"Again!" the commanding officer barked out, and Breck winked at Lira as she lifted her rifle and shot. A perfect bull's-eye in the target.

The other soldiers scrambled to follow Breck's lead. *Lock. Load. Aim. Fire.*

Lira's next shot hit close to her intended mark, but she couldn't yet match Breck's accuracy. Shooting was still so new to her. She'd always preferred to use her own body as a weapon, but there were a lot of old preferences she'd once had that had melted away beneath the weight of Lira's desire to please her new queen.

She'd spent the past two years of her life aboard the *Marauder*, a glass starship where her piloting skills were used to gallivant across the skies, following the lead of the Bloody Baroness, a space pirate notorious for raising hell.

Lira could see Androma's face now—those metal cheekbones, the bloodlust in her eyes. What waste Lira had once laid to Queen Nor's precious planets at the Baroness's command.

Sometimes, when she thought of her past life, Lira still felt the ghostly heat of her scales warming on the surface of her skin. A lifelong struggle she'd tried to harness, her emotions getting the better of her far more often than they should. Those out-of-control emotions had hurt people, ruined her relationships, left her feeling like a weapon always on the brink of a misfire. But now, with a deep breath, a mere thought of Queen Nor...

Lira felt nothing. As if she were a hollow shell, blessedly free of the stresses she'd spent so many years trapped beneath.

A soldier groaned suddenly as the butt of his rifle smacked him in the eye. Horrific form.

"Not good enough, Krisson!" their commanding officer shouted, stomping closer to the line of soldiers clad in black, the Solis crest stamped on their backs and chests. Lira wore it on her own chest now, and it was displayed all across the city, waving from flags, brightly flickering on holoscreens across the glass towers that made up much of Arcardius. "Tighten up your grip. Deep in the shoulder. Fix your form, or I'll tell the entire barracks that bruise on your eye is from Gilly!"

A small redheaded girl turned around from the line, a wicked grin on her youthful face. "Who's to say I didn't beat the shit out of him already?"

"Language, Gil," Breck huffed under her breath, but she smiled as all the soldiers laughed, men and women alike, when Gilly turned back around and fired three consecutive shots dead-center in the target, three hundred yards away.

Lira smiled. Gilly knew her way around a weapon, and it was with the greatest joy that she got to watch the youngest member of her old crew serving the queen in such a spectacular fashion.

Together, the three girls were finally fighting for a cause that mattered.

Hoots and hollers sounded down the firing line as their commander signaled the end of their training session.

It's about time, Lira thought. They'd been at it for hours. She slung her weapon over her shoulder and stepped away from the larger group, joining Breck and Gilly at the edge of the warehouse. The girls took seats together by the watercooler, where the next formation of soldiers waited for their turn at target practice.

Gilly's red braids bounced as she slumped into the bleachers, craning her neck to look the other two girls in the eye. "Go ahead and try to tell me that shot wasn't sexy as hell."

Lira gave her an indulgent smile. "You're talented, Gilly. A true asset to our queen."

Breck nodded in agreement, taking off her cap, the golden Solis sigil on it sparkling as she set it down beside her. "Sexy. As. Hell."

They were like sisters, the three of them, their bond forged through a past they all wished to forget.

"But seriously. You're doing good, Gil," Breck added. "Keep it up, and you'll be out there in the galaxy soon, shooting Unaffecteds, clearing out the nonbelievers."

"Do you think Queen Nor will ever come down and visit us?" Gilly asked.

Everyone wanted a chance to see the queen, to kiss her hand or simply gaze upon her. She'd turned Mirabel from a place of hatred and darkness to one of glorious, peaceful light. Under her reign, everyone was united behind one cause.

Lira shrugged. "She's so busy, ensuring Nexus is built and the plans for Phase Two are set in place."

"Let's not forget her efforts to take down Arachnid and his so-called resistance," Breck added, her face set in a grim expression.

Lira's blood went hot at the thought of those betrayers. Ever since they'd seen Arachnid's threat playing across the feeds, Lira had felt even more committed to protecting Queen Nor's rule. Arachnid and his rebels had no place in this galaxy, and Lira would make sure they bowed down to their rightful queen, even if she had to hunt them down one by one herself.

"They won't be a problem for much longer," Lira said. The Unaffected numbers were few, and Nor's army was many, spanning all the planets across the galaxy.

"I wonder how the queen is feeling about all this. What is she going to do?" Gilly asked. Although Gilly was brave, she was still very young, and she tended to worry about things Lira generally didn't even think about. Their queen was strong, of course, but with so many factors demanding her attention, Lira hoped she was aided by loyal aides and advisers. All-powerful or not, Queen Nor was still just one person.

"I'm sure she's doing fine," Lira told Gilly reassuringly. "Especially knowing how capable her army is. We lessen her burden, and we'll do whatever it takes to stop the rebels."

"Right now, there are more important things for the queen to handle, like Phase Two. A few rebel sympathizers are nothing but pesky insects," Breck added, giving Gilly's shoulder a squeeze. The small girl smiled.

"What *is* Phase Two?" Gilly wondered.

Phase Two hadn't been shared with the grunt soldiers like them yet—the queen needed to keep many of her plans under wraps for now, until the Unaffected threat was eliminated. But Lira knew it would be glorious, and she'd do whatever was asked of her when the time arrived.

"It doesn't matter what it is," Lira said. "We're blessed to be able to serve her together. That's enough for me."

Breck lifted her cup of water in agreement.

"I served beside you both for two years on Andi's ship," Gilly said, draining her water and tossing her metal cup into the bin beside the bleachers. "That traitor."

The sound echoed like a tiny gunshot that Lira felt in her chest. Sometimes, she still thought about Androma and wondered where she was. But then guilt riddled her insides for spending even a moment thinking of the traitorous young captain of the *Marauder.* If Andi was on Nor's side, she would have been here now, with the three of them. She would have put her skills to use serving the rightful queen.

Instead, she'd taken the *Marauder* and soared away, with Dex and Lira's twin brother, Lon, in tow. A coward's move, if ever there was one.

Lira could still see Lon's face, so much like her own—the same smile, the same ocean-blue skin. But he'd chosen the wrong side. Andi, too. Lira had once considered Andi to be her family, every bit as much as Lon.

Now she felt ashamed to have ever been so closely connected to two Unaffecteds.

A bang came from Lira's right, drawing her gaze as the double doors of the warehouse suddenly hissed open.

"Looks like it's showtime," Gilly said, eyeing the new arrival. She began to bob on her toes expectantly. "Aclisia's here!"

As Queen Nor's head scientist entered the range, every soldier snapped to attention.

And how could they not? Lira thought, watching Aclisia march across the oil-stained concrete floor. It was like being in the presence of a legend, albeit a strange one. Aclisia possessed two heads—one of the few left of her race in Mirabel. They both worked in tandem, yet had personalities of their own.

Lira gazed upon her in awe. *This* was the woman who'd taken a single drop of blood and transformed it into the cure for ignorance. A single shot from one of the silver bullets Aclisia had created, and the victim's eyes would be opened. They'd see Queen Nor for who she truly was: a goddess, worthy of their worship.

Aclisia ordered the soldiers to gather in the bleachers. The sea of black uniforms obeyed, moving as one to find seats. Two soldiers in the bloodred uniforms of Queen Nor's personal guard hauled in a pair of struggling, hooded prisoners, glowing magna-cuffs binding their wrists, the molten metal swirling around them like a trapped snake.

"This is going to be wicked," Gilly whispered. Breck shushed her with a wave of her hand. The other soldiers were a thick wall behind Lira, every one of them watching with bated breath.

"Today, we prove to you the power that Her Majesty's weapon has over her enemies!" Aclisia's right head addressed the soldiers, her voice ringing out across the warehouse. "The galaxy belongs to Queen Nor. And yet some still fight against her reign. Her Majesty thanks you for your service, and wishes to inspire you."

The soldiers roared in response. Lira joined them, Breck and Gilly shouting, too.

When they'd quieted down, Aclisia removed the hoods from the captives. The first was a young woman, red-faced from screaming, sweat plastering her white hair to her forehead. For a moment, the woman's pale locks reminded Lira of Androma Racella, seated behind the dash of the *Marauder*, scratching tal-lies into a sword.

If only she'd been here. If only she'd been brave enough to serve Nor, too.

The second captive was a man, round and well-fed, with powder-blue skin. An Adhiran, like Lira.

"We must ask each person we encounter a vital question, in order to determine who they truly serve," Aclisia said. She nod-ded to the guards, and they removed the gags from each captive's mouth. "Who is your queen?"

The prisoners gasped for air, gulping in weighty breaths. The woman sat still, her eyes wide and roving over the group, but the man began to curse in Adhiran.

"Nor's a demon!" His voice was ragged, as if his vocal cords were tearing in two. "She's turned you all against what's right!

That monster is *not* your queen, damn it! Why can't you see that? Why can't you see what she's done to you?"

Beside him, the woman simply shook as silent tears streamed down her cheeks.

The word from soldiers already out on the front was that all the Unaffecteds said similar things, but Lira had not yet seen it with her own eyes. The audacity of the man's words made Lira's blood boil with rage.

"Who is your queen?" Aclisia asked again.

"She's brainwashed you all!" the man howled, veins popping out from his neck. "SHE'S TURNED YOU INTO—"

A guard stuffed the gag back into the man's mouth, and his cries were cut off short.

"Pathetic," Aclisia's left head said.

Her right head nodded. "This is what our enemies believe. That we are all beneath a spell, following a queen who has wrongfully stolen her throne."

Behind Lira, the soldiers cursed and spit at the captives. She joined in with eager haste.

"We have peace in Mirabel for the first time in decades. We have a queen who wishes to treat us all equally, and all she asks in return is that we serve her. That we continue to spread her vision across the galaxy, so that everyone will believe. Time is of the essence now, in the building of Nexus. And when it is completed, Phase Two will begin."

Murmurs of agreement sounded down the line. Lira felt the truth of it in her heart, felt it beside that ever-constant whisper that seemed to ring out in her soul, keeping her eyes open and her loyalty true.

Nor is your queen, your goddess, your savior.

"A gift from your queen," Aclisia said, lifting the rifle handed to her by one of the guards in red. The crowd roared in antici-pation, eager to see another join their ranks. "Let's show him the true power of the woman he claims is not his queen."

When Aclisia squeezed the trigger, the round was silent. It slammed against the man's forehead, knocking him back with the intensity of it. His eyes closed, as if he were dead. But in the center of his forehead, instead of a hole, instead of blood and brains…

Silver liquid swam against the man's pastel skin, like a gentle caress of liquid moonlight. Then it began to fade, sinking beneath the surface until the liquid disappeared entirely. Lira waited for the change to take effect. For the man to finally see and believe the truth, to fully understand what light Nor could bring to his life.

His eyes fluttered open, his head bobbing slightly on his shoulders, chin dipping before a guard helped to lift his gaze to Aclisia.

"Who is your queen?" Aclisia's two heads asked softly, the words as delicate as a kiss.

The man's blue eyes lost their fog.

"Queen…" He seemed to fumble for the words, as if he were listening to the voice in his head. As if he were a child, learning the truth at last. "Queen Nor."

Then he wept tears of joy, whispering Nor's name over and over like a song, the words pouring from his very soul. Lira leaped to her feet, cheering alongside the other soldiers.

But beside him, the female captive began to scream. It broke through the power of the moment, through the joy of the man's transition into the light.

"Enough!" Aclisia shouted. She lifted her rifle, set the woman in her sights and fired.

The scene was the same as before…and yet the effect was not.

For the woman did not lose consciousness. The liquid spread against her skin, but her eyes never closed. She kept screaming. "Let me go! Please, Godstars, let me go!"

The room should have felt frozen, a horror scene unfolding in rapid time. But Lira only felt calm as the woman began to howl and writhe against her bindings. Blood dripped from her wrists as she fought, shaking like a demon was clawing at her from the inside out. "LET ME GO!"

"Unaffected!" one soldier shouted. The others joined in, beating their fists and stomping their boots against the bleachers.

But Aclisia held up a hand. "Inject her."

At once, the guards sank a tranq needle into the woman's neck. Immediately, she fell silent.

"Do you see?" Aclisia asked, turning to the crowd of soldiers, now quiet, as well. Lira chanced a look at Breck and Gilly, their expressions stony as they looked forward. "This is what happens to those who do not believe."

The guards cut the woman's bindings loose, and Lira watched as they hauled her away, the woman's pale hair dragging against the ground as they disappeared through the double doors. Lira continued to stare after the woman, even as the crowd came to life again.

She never wanted to return to that state of desperation. Never wanted to return to that place of *feeling*, of running and wishing to hide from the truth.

When she left the warehouse with the rest of her unit, Lira's heart beat steadily in her chest as she stared out across the silver city all around her, as she saw the glorious banners, the Solis crest displayed for all to see.

I will always serve Nor Solis, Lira thought, saluting the symbol of her queen.

She turned her eyes to the sky, the ghost of a smile kissing her lips as she stared up at the distant floating mountain that housed her one true queen.

Beside it, the Nexus satellite winked beneath the starlight.

And all was well in Lira's soul.

CHAPTER 7
NOR

Her hands wouldn't stop shaking.

That armor. That *voice*. Nor's heels clacked on the polished marble floors as she paced, her mind racing in circles. Who was behind that crimson helmet? She wished, desperately, that her gift went beyond compulsion, that she possessed some greater power that would allow her to see through the shield to the enemy beyond.

"Nor?"

Darai's voice yanked her back into the present. He pressed his cold hand to her wrist, the feeling like an electric shock. She backed away, her heart racing. Beside him stood the producer, his four arms crossed as he waited for her orders. Despite the sudden shock of the moment, he still looked at her as all the others did—like she was a goddess come down from the stars.

"We've managed to trace the origin of Arachnid's message, Majesty," the producer told her. "It seems he was filming in a cave on Sora."

Sora. A moon in the nearby Prime System, virtually uninhabitable due to the poisonous gases in its atmosphere. The perfect place to hide, shivering in the shadows like a spider.

Nor would see the fool squashed beneath her heel.

Zahn's eyes met hers from across the room. She gave him a quick nod, and though they didn't share a mental link like she and Valen did, a silent message seemed to pass between them all the same. *I'm okay. We're okay.*

Nor lifted her chin and turned to Darai. "His armor is likely the only reason he was able to survive long enough to send us a message from Sora. A clever place to hide, where I cannot easily reach him."

"Could we send drones in to find him?" Zahn asked as he began to pace, already trying to solve the problem for her. She loved him for his effort, but it would take more than what Zahn could come up with on his own to silence this threat.

For Arachnid *knew.* Somehow...the man behind that red helmet knew about Nor's and Valen's compulsion. But how? It was impossible, and yet Arachnid's final words were all Nor could hear. *You cannot compel me.*

"Clear the room," Nor said. She reached for her crown, straightening it against her curls.

Darai's jaw looked to be hanging on broken hinges. "My dear…"

She held up her hand, and her adviser fell silent. "I said, *clear the room.*"

Darai snapped his fingers, ushering the others out. They raced from the room as if it were on fire. As the doors closed behind them, Zahn rushed to her side. Years before, when Xen Ptera was attacked and everything was stolen from her, it was *Nor* who had picked herself back up. She'd had Darai and Zahn at her side then, as support. But ultimately, the decision had been *hers* to stand up. To carry on with her life, and make something more of it.

She'd never believed she needed to depend on others until Valen came along—and until Zahn's heart had merged with hers. She let her lover press his hand against the small of her back as he gazed at her with worried eyes, his soldier's mask gone now that the room was empty of watching eyes.

"He knows," Nor said shakily. "If he knows about the compulsion, then there's a chance he knows about Exonia. And he will try to stop us from reaching the other side."

"Then we will destroy him before he takes another breath," Zahn answered. "We'll tighten the security measures around Nexus, too."

Nor fell silent as she considered what to do next. She was the queen of Mirabel. The savior of this planet and the many beyond it. She would not bow to any man, especially one too cowardly to show his face.

"Please, Nor, you must tell us what it is you wish to do," Darai begged. "Do you want to send a team after him? Give another speech? Do you want to have Valen—"

"Valen is not to be disturbed in this chaos," Nor said. "He needs peace. Time to focus *only* on his compulsion. If anything, we need to move more quickly now. For if this Arachnid poses a true threat, if he manages to share his knowledge of our compulsion with the other Unaffecteds... Exonia could be at risk."

"I'll do whatever it takes to stop this man," Zahn said. "You give the command, Nor, and I will send every soldier we have." His dark eyes could have burned a hole in Nor's soul, for all the fire in them. He'd always been a fighter, leaping to her defense the moment anyone dared speak ill of her name.

"I know what needs to be done," Nor said, moving toward the window to look out upon her estate. Her kingdom. Zahn shifted to stand behind her, his warm hands closing around her shoulders. She sank back against him—not because she needed his strength, but because she *wanted* it. Because when he was at her side, she knew she had all the loyalty in the world.

"Phase Two will come soon," Nor said, pulling away from his touch, turning to face him instead. Darai hovered in the background, a bitter expression on his lips. "But we may as well conduct a test fire, in light of Arachnid's message."

She typed a code into the holoscreen on her desk. The lights overhead responded at once, fading to near-darkness. A few more codes, and a map of the galaxy materialized in the office, beautifully rendered orbs of light representing each planet. They danced across the ceiling, and the stars flickered across Zahn's face, showing his determination.

Nor walked to the front of the desk, her body passing through the holographic orb that represented Arcardius. Just past it, at the edge of the galaxy, was the Void.

A place without any light. Not a single star shining. Not a single planet or satellite to break through the blackness of it all. Soon, it would be torn open, and the people who truly held her heart would come through, to live safely and prosperously under her rule.

Some nights, Nor feared her plan wouldn't work. That she'd never see Exonia; that Nexus would fail to break open the doorway that kept Nor from her true home.

But that wasn't an option. Nexus would be finished soon, and as long as Valen held on, his exhaustion carefully monitored, his mind occasionally given time to rest from the compulsion... then all would be well.

"It's beautiful," Nor said, trailing her fingers through the dark expanse that was the Void. An entrance to another world. In her mind, she saw the future, the sky opening wide. She saw not one galaxy, but two, bowing to her command.

It would be the greatest achievement Mirabel had ever witnessed. Nor was sure that the story of her reign—the creation of the Nexus satellite, the complete command of every planet in Mirabel—would be written down in the archives. Songs would be composed about it, paintings created in reverence.

"I can taste it," Nor murmured, closing her eyes. "I can taste the glory, not only of Mirabel, but of Exonia."

Across the room, Darai cleared his throat. "Majesty. While it is good to see you leaning toward the positive… I implore you. We must make a decision about Arachnid."

Despite his words, Nor lingered for a moment longer in her vision of the future. It was her driving force. Her passion, to continue in her mother's footsteps.

Then she felt Zahn touch her hand, trying to draw her attention back.

If anyone else had done that, they would have found themselves without hands for such an impertinence. But not Zahn. He was different in so many ways. He helped smooth her sharp edges, helped her to become the embodiment of strength and softness, easily able to work between the two in harmony.

Nor took a deep breath.

"Arachnid wishes to thwart our plans to reach Exonia," she said, this time allowing herself to lean deeper into Zahn's touch. His warmth mingled with hers, eliciting a sigh of relief.

"That's impossible. No one else knows of the compulsion," Zahn insisted.

"But it isn't," Darai replied grimly. "I feared this would happen—have feared it since the day your mother ran off to this planet. General Cortas knew. He found some way to resist her power."

"He's dead," Nor said flatly.

"But it's possible he shared the information with someone else," Darai told her gently. "His body was never found, after all."

"His wounds were fatal," she snapped. "Valen gave me his word."

Darai inclined his head. "I have no doubt that his aim was true, Majesty. Nevertheless, if he somehow made it off-planet before he died... Perhaps he managed to send a message."

"Then we will send Arachnid a message of our own."

"Nor," Zahn started, his voice pleading. "Not another speech? There have been a great many deaths since your reign began. The Unaffecteds are revolting. Rising up. Just imagine, if there were a band of them on this very planet, following the orders of Arachnid, in hopes that you would respond with a speech the moment his video overtook the feeds... They could be just waiting to attack."

"I am surrounded by believers," Nor said, though Zahn's words rattled her very core. "Any of them would lay down their lives to see my plan succeed." She reached out to cup his cheek. "But you need not fear, my love. Arachnid needs a demonstration of our power that's far grander than any speech I could give."

Nor turned back to the map, still illuminating the large office. She could practically feel the heat thrumming through her veins as she studied the projection of Sora and imagined what was soon to come.

For on Cyprian's old desk, beside the holoscreen, was a scanner keyed to Arcardius's leader, kept covered by a sheet of impenetrable varillium so that it was not engaged accidentally. Nor slid the covering open, placing her palm across the scanner to activate it. She typed in the access codes the late general's team had given her, her body almost buzzing with delight as she entered the coordinates for Sora.

"We'll see how the spider survives this," Nor said as she typed in the final code to access the top secret arsenal carefully hidden on Arcardius. Every capital planet had one—a massive array of nuclear weapons that were created toward the end of the Cataclysm, ready to be sent out across the stars should the threat of another war ever resurface.

Somewhere across Arcardius, one of those enormous missiles would respond, angling toward Sora, ready to blast it from the sky.

"A test fire of sorts?" Darai asked from across the office.

Nor nodded. "The moon is small enough that just one missile should be able to handle it."

A triumphant smile was just broadening across her rouged lips when a beep sounded from the scanner. Nor blinked down at it as two words suddenly appeared, glowing red.

ACCESS DENIED

"That can't be," she said. Zahn and Darai joined her on either side, looking down at the screen with twin frowns on their faces.

Nor typed in the code again.

But the same message flashed back at her.

"The code must be wrong," Zahn said, reaching up to access the com behind his ear. "Perhaps we already have some Unaffecteds beneath our noses."

"They're loyal," Nor argued, shaking her head, her crown suddenly too heavy. "Everyone on this estate is being compelled. Valen is certain of it."

Zahn mumbled something into his com. Moments later, the doors to the office opened as a team of tech droids and their analysts arrived, shuffling inside with portable holoscreens clutched in their arms. Nor stood aside, watching as they tried to override the system, to no avail. The same response came up every time, that hideous message in bold, bloody red.

"What's the problem?" Nor demanded. She was pacing now, the long train of her gown tangling beneath her spiked heels. The head analyst stepped forward, a beautiful woman from off-planet, her orange eyes downcast as she studied the curved screen in her hands. "Well?" Nor snarled. "Speak!"

The analyst looked up, terror written across her face. Her Adhiran accent made her voice sound calmer than the words should have. "I'm so sorry, Majesty. But it seems…it seems there was a fail-safe set in place."

"What fail-safe?" Darai asked, stepping up beside Nor.

The office suddenly felt too stuffy, as if too many warm bodies were packed inside at once. The analyst blinked slowly, seemingly trying to decide what to say. "It seems that when General Cortas died, this fail-safe was activated."

"Speak plainly," Nor growled, her patience growing thinner by the second. "Explain what that means."

"It sickens me to say this, Majesty," the analyst began, "and I beg that you please take no offense at my words, for the fault is not mine."

"Go on," Zahn encouraged gently. The analyst nodded, likely reassured by the calmness of his voice. Zahn was the only one holding it together right now, still steady and true as the day continued to fall apart around them, and Nor felt another wave of gratitude for his support.

The analyst turned her holoscreen, so that Nor could see numbers running across it, symbols and shapes she didn't know how to decipher. Beside the analyst, a small red tech droid beeped sadly, its clawed hand drawing away from the screen on Nor's desk to retract back into its torso. Apparently even the droid had given up.

Nor took a deep breath and faced the analyst as the woman tried to explain.

"According to the system…it says here that you, Majesty, are technically *not* the General of Arcardius. I'm ashamed to admit that we had no reason to know this before now, but in any case, when you tried to access the nuclear arsenal, the fail-safe responded, revealing itself for the first time. So I'm afraid that, even with the correct codes, you will not be able to activate those weapons."

"Cyprian Cortas is *dead*," Nor snapped. Her hands were curled into fists now, so tight that her nails nearly broke through the skin. "He was executed when I arrived here, and I took his place. Therefore, I *am* the rightful General of Arcardius. I am *queen* of this entire galaxy."

The analyst swallowed hard, taking a subtle step backward. "I'm afraid the fail-safe does not see reason. It only understands numbers and coding. And the coding, Majesty, has told the fail-safe that though you are *my* queen, and everyone else's in this room, long may you reign…"

Polished words.

Words spoken out of fear, even through the compulsion.

Nor's teeth ground together as the analyst finished her thought. "Therefore, you will not have access to the arsenal until you are the rightful General of Arcardius—until the system deems it so."

The room was so silent, Nor swore the others could hear her heartbeat pounding from within her chest. She stared at the screen on her desk, wishing she could compel it to obey her. But her compulsion, and Valen's, only worked on the living.

"The other planets," Zahn suggested suddenly, his voice still level despite the unease spreading like a poison through the office. "We can use their weapons instead. We have the codes for them, as well."

The analyst's words were barely a whisper when she spoke, her little droid sliding closer to her side. "I thought so, too, but the fail-safe's reach stretches across *all* of Mirabel, Majesty. I'm so sorry. We didn't know… We didn't anticipate…"

Ice had encased Nor's body. She had killed all the leaders, killed them with one swift slice of her blade so that they would not stand in her way. And now, a month after taking over, it was as if their ghosts had suddenly come back to haunt her.

Or perhaps they'd been lurking on the fringes this entire time, waiting for the right moment to strike.

"There is a ceremony of sorts," the woman said tentatively. "When a leader passes on, a new heir is chosen. Not just by words or oath, but by the system, as well." She looked down at the screen in her hands again, its dim light reflecting in her orange eyes. "But in the event that the other leaders fall without an heir, and only one remains, that single remaining leader gains total control of the weapons network across the entire Unified Systems."

"Then we must do that now," Darai said, nodding his head as he came around to the front of the desk. "We will enter Nor into the system here as the sole leader of Mirabel, so that she can access the arsenals."

The analyst's knees began to shake. "That's simply not possible, sir." She looked to Nor. "Unfortunately, according to the system and the fail-safe… Another leader has already been chosen."

All eyes fell upon her as Nor gripped the desk for support. It couldn't be true.

She'd made sure everyone was dead.

Nor's body felt strangely light, while her head felt too heavy on her shoulders. "Who?" she asked softly, menacingly. "Who is it? We will find them and kill them."

"That's the other problem," the analyst said with a grimace. "The system's firewalls, its back-door fail-safes…they're all heavily protecting the identity of this chosen leader. And merely killing this person won't give you access to the weapons. It would be too easy for leadership to fall into enemy hands if that was the case. The new leader has to pass on the power, to freely hand it over and enter their chosen heir into the system."

"THEN BREAK THROUGH THE SYSTEM!" Nor screamed as fury roared within her blood. She hadn't come all this way just to be stopped by some technological *glitch*.

She picked up a glass bauble from the desk and launched it across the room, where it exploded against the wall in a shower of gleaming shards that looked like falling stars.

At a quick nod from Zahn, the analyst ran from the office, her droid trailing in her wake. The room turned to chaos, Darai commanding orders, the other workers and droids scrambling to obey. But all Nor could hear was the blood roaring in her ears, a heavy thrum as it pulsed hotly through her body.

She was queen. The *only* leader left in Mirabel, all others be damned.

Nor stormed out of the office, Zahn and Darai hot on her heels, and she did not stop until she reached the front doors of the estate and stepped out into the cold night. She stared up at the stars, gazing out across the sky, as if she could see this so-called *other leader* hiding in the shadows.

For when she discovered who it was…

Not even the Godstars would save them from her wrath.

CHAPTER 8
ANDI

Her hands were covered in blood.

An ancient obsidinite dagger, the color as dark as pitch, lay forgotten on the metal floor of the Marauder. The blade had broken in two during the fight. Unsurprising, for Androma had fought hard in the skirmish. The weapon itself was old and somewhat dull, but the wounds it had inflicted upon her fallen enemies were not.

It's over, she told herself. You slayed them all. You won.

And yet, as Andi stood on trembling legs, surveying the cargo bay of the Marauder, the feeling in her bones was not one of victory.

Rather, it was one of defeat.

Loss was a crippling thing, a beast that did its very best to conquer even the strongest of souls. With each life she took, a voice in the back of Andi's mind whispered the same question.

How can one truly be an enemy, if they're being controlled?

Andi staggered forward, a pinch in her side alerting her to the presence of a wound. There was too much blood on her to discover the source, too much exhaustion for her to care.

They'd come for her, knowing she'd survived the attack on Arcardius weeks before. The fight had lasted mere minutes, and the bodies were now scattered all around the cargo bay, still fresh, still bleeding out. All of them wore the sleek, dark uniforms of Xen Ptera. The queen's sigil, shining gold on their armored chests, glared at her from all around.

She'd won this time, but more would come.

More always came.

Andi growled a curse as she saw movement in the corner, behind the rubble of a smashed crate. A gloved hand, stretching out from the shadows. One of the soldiers, mask still in place, was struggling to hold on to life.

She thought she'd finished them all off.

Andi stumbled forward, and the room wobbled, going in and out of focus. She blinked, suddenly realizing that much of the blood must be from her own wound, and pressed onward, stepping over fallen soldiers until she reached the only other living soul on this ship.

"Please," the voice begged, the exterior com of the soldier's helmet crackling. Half of it was bashed in, likely from one of Andi's hits. "Please."

The sound of that voice…

Something tugged at Andi from within.

The soldier's hand lifted, reaching for the helmet, trembling as it moved upward.

Andi leaned forward and removed the helmet herself, wondering why she was doing it, even as the soldier's face was revealed.

"Help me," the soldier gasped, this time not through a com, but through bloodied lips.

A young woman with eyes the color of a clear sky. Her skin was an ashen gray instead of its usual ocean blue, and pain filled her eyes as she stared up at Andi, breathing her last few breaths.

"Lira," Andi whispered. "What are you doing here?" The shock

faded, giving way to horror as she stared at Lira's rapidly paling face. Andi gathered her friend's fallen body into her arms, choking on a sob. "I'm so sorry, Lira. I can stop this. I can fix you."

But the blood was pooling out of Lira's lips now.

"Come closer," Lira whispered. Her chest rattled, heaved, as she sucked in a breath.

Andi bent down, agony shredding her heart. How had she done this? How had she not known her best friend was inside that uniform?

She felt Lira's wet lips touch her cheek as she spoke again. "You killed me. You killed us all."

Then Lira began to laugh. A sickening, howling laugh that struck Andi deep, rattling her bones. She skittered backward, away from her friend's dying body. Her head spun as she turned, realizing Lira's laughter had multiplied.

The fallen Xen Pterran soldiers were gone.

In their place, it was her crew who lay dying.

Gilly, with braids the color of fire.

Breck, her beautiful dark skin now coated with blood.

Lira, those sky-blue eyes growing empty and cold.

All of them, barely alive and bleeding out.

"No," Andi said, nearly choking on the word. "No, this can't be happening."

She lifted her hand, realizing she was gripping the dagger again. It was wet with their blood, and yet she didn't remember any of the hideous act. Andi's body felt a million miles away, her mind screaming at her to make sense of the scene. To change it.

"Very good, Androma," a woman's voice said from behind her. "Now bow to me, before you become like the rest of them."

Andi turned slowly, her heart filling with dread. For she knew that voice, and the monster who possessed it.

Queen Nor Solis, the leader of the Olen System, stood in the cargo bay of the Marauder. *Valen hovered beside her, both of them smiling like demons released from the mouth of hell.*

"I will never bow to you," Andi seethed.

Then her crew members stood, dead no more. They moved to flank the queen, expressions of adoration on each of their faces. And seeing her girls at Nor's command, like a pack of smiling wolves...

The sight brought Andi to her knees.

She'd lost them.

She'd failed them.

And now she would die.

Andi woke with a start.

The horrors of her dream were vanquished as a new nightmare materialized before her bleary eyes. Red lights flashed in the doorway to her quarters, in unison with the blaring sirens that resonated across the ship. Confusion racked her brain until realization came rushing inward.

She'd fallen asleep studying a map of Solera, Lon and Dex in charge of charting their course...

Something was very wrong.

Andi leaped up from her cot and ran into the main corridor. With each step, the clamor of the alarms felt as if it was vibrating in her bones. Her tired muscles screamed as she hoisted herself up the ladder, almost running into Lon as she scrambled onto the landing. He was kneeling on the ground before the door to the bridge, twiddling with wires.

"What's going on?" she demanded.

"The ship is going into meltdown," he told her. "I don't know why. But everything is shutting down, including the doors. I can't seem to get them open." He dropped the two multicolored wires in a huff.

"Where the hell is Dex?"

Lon helplessly held out his hands, and Andi let out a growl of frustration. "Move aside, unless you want to land your ass in the med bay." Lon hurriedly backed away as Andi pulled Gilly's double-triggered gun from her belt and fired the stunner at the door's scanner in a hail of sparks and smoke.

The door teetered on its hinges for a moment before falling inward with a rattling bang.

"There, it's open."

Lon whistled as he looked at the gun. "That thing is awesome."

Andi rolled her eyes and rushed inside.

The control panel on the dash was going haywire. Holographic blueprints drifted across the console, lighting up many areas of the ship in flashing red. Too many.

"Memory?" Andi called out as she slid into Lira's pilot seat. "Run a diagnostics scan."

Memory's voice crackled over the ship-wide com, weakening with each word. *"Fuel leak in the engine room. Oxygen levels at thirty-four percent and dropping."*

Both of which were their lifelines—though by the looks of it, neither would be viable for much longer, at the rate they were dropping.

"Well, that's just great," Andi said sarcastically. She wished, desperately, that Breck was here. Her head gunner knew the ins and outs of the *Marauder*'s mechanical room like the back of her hand, and while she couldn't always fix the problem, Andi knew she could've at least bought them more time.

But she wasn't here. And any attempts they made to fix whatever was wrong would waste time they didn't have.

"What the *hell* is going on?" Dex cursed as he came running through the door, Havoc hot on his heels. The creature leaped for his legs, but Dex kicked it off.

"Easy!" Lon shouted, reaching out his arms as Havoc yowled and barreled into them, horns just visible beneath his layers of fuzzy orange.

"The damned thing is trying to kill me before the ship does!" Dex snapped.

"Took you long enough to get here," Andi said, sending him an annoyed look.

"I was having a great dream." He came up next to her and nudged her shoulder. "You were in it, actually—"

Andi cut him off. "Spare me the details."

Dex glanced at the floating blueprints. "Well, this looks bad," he said, stating the obvious.

Lon stepped up to the console, Havoc cradled in one arm as he entered in a code that blessedly turned off the alarm. He'd learned a lot in his time on the ship. Lira would have been proud.

He turned back to Andi and Dex. "I know we wanted to have a better plan before jumping to Solera, but I don't think time is something we have anymore."

"Do we have enough fuel to make the jump to hyperspace?" Dex shifted his gaze to the fuel gauge, which was running dangerously low. The control panel still blinked a furious red.

Lon scrutinized the fuel level. "Barely."

If they had enough fuel to make the jump, it would be a miracle. And if they didn't?

Well, they'd likely burn up in hyperspace.

"It's a chance we're going to have to take," Andi stated, seeing no other viable options. She buried her nerves deep as she typed in the coordinates for Solera, fingertips flying across the dash. "Dex, why is it that ever since you first boarded this ship, we always seem to be crash-landing?" she asked.

"Because our love is impossible to keep afloat?" Dex suggested jokingly.

Andi let out a shaky laugh.

She wanted to be confident, but her hands shook, the traitorous things. She hadn't known how much strength she'd actually pulled from her crew until they were gone. Lon and Dex were worthy partners, but they weren't her girls.

You'll get them back soon, Andi told herself. To Lon and Dex, she said, "Time to make the jump."

"You sure?" Dex asked, furrowing his brow.

"Yes," she confirmed. They couldn't risk waiting for something else going wrong, if that was even possible. Everything that could have gone wrong just had. So Andi entered in the last command and offered up a silent prayer to the Godstars.

"Destination confirmed: Solera," Memory announced. *"Warming engines for full thrust to hyperspace in ten…nine…"*

The ship jolted, throwing them to the ground. "Crap!" Andi said, grappling to stand and read the control board. One of the ship's engines had just blown.

"Can we still make the jump?" Lon asked, pulling himself up into a chair, his eyes wide as he looked between Andi and Dex. Havoc clung to his shoulders like a rabid leech.

Andi shot a questioning look at Dex. He knew this ship as well as she did, and right now, she didn't know the answer.

"I'd say it's a forty percent chance," Dex said, looking at the stats.

"Thirty-five percent," Memory corrected in a crackling tone. Even the *Marauder*'s AI was failing.

"I'll take it. Strap in, boys," Andi said, settling into her captain's chair. Even in the middle of this disaster, she couldn't help but melt back into the smooth leather, perfectly molded to her form. Like a queen sitting upon her throne.

Dex took the pilot's seat and Lon buckled himself in behind them. The ship shuddered again and dipped to the right. Andi's head smacked painfully against the headrest.

Damn things were supposed to protect her head, not give her a concussion.

"Make the jump, damn it!" Andi growled, looking sideways at Dex. They *would* get to Solera. They had to, even if the ship was just a husk when they landed.

They had to make it.

There wasn't any other option.

Dex hit the throttle, launching them into hyperspace.

Rainbow streaks streamed past the windows, but Andi didn't have any time to marvel at the sight. She was too busy watching the *Marauder*'s diagnostic array to make sure the ship wouldn't explode around them.

At this point, there was no going back.

"May the Godstars guide us," Lon prayed. Andi hoped they were listening—otherwise, they were essentially screwed. And not in the way Dex enjoyed so much.

The three of them fell into a tense silence for a few minutes as they hurtled through space toward Solera. Andi typed some calculations into the navigation system and readied the ship for arrival—or at least she tried to. Half of the systems were off-line and the other half weren't functioning correctly.

"What are we going to do when we get there?" Lon asked.

That was a great question. Andi thought they'd have more time to plan, but with the current situation putting a huge snag in their mission, she wasn't quite sure.

"We need to fix the ship," she said. "That's our top priority right now. Without the *Marauder*, we can't do anything."

"But how will we get the parts we need when we don't look like Nor's followers? You know, those silver veins?" Lon wondered.

They were going to have to improvise. Andi had done it before—with Dex, actually.

She turned to him. "Do you remember Ricar?"

Dex smiled wide. "I was just thinking the same thing."

"What's Ricar?" Lon asked nervously.

"It's a small planet in one of the rogue systems. Dex and I had to stop there once for fuel, and it didn't work out too well."

"You see," Dex continued, "Ricar is essentially a terraformed planet made of metal. Most of the people who live there fancy being more machine than human. We didn't think stopping there would cause any issues, but apparently the locals aren't too fond of outsiders."

"So what happened?" Lon pushed.

Even in their current situation, Andi had to laugh as she

glanced back at him. "We had to become one of them. So we took wires, metal plates…really anything that might seem mechanical, and we dressed ourselves up."

Andi could still remember how Dex had wound a metal coil around her neck and arms to hide her skin. He, on the other hand, had glued small aluminum sheets to his face for his disguise. Surprisingly, it had worked. No one batted an eye at them as they refueled. Everything went smoothly, at least until they were back on the ship.

She took off her disguise easily, but Dex… Well, he hadn't really chosen wisely when he'd adhered the metal to his skin. The glue turned out to be rather permanent, and the tiny sheets of metal were stuck to his face for a full week before they finally managed to pull them off.

"Let's just say we got the fuel, but it wound up causing more problems in the long run." Dex rubbed a bare spot on his stubbly cheek.

"Still can't grow hair there, I see." Andi smirked.

"Shut up," Dex mumbled.

"It's time," Lon said, pulling them back to the present.

The radar flashed, marking the Tavina System up ahead.

Dex placed his hand on the throttle and eased it back, exiting hyperspace as they approached Solera. The ship shook around them, far too aggressively as it entered the planet's atmosphere.

They'd made it. The ship was breaking apart around them, but against all odds, they'd made it.

Andi let out a sigh of relief. The Godstars must be liking her today.

Using the last dregs of fuel, Dex directed the ship toward the planet's icy surface. But as they passed through Solera's outer rings, Andi realized that they were utterly alone. It was a known fact that Solerans didn't like mingling any more than necessary with outsiders, but every populated planet had some type of space traffic around it.

It was beyond eerie that this one didn't.

So when a pulse of light shot through the empty airspace toward them, it caught them unaware. The light encased the *Marauder* for a moment before resuming its path in their wake.

Dex swore. "What the hell was that?"

"Solar ray?" Lon guessed, but Andi shook her head.

"Let's just get down there," she said. "We don't have much fuel left. Bring her down nice and easy, Dextro. You wreck my ship, you pay for it."

Dex grunted. "I can't," he gritted out as he tried to engage the thrusters.

"What do you mean, you *can't*?"

"The thrusters aren't at full power."

"They're only giving twenty percent thrust," Lon said, furiously typing on the holoscreen in his hands. "And the backup system is off–line."

Of course it is, Andi thought grimly. That light must've done something to the ship.

Solera was growing larger and larger by the second.

"Brace for impact," Memory said calmly from the speakers as fire engulfed the exterior of the ship, so at odds with the icy world they were quickly approaching.

Andi gripped the edges of her seat and watched helplessly as Dex white-knuckled the wheel, trying to keep the ship steady.

She took back what she'd said about the Godstars liking her.

They really must hate her guts.

CHAPTER 9

DEX

There had been plenty of times in Dex's life when he'd thought he was dead.

When he was a child, he'd been told stories by traveling missionaries of what the afterlife was like. If you were good, and had no sin, you'd go to the Godstars' palace in the sky. But if you were bad, you would be sent elsewhere, to be tortured for all eternity.

Of course he'd thought about the afterlife, and what lay beyond this existence, but he always thought when he experienced it for himself, it would be unlike anything his mind could've conjured up. Now, as his eyes cracked open, he was almost blinded by whiteness. It was the purest color he'd ever seen.

If those missionaries were right, and there was a palace in the sky where the righteous went after death, then he had not a damned clue why he was there. He wasn't trying to say he deserved to be tortured, but hey, there were far better people than him in this galaxy.

That was how Dex knew he must be alive.

That, and the searing pain that pulsed within his head.

Dex could feel his heart beating inside his skull, like a hatchet against stone, chipping away bit by bit. The acidic smell of burned metal wafted into his nose, and something sharp jabbed his side.

"You with me, Dex?" a voice said from what seemed like a mile away. Then a hand connected with his cheek with a sharp sting, jarring him out of his haze.

The world of white came into focus, and at its center was a pair of stormy gray eyes.

"I'm with you," he croaked, rubbing his sore cheek. "You didn't have to smack me, though."

"It got your attention," Andi said, looking unabashed as she stood.

"That it did."

He was still buckled into his chair. The reason everything looked white when he'd awoken was now obvious. Through the viewport of the *Marauder*, as far as he could see, was an endless expanse of snow, filling the entire front window as it stretched into the distance.

Everything came flooding back to him at once.

The ship shutting down, leaving the nebula behind. The frantic jump to hyperspace. The jarring screech of metal hitting the planet's frozen surface.

They had survived the crash, but he wasn't sure how long they'd last now. Solera was an unforgiving planet, and with Nor's soldiers having swept across the galaxy... He wasn't sure if anywhere was safe.

"Any idea where we are?" Dex asked, blinking stars from his eyes. His head throbbed angrily.

Andi stared out the viewport. "Not a clue."

Dex grimaced. Nothing but frozen terrain out there, as far as he could tell. The ship rocked in the howling winds, and giant shards of ice jutted up from the white plain, towering hundreds of feet in the air. One of them, half a click away, was broken in two, a great gouge in the ice revealing where the *Marauder* had crashed into it before sliding to a stop here.

He unbuckled himself and slowly rose to his feet. "Memory, how bad is the damage?"

"Catastrophic," Andi answered from the dash, which was flashing erratically with glitching blueprints and radar screens.

Memory's absence echoed Andi's point.

Across from them, Lon groaned in his seat, straps still secure across his chest. "I'm fine, guys. Thank you for your concern."

"We're a little busy, Sentinel," Dex said, just as the ship groaned a final time and silence rushed through the bridge.

The lights on the console blinked out entirely. The only noise came from their hitched breaths and the freezing winds outside.

And Havoc, screeching wildly as it ran circles around the bridge, horns protruding from its fur. Apparently the creature had enjoyed the ride. Lon scooped him up, and the beast instantly fell as silent as the ship.

Well, hell, Dex thought as he looked around. This wasn't good.

"Did the ship just…?" Andi started.

"Completely shut down, leaving us to the mercy of the elements? Yes, yes it did," Dex said. "Godstars, I hate Solera. I managed to deploy the backup shields so our landing wouldn't damage the ship too badly, but I guess it didn't help much."

That explained why the air smelled like burned metal. He didn't want to imagine what the exterior of the ship looked like. Varillium was supposedly impenetrable, but how many times could they crash-land the ship and have it remain so?

"Thank you," Andi said suddenly.

Dex stared at her in shock, his eyes widening. "Did you just… thank me?"

Maybe he *was* dead after all.

"Don't get too cocky."

Still dazed, he said, "I should crash the ship more often."

Andi glared at him. "Don't push your luck, Dextro."

He laughed, then winced at the ache in his head.

Lon gasped from across the bridge. They turned to see him glued to the small window on the starboard side of the ship.

"What's wrong?" Andi asked.

The window fogged up as Lon spoke. "It's so beautiful," he said in a daze, making Dex wonder if he was okay. "I've never seen snow before."

It took a moment for his statement to register. "Never?" Dex asked, stunned.

"Never," Lon confirmed, wiping at the clouded window. "It doesn't snow back on Adhira, and until we went to Arcardius, I'd never once left home. My job was to protect Adhira, not leave it. All the Sentinels made vows to my aunt Alara, to protect the Mountain of Rhymore."

"A soldier's vow," Andi aknowledged with a curt nod. "Something I broke long ago."

"Looks like we're all deserters," Dex said, thinking of how he'd lost his Guardian status years before, too. General Cortas had promised to reinstate him after he and Andi had retrieved Valen from Lunamere, but the general's manipulations and untimely death had prevented him from fulfilling his end of the bargain to Dex.

Lon looked down at his boots. "How far we've fallen."

"You didn't break your vow to Alara," Andi told him. "You served her and Adhira faithfully, until her death. Now you can serve whomever you wish."

Dex nodded in agreement. He'd been just a few months old when he left Tenebris for the first time. Although he didn't remember the journey, he knew it must've been the first time he'd bonded with the stars. Ever since, he'd longed to be among them, traveling to the deepest corners of the galaxy. That bond was what had initially connected him to Andi. They both saw an opportunity out there, in the spaces between the stars—a place where they could live out the wildest parts of their dreams.

"We need a plan," Andi said, drawing everyone's attention back to the matter at hand. She grabbed the portable holoscreen off the console, which fortunately hadn't been damaged in the crash. Dex joined Andi as she pulled up a miniature rotating Solera, wrapped by its rings. She zoomed in on a spot in the middle of a jagged ice field. "This is where we landed—the closest city isn't for a thousand clicks. We'll need a ship, or a transport of some kind, to make it there alive in this weather."

Solera was an ice giant in the Tavina System. It was heavily populated, but every resident lived within one of Solera's seven domed cities, as the elements were too harsh to bear year-round. As a result, most of the planet's surface was uninhabited and devoid of civilization, which meant they were unlikely to find help all the way out here.

"How long do you think we have before we freeze?" Lon paced the length of the bridge, his breath already rising before him in small clouds.

"Depending on how damaged the hull is… I'd say six hours," Andi said, handing the holo to Dex and peering out through the window. The sky above them was an icy blue, but beyond, it turned into an angry gray. A storm was rolling in. "I take that back—maybe three, max. The girls and I came here for a job a while back. Solera is merciless."

She was right. If there was one thing Dex knew about this planet, it was to beware the shifting weather. Solera's storms were renowned across Mirabel for the lives they'd stolen over the years, the planet's icy surface like a glittering grave.

"Have you looked for military outposts in the area?" Lon said, coming up beside him. "On Adhira, during the Cataclysm, they had outposts built across the planet for the military to be stationed at. There may be some here, too, and if they're anything like the ones back home, they should be full of supplies and tech."

"Worth a shot," Andi said with a shrug. "Dex, can you do a search?"

"Can't," Dex said. "No access to the feeds on this thing." He looked at the silver band on his wrist, hoping Alfie would have established a connection by now. But alas, the AI was still silent. He was about to set the holo down when Lon cleared his throat.

"We've got company."

Dex turned to look out the window, across the ice field. Beyond the snow whipping in the wind, a triangular shape appeared, moving quickly as it hovered over the landscape.

A transport.

"Who do you think it is?" Lon asked.

"Memory's down. Can't ask her," Andi replied, grabbing her sheathed swords from their spot on the back of her captain's chair. She buckled the twin belts across her chest, looking more like herself than she had in weeks.

"Looks like we're about to find out." Dex unholstered his gun. "They're almost here."

As if the mystery passengers had heard them, a voice suddenly blasted from the transport's speakers.

"Come out, weapons down, or we will fire!"

"Think they mean it?" Lon wondered, brows raised.

Dex shrugged. "I don't plan to find out. Arm up and meet me in the cargo hold."

"You can't be serious, Dex. You want to walk into enemy hands?" Andi huffed.

Dex felt a flicker of annoyance. "We don't exactly have many options. We either take our chances with these people," he said, checking the clip on his gun, "or we freeze to death in here. You decide, Androma."

"I have a better idea," Andi said. "We need a ride to the

city…" She looked out the window at the transport, her hands clenching around her sword hilts. "So let's take it."

"Where's Lon?" Andi asked, running into the cargo hold.

"He had to grab something from his bunk," Dex said, handing Andi a planetary suit and grabbing one for himself just as Lon rushed in the door as well, carrying a small backpack.

It was squirming.

"Nope," Dex said, shaking his head. "Hell no, Lon. You're not bringing that thing with us."

Havoc's telltale yowl sounded out from inside the pack.

To Dex's surprise, Andi responded this time. "We have to."

"You hate that thing as much as I do!"

She shrugged. "You want to face Gilly's wrath when we free her, and Havoc isn't in tow?"

Dex imagined the little girl's classic, mischievous snarl. "No," he said, sighing and looking back at Lon. "Keep the Fellibrag under control, Sentinel, or I'm putting a bullet through its brain."

"I'm not entirely sure it has one," Andi said with a laugh.

They each pulled on their suits, and although the material was thin and light, that didn't fool Dex. It was designed to protect its wearer from the harshest environments, ranging from lava worlds to frozen wastelands, like Solera. They'd cost him a hell of a lot of Krevs, and while Dex had once been furious that Andi had stolen the suits, along with the *Marauder*, years ago, he was glad for her thievery now. Without the suits, they'd be screwed.

Dex buckled his weapons belt around the suit, as did Andi. But Lon carried no visible weapons, simply slinging the pack he'd retrieved over his shoulder. Havoc hissed in response.

The only thing left for them to do was step outside and face their fate. Whether that be death, imprisonment or freedom, they had yet to find out.

The three of them traded looks.

"We go in as a team, and come out as one," Dex said.

"No one gets left behind," Andi agreed. Dex could see the pain flickering in her eyes as she uttered those words and knew she was thinking of her crew. She swallowed and glanced away from him.

"We might be going into this blind, but we'll try negotiations first," Dex instructed them. "If that doesn't work, we shoot. Getting captured is not on the agenda for today." He pressed the button on the side of his neck, and a helmet engulfed his head. Andi and Lon did the same.

They lined up together on the edge of the loading dock. Andi pulled a lever, and the giant door yawned open. Solera greeted them with a rush of wind that Dex assumed would've frozen them in place if it weren't for the protection of the suits.

"Let's not keep them waiting."

They left the cover of the *Marauder* and stepped onto the open ice field. The transport ship had landed a few paces away, and a group of six figures now emerged from its belly in black suits. There were no sigils on their uniforms, providing no indication of whether they were friends or enemies.

To be honest, Dex didn't even know if they had any friends left in this galaxy anymore. Everyone he knew was compromised, or at least he assumed they were by now. He'd never forget the glazed expressions of the people who'd turned to Nor, and he was certain they'd do anything in her name.

Including killing Dex and the others in cold blood right now.

The group stopped a few paces away from them. Dex put a hand on his gun, noticing Andi's body tense beside his as the leader of the group froze in place.

For a moment, Dex thought he saw the person reach for a weapon. But his eyes widened when they instead lifted a hand in greeting.

"Dextro Arez. It's been a while."

Dex's eyes widened as the speaker's face came into view behind a clear helmet.

"Klarisa?" Dex asked, utterly aghast.

"The one and only," Klarisa said with a wicked grin.

Dex wanted to rush forward to greet his old comrade, but he held back, knowing he couldn't allow his emotions to rule him. There was only one way to determine whether Klarisa was still herself, or if she was in Nor's thrall.

"Who do you serve?" Dex said carefully, remembering the question that had been asked of the guests in that Arcardian ballroom, just after they'd been shot with the silver bullets and rose again.

Klarisa thudded her right fist against her heart. "I serve my galaxy, as do you. As do all Guardians. But I serve no queen."

Dex took a few steps forward, surveying her face beneath her helmet for the telltale silver veins, but there was no trace of them on her dark complexion. She looked him up and down as well, as if she, too, were trying to see through to the blood beneath his skin.

"Who do *you* serve?" Klarisa asked pointedly.

Dex shrugged. "It depends on the time of day. Griss in the morning, Jurum in the evening."

The woman stared back at him for a moment, her comrades utterly silent behind her. Then she burst into laughter. "Arez, you sorry bastard. You haven't changed a lick since we last saw each other."

"Much to your satisfaction," Dex said, finally allowing himself to step forward and engulf her in a tight hug.

He hadn't seen Klarisa since they'd graduated from the Academy. She'd also gone on to become a Guardian, but their paths hadn't crossed since he'd joined the Bounty Hunter's branch. He felt a twinge of guilt for not following up with her these past few years, but this surprise reunion gave him the first bit of hope he'd had in three weeks.

"Sorry to ruin the moment, but what's going on?" Andi said, coming up next to them. Her hand rested lightly on Gilly's double-triggered gun at her hip, though Dex was relieved to see she wasn't yet reaching for her twin swords.

"Andi, this is Klarisa, a fellow Guardian," Dex told her. "We attended the Academy together."

Andi remained tense, despite his words. "Who are you with?" she asked Klarisa.

Klarisa looked back at her group. "We're with the Underground, led by Arachnid. But we choose our own paths—and control our own minds."

"Did you bring my ship down?" Andi demanded.

"We've been doing that with any ships that enter this airspace," Klarisa replied apologetically. "We've saved many Unaffecteds this way. Some people were traveling when the attacks happened and weren't infected with the virus."

"You almost killed us, and you ruined my ship."

Dex knew then that Andi and Klarisa would never be friends.

"Usually the ships we bring down are in better shape than yours was," she explained, surveying the damaged hull of the *Marauder*.

"My ship was perfectly fine before you interfered," Andi hissed, glaring at the woman. Dex tried not to snort at the obvious lie. "So you've been doing this a lot? How did you know we weren't a ship full of Xen Pterran soldiers?"

"We've been monitoring the flight patterns of Nor's ships, and none of them have taken the route yours did. They usually come and go from Craatia, so we assumed your ship was an anomaly, like the other Unaffected ships we've encountered."

Andi nodded. "Where is your base?"

"For safety precautions, I cannot tell you its exact location, but I can tell you it's in the Briog Sector. Arachnid likes to keep things under wraps, until we know who we can trust. The galaxy isn't what it used to be."

"It's still a shitshow," Andi said with a grumble.

Klarisa barked out a laugh in agreement.

"How do we know you're not lying about the Underground?" Lon asked, speaking up for the first time. Dex had come to realize that Lon never asked questions until he'd ascertained a certain amount of information. He was very much a listener in that respect.

"Who's this?" Klarisa asked Dex.

Lon spoke for himself before Dex could answer. "Lon Mette, a Sentinel hailing from Adhira. Nice to make your acquaintance," he said formally. The backpack slung over his shoulder howled furiously.

"Adhiran Sentinels never leave their posts," Klarisa said, eyeing the backpack as Lon shushed it. "Must have been a hell of a choice, leaving your planet behind."

Lon nodded, his eyes downcast. "There's nothing left there for me now."

"And you?" Klarisa asked, looking back toward Andi.

When Andi simply glared at her, Dex rolled his eyes and said, "Klarisa, meet Androma Racella."

Klarisa's eyes widened. Dex smiled, knowing that Andi's name would give the woman a reason to respect her. A reason to want them to join this so-called Underground led by the red-armored soldier from the feeds.

"The Bloody Baroness," Klarisa said, her tone changing as she looked back at Andi, angling her chin high. "I've heard a lot about you."

Andi smirked. "I can't say the same about you, unfortunately. So tell us, why should we trust you? Seems all too convenient that you found us, and of all the people in the galaxy, Dex just happened to know one of you. And you're supposedly Unaffected, working for the one man in the galaxy who might be able to fight back against Nor."

"I don't argue with fate, Baroness," Klarisa said. "And by the looks of you three, you'll likely be captured the moment you get within a rifle scope's view of any domed city. There are

Guardians," she continued, glancing at Dex. "A whole legion of them, manning the outskirts of each dome. All of them loyal to Nor's cause."

"Silver veins?" Dex asked.

Klarisa nodded.

"I don't suppose you've got a way around that?"

The woman smiled. "The Underground has its ways. We're not without specialists in…certain areas."

"What's that supposed to mean?" Lon asked.

"One of our comrades disabled the heating systems in Craatia a few days back," Klarisa told him with a smirk. "It used to be as warm as a summer's day, and now? Well, let's just say the good citizens of Craatia are mourning their summer fashions now that they have to don their best winter gear. You'll be safe in your suits and helmets—that will do as a disguise, for a time."

"Good," Andi said. "In that case, will you take us to Arachnid?"

"We have skills to offer," Dex added, raising a brow at his old comrade. "We made a vow to each other, Klarisa. Ages ago. To protect each other, and to protect the galaxy."

The woman considered, looking him up and down before glancing at Andi and Lon again. She was a good soldier, having earned top marks at the Academy, and Dex would never forget all the late nights they'd spent together during their years of training, with countless other Guardians, playing games of Fleet and swapping bottles of Griss until the suns rose.

The very best kind of bonding happened when bottles were passed around.

"We'll give you a ride to the domed sector," Klarisa said at last. "As for joining the Underground, Arachnid wants every free mind to decide for themselves. But there's a gatekeeper. You'll have to get past her if you wish to join. She'll check to be certain you're not a Solis spy."

"And if she lets us in?" Andi asked.

"Then Arachnid will welcome you into a tangled web of—" Klarisa's response was cut short as a boisterous crack split through the valley. All nine heads turned toward its origin, past the *Marauder*, as the very ground trembled.

A wave of dread swept over Dex's body, making his hair stand on end. Wind gusted across the ice field, sweeping snow from the ground, tossing it into the skies so that everything looked clouded.

Another crack sounded out, and the ground shook again.

"Defensive positions!" Klarisa exclaimed. Andi followed suit, pulling her swords free of their sheaths as a deafening roar resonated around them, the sound unlike anything Dex had ever heard.

He pulled his gun from its holster and Andi ignited her swords, swaths of electricity casting a hazy purple glow on the snow swirling around them.

"What the hell is that?" Andi asked. Dex didn't have an answer—he was just as confused as she was.

"The locals mentioned a beast in the icelands," Klarisa said. Her comrades closed in around her in a half circle. Dex, Andi and Lon joined them, backs pressed together. "We thought it was just a story rooted in superstitious lore. We've been out in the icelands many times, but never encountered anything living. But if the stories are true—"

Klarisa was cut off again as the ice around them exploded into fragments. Dex was thrown backward, but as he sailed through the air, he got a glimpse of what he could only describe as something from legend.

An ice dragon.

He landed on the ice-encrusted ground. Pain shot up his spine, spreading through his nervous system like lightning. The planetary suits were made to protect them from the atmosphere, not bodily harm caused by the planet itself.

Dex rolled onto his side, his lower back screaming in protest. He didn't think he'd broken anything, but he would surely end up with a wicked bruise. But that didn't matter now—what *did* matter was that he couldn't see more than a few feet in front of him, and a predator was on the loose somewhere among the flurries.

Snow drifted around him like slinking ghosts, obscuring his view. Someone else groaned in the distance.

"Everyone alright?" Dex called, grabbing his gun from the ground beside him and struggling to his feet.

"I'm here," Andi answered from close by. Two more voices he didn't recognize yelled back, as well.

The air had cleared enough for him to make some shapes out through the white veil of snow, but the ice dragon's lumbering form was nowhere to be seen. It must've gone back under the ice, but somehow he knew, deep in his bones, that it would be back.

Someone touched his shoulder, and he whipped around to find Klarisa standing there, her arm twisted at an odd angle.

"You're hurt," Dex said, stating the obvious.

She shook her head, batting him away. "Nothing I can't handle. Better than half my crew—that thing took them into the ground with it."

"Godstars. I'm so sorry." Even as Dex said the words, he realized they fell short. But this wasn't the time to grieve, and he was sure Klarisa knew that, too. "If we wait around here any longer, we'll be monster bait, as well. Where's your transport?"

Klarisa pointed off into the distance. Dex scanned the horizon—the transport's sleek form was nearly a click away. That beast had really tossed them on their asses.

"Let's find everyone and get the hell out of here," Dex said. Klarisa nodded in agreement.

They came across Andi first, who was helping Lon stand. Dex let out a breath, thanking the Godstars for sparing his small crew.

Then the ground rumbled beneath them again.

"*Not* good. We have to run," Andi said, supporting Lon, whose leg was bleeding through his suit. A jagged ice shard lay on the ground behind them.

His suit was compromised. They only had a few minutes before Lon would die of exposure out here on the frozen tundra.

Andi must've seen his gaze wander. "He'll be fine as long as we get to the transport before the cold gets him first." Her eyes pleaded with him not to put voice to the thought that was in both their minds.

If they could get him to the transport in time. Which was looking less and less likely by the minute. Lon's backpack, somehow, was still squirming, Havoc hissing furiously inside.

The only casualty Dex *had* hoped for had survived.

Dex turned to see the two remaining members of Klarisa's crew running toward them. But before they'd taken more than a few steps, the ice splintered in front of them and a new hole formed, sucking the two men below the surface. Their screams were cut short as the dragon, twice the size of the *Marauder*, shot through the jagged hole and hundreds of feet into the sky, its long body whipping through the air effortlessly. It looked as if it were made from ice crystals, carefully arranged into a skeletal structure, and Dex was momentarily struck by the harsh beauty of the creature.

Then transparent wings unfurled from its back, making the beast arc through the sky. It looked graceful, but Dex knew that beautiful things were often the most deadly. Its body did a dance midair, its bones clinking together as it turned and nose-dived downward, its mouth yawning open, razor-sharp teeth glinting in the fading light of the approaching storm.

Dex didn't plan on becoming monster food tonight. But it was Andi who was the first to move.

"To the ship, now!" she roared, pulling Lon with her. Klarisa and Dex followed in their wake just as the beast landed behind them.

Dex jumped over a crack that split the ice a few feet wide. Once clearing the rift, he pointed his gun behind him, shooting at random, but even when his shots met their mark, they didn't slow the beast. It was as if there was nothing to penetrate, all its organs protected fiercely by its bone-work scales.

The transport ship slowly came into view. A shard of ice shot through the air, narrowly missing him.

It struck a different target instead.

Klarisa screamed and fell to the ground, blood quickly drenching the snow.

"No!" Dex dropped to his knees beside his old friend, staring at the ice shard embedded in her stomach. Klarisa looked up at him through her helmet, eyes full of pain, but determined.

"Save yourself," she whispered. "Get to the ice pub."

"Dex, come on!" Andi yelled, hurtling past him, Lon close behind.

"Back to the stars, Guardian," Dex choked out, reciting the words he'd said to fallen friends before. Klarisa's eyes closed for the last time just as the ground trembled again.

With a final glance at her still face, Dex ran for his life. The ship was just a few paces ahead, but the dragon was closer.

"How are we going to get the ship in the sky before that thing takes it down, with us inside?" Andi asked through the com in their suits.

She had a point. The beast could fly, and if this transport went down, they'd either be dragon food, or scorched to death if the ship blew. Either way, dead was dead.

Dex got to the loading ramp first, shooting rounds at the beast to give Andi and Lon time to board. Finally, the two of them reached the ramp. Lon dumped the backpack on the floor as he slumped into a chair, breathing heavily.

Blood pooled from his suit.

"Now what?" Andi panted, ripping a medkit from the paneled wall as she turned to Lon.

"We fly this bird," Dex said, racing to the front of the hull. He buckled himself into the pilot's chair and turned on the engines. They made a satisfying hum.

"It's almost on top of us!" Andi shouted in warning.

Havoc screeched, claws lacerating a hole through the backpack as the dragon's roar closed in.

"Andi," Dex heard Lon say. "It's useless."

"No," she growled. Dex looked over his shoulder to see her hands shaking as she sliced Lon's suit leg open wide and frantically pressed gauze to his wound. The gauze soaked through instantly, and she cursed. "Dex! Get us the hell out of here!"

Dex punched the throttle and lifted the ship into the air. But it wasn't fast enough.

The dragon's claws raked down the open ramp, lurching the ship back toward the ground. Dex pushed the thrusters to full power, but it did little to dislodge the beast.

"Andi! Get over here now!"

He heard her muttering under her breath as she joined him. Together, they searched the console for something, anything that might help them fight back, until Dex heard Lon's weak voice behind them.

"Tell Lira I love her, and I will see her in our next life," he said. Dex jerked his head around just in time to see Lon pull a grenade from the backpack. Havoc launched out as well, scurrying into the shadows beneath the dash.

"Lon, what are you—" Andi started.

The Sentinel met Dex's gaze. "Tell her the truth, Dex. Tell her what she truly is." His eyes flitted toward Andi briefly. Then he turned, before either of them could stop him, and launched himself out of the transport, toward the beast.

Andi screamed as the dragon swallowed Lon whole and released its grip on the transport.

Then the beast exploded into flames as the transport took to the sky.

CHAPTER 10
VALEN – *THREE YEARS AGO*

*T*oday, Nor gave him the sun.

Or, at the very least, she'd tried to.

Valen stood in his older sister's crumbling tower, peering up at a sky that refused to open wide and reveal that blazing orb of light he'd missed so deeply during his months in Lunamere.

"I know it's not as you'd hoped it would be," Nor said, stepping up beside Valen to rest her palm against the glass window that protected them from the acid rains. "I've heard stories about the sun on Arcardius. They say it shines so bright, it's blinding."

Valen shrugged. "It hardly matters now. Arcardius isn't my home any longer."

His real home was a place that existed beyond where he could see, far in the depths of outer space. In another galaxy entirely. Exonia.

Valen often wondered if anything from his past had ever truly been real. He saw his sister Kalee in his mind's eye. Not a full sister, as he'd always thought, but a half sister, like Nor. He could still see Kalee's smile, still hear the fading remnants of her laugh. Those memories were the ones he'd hung on to while he rotted inside his cell in Lunamere, completely unaware that his imprisonment was all part of Nor's plan to help him discover his true self.

Kalee's laugh, when he tried to conjure it up now, fell flat. The sound was off, like a melody sung out of tune.

He saw his mother, Merella—the only mother he'd ever known. He remembered the way she'd always been so gentle with him, so kind. Perhaps it had been out of pity, for she had always known that Valen wasn't truly her flesh and blood.

Most frequently of all, he saw his father. The ruthless General of Arcardius.

A man who'd killed Valen's real mother—murdered her in cold blood, when she was meant to be set free, delivered safely back to Xen Ptera with Valen. But on that Arcardian warship, during the final moments of the Cataclysm when his father and mother, Klaren, had hovered above Xen Ptera, Valen supposed that Cyprian had never planned to let Klaren live to see her two children united.

Somehow, he'd discovered a way to fight Klaren's compulsion. And because of that, he'd broken her, refusing to allow her to raise Valen and Nor together, as a family.

Perhaps that had been his father's mission all along. For he surely knew that if Klaren's two children ever found each other, they'd become powerful beyond measure. Ruthless, perhaps even more than Cyprian had ever been.

"The sun is a reminder," Valen said now, sitting down on a small stone ledge carved into the tower. His body still ached, but Nor had assigned her personal physician to look after him, a cyborg woman who had come to his new suite of rooms and spread oils and tonics across his back until the lash wounds stitched themselves back together.

Nor had given him more food than he'd eaten in months—the best she could offer from Xen Ptera's limited supply, to help him grow strong.

And now she'd done what she could to give him a ray of sunlight to cast away the shadows of his past.

"A reminder of what?" Nor asked.

Through the glass, Valen surveyed the streets of Nivia, Xen Ptera's capital city. "That there will always be a new day."

"And if you can't see the sun?" *she wondered. Her expression was full of grief as she gazed down at her people below—as if all she could see was death.*

"Then we will make our own," *Valen swore.* "Together. And then the world will be ours, and bow beneath our will."

Nor looked slightly heartened at his declaration. "The message our mother sent to me before she died… It wasn't only about you. She told me that Exonia was dying, too. Imagine it, Valen. Our true home is an entire galaxy like Xen Ptera. Desperate for escape. We can be that escape for them, when we tear open the Void."

They would do it. He knew, just from the look in her eyes each time she spoke of the future, that she would help him hone his power to its greatest potential. And someday, they would change the fate of not just one galaxy, but two.

"That's why I come up here," *Nor said quietly.* "I force myself to stare down at this hideous place, because it reminds me of what's at stake. And now I hope it reminds you, too." *She glared at the skies, with that icy gaze he had come to know as strength.*

It made Valen itch with the need for revenge.

Not for himself. But for these people. For his sister.

For all the lies his father had ever told him.

For Exonia.

One moment, Valen was lying on a soft pillow of moss in Kalee's garden, feeling Nor's presence fade away from their mental doorway. The next…a deep breath, a press against that thread of power within his soul…

Valen stepped into the confines of his mind.

Here was the threshold of his power.

The sky was dark overhead, clouds rumbling as the wind howled like a wounded beast. A battlefield lay before him, heavy with the corpses of dead demons from his past. Fear, and insecurity, and the certainty that he would never amount to anything. Valen himself had slain them all on his journey to unlocking his compulsion.

He'd left their bodies to rot. Physical reminders of how far he'd come, since that very first time Nor and Darai had shown him how to craft this domain.

Some of those dead demons would rise again, as they always did.

But for now, they remained motionless. And that was fine with Valen, for he had work to do. Minds to connect with, orders to give.

The frozen grass crunched underfoot as he walked down the sloping hillside, a torch held tightly in his fist. The flame flickered, but did not give out, even with the power of the wind.

For Valen controlled all things here.

This was his kingdom. *His* domain.

And far across the battlefield, waiting for him, like a monster in its own right—a dark fortress. The place where his compulsion, the height of his ability, the center of everything for him and Nor, stood. Valen smiled, his first real smile in days, as he stepped over the dead, his eyes on the giant obsidinite castle that cast a shadow across this land.

Here, he was a king without a crown. But he didn't need one—not in this place.

Here, there were no limitations on what he could do.

Valen visualized himself wearing a cloak of deepest crimson—Nor's favorite color—as he did each time he visited the castle in his mind. In the space between one breath and the next, the cloak appeared, fabric snapping in the wind like the crack of the whips that had once been used to drag him down to the depths of humanity in Lunamere—to force his compulsion to manifest, if he wished to survive.

The fabric shimmered with each step he took, illuminated by the steady flame of his torch, and bones shattered beneath his boots as Valen reached the edge of the battlefield. The wind, howling at his back, seemed to quiet. It had always talked to him, the wind. Whispered little things that were like secrets from deep within his own soul.

But tonight, it was silent. As if everything came to a sudden stillness when he reached the threshold of his domain.

Valen looked up, craning his neck toward the top of the castle, taking in each perfectly aligned black obsidinite stone. This fortress housed every mind he compelled across Mirabel. Hundreds upon hundreds of thousands, all bent to his will.

Home, his body hummed. For a moment, he thought he heard Nor's voice calling his name. A flicker, distant as he glanced back across the battlefield, to that dark tunnel that led to their linked doorway. But the sound faded almost as soon as it began, and he carried on, dismissing it as he drew closer to his castle.

It was a shadow even darker than the battlefield, spreading as far as his eyes could see, left and right, the rigid walls snaking across the horizon. The irony of its resemblance to Lunamere was not lost on him, as the mere mention of the prison moon had once caused his knees to quake. But Valen chuckled to himself now at the thought of that wretched place, where he had spent months weak and shivering, because it was now his greatest memory in life.

It was there where Valen had first tasted power.

Where he had first learned who he was…and who he could be.

He reached the castle doors, towering masterpieces made of obsidinite. A carving of the triangular Solis family crest was spread across the two doors.

Gold, the color of Nor's eyes.

Valen ran his fingertips across the symbol. He could feel his power purring in response, like a great beast awaiting its master's return. If Valen listened closely enough, he could hear the murmurs of those beneath his compulsion. Like whispering souls, wandering aimlessly through the black corridors.

He took off his boots as he entered, placing them down gently on the dark stone floors.

"Home," Valen said.

His voice echoed across the walls. There were no portraits here. No fine decorations. Just dark, endless hallways that stretched on for miles.

Valen set his torch in an empty bracket on the wall. Immediately, the other torches in the corridor flared to life, stretching on forever, as far and as wide as Valen's mind would allow, illuminating the vast space.

Lining both sides of the halls were doors, nearly identical to those that had once caged him in his cell on Lunamere. But inside these cells, the prisoners were not people.

They were *minds*.

The very essence of a person. Their hopes, their dreams, their desires. The minds of nearly every man, woman and child across Mirabel resided in this castle. Or rather, Valen's connections to those minds.

He still shivered every time he felt a new mind join his network. It was like another piece of himself clicking into place, and with each addition, his castle walls had expanded. They'd grown taller. Wider. Until the castle became a fortress that could not be shaken or overtaken.

Valen took a left now, striding down the first hallway. As he walked, he occasionally glanced through the barred windows of each doorway. Eventually, he slowed to a stop before one door and peered inside the cell, pressing his face to the cold bars.

As soon as he made contact, it was as if Valen had suddenly been transported across the stars, soaring through darkness until there was a spark. A jolt. A scene materialized before him, images flickering into existence as Valen saw into his victim's mind. As he saw the world through their eyes, like they were his own.

A young child, judging by the size of her hands. She was sitting crisscross in a patch of amber grass that swayed in the wind. Native to Uulveca, Valen realized.

The girl was playing with a doll. A newly fashioned one, for when the child turned the doll around, Valen saw the rouged lips, the ringlet curls, the golden crown nestled atop the doll's head.

It was Nor.

The child giggled as she made the doll dance.

"Worship your queen," Valen whispered into her mind. "Worship her, carry out her commands, and you will have peace."

He felt the compulsion sink into the child. Like a parasite nestling in deeper, beside one that had already been there, growing steadily day by day.

Valen extracted himself from the child's mind, pulling away from the cell door and back out into the hallway of his castle. He took a few steps farther, whistling to himself, his cloak dragging soundlessly across the stones behind him. The cold kissed his cheeks, and he felt *alive.*

Electric.

When he was doing this work, he mattered. No one disobeyed him. No one dared to defy him, for how could they, beneath the weight of his compulsion?

He picked another cell door.

An elderly man stood at the bow of a hovercraft, the glistening silver ship soaring just above the surface of a flat, motionless sea. The terraformed water sector of Adhira. Valen had always wished to visit, and now he could, through the mind of this man.

"We'll find it today, won't we, Oyneko?" a voice asked.

The old man turned, and Valen saw as he saw. A young Adhiran man, skin purple and smile bright, held a torpedo-shaped camera in his hands. He wore a gray work suit, salt stains crusting around the collar from his sweat.

"If the Godstars shine their light on us today, then perhaps we will," the old man said. "There were hundreds of varillium ships lost in this sea during the war. If we can find them, Rantyi, we'll have served the queen in a way few ever could. She'll finally be able to finish building Nexus."

"All hail the queen," the young Adhiran said, then tossed the camera into the sea.

Valen whispered his compulsion into the old man's mind, pressing in the desire to serve Nor. Igniting a hunger to keep working until he uncovered the lost varillium for Nexus. Then he pulled himself away from the old man, back into the castle halls.

Valen didn't know how long he spent pressing thoughts into minds, compelling them to stay loyal, to stay true to his sister's reign. Time moved differently inside his mind fortress.

Usually, Valen's energy heightened in this space. But as he worked today, he found himself beginning to grow tired. He walked more slowly, stopping often to catch his breath as he passed by aisle after aisle of cells.

Then he heard the faintest echo of a whisper resonating throughout the castle. A little tugging on his thoughts, from far off.

"Nor?"

The sound of her name was labored on his lips—though he shouldn't be breathless, shouldn't even feel the need to breathe. For here he was all mind, no body.

And yet he felt heavy, as if weights were tied to his limbs.

Valen turned, a sigh pulling at him, and headed back toward the front doors to his castle. He'd just made it to the threshold when the torches behind him began to gutter out. His vision dimmed, dark spots appearing before his eyes…

And then he found himself waking up, lying on his back in Kalee's garden, blood crusting the skin beneath his nose.

The sky above was dark, the twin moons blinking down at

him as if they'd been watching. Valen sat up shakily, his head throbbing with the awful, persistent headache he hadn't been able to shake in days.

"*Valen.*"

This time, he was certain he'd heard Nor's voice. The ghost of it, perhaps finally reaching him now that he was back from the depths of his mind castle. But when he prodded at the doorway that linked them, he couldn't find any trace of his sister.

Just the lingering feeling of fear.

Something had gone wrong, while he'd been away.

Valen stood up, head throbbing with the effort. He wiped the blood from beneath his nose as he headed toward the mansion, eager to find his sister. To make sure she was alright, and to tell her what had just happened—how for a moment, he swore his power had flickered.

Like a dying star.

Nor couldn't shake the chill in her bones, even with the roaring fire in the marble fireplace of Averia's great room. The walls around her were gilded in gold, the ceiling stretching high into a towering dome. The Godstars were painted there, likely meant to be a comfort to anyone who found themselves lying on one of the plush couches, staring up as they lost themselves in their thoughts.

But tonight, Nor felt like the Godstars were glaring down at her. Just waiting for her to fail in the mission laid before her, broken now in the shadow of the unnamed general who'd taken her rightful place.

"We'll figure it out." Zahn's voice drew Nor's gaze from the shining ceiling and back toward the fireplace, where he stood before the flames, his muscular arms crossed. "For now, you may as well rest. Give yourself time to gather your strength for the days to come. You'll be no good to anyone exhausted."

Nor sighed and lifted a hand for him to help her from the couch. "I can't rest, Zahn. Not until we uncover the fool who has control of this galaxy. Nothing is relaxing when you feel as if your chest is wound so tight, it might burst." All she could think of, all she could see, was the hellish red armor of Arachnid, coupled with the faceless, ghostly form of whoever had stolen her command of Mirabel's weapons.

Who was behind that mask?

Worse still…who was the General of Arcardius, now that Cyprian Cortas was gone?

The last place Nor had seen the awful man was on the stage of the ballroom, during the Ucatoria Ball. He'd been bleeding out, at the end of his lifeline, thanks to Valen's blade. Had it been in his final moments that he'd passed the power on to someone else? Or had he set it in motion long before? Had all the leaders known upon their deaths, as they let Nor slide a blade across their own throats, that the galaxy would not fully belong to her once they were gone?

Was she truly a queen, when she felt as if someone else was wearing her crown?

"Nhatilya," Zahn said, effortlessly lifting her from the couch and guiding her closer to the flames. Her arms, bare without her cloak, were covered in gooseflesh. She hadn't realized how cold she was. Zahn ran his fingertips across her skin, smooth and strong as he pulled her close, trying to chase the chill away. "You're shaking."

He held her tighter, and she leaned into him, wishing she could forget, just for a moment, the weight she carried upon her back.

It had been there for so many years, growing heavier day by day.

"What if we don't find the new general, Zahn?" she asked,

looking up at his face. "What if all of this has been for nothing, and Exonia fades from existence? My true home… I'll never be able to call it mine."

"It's already yours, Nor," Zahn said. "And you *will* succeed."

He had the kindest eyes. He'd always looked at her with dedication and loyalty, since the moment he'd pulled her from the rubble as a child. As if she truly had always been his queen, even when she didn't yet wear a crown.

"Nexus is nearly complete, and even if we manage to amplify Valen's compulsion forever, long after he and I are gone… What's the point, if we can't access those weapons?"

What if I become just like my mother? she wanted to ask. *What if I'm a failure far worse than she ever was?*

If I fail, Exonia will be lost to the mists of time and space.

But she couldn't bring herself to utter those words. That fear. Saying them aloud would be like giving her fear wings, allowing it to take flight and carry her away.

"Exonia has waited a long time for their queen," Zahn whispered, his fingertips running up and down the small of her back. "They will not have to wait much longer. I'm certain of it. You've conquered so much in your life, Nor, but you've still so much left to live. So much left to make yours. With Valen's compulsion, with Darai's guidance, with the loyalty of Mirabel behind you… We will succeed. Together. For you."

Nor sighed, her face pressed against his chest. "You think too highly of me."

"No." Zahn angled her face upward, to look at him. "You are my *queen*. But more than that, you are my heart. There is nothing I won't do, Nor, to help you succeed in your life's calling. And if rooting out Arachnid, if rooting out this estranged general, is what you wish…then I will see it done."

"You're too pure for this galaxy," Nor told him.

Zahn raised a playful brow. "I can think of a few ways to change your mind about that."

He pressed a tender kiss to her lips, warmth flooding through her just as the doors to the great room burst open.

Nor sighed and pulled herself away from Zahn, turning toward whatever responsibility had found its way to her. It seemed impossible to find time alone with Zahn these days—or even time by herself, for that matter.

But it was only Valen, walking inside, tension in his thin shoulders. "What's going on?" he asked. "I felt something happen while I was away." He ran the back of his sleeve across his nose, as if he were rubbing away dirt that Nor couldn't see. "Are you alright? I thought I heard you calling, through our link."

"I *did* call," Nor snapped, annoyed. "I needed you, and you wouldn't answer."

Valen looked taken aback, and Nor immediately felt guilty for lashing out at him. She knew the work he was doing was important to their cause—perhaps more than ever, now. But sometimes she wished he was more present for her out *here*, instead of in his mind.

It was hard to feel connected to a ghost.

"Nice of you to join us, finally," Zahn said, pulling away from Nor with a sigh of his own. But he smiled at Valen all the same as Nor sat back down on the couch, allowing Zahn to relay the events that had taken place while Valen was likely traipsing the halls of his mind castle.

She felt so tired. And yet Nor knew she wouldn't be able to sleep until they discovered the identity of the general and found a way to take back what was hers.

"Well, that's…" Valen's words trailed off as Zahn finished his recap. He slumped down onto one of the couches, looking weary. "That's just great."

"Not the word I'd use to describe it," Nor said. "But now that you're caught up, we have a lot to discuss."

Zahn nodded and said, "I have to go check on a few things,

so I'll leave you to it." Then he pressed a kiss to Nor's forehead, leaning in to whisper, "Later, I'd like some time with you alone."

Her cheeks heated with pleasure as she watched him walk briskly away, a smile on his lips as he exited the room.

"So tell me, sister," Valen said, as he leaned back into the cushions. "Why can't we just blast this fool into bits, like my dear father did to Xen Ptera during the Cataclysm?"

Sometimes, at night, Nor still dreamed of the horrors that had befallen her home planet. The crushing decay that Xen Ptera still suffered from. She'd evacuated her people in the days just after her crowning, sending ships to bring them to the many flourishing planets across Mirabel. But she still felt a burning hatred for the Unified Systems because of what Cyprian had done when she thought of how long Xen Ptera had suffered. The planet might never come back to life again.

"That was my initial thought," Nor said. "But we can't destroy Sora, even if Arachnid is somehow still there, though I doubt he lingered long after sending his message." Nor massaged her temples. "It turns out we can't access the nuclear arsenal while the new general remains in power. Did you ever, in all your years spent around your father, overhear him speaking about the possibility of an heir?"

Valen shook his head, his eyes darkening. "No. He never chose. It was supposed to be Kalee, but when she died... There was no one else. He certainly didn't want me."

Bastard, Nor thought. She was glad Valen had been the one to drive the blade in deep.

"And on his deathbed?" Nor asked. "When he escaped from Ucatoria? The leaders of Mirabel were dead. Who would he have chosen in those final moments? Can you think of anyone he would have turned to?"

Valen shrugged. "I have no idea, Nor. My father had plenty of comrades, but he had plenty of enemies, too. I was gone for two years, Nor. There's no telling what relationships he made during that time. He traveled all across Mirabel, always making new acquaintances, forging alliances. And even if he *had* someone in mind… I'm surprised he would have given the command, or transferred that level of galaxy-wide power to anyone. There's no one my father trusted to run things but himself."

"But he did choose someone," Nor insisted. "The fail-safe demands that there be a leader, and according to the system, there *is* one. But it's not me." Her body was tensing up again, that chill returning as she thought of all the weapons on the capital planets that were just waiting for her to use them. To blast through the Void and reach Exonia.

And yet she could not use them.

Even when Nexus was completed, she *still* wouldn't be able to use them.

To be so close, yet doomed to fail… The thought made Nor sick.

Valen yawned—not from boredom, but from that pure exhaustion Nor was so used to seeing in him these days. "I could look into the minds of everyone beneath my compulsion. Perhaps I'll find this new general, and I can command him or her to hand over the access."

Nor felt her spirits lifting at the possibility. "Yes, see what you can find." Then her heart sank again as another thought occurred to her. "But if they're Unaffected, we'll be out of luck. And we'll never reach Exonia."

"So close," Valen said, echoing her earlier thoughts. "And yet so far."

"Thank you for the reminder, little brother," Nor retorted. "We'll work day and night. We'll search every corner of this damned galaxy until we find the usurper. Until we force them to give me full control of my rightful reign."

"And then we'll finally see our true home," Valen said quietly, staring into the fireplace as if he were gazing through the Void to Exonia.

Darai had grown up there. He'd spent his earliest days wandering that strange, formless place. He'd often told her about a great sea of color, the swirling abyss that had allowed him and her mother passage to Mirabel.

Nor had seen only a glimpse of it—a memory that was not her own. Her mother, with her own gift of compulsion, had found a way to send Nor that flash of memory before her death.

Nor had never seen anything like it. So *other*, so blessed by the light of the Godstars.

She'd tear open that space between worlds, soon enough. Darai had promised her, all these years, that it could be done. *No thanks to your own power*, Nor thought with a fleeting sense of sadness. Because her power, her blood, wasn't strong enough. But Valen's was.

That was Nor's own demon to battle—the constant disappointment in herself, for not commanding enough of their mother's power. She wasn't sure how it had happened, that uneven passing of Klaren's ability. She was the firstborn, and she'd expected, as her mother and Darai had, that most of it would have gone to her.

But Nor knew better than most that looking upon the past and wishing for a different outcome was futile.

Sometimes, she wished she could be Valen. Switch places with him for a day, and feel what it was like to reach the greatest heights of compulsion. Valen was the strongest person Nor had ever known—so strong that Darai could no longer train him. The old man had stopped even trying only weeks after Nor pulled Valen from his cold, empty cell in Lunamere, taking to the shadows instead.

He was likely jealous, in much the same way that Nor sometimes was. But she knew everyone had their place. Valen was their power source; Nor was the face of their mission. And Darai was indispensable as well, with all his knowledge of Exonia.

"There's something else," Valen said softly.

Nor looked up at him, raising her brows in a silent question.

"You know I visit the castle in my mind quite often."

It probably sounded silly to anyone who didn't understand how deeply he was speaking the truth. Valen wasn't one for jokes—Nor had learned this about him early on. It was one of the things that connected them, besides the obvious. It had taken time and effort to develop a relationship that existed outside of their shared blood.

After all the years they'd spent apart, she'd often wondered if they would ever have any sort of bond beyond the compulsion. But little by little, she'd grown to know Valen. He was a creature of complexity; a young man who lived in constant darkness, yet found such fascination with painting the light. And she could no longer imagine a life without her brother.

"Yes," Nor told him. "I'm aware."

"I think…it's beginning to take its toll," Valen said carefully.

"In what way?" she asked, looking him over intently. His golden eyes were dull, with dark circles marring the skin beneath them, and Nor felt a twinge of guilt, as she often did, for what she'd done to him in Lunamere. For the massive weight she'd placed on his mind, with all the energy the compulsion required.

"Today, when I left the castle… There was a flicker, of sorts."

"A flicker?" Nor echoed, confusion sweeping through her.

Valen nodded. The firelight illuminated the shadows beneath his eyes.

He needed rest. Darai had warned her of this—that the power would demand a price. But Nor hadn't wanted to ask Valen about it, for fear of discovering just how bad it truly was.

Her stomach clenched as she looked at him, so burdened. Perhaps he simply needed a reminder of what they were both working toward. For if Valen faltered now, when they were just beginning to feel the pressures of their mission…what would she do without him?

"Can I show you again, Valen? Our home?"

He nodded.

Nor closed her eyes and took a deep breath. She felt his mind reaching for hers, and as their power collided, Nor was suddenly transported away from her seat on the couch and into the recesses of her own mind, into that mental tunnel that sat between them, a doorway at the opposite end.

It was there, through a crack in the door, that Nor sent the vision she'd once been given from her mother. The memory that Klaren had sent down to Xen Ptera, when Nor and her father were lying crushed beneath the palace rubble.

The Void was the only place lacking stars in the entire galaxy. A blanket of nothingness that spanned from one end of the Phelexos System to the other. But beyond the Void, unbeknownst to Mirabel, was the root of Nor's and Valen's true allegiance.

Exonia.

Nor pushed the vision deeper into Valen's mind, and she heard him sigh longingly.

A galaxy that had once been full of light and grace, blessed by the mighty Godstars. Its inhabitants the chosen heirs of the Godstars' mighty powers, like the compulsion Klaren had gifted to her children. A realm that had long been decaying, even more so than Xen Ptera, putting their mother's people in danger of extinction. They clung to life by the thinnest of threads and dreamed of a savior, in the form of a mighty queen, a powerful brother at her side.

Soon, they would open the Void, using Nexus's power to command all the weapons at once. And when they tore open that hole in the sky, the Exonians would enter Mirabel like a flood. Hundreds upon hundreds of thousands who would soon find deliverance here.

Nor's vision ended, and she and Valen blinked at each other as they returned to the present. It was a sobering memory that Klaren had sent down to Nor so long ago. Each time Nor felt exhaustion weighing on her, each time she felt the fear of failure breathing down her neck, she remembered Exonia. She remembered the lifetime she'd spent fighting for Xen Ptera—

only a small taste of what Exonia had been experiencing for untold years.

The door to the great room swung open, and Darai swept in, cloak billowing in his wake as Zahn and the orange-eyed analyst from earlier followed on his heels.

"We have news, Majesty."

Valen looked away, wiping quickly at his nose again. Nor could have sworn she saw a glimpse of red there, but when she looked back, there was no trace of it.

"What is it?" Valen asked Darai with a deep sigh.

The analyst stopped before them and bowed, her sleeveless outfit revealing arms covered in glowing, silver veins. They were bright reminders of Nor's cause, of Valen's power. "We've been working around the clock, using every resource at our hands to uncover the identity of the false general. I'm delighted to report that just a few minutes ago, we had a breakthrough."

Nor's blood went cold.

"Who is it?" she said, the words a mere whisper.

"It's…rather unexpected, Majesty," Darai said. "And it will likely be a challenge to track her down."

"Just tell me," Nor snapped.

The analyst cleared her throat. "Androma Racella, Majesty."

The name sounded strangely familiar, but Nor couldn't place it. "Who?" she asked.

It was Valen who answered this time, his face paling as he turned to look at Nor. "Andi," he said faintly, his eyes wide with disbelief. "The Bloody Baroness."

CHAPTER 12

ANDI

The transport shot across the landscape, leaving the icy battle-field far behind them. A plume of smoke spiraled up from the attack site, trailing into the sky as if marking Lon's final resting place.

Andi buckled herself into the passenger seat as Dex angled them toward the ghostly outline of a domed city in the distance. But she found that she couldn't look away from the carnage in the distance, couldn't stop seeing the dragon's gaping jaw.

"This can't be happening," Andi said, as Dex laid on the throttle. "Godstars, this isn't how it was supposed to go."

All she could see was Lon's face as he slipped between the dragon's teeth. All she could think of was the horrific death that had followed. The fiery explosion. And Lira… Oh, Godstars, *Lira*. How would she react when Andi freed her someday, and

Lon wasn't there waiting for her return? She'd already lost her aunt Alara at the hands of Queen Nor, and now…

"He made his choice," Dex said quietly.

But again and again, Andi saw his face. The calmness in his eyes, so willing to give himself over to the other side as he leaped from the transport into the literal jaws of death.

"He did it so that Lira could be saved."

"Don't say her name," Andi hissed. Grief enveloped her in its all too familiar embrace. "She'll never forgive me for letting him go. Godstars, I should have *stopped* him!" She slammed the dash in fury.

"There was nothing we could have done!" Dex insisted. "He was probably planning to sacrifice himself the moment his suit ripped open."

"We could have made it to the city before he bled to death!"

"We wouldn't have," Dex said. "And he knew that. He saved us, Androma. So that we could continue on and save the girls. Save Lira."

Andi's body was rigid, every muscle tense. "We don't know for sure if… We should turn around, go back…" But she knew her own words were foolish even as she uttered them. That Lon's soul no longer existed in this galaxy.

"Andi." Dex's shoulders rose and fell as he took a deep breath. "You know as well as I do that turning around would bring us nothing but grief. He's gone. He died a hero. A worthy death, for a Sentinel."

The transport was finally growing warm inside, the old heating system kicking into gear, but Andi's hands still shook as she gripped them together. She knew it wasn't from the cold.

Dex reached over, carefully, and wrapped one hand over hers. She tensed beneath his touch, so lost in her pain. But he felt it, too. The others had been Guardians, his brothers and sisters from Tenebris, and they had died alongside Lon.

Andi hadn't been the one to bring about their deaths, and yet her swords seemed to sing her name, begging for more tallies. How had they already lost another of their crew, so soon? In the short time he'd spent on the *Marauder*, Lon had become a part of them, saving Andi's life with his own blood after they'd fled Arcardius. And now… He'd traded his life for theirs. Again, he'd saved her.

But for what purpose?

Now she had no crew. And no *ship*.

The realization of that finally hit her, too. The *Marauder* was gone. Frozen and forgotten in the Soleran wastes, the cruelest reminder that without her girls, without her ship…

She was nothing.

She thought of Lon's final words. "What did he mean?" Andi asked. "When he said…" Again, his face flashed in her mind, like the countless others that had died because of her. "When he said to tell her what she truly was?"

Dex's jaw tensed. He swallowed and looked away. "I…I don't know."

He knew something. Or perhaps that was just Andi's own guilt tugging at her, trying to project onto Dex. She cracked her knuckles, a habit she'd always resorted to in times of stress.

It was calming, the act of doing *something*, however small.

"Lira always spoke so hopefully about the dead," Andi said, remembering her friend's words about those who'd fallen in the attacks on Adhira, after they'd crash-landed there in the *Marauder*. It seemed so long ago now, though it had been little more than a month since the Xen Pterran forces had invaded that peaceful planet.

How many others had fallen in the weeks since?

"She said that they live on, in the world around us," Andi continued. "In the wind. The trees. The stars."

Dex nodded, his eyes locked on the landscape ahead. "Then Lon is with us still, even now."

Andi didn't know if she believed that was true. But for this moment, for today… She wanted to believe it.

For she and Dex were now a crew of two. Alone in a frozen land that cared little for its inhabitants, and even less for its visitors. They had no idea where to find safety, other than a fragmented instruction to find the Underground, somewhere in the Briog Sector. In an ice pub.

That was practically *nothing* to go on.

"Klarisa was a good soldier," Dex choked out. "A Guardian with a lot of marks upon her skin. But she had no one. She died alone."

"That's not true," Andi protested. "She had you."

Both Dex and Andi had been responsible for countless deaths over the years. Her victims had always haunted Andi in her dreams, ghostly bodies that she danced with until her guilt eddied and she woke in the morning, finally able to face up to what she'd done. Able to scratch their tallies into her swords.

But those deaths had always been at *her* hands. And yet somehow, even though Andi hadn't brought about these recent ones, the faces of those rebels from the Underground tugged at her in the same way. They had been so eager and excited as they shared the hope that there were more Unaffecteds out there, their minds still free of Nor's power.

Now they'd never see the galaxy freed from the queen's clutches.

"We'll make it to the Underground," Dex said, determination filling his voice. "We'll make sure their deaths weren't in vain. And then we'll make a plan. Figure out what the hell is going on across Mirabel, how we can get back to the girls. We still have a mission, Andi. We need to focus on that."

He sounded like he was saying it as much for himself as he was for her.

On the dash before them was a screen, its glow barely visible beneath thick layers of dust and grime. Dex wiped it with his gloved hand, revealing a map of the planet's surface.

A small red dot showed where they were headed—Craatia, the capital domed city of Solera. It was a straight shot from here, three hundred clicks away.

The Soleran landscape was known for being one of the harshest in Mirabel, but it was beautiful all the same. As they journeyed on, their transport hovering a few yards above the snow, Andi took in the view, willing it to overcome her mind. To make it as numb as her body was from the cold. But all she could think about was that damned ice dragon. How it had erupted from the earth out of nowhere, overtaking them in an instant.

It only made her think of Nor's power, and the might of her threat to Mirabel.

"It's so empty here," Dex said, clearing his throat. Andi looked at him as he ran a hand through his hair. It was getting longer, the front now shaggy enough to cover his brows. "Sorry. It's just…talking helps. To distract my mind."

Left and right, spanning as far as they could see, was a world blanketed in white. There were countless frozen lakes across Solera, snow bounding across their surfaces in a dance that went in time with the wind. The wreckage of the *Marauder* was long behind them, the poor ship abandoned to the cold, half-buried in the ice. Already, it probably looked as if it were becoming a part of the planet. As if everything that visited Solera was claimed by it eventually.

Jagged ice mountains, like splintered bones, were scattered across the landscape, some of them twisting in spiraline forms, purple and deep blue in color. But Dex was right—there were hardly any signs of life, save for the few scattered outposts that they passed. Many of them looked abandoned, as if everyone had picked up and left for more populated areas, perhaps the better to find a place where others praised Nor.

It made Andi want to scream—or drive her swords through

the queen's throat, the way Nor had done to all the other planetary leaders.

"How did it happen so quickly?" Andi asked. Grief still marked her heart, but Andi had lost enough people in the past to know that Dex was right—talking about something, *anything* other than the loss, would help make it easier to bear.

"I guess Nor had more resources on Xen Ptera than we always assumed," Dex replied. "Or she used the advanced tech on Arcardius, once she gained control. I hate to say it, but she was smart to pick Arcardius as her target for setting up shop."

"Did you just compliment that witch?" Andi growled.

Dex looked like he regretted it already.

"Smarter, still," Andi said, changing the subject, "for Arachnid to choose one of the most unforgiving planets in the galaxy for his headquarters. Nor would have a hell of a time bringing the battle to this tundra, especially if the Underground has already overtaken some of the domed sectors. She'd have a hell of a time infiltrating it, too, if it's really underground."

"Doesn't bode well for us," Dex said with a deep sigh.

"We've made it through worse," Andi said with a shrug. "Or have you forgotten Lunamere so quickly?"

Dex muttered under his breath, his hands gripping the wheel tighter. "You know, I never suspected Valen was a part of this. Did you?" When Andi remained silent, he added, "You didn't see the way he bowed to her that night. Like she truly was his goddess come down from the stars. To think, you're both from the same planet, born and raised, and yet somehow, he has this impossible power to—"

"That is incorrect, Dextro Arez." A voice squeaked out from Dex's wrist.

"What the—" Andi yelped. Dex nearly crashed the transport into an ice spiral as he whirled around, forgetting the gears for a moment.

"Dex!" Andi screamed, reaching over and grabbing the wheel.

The transport spun as both of them grappled for control, finally slowing to a near-stop. They hovered over a broad expanse of frozen lake, colors shifting beneath the surface.

Dex looked down at the watch on his wrist. "Alfie?" he asked incredulously.

"Artificial Life Form Intelligence Emissary," the droid reminded him.

"You scared the hell out of us, Alfie," Andi gasped.

Alfie's voice was as dry as ever. "Impossible. Hell cannot be contained in a human body, nor can it be proved that it is, in fact, real."

Dex burst out laughing, the sound strangely out of place after the attack, but welcome all the same. "Took you long enough to show up. Finally found a connection?"

"We are on Solera," Alfie said, as if he'd just noticed. Likely his chip was finally done calibrating into the watch, re-tethered to the feed. "Why are we on Solera?"

Dex kicked the engine back into gear, turning them back toward Craatia. "You've been a little under the weather, pal. Last we saw you, you were supposed to be delivering the results of those blood tests you performed on Valen, before the *Marauder* crashed on Adhira. You said there was a team of scientists in Averia that needed the information."

"Then someone murdered you," Andi said. "But I saved your memory chip, so you could tell us what the hell happened, and who did it."

"Incorrect again," Alfie said. "I cannot be murdered, for I am not alive. I was dismembered by Sir Valen Cortas. He commanded me to allow him to do so."

Dex cursed. "Of course you were. What was he trying to hide, besides the fact that he was related to Nor? And why am I incorrect *again*?"

"You said Valen Cortas was Arcardian, born and raised. Valen is half Arcardian, yes," Alfie said. "But according to his DNA, he is also half…"

His words trailed off. Dex's watch screen flickered, as if it were malfunctioning.

"Alfie?" Dex asked. He shrugged and knocked the watch against the transport's dash.

The screen flickered back on. "I cannot compute."

"What the hell is that supposed to mean?" Dex sputtered.

"He should be half–Xen Pterran, right?" Andi asked. "Because of Klaren?"

"Evidently Klaren Solis was not Xen Pterran," Alfie replied. "But there is nothing in the entire Mirabellian database that explains where her DNA originates from."

Andi met Dex's gaze, the uneasiness in his expression mirroring her own feelings. "So you're saying that Valen's mother isn't from Mirabel?" Dex asked. "But how is that possible? Maybe her people just haven't been discovered yet?"

Andi relaxed a bit. Mirabel had countless races, some of which kept themselves very secluded. Surely Klaren hailed from one of those, though how she'd then ended up marrying Xen Ptera's former king was a mystery.

"Still incorrect," Alfie responded. "There are no more undiscovered races in Mirabel." The transport lurched with a gust of frigid wind, prompting another round of cursing from Dex.

"So what is she, then?" Andi prodded, tired of the questions, eager for answers.

It was Dex who spoke next. "She's not Mirabellian at all."

Alfie nodded. "That is my calculation. The DNA strands that make up half of Valen Cortas's blood are not Mirabellian. Nor are they from any of the known galaxies nearby, many of which would have been too far for Klaren Solis to travel in a lifetime. Even with cryogenics."

The transport fell silent, as both Dex and Andi were lost in their thoughts. Alfie's revelation was a welcome distraction from their grief, albeit a disturbing one.

"So he's not from here," Andi mused. "I mean, Klaren wasn't from here, anyway. And I'm willing to bet that means Nor's DNA is the same. And if Valen knew Alfie was delivering that news to Cyprian before their planned attack on Averia...then trying to murder Alfie makes sense."

"Not murder," Alfie corrected.

Andi ignored him, turning to face Dex. He held himself rigid, chewing on his bottom lip as he seemed to process all of this.

"Was Kalee...?" Dex seemed like he didn't know how to form the question.

But Alfie seemed to sense what he was getting at. "The late Kalee Cortas was the daughter of Cyprian and Merella Cortas."

Andi loosed a sigh of relief, but the feeling was short-lived. "So we have no idea who we're really dealing with, as far as Valen and Nor are concerned," she said, watching the landscape outside. The snow was scattered with what looked to be purple clouds, thick groups of them clustered together, their heads to the ground.

One of them bleated as the transport passed by. Roaks, a species of feral sheep native to Solera. They were known for their thick furs, which could withstand the cold—and the fact that when food was hard to come by, they often feasted on the weakest from their herd.

"Do you think the Underground knows about Valen and Nor's DNA?" Dex asked Andi.

"I don't know what I think about anything anymore," she admitted. "But we're not going to tell them anything until we learn if we can trust them or not. Hopefully we can use the information as a bargaining chip. A way to get them to help us with supplies and a ship, to get to Arcardius and the girls."

"Agreed," Dex said, nodding. "So...it seems like Cyprian was telling the truth when he died. That Valen was a monster.

That he feared for his life when he was around him, and even more so, the possibility of Nor and Valen getting together and combining their abilities."

"Then the general was right about one thing, at least," Andi said.

"He is not the general anymore," Alfie answered suddenly, his voice sounding so matter-of-fact from Dex's wrist, like a child insisting they were capable of eating their dessert before dinner. "The General of Arcardius is—"

"I think that's enough out of Alfie for now," Dex said quickly, turning off the watch in one swift motion. The silver band went dark.

"What the hell?" Andi glanced at him, suspicion creeping up her spine. But Dex only stared straight ahead, his teeth still worrying at his bottom lip—as if he had something to hide.

"I could use some quiet time," he explained at last. "Enough has happened to us already, and a hell of a lot more is soon to come. We'll be in Craatia in a few hours—why don't you take some time to rest?"

"What are you, my mother?" Andi asked blankly.

Dex quirked a dark brow. "I hope to the Godstars that I'm not." He swallowed and repositioned his hands on the wheel. "I just think you deserve a rest, Andi. After everything. That's all."

He was right. They'd had enough talking, enough contemplating the new world around them. Still, Andi watched him a moment longer, eyeing his tense jaw and tired eyes. She knew him well enough that she could tell he was hiding something, though she had no idea what it could be. Either way, it was clear he wasn't ready to talk about whatever it was.

Right now, getting to the Underground headquarters was of the utmost importance, and they needed to be alert when they got inside, for they had no idea what awaited them there. Once they made it through, *if* they determined the Underground was completely free of Nor's power…they'd use Alfie's knowledge to negotiate the help they needed to rescue Andi's crew.

So Andi sat back and closed her eyes, Dex a silent presence beside her as they soared over the icy tundra toward Craatia.

A storm began during the second half of their journey.

If it weren't for the radar equipment on the transport, Andi doubted they would have been able to navigate their way through the snow and sleet. The wind on Solera was a beast in its own right as well, kicking up the snow beneath them until everything was a sheet of white.

"We should be getting close," Dex said. "Radar shows that it's just ahead."

"It better be, otherwise we won't have enough fuel. And I'd hate to think of what we'd become, out here in the cold."

Though they'd last longer than Lon would have, since their planetary suits were still intact, they *would* eventually die of exposure. The memory of Lon surged through her again at the thought—how determined he'd been to save them, ready to die as he leaped toward the dragon's gaping jaw. Andi gritted her teeth and changed her focus, thinking of Valen and Nor instead. She was desperate to remember any clues or signs that Valen might have given about the truth of who he was.

But of course, he'd fooled them all.

She hated the cautious friendship that she'd allowed to blossom between them after his rescue. The conspiratorial smiles, the quiet conversation they'd had by the water on Adhira, speaking of their shared past with Kalee. Forgiving each other for the mistakes they'd both made. Attending the Ucatoria Ball at his side.

Now Andi wondered if Valen had been holding back the desire to murder her the entire time they'd been together. She wondered if any of his so-called forgiveness was ever truly real.

And her girls had so often been *alone* with him during their journey. Gilly in particular had been fascinated by Valen.

That should have been warning enough, Andi realized. For Gilly had always been drawn to the darker things in life. The backpack, now nearly ripped to shreds by Havoc's claws, was proof of that. And judging from the ache still present in Andi's chest when she moved, the wound that had closed over but wasn't even close to healed...

Valen had been the darkest of them all.

Andi's thoughts wandered to her crew. She often feared what they were being commanded to do. If they were out there in the galaxy somewhere, killing in Nor's name. Or if they were still on Arcardius, silently doing her bidding, or falling on their faces in worship of her.

"There!" Dex shouted, drawing Andi's attention as he leaned forward and pointed. The radar beeped, signaling that they were closing in on their target. "I see them."

The domed sector of Solera appeared from the snow like a cluster of ghosts upon the icy surface. The radar showed ten domes spread across the expanse, and Andi knew from her previous visits that each of them had their own unique feel, as if every one contained its own little world.

This part of Solera was densely populated, and the domes varied in size. The spring domes, Mravio and Devtraci, were meant to look similar to Adhira, and had been terraformed into dense jungles, the greenery lush and overflowing with waterfalls and rivers. The weather inside was warm and beautiful at all times, and flowers the size of Andi's head bloomed year-round. Then there was the summer dome, X'Ani, its landscape like that of a sprawling desert, with sand dunes instead of snow mounds and buildings like sand castles sprouting from the earth.

Craatia, as Solera's capital, was the largest and most central of the domes in this sector. It was a city that still honored many of the planet's most ancient customs, filled with sparkling glass bridges and buildings designed to resemble ice castles—though the temperature inside was warm enough for its inhabitants to shed their coats and grow food that otherwise wouldn't survive on Solera.

As they sped closer to the domed cities, Andi felt a slippery sense of fear wash over her. Not fear of the job at hand, because she'd learned to shove that away, ages ago. Jobs like this always pumped her full of adrenaline.

No—this was a different sort of terror, the kind that whispered into her ear that she would not succeed.

And that if she failed, she'd unwittingly destroy the future her crew deserved.

"Hey," Dex said, his voice quiet beneath the hum of the transport. "We're going to make it. Even if we have to take out everyone we come across to get into the Underground."

For the first time, Andi considered something about the people inside those domes, the ones whose blood truly *did* glow silver with the Solis curse... Were they really enemies, when they weren't in control of their actions?

Andi had a code that she obeyed fiercely, the way a soldier obeyed a commanding officer's orders. No death blow, unless the enemy was endangering the life of Andi and her crew. She would never lift her sword to harm an innocent.

But when they entered Craatia, it was possible that nearly *everyone* would be trying to kill or capture her and Dex. Yet under normal circumstances, none of them would blink an eye as the two of them walked through the streets. The thought made her wonder whether other Unaffecteds shared that opinion— whether or not they felt any hesitation or remorse over killing Nor's mindless followers, even in self-defense.

So as Dex eased up on the throttle, slowing the transport for their approach, Andi said, "We can't handle this like our other missions, Dex."

He turned to stare at her, a silent question in his eyes. "Think about it," she told him. "The people inside—they're just like Lira, and Gilly, and Breck. They don't know what they're doing.

If anyone comes after us…we can't just take them out, like you said."

Dex's expression grew thoughtful. "I hadn't thought about it like that," he admitted. "I've just been so concerned with trying to stay alive, and keeping you safe. But…you're right." Dex took her hands in his for a moment. "Incapacitate only. No killing."

"Not unless they're aiming to kill us," Andi said.

He nodded, his eyes full of understanding. As he pulled on his hood and mask to conceal his face from view, Dex said, "Remember—we're worshippers of Nor. Just like everyone else we pass. We blend in, as best we can."

"And if they see through it?"

"Then I guess we'll die together."

Andi glared at him, all earlier gratitude disappearing. "Thanks for the positivity."

He leaned over and kissed her on the cheek. "I learned it from you, love."

The wind was howling outside now, a mighty and furious roar. Snow tumbled from the banks, whipping by them as it went, but when it touched the exterior of the domes, it melted away, their heating systems designed to keep the domes from being buried in the landscape.

Andi knew they shouldn't stay exposed for much longer—they needed to find the Underground as soon as possible. She had no idea what awaited them, deep in the belly of the dome. But the longer they dawdled, the more likely it was that they'd get caught—or freeze, once the fuel in their transport ran out.

The dome's main entrance came into view, a steel-reinforced opening where a few other transports were lined up, waiting to gain entrance inside.

"Here goes nothing," Dex said with a sigh.

As Andi allowed the mask of the Bloody Baroness to over-take her, slipping into that place of darkness and death, she knew that she would have the strength, the fury, to face whatever lay ahead.

There was no other option.

The doors opened to reveal the splendor of Craatia.

Buildings towered up to the farthest heights of the dome, glorious in their make, as if a mighty architect had come down from the stars to shape this place. Some of them looked to be carved out of ice, shimmering as they stood above the rest. Others were blue or purple in color, spiraling and twisting like the horns of a mighty beast. Magnificent statues overlooked it all, and an engineered snow trickled down from the dome's ceiling, falling gently upon Andi's visor as she gazed upward.

Birds soared through the city, their feathers morphing colors with each flap of their wings. Great, sweeping silver tunnels passed through the dome from street to sky, a network of passenger pods that allowed the citizens to travel quickly from one end to another.

A frozen lake separated the docking sector from the city's entrance. Hovering boats glided above the ice like slinking ghosts.

"Wow," Dex breathed. "Hard to believe this place harbors the Underground."

A yowl sounded over his shoulder, from inside the squirming, half-shredded backpack that Andi had shoved Havoc back into before they'd disembarked the transport, much to Dex's dismay. But she knew Gilly would murder them both, probably slowly and painfully and *creatively*, if they'd left the creature to die in the snow.

Then again, if Havoc didn't stop kicking up such a fuss, they'd likely wind up attracting the wrong sort of attention, and die at the hands of Nor's minions instead.

"Glorious, isn't it?" Dex asked, drawing Andi's attention back to the view ahead.

It was true—Craatia was a glorious city.

And so full of people that it made Andi feel as if she were being crushed.

All around them, Craatia's citizens moved as one, heading toward their homes, their jobs, all manner of errands and entertainment. But no matter how different everyone looked on the outside, it was impossible to overlook the fact that they were all united in one dark, hideous cause. Prisoners whose chains lurked in their very veins.

Andi wondered if they were stuck screaming from within their own minds. If they screamed endlessly, wondering if anyone would ever hear them, or if they were happy to serve Nor, mindless in their devotion to her.

"Andi?" Dex said, turning his face toward her.

"So many of them," she whispered. "How do you think it happened so fast? The feeds spoke of silver clouds that filled the galaxy, but with the domes…"

Dex shrugged. "Klarisa said there were Guardians here, ones loyal to Nor's cause. They likely stormed the domes one by one and used the bullets to overtake everyone in sight." His eyes turned distant and troubled, the way they often did when he remembered the night of the Ucatoria Ball. "It happens almost instantly, once they're shot. All these people…"

"Five hundred thousand and seventeen, to be exact." Alfie's voice buzzed into her com. Andi flinched at the sound of it. "I have connected to the communication systems housed in your suits, Androma Racella and Dextro Arez."

It was strange, hearing a different voice where the girls' used to be. As if someone else had occupied a space that should have been *theirs*. It filled her with a guilt she knew she shouldn't need to carry, but it was there, all the same.

"No more numbers or stats, please, Alfie, unless you want me to unleash Havoc on you," she told him, muting her com with a swipe of her fingers across the brim of the helmet. "And stop popping into my mind unannounced."

Dex jostled the backpack a little too roughly over his shoulder, silencing the angry feline.

A mother and child walked past, heading for the loading dock of a giant freight ship. On its bow, a flag bearing the Solis crest waved proudly, the false snowflakes landing upon it like gentle kisses. And all across the city—on the sides of the icy buildings, flickering atop the turrets of the castles—were massive holograms of Nor Solis. Her rouged lips were curved in a deceptive smile, and her eyes bore down on the city, as if she were demanding any of them to defy her.

Andi felt her hands balling into fists, nails digging into her palms beneath her gloves.

"I know," Dex said, stepping closer. "Trust me. I know."

Seeing this display of power made anger well up in her chest. It was as if the queen was teasing her, testing her, waiting for Andi to crack under her watchful gaze.

"We have to move," Andi said. If she stood here any longer, staring at the people, staring at the massive hologram of her enemy, she might very well rush into the writhing crowd and tear everyone apart, limb from limb. Or she'd unzip Havoc and let him loose in the hope that, with everyone she took down, she could somehow weaken Nor, bit by bit.

A million tallies on her swords.

A million deaths to mourn, at her own hands.

Her girls, her crew, wouldn't have to wait much longer for her. For when they found the Underground, Andi wouldn't rest until she made it back to Arcardius and ripped them away from Nor's iron grip.

With a deep breath, Andi stepped forward, Dex behind her as they followed the citizens of Craatia onto the waiting ship.

CHAPTER 13

DEX

It took no more than ten minutes for the ship to traverse the frozen lake and enter the city. The outskirts of Craatia contained the financial district, its castle-like structures overflowing with Soleran men and women dressed in the latest cold-weather fashions. Their brows were crusted with false icicles, their hair dyed shades of blue, purple and white to match the wintry cold beyond the dome.

"Klarisa said the entrance to the Underground is within an ice pub in the Briog Sector," Dex said, reciting what the Guardian had told him in her final moments. "But in the capital city of an ice planet, how many of those pubs exist?"

"A hell of a lot," Andi said. "Or perhaps not enough, depending on how you look at it."

He could use a drink. Or two or three. The bag over his shoulder hissed again as Dex and Andi disembarked.

Okay, perhaps four drinks, he thought.

"How will we even know when we've found the right one?"

"I imagine we'll ask the same question Klarisa asked us."

He hated to think what would happen if they asked the wrong people that question. In this city, *everyone* seemed like the wrong people.

They walked in the midst of a pack of citizens crossing a busy intersection, heading for one of the pod stations that filled the city. It was what set this place apart from Arcardius, where the sky was often overflowing with transports and personal drivers taking their wealthy passengers from place to place. Here, people climbed spiraling sets of stairs and slipped into the waiting passenger pods that took them where they wanted to go.

"Fastest route to the middle of the city," Dex said, nodding to a pod station overhead. Holographic maps hovered in the air in front of the station's stairwell, noting the different sectors of Craatia. The dome was enormous, large enough to rival some of the cities on Arcardius.

"Briog," Andi said, pointing to a glowing line on the map that intersected the city center. It looked to be an industrial sector, likely full of pubs and the sort of people Dex wouldn't mind being around, if the galaxy wasn't wrapped up in Nor's clutches.

"We'll start at the front, stop at every pub that fits the bill," Dex said.

"You should be good at this," Andi commented with a wink in his direction. "Being a bounty hunter and all."

In a sense, Dex *was* bounty hunting again. Though he'd never had to find an entire group of rebels before, especially not with a demon Fellibrag slung over his shoulder.

"I'll try not to impress you too much," Dex told her.

Andi huffed out a laugh and sauntered past him, beginning the climb up the stairs. Dex followed behind her, and they boarded the moving walkway together. He could see the pods in the distance, but there was a lengthy line ahead of them. As Dex settled in to wait, scanning their surroundings for potential threats, a nearby conversation drew his attention.

"They discovered an Unaffected child last night," the man ahead of them said. "Hiding like a city rat in the pod maintenance bay south of this sector. Said he'd been living on rodents for weeks."

He gasped as he said it, as if he were shocked by his own news. His hair stuck up from his scalp, glitter flecking each strand. His chin jutted out several inches, leading to a sharp point. A body mod, no doubt, that seemed popular in this city.

"What did they do with the Unaffected?" asked his friend, a woman with purple eyelashes whose pupils were white and slitted like a feline's. Perhaps Dex should offer *her* the backpack. "I've heard that the queen personally thanks each person who turns them in," the woman added reverently. "That her blessing is like a kiss from the Godstars."

The man nodded. "Word is, they turned the Unaffected over to the Guardians manning the sector."

"Good riddance," the woman said, clucking her tongue. "All glory be to the queen."

The man repeated her words, pressing his hands together and holding them out toward a Solis flag that hung from a building nearby. "Just wait," he breathed. "Once she completes Nexus... We'll root out the Unaffecteds forever."

Dex's stomach clenched at the thought of more innocents dying because of this new world of Nor's. The depth of grief he'd felt at Lon's death had surprised him—though the two of them had bonded over their need to survive on board the *Marauder*, Dex hadn't realized how much he'd come to depend on Lon's calming presence until it was gone.

Klarisa's death...that had struck him with the same devastation that the death of a fellow Guardian always had. Though

Guardians protected Mirabel—gave their lives up to do it—they protected each other first, always, no matter the cost. And Dex had failed to protect Klarisa.

He could hardly even begin to imagine how Andi felt, with all she'd lost.

"There haven't been any other signs, have there?" the man said, drawing Dex's attention back. "Those Unaffecteds have been leaving their mark on this city far too often."

"Not as many lately," the woman answered. "Soon Craatia will be as clean as Arcardius."

Dex cast a glance at Andi, who was glaring at the citizens with furious eyes, as if the mention of her home planet only added to her rage.

If only she knew just how much the mention of Arcardius made *him* bristle—made guilt pick at his insides, for the secret he still harbored about what he'd helped Cyprian do.

In time, Dex would tell her. But not today.

"Where have those scum been lurking this time?" Dex asked the duo, pitching his voice so that he sounded like a confident businessman.

The man barely cast him a second glance as he stepped into a waiting pod. "Mostly in southern Briog, with the other scum of the city."

The woman tsked as she joined him, and they were off, what little bit of extra information they may have had gone.

"Southern Briog," Andi said. "Well, that narrows the search a bit, I'd guess."

The line moved forward, and they boarded a glass pod meant to hold four. "Sorry, my friend," Dex said as a man with icicle hair tried to climb in with them. He lifted the backpack with Havoc yowling inside. "Not friendly. Pisses quite a lot, too."

The man's eyes widened in horror.

Andi kicked Dex's heel and stepped past him, giving the man a sweet, vacant smile. "We wish to…sing our praises to the queen in private, while we ride."

"Of course," the man said, bowing out of the way, careful to avoid Dex and his backpack.

"Are you trying to get us killed?" Andi murmured to Dex.

"I can't have some fun?"

Andi sighed as the door slid shut behind them, and with a quick voice command, they were off to the Briog Sector.

A small holoscreen sat inside the pod, playing ads that were similar to many Dex had seen in his lifetime, for beauty products and restaurants and the latest transport ships. But as they watched, the city flying by them on all sides, a familiar voice suddenly spoke from the screen.

Dex saw Andi's body go rigid beside him as Nor Solis's face appeared. Music played in the background, a sickeningly sweet instrumental tune.

"People of Mirabel. A new future awaits us all," Nor said triumphantly. She was clad in a glorious bloodred gown, a golden crown balanced on her dark curls as a camera panned slowly from left to right, showing every side of her. *"We must root out all who seek to defy me, all the Unaffecteds who cannot be convinced to see the light. We must shed our brightness across the galaxy, before the dawn of a new day approaches. Let no man, woman or child be left in the dark. Discover them. Turn them in to the authorities, who can guide them to new light. For I am the One True Queen, and I have come to bring a new dawn to Mirabel—a future that will unite us all."*

"Turn it off," Andi growled.

Dex looked out the pod windows. All across the city, people had stopped moving, watching the buildings above as holograms echoed what they saw now in their pod.

Nor's face, magnified and on display for all to see and praise.

A cry went out across the city as the image of the queen disappeared—a roar that seemed to make the pod tremble on its track. It silenced just as quickly as it had begun.

"I hate this city," Andi said. Her words came out like a curse. "I hate every part of it."

"We need to get to the Underground first," Dex said matter-of-factly. "Then you can set this place on fire."

She sat back in her seat, but her body didn't relax. Her hands curled across her thighs as the pod slowed, arching down toward the ground. The city changed as they approached their destination. The buildings took on a darker sheen, as if they hadn't been cleaned or taken care of. They looked more like warehouses, or pleasure palaces packed tightly together. Music filtered out from bars with androids dancing in the windows, and fights broke out in the street. Weapons were sold in shopfronts, and smoke curled from open windows, where inside, Dex could see the shadowed outlines of people doing what black marketeers did best.

Making dangerous—and often deadly—deals.

"Now, this," Andi said, as a headless droid wheeled past outside, a man stumbling after it, hefting a bag twice his size behind him, "is much, much better."

Dex saw her reflection in the glass then. The way her eyes had darkened. The way her jaw was hardening, her head tilting slightly to the side as if she were an animal about to choose her prey.

"Let's find the Underground," Andi said. "Even if it means tearing apart every pub we see."

Her voice was rough, her body lithe as she opened the pod door and stepped out into the street. Dex knew what it meant, and he found himself filled with an equal amount of joy and fear as Andi crossed her arms and watched the passersby, each one a possible victim.

The Bloody Baroness was here.

And she was ready to play.

Andi and Dex made their way through the congested streets toward the Sharp Spire, the first stop on their pub crawl. Alfie had gathered a list of all the ice pubs in the sector, seven in total, his voice spouting useless facts about them from Dex's wrist. Four of the pubs were located in the southern portion, so they'd decided to begin their search with those. Dex just hoped one of them would lead to the Underground.

The rich smells of roasted meats and spices drifted around them, making his stomach rumble. It had been some time since their last meal, and he was starting to feel the debilitating effects of hunger. The feeling only heightened as they entered the Sharp Spire.

The pub was scattered with patrons sprawled across ice couches and lounge chairs, droids rolling about and offering drinks on ice trays. Andi and Dex split up, moving about the place, prodding with simple questions about Nor and the Unaffected, but no one offered any information worth their time. The entire pub had the feel of Nor's hands on it, with patrons bearing her crest on their clothing and the queen's face displayed on holoscreens around the room, playing the same video they'd seen in the pod earlier on a loop.

Dex and Andi regrouped next to a dented droid offering fur blankets for rent.

"I rented a blanket once," Dex told her, sidestepping the little droid as its face-screen flashed him a discounted price. He was tempted to offer up Havoc in exchange for a few Krevs. Surely the Fellibrag would make a lovely blanket.

"How'd that go?" Andi asked, her lip curling in disgust as she nudged the droid away with her knee.

Dex shrugged. "It gave me fleas."

She snorted, then said, "The Underground isn't here. Let's go."

He laughed as she turned on her heel and exited the pub like it was on fire.

"Alfie," Dex said to his wrist once they were back out in the street, hiding in the deep shadows cast by the towering buildings overhead. They could see the top of the dome from here, where night and the storm darkened the outside world. Dex thought of Klarisa and her comrades, their bodies now frozen and covered by the snow. He sighed deeply and looked back at his watch. "Where to next?"

"Dragon's Breath," Alfie's voice said.

"That's very rude, Alfie."

"I do not compute."

Andi rolled her eyes at him. "He doesn't understand jokes. You know that."

A group of people approached them, hefting a Solis banner over their heads as they cheered Nor's name. Dex plastered on a smile and took Andi's arm, and they both waved at the silver-veined citizens.

"It was worth a shot," he murmured to her as they made their way to Dragon's Breath.

Over the next couple of hours, their visits to the other pubs offered little to nothing, and Dex began to feel like their efforts to find the Underground were doomed to fail. They had hardly any information to go off of, and the longer they stayed out in the open, the more dangerous their situation became. At some point, he knew someone would see the truth written across their faces, behind their false smiles.

"That's it," Dex said wearily. "We've checked them all."

Alfie spouted off the list of pubs again, and sure enough, they'd been to them all. Yet there was no sign of the Underground.

"We're not going to find them, are we?" Andi said, stopping short before a narrow entrance to an abandoned stone storefront, its sign barely visible under the awning.

Iceman Antiquities.

Dex leaned against the frosted glass shop window, eyeing the pile of strange old antiques. Rusted old war helmets and ancient-looking weapons, broken bottles of Griss long since forgotten. The place had clearly gone out of business ages ago.

It struck him suddenly that he was standing with the General of Arcardius. Andi had no idea of the truth yet, but when she did, she'd have the resources of an entire *planet* available to her. How different their situation would be, if Andi had gained the title another way, instead of in desperate response to Nor's attacks.

They certainly wouldn't be hopeless and shipless, hungry and without any Krevs, hiding in the middle of some dingy street outside an abandoned shop in Solera.

He needed to tell her. Lon's last words still haunted him. *Tell her the truth. Tell her what she is.*

But not now.

Not until they had a moment to regroup. To recover. He knew the news wouldn't be welcome. She hated Arcardius, hated the people who had chased her from it years ago. No, the secret would remain his for a time—and the guilt over not telling her would remain, too.

Another demon to hang on Dex's back.

Something in the shop window caught his eye. "Andi," Dex breathed. "Look at that."

She turned to face him as he pointed through the frosted glass. Inside the old shop window, hidden among the strange, useless items, was a painting. Everything else was old and covered in dust, but the painting was *new*.

A spider's web, painted in bloodred against an expanse of black.

Klarisa's words suddenly came back to Dex. *Then Arachnid will welcome you into a tangled web of...*

She'd never gotten to finish that statement, for the ice dragon had broken through the ice moments later. And then she'd died.

"That's interesting," Andi said. "It could mean nothing, but... Alfie, what is this place?"

"Out of business," Alfie's voice said a moment later. "Though it is labeled on the Craatian feeds as a speakeasy."

Dex barked out a laugh. "Alfie, you idiot. That's a pub. Just a hidden one."

He smiled as he pushed away from the window and tried the

shop's ancient door handle. The door creaked open, revealing a tunnellike hallway. Inside, the shop itself was cold and empty of items. The rows of metal shelves had been cleared away, nothing but dust and empty boxes for the taking. But Dex was certain there was something else here. His spine tingled in anticipation, as if he were fresh on a blood trail.

"There," Andi said. She pointed to the floor, where a mess of footprints had disturbed the dust. They led toward a heavy metal storage room door at the back of the shop. Just beneath the handle of that door was another small painting of a spider's web, no larger than Dex's fingertip.

Dex's heartbeat was heavy in his chest. He looked over his shoulder, back at Andi. She nodded, her face barely visible in the shadows of the abandoned storefront. "What's the matter, Guardian? Scared?"

"As hell," Dex said, thinking honesty was always the best policy. But he stepped forward anyway and, with a deep breath, turned the handle. He heaved, pushing the heavy door inward...

And was greeted with a cold kiss of icy air, cool blue lighting and the rhythmic pulsing of dance music as the hidden ice pub was revealed.

It was stuffed full of people, all of them wearing the thick furs of Solera as they milled about. The dance floor was littered with giant icicles that resembled stalactites, and the bar itself was an entire wall of ice, holes carved out to fit bottles within. Drones strung with old, twinkling holiday lights soared around the ceiling, casting the entire pub in a flickering glow. In the corner, a fireplace from frozen blocks of ice boasted a purple fire within—some sort of chemical substance that looked pretty, but did nothing to chase the chill away. Patrons lounged before it, laughing as they enjoyed their drinks.

"Damn," Dex muttered. A woman waltzed past, her hair piled on her head and braided in the shape of a snowflake. With a start, he noticed that her veins weren't silver. Her skin was blessedly free of Nor's stain, and as he looked around, Dex realized with glee that everyone else was free of the veins, too.

"I think we may have found the Underground," Andi breathed. "What now?"

Despite his better judgment, Dex reached up and removed his helmet, gulping in the cold air. The whole place was thick with the smell of smoke and Griss. Someone shouted in the corner of the room, where two mini-droids were boxing in the center of a carved, frozen table. A large crowd surrounded it, throwing in Krevs and spilling their drinks as they clashed their ice mugs together, sealing bets.

"We look for another sign," Dex said, scanning the pub. "A spider's web, maybe painted somewhere, or on a bottle of Griss, or—"

"There," Andi said, grabbing his shoulder tight. Her helmet was off now, too, and nobody looked twice at the two of them.

She nodded in the direction of the bar, where a woman sat with her back to them. Woven into her clothing, as if a spider had stitched the design right into the fabric, was an intricate black web.

"We question her slowly," Dex said. "We feel her out first, just a gentle nudge, and if she gives any indication that she's one of the Underground…"

"Godstars be damned," Andi said, cutting him off.

The woman had turned, the side of her face visible now as a droid refilled her cup.

Dex almost couldn't believe his eyes. It felt like he was having a very real case of déjà vu—or like he'd been thrown back into one of his worst nightmares.

For it was Soyina who sat at the bar, a finger lazily tracing the rim of her glass. Her tattoos swam around her skin like fish in a pool of water as she surveyed the room.

"What are the chances…?" Andi started.

"What the hell is she doing here?" Dex wondered aloud. The

last time they'd seen Soyina, she'd put a bullet through them both and dumped their bodies—and Valen's—on a Lunamere corpse ship.

Of all the people in the galaxy, it had to be *her*.

Soyina turned around as they approached the bar. "My, my," she said, eyes just barely widening in surprise at the sight of them. "If it isn't Dextro Arez and his pretty Baroness, back from the dead."

"Thanks for the warning about that, by the way," Andi growled. "I'm pretty sure I still have a bruise on my chest from your stunner bullet."

Dex glanced between the two of them as they stared at each other, a mirror image of the night they'd first met with Soyina at Dark Matter, when they'd asked her to help them break into Lunamere and free Valen.

She couldn't be trusted, Dex knew.

Yet she had Arachnid's mark stitched plainly across her back, and there was no sign of silver glowing beneath her skin.

"Before you speak, I've a question to ask of you, dearies," Soyina said as she signaled for the bartender droid to return. It rolled over, offering two frosty mugs full of liquid. Neither Dex nor Andi took them. Soyina only shrugged and smiled up at them as she added, "Be careful how you respond, for it will decide your fate. Who do you serve?"

Neither of them answered. But Andi's face, so full of hatred at the mere thought of Nor, gave the answer away.

Soyina sighed. "Klarisa's team radioed in about a certain battered glass starship crash-landing before they went radio silent. I figured you two would show up eventually, and when you did… Well, I also figured your stubborn asses would be on my side of things."

Dex whooshed out a breath. "Klarisa told us to find you," he said. "She said there was a gatekeeper of sorts—"

Soyina laughed, but leaned in close, eyeing Dex's backpack

first. "Lower your voice, you delicious thing." She sighed as she looked at Andi, whose back had stiffened at her comment. "Of course. You're in love again, aren't you? Ah, well, it was fun to hope." She turned back to Dex. "I'm the gatekeeper, Dextro. And I'll need something from the two of you, if you're to join me."

She stood, downing her mug before she reached into her jacket and revealed a small blade.

Dex had his gun drawn before Soyina could take a breath, Andi reaching for her swords in an instant. But the woman only laughed at them both. She reached down and drew the blade across her own fingertip. Crimson welled from the wound, a color that stole the tension from Dex's shoulders. Because it was truly evident now that Soyina was not one of Nor's minions.

"I've shown you mine. Now you show me yours," Soyina said, passing the blade, handle-first, to Dex.

He wiped it off, then removed his glove and ran the blade quickly across his palm. His green Tenebran blood oozed from the fresh cut. Andi followed suit, red weeping from her skin.

"I had hoped, in some way, that I would have been able to kill you," Soyina said with a sigh as one of her galaxy tattoos snaked across her brow. "But this will be more fun, anyway. Think of all the time we'll spend together now that I know you're not silverbloods." She stood, took the knife from Andi's waiting hand and wiggled a finger over her shoulder at them. "Follow me, Baroness, Dextro. And for the love of the stars, *do* please try not to look so glum. I've saved you once again, ever your loyal heroine."

She slipped behind the bar, where two droids were busy carving fresh mugs from a block of frozen ice. "Well?"

"Should we go?" Dex asked, looking helplessly at Andi.

"We don't have much of a choice," she said. "Where else are we going to go?"

Dex sighed. "I swear, if she handcuffs me to a toilet again…"

"You know," Andi said, as she followed after Soyina. "I think I'd pay to see that."

They moved past the droids to the entrance to the kitchen, past rows of more liquor bottles and frozen meat awaiting a fire. The entire pub staff, it seemed, was mechanical. Not a single human in sight; no one to look twice as Soyina approached the huge meat storage freezer, swinging open the thick metal door.

Cold, even colder than the pub itself, filtered out, along with thick clouds of chilly steam. Rows upon rows of frozen animal carcasses hung inside, some clearly roak-hunted on Solera and others imported from other warmer planets across Mirabel.

"Always around corpses, Soyina," Dex commented.

She smiled over her shoulder. "I find them fascinating, and beautiful. The Baroness would likely agree."

Andi shook her head silently at Dex and mouthed, "Nope."

Soyina stopped at the back of the massive freezer, turning to face them again.

"Before we proceed...what's in the bag?"

Dex shrugged, Havoc finally having gone silent inside. "The devil incarnate," he said with a wink. "A Fellibrag from Adhira."

Soyina seemed to accept that answer, sweeping aside a huge hunk of frozen meat.

Behind the carcass was a hole carved into the wall. And beyond that, a tunnel that led downward into the earth, into a seemingly endless darkness.

"After you, Baroness, Bounty Hunter."

When neither Dex nor Andi moved, Soyina laughed softly, but the sound held a bit of chaos within. "What? You thought the Underground was just some kind of code name?" She waved a hand as she slipped inside. "Follow me. We shouldn't keep Arachnid waiting."

CHAPTER 14
ANDI

The darkness was not complete for long, for as soon as Andi pressed the button on her varillium cuffs, cool blue light bounded off the rock walls.

Eventually, the rock gave way to ancient, deep blue stone, the substance that made up most of the Soleran landscape beneath all the ice and snow. As they journeyed deeper underground, Andi began to notice rough carvings on the walls, driven deep into the stone by hands long since buried in the grave.

"I haven't been to this planet in years," Dex said. "But we studied all the planetary systems in Guardian training. I never knew there were tunnels like this one on Solera."

"Every planet has their secrets," Andi said, thinking of the hidden tunnels within Averia that she'd learned of when she became Kalee's Spectre. How much her life had changed, since those days.

The symbols on the stone walls only grew in number as they walked, until they came upon fresher carvings gouged deep into the blue. Spidery etchings, arrows leading downward, words scratched in a language that Andi had never seen. They looked like constellations, and yet they were different, somehow.

As if someone had swapped the angle of the Godstars.

Andi reached out a hand, inexplicably drawn to the images.

"The boss doesn't like the carvings being touched," Soyina said. "The boss doesn't even like people looking at them, actually. Art is a private thing. Even more so when it's been your greatest companion for so many years."

"Where are these symbols from?" Andi asked, running her fingertips over them, as if she hadn't heard Soyina's warning—or didn't care about it.

Soyina sighed, but didn't scold her further. "Patience, my dear. Answers will soon follow."

As if in response, a voice called out from the darkness. "Back so soon? And with stragglers, I see."

The tunnel finally came to an end at a heavy silver door, nestled into the rock and firmly shut. On its front was an archaic keypad, the kind that only existed in stories of a time long before the Cataclysm. A blue lantern, housing the same cool flames from the ice pub on the surface above, hung beside the door, revealing the fact that no one was there.

But the voice had come from someone other than Andi, Dex or Soyina. For a moment, Andi assumed it was just an external com.

Then the voice spoke again, loud and clear, only a pace from her. "Where's Klarisa?"

Dex yelped as a young woman suddenly materialized before the door, like a spirit from another world. She wore a tight-fitting suit of purple and black, her curves outlined for all to see. Her hair was a perfect mixture of metallic strands interwoven with natural brown, bangs splitting the two right down the center of her forehead.

Andi had reached for her swords at the woman's sudden appearance, but slowly lowered her hands when Soyina nodded in greeting. "Klarisa sent them."

"As she does," the girl acknowledged. She grinned at Andi with all her teeth.

Then *disappeared* entirely.

"Godstars," Dex whispered, coming up beside Andi. "She must be from Tevara—the moon that orbits Vacilis. I've never met anyone from there before."

"Where did she go?" Andi asked, stepping forward to stare at the space where the girl had just been.

Moments later, the girl's laughter could again be heard, back down the passageway. Andi and Dex whirled, and sure enough, she now stood behind them, arms crossed over her chest, the metallic strands of her hair glinting in Andi's cuff lights. "The name's Eryn Railian. And *you* are Androma Racella."

"Eryn likes to show off," Soyina said, shrugging as if she were used to Eryn's tricks. "She can bend light, make herself and other things seem to disappear. Arachnid was incredibly pleased when Eryn came along. She'd been hiding in the city for a few days after Nor took over, and now she's quite useful as a spy. Gets us a lot of information from the rest of the dome."

As Soyina spoke, Eryn approached Dex and tentatively placed both hands on his arm, closing her eyes and tilting her head at just enough of an angle to still show off her smile. The edges of Dex's body began to flicker beneath her touch, fading from view as if a giant ghostly hand was gradually erasing him from existence.

Andi watched in amazement as Eryn and Dex faded, then reappeared together, Dex's eyes wide with shock as he cursed. "Incredible," she breathed. "How do you do it?"

"With style," Eryn said playfully. She held out a hand, twisting and turning it, making it fade from view and then return, fully formed again.

"Enough of your show," Soyina said impatiently. A tattoo of a dragon danced across the bridge of her nose, reminding Andi briefly of Lon. "Though I do want to see if you can sneak me into the bathhouse later. I'd like to play a nasty, painful little trick on that bastard, Peiter."

"I'd be honored," Eryn said with a small bow. "After my shift is over, of course."

"Eryn guards the entrance," Soyina explained. "There's no one else expected today, so should anyone arrive…" Soyina glanced to Eryn's thigh, where a menacing silver pistol nestled in its sheath. "Blast them sky-high, my little dove."

"With pleasure," Eryn said. She kicked the door twice, two booming *thunk*s of her metallic boots against the steel, then faded from view in a blink, as if she'd never been there at all.

"Theatrics," Soyina said with a sigh. "Arachnid appreciates them so." A booming knock sounded from the other side of the door, and she grinned like a demon. "It seems the show is about to begin."

The door opened slowly, emitting a great groan as someone inside heaved at the weight of it. At first, Andi saw only bright light. As her eyes adjusted, she heard Dex gasp from beside her, and then…

"Godstars be damned," Dex said, stepping past her.

Andi's eyes widened as she took in the scene beyond the open door, the massive space overflowing with warmth and light and the noises of humanity.

An entire *city* was hidden inside.

All this time, Queen Nor had been scouring the surface of every planet for those who hadn't been affected by the Zenith virus. And yet here the Underground was, hidden far below where her drones and droids could reach.

"Welcome," Soyina said, stretching her arms wide, "to the undercity. Underground headquarters, at your service."

The cavern was massive, nearly a quarter of the size of Craatia above. But this city was a natural phenomenon, carved out of the belly of the planet itself. Blue rock walls towered as far up as Andi could see, with stalactites and stalagmites hanging down and jutting up every few yards, like the fangs of a humongous creature.

Woven around them were scaffoldings and makeshift structures of iron and rock, wood and bits of what looked like old spaceships from days long past. Workers climbed all around the scaffoldings, swinging across the bars like they'd done it a thousand times, with the ease of those used to such places.

"We hail from all across the galaxy," Soyina said. "But some of our number are native to Solera, and it's because of them that we were able to find this place. Eons ago, the old Solerans settled in caverns just like these. Of course, many of the old ruins were destroyed during the Cataclysm, their entrances buried in the rubble of the bombings. This one survived, though, and it's been the perfect hideout for us. We're so far below the surface that we're completely undetectable from above. There's natural heat, too, thanks to the insulation from the dome overhead. It's not exactly a summer home, but it stays warm enough." She motioned for Andi and Dex to stay close as she began the descent into the undercity. "Walk with me."

And follow they did. As they walked, Andi's head felt as if it were on a swivel, rotating constantly while Soyina led them into the undercity's depths. Crackling fires, the flames purple and smokeless like those in the ice pub, were scattered about, serving as the main source of light. Groups sat around them, some with children talking and playing with makeshift toys.

They passed a New Vedan man, his great arms swinging in

an arc as he forged a massive broadsword over a fire, the blade easily the size of Andi herself.

Breck, Andi thought, seeing that giant form. Her heart squeezed, thinking of her head gunner. What would Breck have thought, seeing this place? She would have whistled, low and long. She would have sniffed the air and asked about the next meal. She and Gilly would have been fascinated by all the different fashions, hairstyles, makeup looks.

They would have adored this place.

Andi felt, already, that she adored it, too. The cavern smelled like damp earth, human sweat, meat roasting on fires...but that was *life*. That was freedom. She smiled for the first time in what felt like years. If only the girls were here—then she'd smile even broader.

"The looks on your faces," Soyina said, giggling as she glanced over her shoulder. "It's a lot to take in, but by the Godstars, it's glorious." She pointed at something just ahead. "Careful, Baroness. Wouldn't want you to step in that."

She stepped over a crack in the ground, where some sort of pale yellow liquid was bubbling in a stream that fishtailed throughout the place. "Perfectly safe to drink, though it may make you forget your own name."

"How many of you are here?" Dex asked. "Are there other Underground camps across Mirabel?"

"Not enough," Soyina said, causing Dex to frown. "But though we may be only a few hundred, we're mighty. We've made contact with another group on Arcardius, and a couple on Tenebris and Pazus. And we're certain others are out there, hiding. Now that Arachnid's messages are getting through, we expect others to rise and show themselves. If you hadn't been lost in your shiny spaceship this whole time, you'd probably have joined us weeks ago. Worked your way up the ranks. Now you'll have to start as grunts. Ground soldiers. Well...you would have, if it weren't for the Baroness, here."

"Me?" Andi asked in disbelief.

"You," Soyina said with a grin.

Andi sent her a suspicious glance. "What do you want with me?"

"I don't have any opinion on the matter. But Arachnid…oh, the boss can't *wait* to speak with you." Soyina glanced away, pressing her lips together. "I've said too much already. Let's keep moving."

They walked until they reached the other side of the cavern, where a series of tunnels had been sculpted into the blue rock. A group of children hurried into one in the center, carrying baskets full of what looked like soiled blankets and rags.

"Bathhouse is that way," Soyina said, glancing at Dex again, her eyes full of suggestion. Andi's insides boiled a little at that look, but she wouldn't give Soyina the satisfaction of knowing how she really felt.

The woman waggled a finger at Dex, the tattoos on it swirling in erratic patterns. "The things we could do in there, you and I." Then she smiled sideways at Andi. "Hell, I'd take the Baroness, too, if it weren't for the stick she's got stuck up her—"

"We'll *pass*," Andi said, taking Dex by the arm and hauling him toward her. He looked at her in surprise for a moment, then smiled warmly. Andi blushed, annoyed that she'd allowed Soyina to get under her skin.

Soyina stopped just inside the leftmost tunnel, where a group of guards stood at the ready. "Hello, my darlings. Is the boss ready for us?"

An elderly woman, who had a scowl worthy of Dex, nodded curtly and lifted a wicked, curved sword. "If you're certain they're safe, Resurrectionist. It's your head on the end of my blade if you're wrong."

Soyina scoffed. "So doubtful of my science, all of you soldiers. But blood never lies—they're clean. And we all know my brilliance has always exceeded everyone's expectations."

"Science has its shortcomings," the old woman grumbled back.

Soyina stopped before a set of heavy hide curtains, the animal skin old and worn, holes patched up with random bits of fabric and threads.

"If this is some silly game to you, Soyina," Andi said, keeping her voice low. "If you're leading us to our deaths... I'll personally spear your eyes out with a fork."

"It's true," Dex said. "I've seen her do similar things—in Lunamere."

"Oh, that *would* be a pleasant way to go," Soyina replied brightly. "But unfortunately, my time to die hasn't come yet. And neither has yours." She swept open the curtain. "Go in and get your answers, kiddies."

Dex gave her a wary look. "You're not coming with us?"

Soyina reached out a hand, those tattoos swirling again as she patted him a little too hard on the cheek. "I know it's hard for us to part, but Arachnid has requested to see you two alone."

"Joy of all joys," Andi remarked dryly.

"Weapons stay here, though," Soyina added, eyeing Andi's swords and Dex's pistol. "But don't worry. I'll take good care of them while you're gone. We'll have lots of fun."

With a sigh, Andi unlatched her harness and shoved the sheathed blades so hard against Soyina's stomach that the woman let out a grunt and stumbled backward, clutching them haphazardly in her arms.

"If you remove them from their sheaths," Andi said with a glare, "you'll have to remove them from your intestines when I return. Imagine how much *fun* you'll have with that."

Dex placed his gun atop the swords, shrugging as if he hadn't a care in the world.

"Let's go, Androma," he said lightly, taking her by the hand.

Before Soyina could respond, Andi took the backpack from Dex's shoulder and tossed it into the woman's arms.

"Careful," she said as Havoc hissed from within the pack,

and Soyina held it away from her by its fraying strap. "Havoc can smell fear."

She turned on her heel and disappeared through the curtain, tugging Dex in after her.

Andi had never been a fan of movies.

She hated the way they painted a picture that wasn't truly *real*. Illusions, displayed on a grand scale, that told stories that could never really come true.

Most of the movies that were popular on Arcardius ended happily, everyone too afraid of sinking back into that place of darkness so many people had felt during the Cataclysm. But Andi had seen one film, ages ago, that she didn't hate. She'd watched it with Kalee late at night, hidden in the back of the media center in Averia. Kalee had been terrified, watching the lead actress walk through a dark tunnel that would surely lead her to her death.

But Andi had felt *alive* watching that moment play out. She'd known even then that she'd never be so foolish as to walk down a road that led to such an obvious, ominous death. And if she was ever forced to, she'd know how to fight her way back out.

At least she'd always thought so…until now.

"Well, this looks like a cozy place to cuddle up together in the shadows," Dex said softly.

Andi couldn't help but laugh, despite her nerves. "No time like the present, is there?"

The tunnel beyond the curtain *was* dark and narrow, with water dripping down the rocky walls like fresh blood. Had Andi been anyone else, she may have feared taking a step forward.

Instead, she clicked on her cuffs, allowing their light to bathe the tunnel in a cool, muted blue.

"The best gift I've ever given you," Dex said. "Those, and the *Marauder*."

"Oh, was that a gift?" Andi teased. "I thought I stole it, fair and square."

He was right, though. Not only did the varillium cuffs protect her scarred flesh—burned into ruin the night Kalee had died—but they'd helped her get out of many sticky situations. The *Marauder* had, too.

"Let's go," she said. Andi stepped forward, her fists held before her. As she walked, she imagined it wasn't just Dex with her, but also her crew. Breck's tall figure at her back, Gilly's delicate footsteps beside her. She imagined Lira, calmly assessing the situation, beautiful in her fearlessness as she prepared to destroy anyone who laid a hand on the girls.

So much had changed in a matter of weeks. But for the sake of her crew, Andi would bravely walk forward into the dark.

The tunnel suddenly opened wide, revealing another rounded room. Dex stopped and gently guided Andi's wrist to shed light on the wall.

"More of those strange carvings," he whispered.

The symbols truly were like the constellations that marked the Godstars, only flipped. Altered, in strange ways. They followed the carvings deeper into the darkness, until the rock walls began to widen, trailing upward to a spot where a single fire flickered on the rocky ground, the flames spitting embers that danced in the shadows overhead. The smoke escaped somewhere above, likely another clever design by whoever had once turned this place into a hidden home.

Andi walked quietly toward the flames. More carvings were written on the ground with what looked like coals from the fire.

"Someone's slightly obsessed," Dex said as Andi knelt to look at them.

It was then that she felt the presence of someone else shifting in the shadows.

"Interesting, that you would invite us here, but choose to hide when we finally arrive," Andi said softly to the darkness.

She could feel the warmth of the fire, welcome in the chill of the space, and Dex's body close against her back. If she couldn't have her swords, she'd definitely settle for him as her backup. He'd taught her to fight, after all.

"Well?" Dex called out. "We're here for the party."

Silence was their only answer.

But then, across the room, a set of tiny red lights blinked into being. Gone one breath, and there the next, floating in the shadows.

"You must be into games, if you've teamed up with Soyina," Andi said, moving to the side. The red lights followed her as she paced by the fire. They did not blink, only tracked her with a devil's stare.

Andi stopped walking and squared herself with the flames between them. "What do you want from us?"

The red lights shifted, and Andi heard a clicking noise, the tiny *tap-tap-tap* of what sounded like an animal's claws. "Well?" she demanded, even as a shiver ran over and through her. She wasn't afraid. She *would not* be afraid.

Dex pressed a reassuring hand to her back. "If you won't speak to us, we won't waste our time any further. Soyina would be more than happy to play creepier games with us."

The red lights flared as Andi spun on her heel, following Dex's lead away from the fire, back toward the tunnel to the undercity.

"She stole everything from you, did she not?"

The voice that spoke was shockingly deep. Metallic. Inhuman. It sounded even worse than it had on the feeds, somehow more imposing in person. As if it were speaking into her very soul.

Andi stopped, tilting her chin ever so slightly to the side. "Who?" she asked.

"Nor Solis."

From the corner of her vision, Andi could see the darkness moving. She could see the tiny red lights shifting, glowing brighter with each syllable the figure spoke.

"She has stolen a lot of things from a lot of people," Andi answered. "But yes. She stole my crew."

"And what would you be prepared to give, to have them back?" The lights flared again and again, each time that metallic voice uttered a word. "The answer is simple. Get it wrong, and you'll leave here at once, unharmed." The lights moved upward, the *tap-tap-tap* clicking in time with the motion. "Get it right, and I can give you what you desire most."

Andi's heart pounded, furious, in her chest. "I'd give anything to have them back."

"Andi," Dex said, a warning in his voice.

She knew he was afraid to lose her, afraid she'd risk too much of herself for the sake of rescuing her girls. But she couldn't hide from the truth of her heart, and she wouldn't protect him from it, either.

"Most would say the same, after losing what they love," the figure in the darkness said.

"True." Andi raised a brow. "But when I say things, I mean them." She stepped closer, wondering who Arachnid really was, to hide in the shadows like this, and how he dared to ask her such questions.

She stopped at the edge of the flames, feeling the warmth dancing on her face, the firelight flickering off her metal cheekbones. "To have my crew back, to see them walk free from the false queen... I'd give my life."

Dex's breath came out in a whoosh behind her.

Then the red lights blinked out, and only darkness stared back at them both.

"Is that the wrong answer?" Andi asked. Frustration picked at her, an obnoxious little creature she couldn't shake, and she was about to turn away when the darkness shifted once more.

A massive figure, clad in crimson armor, stepped forward from the shadows. Andi couldn't see a face beyond the dented, war-torn helmet concealing the figure from view. But the spidery droid that sat upon its shoulder, red eye-lights blinking to life again, explained the strange voice.

"No," Arachnid said. "I can give you what you desire."

"And what do you want from us in return?" Andi asked, walking closer to the firelight.

"Didn't anyone tell you why you're here?" Robotic laughter filtered from the droid on Arachnid's shoulder. "You came here without knowing why. What if this were a trap? What if it *is* a trap?"

Fury began to writhe within Andi.

"We came here because your people saved us," Dex snapped. He gestured in the direction of the ceiling, indicating the surface of the planet. "No one out there controls their own minds, but your people do. That's enough for me to hope we're on the same side. Call us foolish, stupid or whatever you want, but we can help each other."

"How do you propose to help me?" Arachnid asked.

Andi knew their fighting skills were unmatched, but that wasn't enough to bargain with. There was only one thing they had that could be used as leverage—something that was of the utmost importance.

"We have information." She grabbed Dex's wrist and unfastened the silver band Alfie was programmed into. "Inside this watch is a chip with detailed information about Nor's half brother, Valen Cortas. We believe he's a key to how the virus works."

"And what do you wish in exchange for this information?"

Andi held out the watch. "My crew is stranded on Arcardius, under Nor's control. I'd like your help getting there, so I can set them free."

Arachnid turned his head slightly to look at the watch, seemingly deep in thought. Andi sent up a prayer to the Godstars as she waited, heart in her throat. If he wouldn't help them, they might never find another way to rescue the girls.

Finally, Arachnid said, "I don't need your information. I already have it."

Andi's heart dropped.

"How could you have this information when you've been hiding out here? I doubt Valen gives away his blood willingly," Dex countered, as if trying to call a bluff.

But Arachnid ignored Dex's comment, instead moving his hands up to his helmet, pausing when they reached the back. A whoosh of air escaped the suit, and the droid on his armored shoulder scuttled away, over his back and out of sight. There was a hiss of steam, and then the metal collapsed in on itself.

As the steam cleared, Andi stared at Arachnid in disbelief. For standing before her was not a man, like she'd expected, but a woman.

Small in frame, practically dwarfed by the size of the armor protecting her. Her face was marred with a wicked scar, harsh against her brown skin, but her eyes gleamed in the firelight.

"Who are you?" Andi demanded.

"You don't know me." The woman's lips didn't move as the droid spoke for her. "But I believe you *do* know my son, though perhaps not my daughter. Yet."

Realization began to dawn on Andi as Arachnid stared at her with eerily familiar golden eyes. "My name is Klaren Solis. And I need your help to stop my children from destroying Mirabel."

CHAPTER 15
NOR

Nor had spent most of her life dreaming of growing old on Arcardius. The planet was breathtaking with its crystal clear waters, lush greenery and floating gravarocks—a veritable paradise compared to Xen Ptera's crumbling earth and poisonous atmosphere.

Arcardius's capital city of Veronus was its crowning jewel, filled with glittering towers. But today, Nor found it difficult to appreciate Veronus's glory as she peered out the windowed wall of her office, past the clouds to the cityscape far below. For how could she stand to look upon it when, after all this time, the planet she'd thought was finally *hers* actually belonged to someone else?

With a huff, she drew the curtains closed, suddenly disgusted by the view.

"There must be another way," Zahn said from the opposite side of the office. He sat on a comfortably worn couch beside the window, a near-empty glass of aged Griss in his hand. Weeks ago, it had brought Nor great joy to open the doors of Cyprian's personal cellar and partake of the finest liquors in the galaxy. This particular vintage had quickly become one of her favorite indulgences.

But tonight, the taste was stale on her tongue.

Nor sat down beside Zahn, sighing as she looked at the holoscreen he held in his other hand. Androma Racella stared up at her, a wicked half smile on her lips. It was a photograph of the girl from her days as a Spectre here on Averia, guarding Cyprian's daughter, Kalee. When Nor closed her eyes, she felt as if she could still sense the girl's presence here in this office, where she'd once attended meetings with the general.

"We'll never find her," Nor said, looking down at the amber liquid in her glass. She set the drink aside on the table in front of the couch.

"We will," Zahn said, reaching for her hand. Nor gently pulled away, entwining her fingers around her golden prosthetic instead. "You're not one to give up, *Nhatilya*. Don't change that now."

"Of all people, why *her*?" Nor said, looking at Androma's pale skin, the metallic implants across her cheekbones, her winter-gray eyes. The girl looked like she carried a thousand secrets— and as if she would kill anyone who dared try to pull them from her. "Why the most renowned criminal in the galaxy?"

She knew the story of the Bloody Baroness. The girl who'd inadvertently slain Cyprian Cortas's daughter, the very charge she'd sworn her life to protect. As vengeance, he'd trapped Androma into the task of retrieving Valen from Lunamere, an assignment that would have likely been a death mission if Nor hadn't already *planned* for Valen to be rescued—a ploy to get him back here to

Arcardius without the general suspecting he was an ally of Xen Ptera.

It was clear that Cyprian *hated* Androma Racella.

So it didn't make any sense that he would choose her, of everyone in Mirabel, to take his place as General of Arcardius.

"She's not beneath Valen's compulsion," Nor said. "And her ship has left no trace that anyone can find since she fled."

Again, Nor looked down at the screen. The damned girl had been in her clutches only weeks ago, walking these very halls. Valen had nearly killed her at the Ucatoria Ball. She'd thought the girl would never pose a problem...but now?

With every corner Nor turned, it was as if she saw the ghost of the Bloody Baroness.

"We *will* find her," Zahn said again, turning the screen away. "We'll do whatever it takes to root her out, and make sure you have full command again."

"And until then?" Nor asked.

Zahn wrapped an arm around her shoulder, pulling her close. "There's plenty to occupy your time. The completion of Nexus, the running of your new empire...and I can think of a few other things."

His teeth had just grazed her ear when the doors to her office swung open and Valen swept in. Zahn sighed and pulled away, rising to his feet. Nor followed his gaze to the doorway and was surprised to see that Valen was not alone.

For behind her brother trailed Darai, along with three others—female soldiers Nor only vaguely recognized.

"What is the meaning of this?" she asked, standing and pulling her cloak tight across her stomach to hide her wrinkled gown. She hadn't changed clothes since they'd heard the news about Cyprian's successor, too worried to do anything but focus on finding Androma.

"Majesty," Darai said, bowing quickly before crossing the

room toward her. "My deepest apologies for the intrusion, but—"

"You can stop with the ridiculous adviser act, Uncle," Valen said, cutting the old man off. He looked to Nor, but finished his sentence through their mental link instead. *I made a mistake, letting Andi go. I thought I'd killed her—*

A mistake you will not soon forget, Nor snapped back, surprising herself with her own sudden surge of anger.

Valen cleared his throat and quickly answered back with a nod. *No one could have known, Nor. But these three… I promise you, they will be the answer to our problem. Consider this my apology. I think you will find it perfectly to your liking.*

The young women stepped up behind Valen, all three obediently dropping to a knee in unison. Nor looked at the girls more closely, surveying them one by one.

The first, a giantess with brown skin and hardened eyes, was clearly from the planet New Veda. The one at her side, red-headed and petite, hardly looked old enough to don the black soldier's uniform she wore. The last was a girl from Adhira, judging by her ocean-blue skin and eyes. Her posture was graceful and elegant, and she held her head high even as she bent the knee to her queen.

All of them had a singular trait in common: the silver veins of the Zenith virus spread across their skin, glowing brightly as they waited for her judgment.

"Who are they?" Nor asked, still unable to place them.

"These soldiers used to serve a different master," Darai said, his features broadening in a rare smile. "They were once criminals who worked alongside the Bloody Baroness. Her…crew."

Electricity zinged through Nor's entire body at those words.

"I know Androma," Valen said, moving closer to Nor, his hands worrying away at each other. "She's not beneath my control, and she's going to be nearly impossible to root out. And she's a survivor—she'll do whatever it takes to save herself. She's likely already far away, holed up somewhere none of our soldiers can reach. She may even be with Arachnid himself now, hiding out—"

"Don't say his name," Nor said, clenching her teeth.

"My apologies, sister," Valen said, cringing slightly. "But she *would* be impossible to find, Nor, if it weren't for these three." He looked over his thin shoulder at the trio of soldiers. "They're like family to her, and Androma will do whatever it takes to save them. Always. Even if the cost is her own life."

Nor approached the girls slowly, stopping a few paces away to look down at them. They kept their heads deeply bowed, as if they were too afraid to look upon their queen.

"Rise," she said to them. As one, they stood, their faces full of awe as they gazed at her. Nor's eyes fell on the Adhiran girl. Beautiful, like a delicate flower that had rows of hidden thorns beneath its petals.

"How well do you know the Bloody Baroness?"

The Adhiran girl's eyes met Nor's, and her voice was melodic as she spoke. "My queen... I am ashamed to admit that I was once very close to her. I...saw her as a sister, of sorts." She glanced at the other two girls, both of whom were nodding.

"We all did," the New Vedan girl agreed. "We spent years with Androma, learning from her...learning *about* her, on board the *Marauder*. We can tell you anything you need to know. Her likes, her dislikes, her greatest fears."

"Tell her what you told me earlier," Valen coaxed.

"Androma would do anything to set us free, if she believed we were in danger," the Adhiran girl said in that lyrical voice. "If what Valen says is true, Majesty, and you need to track down our old captain...then you could use us."

"We can find her for you," the giantess said. "Hunting people down was once our specialty, and we know all of Androma's preferred hideouts."

"I believe that you *could* find her," Nor said, her mind churning as she considered the possibilities this crew presented. She looked down at the smallest one, who hadn't yet spoken. She was a tiny thing, red braids dangling past her dainty shoulders. Nor knelt, pressing her golden prosthetic to the girl's chin and lifting it so that their gazes met. To her surprise, the child's eyes held little innocence.

"However, I think there is a far better way," Nor mused. "Do you know, little one, what Androma loves the most?"

The girl smiled. "Oh, yes. She loves her ship. But above all, she loves us."

"And do you know what we do to those things our enemies love?" Nor asked sweetly.

For an idea was brewing in her mind as she took in the three young women. Strong, she could tell. And yet they would break so easily—*had* already broken, beneath the strength of Valen's compulsion.

"No," the little girl answered. "But I'd love for you to tell me already."

"Gilly," the New Vedan hissed. "I'm sorry, my queen. She's as blunt as they come."

Nor smiled. "It's alright." She stood, pulling her hand from the child's chin as she spun to look at Darai, Valen and Zahn. "It's time for me to make a speech. Alert the soldiers. Bring in the camera crew. I'll speak to my people from the Academy's square. I want everyone on Arcardius to be there to see me, and everyone else in the galaxy to hear me."

"Nor, my love," Zahn started. "It's too risky to—"

His words trailed off as Nor spun back to look at the three girls. Her gaze fell on the smallest again—Gilly. A pretty little thing, and so pliable beneath her brother's power.

"The answer to my earlier question, child, is that we crush the things our enemies love. We destroy them. And we will do exactly that with you three." She reached out to stroke one of Gilly's braids. "I will send out an ultimatum, so loud that Androma Racella will have to hear it. And if she does not arrive on Arcardius within three days, defenseless and willing to hand herself over to me…then the three of you will die. And I will personally be the one who swings the blade."

She smiled at the girls, so perfectly willing to obey her—to die for her, should it come to that.

"A wise plan, my queen," the Adhiran girl said. "And an honor, to fall as a sacrifice to your cause."

"Will she come?" Nor asked. "Will it work?"

"Oh, yes," the little girl answered, a smile illuminating her freckled face. "She'll come. Andi always comes for us."

Her small hands touched the Solis sigil pinned to her chest, as if it were a token of good luck.

The transport ship's engine purred as the pilot carried them down through the clouds, toward Veronus.

"I have a number of guards stationed on the Academy grounds, where you'll make the speech," Zahn said. His voice was tense, filling the small space. The transport ship wasn't large, with room enough for only six passengers, plus the pilot in an enclosure at the front and a cargo bay in the back.

Nor knew Zahn feared for her safety, away from the well-guarded estate in the clouds. It was true that Arachnid was a threat as real as any, but Valen held control over most of the minds in the galaxy. She trusted her brother to control the crowds.

"I'll be fine," she whispered to Zahn, taking his hand. She squeezed it gently, but he only nodded and focused on the notescreen he held, scanning the security measures one last time.

"Your speech, Majesty, should last no longer than three minutes," Darai said. His hood was pulled low over his face, the shadows beneath his scars deep in the soft red glow of the ship's dash. "A powerful, impactful performance. Show Arachnid you have no fear. Show Androma she has no options. Show them that you will not bargain, and most important, show the people your power." He smiled suddenly, his teeth glowing almost as red as blood. "You will be a vision before the Academy, my dear."

Out of the corner of her eye, Nor saw a flicker of annoyance cross Zahn's face at her uncle's lecturing. She knew he wasn't a fan of Darai; had never really been. His attempts to offer counsel often felt a trifle condescending these days, but the old man had his uses, especially as a source of information about Exonia. So Zahn tolerated the adviser, but only because Nor insisted on keeping him around—just as Valen did.

Nor's gaze shifted to her brother. He'd been silent this whole time, swimming through the recesses of his mind, desperately searching for anything that could give them a clue about where Androma might be, or any intel on Arachnid. He could see through the eyes of millions, and Nor knew he was doing everything in his power to help her.

Yet still, Valen had come up with nothing.

A shadow fell over them as the transport passed below a looming gravarock. A waterfall pounded down its rocky side, glowing in the fading light of dusk. The wind caught the droplets of water as they fell, carrying them across the sky to sprinkle the windows of their ship.

"They defy the odds, these floating mountains," Nor said quietly.

Zahn's answering smile was tight, but he placed a comforting hand on her knee. "Some might say you have always done the same."

"It's funny," Nor replied, returning his smile. "I've always thought that about you. The boy who cleared me from the rubble. Now you're commanding my soldiers."

Zahn's shoulders loosened a little. "I would have you be safe always, Nor," he told her. "But I would also have you be happy. And if happiness means that I must set aside my personal fears of losing you…then I will shove them far away. And I will support you, my queen. Whatever it is that you wish to do, I will stand at your side."

He leaned over to kiss her gently, sweetly, mindful of the others watching. Nor suppressed a sigh of longing when Zahn pulled away and turned his attention back to his duties. It seemed like they never had enough time together, these days.

Zahn's hands flew across his notescreen, perusing guard orders, communications and whatever else he dealt with so that she didn't have to. "Androma's crew will be stationed as guards to your left and right," he told her. "The cameras will focus on them long enough for Androma to see that they are, in fact, loyal."

"Of course they are. We all know the Zenith virus has sealed my reign," Nor answered. "But we need the Unaffecteds to recognize that truth. That I am no longer the starving, broken princess from Xen Ptera, but a queen who will tear apart the Void and make way for something far greater than Mirabel has ever been capable of before. Nobody will harm me—not here. Not today. They will help me bring Androma forth, and Arachnid's threat will falter."

Nor felt in her heart that it was true.

Behind her, Valen suddenly groaned, as if he were in pain. Nor glanced over her shoulder, but her brother was still lost in his mind, eyes clenched shut. For a moment, she debated trying to reach him through the mental doorway between their minds, to see if he was alright, but Nor knew he would resent the intrusion. Valen needed to remain strong, to believe that she trusted in his ability to see this through.

"I want extra guards stationed around Valen," she said, looking to Darai this time and lowering her voice to a whisper. "It's not safe for him out there."

Her adviser gave a curt nod, the metal etchings on his face catching the light from the sunset outside the transport window.

"I agree, my dear. We must keep him as safe as we can, in the event that an attack occurs."

"It won't," Zahn interjected. "My guards will be on high alert." He glanced back at Valen's thin form, too. "But I agree. We'll make sure he's looked after. And Androma's crew will be at your side, willing to die for both of you, should they need to."

"I hope she sees the message," Nor said gleefully. "I hope she sees their faces, full of adoration for their queen, and comes running like a loyal dog."

"She will," Darai said with confidence. "After today, there will be nothing, and no one, who can stand in your way. Exonia will be ours once more."

Nor raised a brow at him.

"Yours, my dear," he corrected hastily. "Exonia will be *yours*, and you will reign supreme until the end of your days." Darai smiled. "I can see it now. A lifetime of patience, and pain, finally coming to fruition."

"And then our children will reign after," Nor said, taking Zahn's hand again, nodding along to her uncle's words. "Valen's message will ring out for eternity, and the Solis bloodline will rule forever."

Though Arcardius wasn't her true home, and though she'd had to fight tooth and nail to win her place here…this planet was nearly hers now. These people, these floating mountains, the Nexus satellite floating in the sky, almost complete. All of it would belong to Nor the moment Androma came for her crew.

So it was with confidence that Nor relaxed back into her seat and turned her gaze to the window, drinking in the sight of her domain. For Arcardius *would* be hers—it was only a matter of time now. And once she had Arcardius, and Mirabel, firmly in her grasp…

Then Exonia would finally be free.

CHAPTER 16

VALEN

Valen pulled himself from his mind castle as Veronus came into view, his head wobbling and pulsing from the effort. Still, he smiled through the pain as he saw the city that was no longer trapped beneath his father's iron rule.

To Valen, Veronus had always seemed to be made of stars. The buildings, largely crafted from glass and steel, glowed in the moonlight as the ship landed among them like a bird, polished silver wings outspread to catch the reflections of every admiring face in the city.

For the queen was coming down from her castle in the sky.

The tiny tendrils of fear Valen had felt as the ship soared away from Averia gradually melted away. As the ship's loading ramp lowered, steam hissing from the cooling vents creating a gentle

curtain of clouds, he heard the sound of his people cheering—
a mighty roar that could not be silenced.

Everyone wanted to see the queen. Innumerable flags with
the Solis family crest waved in Valen's sights as soldiers lined up
to escort Nor through the flanking crowds.

"Nor!" the people screamed. "The true queen!"

He had done this. Valen had never accomplished anything of
true merit in his life until he'd met Nor, and even now, there
were days when he had doubts about himself.

But this? This had been worth the wait.

Zahn called for his squadron to fall into formation, and they
cut a solid pathway through the crowd, leaving just enough space
for the queen's group to pass through. Nor and Zahn walked
side by side, guarded by Lira, Breck and Gilly, while Darai and
Valen followed close behind.

"Stay close," Zahn said over his shoulder to Valen as they
moved toward the Academy. He felt a surge of irritation at the
command—Zahn didn't need to talk down to him as if he were
a child. And where else would he be right now, but by his sister's
side?

Yet as the roar of the crowd pressed in around him, Valen's
annoyance gave way to awe, his eyes widening. His father had
been adored by the Arcadian people, his speeches and rallies
full of supporters…but this was something entirely different.

When Nor passed by, mothers held up their infants, desperate
for the queen to press a kiss to their foreheads. Children called
his sister's name, some of them singing songs of adoration. A
man in the crowd had fat tears rolling down his cheeks at the
very sight of Nor passing by.

It was everything she'd ever wanted—and it was all happening because of Valen.

The Solis name was now adored instead of cursed. And today,
his sister would give these people a great gift, by not showing

any fear of Arachnid's threats. She would also give them a purpose; a mission they would surely be able to help her complete.

Stay safe, Nor told Valen through their mental link. *Stay right at my side, Valen. Promise?*

I promise, Mother, Valen said, his voice carrying a hint of laughter through the link.

Zahn shouted out an order, and the soldiers escorted Nor onto a makeshift stage. Valen stepped up beside her, watching the people swarm around the stage, as closely as the soldiers would allow. Behind them stood the Arcardian Academy, a pyramid-shaped structure made entirely of glass. This very place was where Androma had first met Kalee and Valen. Where her strange connection to Valen's father had originated, though none of them could have possibly imagined then that she'd someday be given his title when he passed on.

This was where the Arcardian military students trained. Where they had once learned to call the Olen System their enemy.

Now they praised the very queen their mothers and fathers had tried to kill, long ago. Everything had come full circle. Valen looked to the sky, imagining he could see the Nexus satellite, and the Void far beyond. Soon, this crowd would have a new group of people to join them in their praise of Nor Solis.

"Show them you will not bow to fear," Zahn said as he joined them on the stage, taking his place between Nor and Valen. Camera droids buzzed about, bobbing up and down, ready to record Nor's message and send it out across the galaxy as Zahn's intelligence team worked to combat Arachnid's constant looped messages.

They'd take back the feeds. Then they'd root him out once and for all—and crush him like the bug he was.

Show them their queen, Valen thought to Nor.

Together, they looked out upon the crowd. A million faces looked back. Faces of every shape and size and color, all of them looking at Nor as if she were their one true ruler. The woman their mother, Klaren, had tried and failed to be.

"People of Arcardius," Nor said, and the crowd fell silent at once. "I come to you this evening in the wake of a message sent out by a monster. A man who hides in the shadows, who threatens the well-being of many others. He calls himself Arachnid. He dares defy the truth I was sent here to spread across every system in Mirabel, the truth that you now all know: that if you follow me, I will bring new order and new light to this galaxy. I will wipe away the bloodstains of the past, and remove the need for war and terror and destruction."

Murmurs spread through the crowd at the mention of Arachnid.

Still, the adoration hung like a perfume in the air, thick with Valen's compulsion. His head buzzed from the noise, but also from the effort of commanding all of them. He needed sleep— sleep, and time to dwell inside his mind and compel more people.

Valen tried to focus on Nor's voice as it rang across the Academy grounds like a song.

"I refuse to hide the way Arachnid does. The message that I have shared with you, since the beginning of my reign, still remains. We must carry on building Nexus, our shining beacon in the sky. We must dedicate every ounce of our energies to ensure that it is completed on time." Nor paused a moment for effect, then added, "But there is another mission I must now call upon you to complete."

Her gaze swept across the crowd as they roared.

As her name formed again on all of their lips.

"Arachnid is our enemy. But there is another who dares to defy me and my name. Androma Racella, known widely as the Bloody Baroness, has spread a reign of terror across this galaxy for far too long. She is my enemy—the only other person standing in our way as we aim to bring peace to Mirabel." Nor lifted her hands to the sky, smiling triumphantly. "I implore you, my beloved people, to rise up with me, and bring this young woman forth. Anyone who has intelligence on Androma, or who delivers her to Averia, will have my favor until the end of my days."

Valen watched as Nor directed her gaze right into the cameras, smiling to himself as she spoke her next words. As she laid the trap for their enemy.

"Androma, if you are watching, I offer you a gift in exchange for your compliance."

She glanced back at Valen then. He motioned for the girls to step forward from the background, into full view of the camera droids.

Breck, towering over everyone, held her chin high as she moved to stand by Nor's side. Gilly bobbed excitedly on her toes, the very same way she always had, but now her excitement was for *Nor*. And Lira, delicate but brave, simply stared ahead, face expressionless as she looked at the cameras.

"Your crew has given their fealty to me. They are loyal to me now, and me alone," Nor declared, her voice ringing out over all. The droids hovered closer, filming the three girls from all angles. Valen could just imagine the look on Andi's face when she saw her crew. Alive, and well, but no longer *hers*. It would hurt her more than any weapon ever could.

Triumph flared in his chest at the genius of his plan.

Nor motioned for the girls to kneel. Valen could feel the dedication pouring off them in waves, see the adoration in their eyes just before they knelt, heads bowing low before their queen. All of them, once mighty soldiers as free as the stars, now fully in bondage to a new leader. So perfect was their commitment to her that they had freely offered up their lives.

Nor lifted her chin in challenge. "Pay close attention, Androma, for I will only say this once. You have three days' time to arrive at Averia, ready and willing to hand yourself over to me without defiance. Should you fail to arrive on time... I will slaughter your beloved crew, one by one by one."

Nor smiled as she finished her demand, looking beautiful as a rose. The droids closed in, red lights blinking on their fronts to show that the message had gone out, loud and clear, across the galaxy.

Androma would hear it. She would come, without a doubt, the moment she saw the feed.

Well done, Valen thought to Nor.

Her answer was just filtering back through their link when a sudden cry overtook it.

"ARACHNID LIVES!"

The scream cut through the crowd like a bullet.

Valen's gaze fell away from his sister as he searched for the source of the words.

Then the world turned to fire as a bomb exploded into the night.

Valen was blasted off the stage by the power of it, a sudden force of wind and dust that had his back slamming into the pavement below. The air rushed from his lungs in a single breath.

He was vaguely aware of his body twitching, his legs numb beneath him as he saw the source of the bomb. Half of the Academy building was gone, the glass structure destroyed in the explosion, like it had never existed at all. Smoke poured from the gaping hole in the pyramid, the world beyond it quickly disappearing as the thick black clouds poured into the city streets.

Valen gasped, trying to stand, but he couldn't see through the smoke. *He couldn't see.* Pain lanced through his body as he tried in vain to catch his breath. He was suddenly back in Lunamere again, before Nor had come to save him. Before he'd chosen to save himself. In his mind, he only saw darkness, and cells lining the sides of an endless black hallway.

He wasn't strong enough to break himself out. He was a prisoner, set to spend eternity in this cold, empty hell.

Not real, Valen told himself. *This isn't real.*

Hands grabbed him from behind.

"Get up, you fool boy!"

Valen yelped and scrambled to get away.

"I said, get on your feet! Get a hold of yourself, princeling!"

The world slowly came back into focus, and Valen realized it was Darai kneeling over him, the adviser's face twisted in rage. Blood trickled down the side of his cheek, and a shard of glass was lodged in his skin, but he was the most welcome sight Valen had ever seen.

"Can you stand?" Darai asked.

Valen nodded, allowing Darai to help him to his feet, shameless in this moment. His back screamed as people sprinted past, trying in vain to escape the Academy grounds. He watched it all with a strange sense of detachment. As if he were not here, as if this were not truly happening.

"You have to calm them," Darai insisted, ushering Valen back the way they'd come. The transport still sat waiting, the pilot waving his arms as he ushered them over. Someone shoved past them both, nearly knocking them back to the ground. Darai leaned on Valen for support, and a sharp spike of pain slammed into Valen's ribs. "Can you hear me? I said you have to calm them! Reach into your mind! Compel the crowd to relax, so we can get to safety!"

"I can't!" Valen said. He was already so weak, his mind so labored from searching for traces of Andromia, from commanding so many to find her and Arachnid and bring them forth.

The old man shook him by the shoulders. "You've grown soft, lazy in that damned estate. I said, *compel them!*"

Amid the chaos, Valen sank into his mind. He realized that he'd had the door closed, but now that he'd opened it, he heard another voice, screaming his name.

VALEN! Valen!

Nor! Valen thought back to her, relief flooding through him at the sound of her voice. *Are you alright?* But when he looked up, he couldn't find her. He only saw a sea of soldiers—reinforcements arriving from their barracks in the city. He could just make out Breck's towering form as she moved closer to the back of the stage, likely closing in on Nor.

"I have to get to my sister!" Valen said wildly.

"She's just as big a fool as you are!" Darai shouted. His eyes were dark, spittle flying from his lips. "You want to help your sister? Then compel these people, before we all get killed in this chaos."

Valen closed his eyes, readying himself to obey, to calm the storm around him.

Then the first gunshot went off.

CHAPTER 17
LIRA

All her life, Lira had trained for battle.

Not by force, but of her own sheer will to prove her worth to the galaxy.

When she was only a girl, her aunt Alara had not allowed her to join the Adhiran Sentinels in their daily training. Lira had begged Alara to let her go, *longed* to fall into step alongside them on their endless runs around the mountain, their days-long treks through the jungle and desert from one terraformed section of the planet to the next.

Alara had refused, but Lira had decided she'd do so anyway, for was life truly worth living when you were only walking in the footsteps someone else had laid out for you?

Her aunt had been furious when she'd discovered Lira spent most of her time fantasizing about flying ships or fighting with her fists, instead of learning how to rule Adhira. And when Lira had finally run, desperate to escape the future her aunt had chosen for her, each life decision like a perfectly stitched portion of a quilt that had been designed just for her...

Lira had taken up fighting in the pits of Zerpro7. Both to hone her skills and to remind herself that sometimes the greatest strength came from a place of pain. Each hit she'd taken, every bruised jaw and bloodied knuckle and swollen limb, had brought her to where she was now.

And so when the explosion went off, knocking her off the stage, Lira recovered quickly and fell into action, her body responding out of memory—and a drive to protect her queen, who'd taken away all the pain of her past life. Who'd given her a new life, and would give countless others new lives, as well.

Smoke filled the streets as she rolled to her feet, Gilly close by. Citizens screamed, tripping over each other to escape the chaos. Commands crackled through the soldiers' earpieces.

A familiar voice rang out in Lira's ear now, through her com. *Breck.* She and Gilly were the only two people who had access to this com since she'd had it fixed—altered to block out any possibility of communication from Androma after that traitor chose the other side.

Traitor.

The word felt strange in her thoughts.

Was Androma a traitor?

The doubt didn't last long. A fog from the outer stretches of her mind came rushing forward, shutting all uncertainty out.

Traitor.

Androma *was* a traitor.

"Create a perimeter around the queen! Protect her at all costs!" Breck shouted, her voice booming in Lira's ear.

But it couldn't block out the sounds of the gunshots.

At her side, Lira glimpsed a flash of red as Gilly closed in on the stage where Nor had just been, the other soldiers in their unit following suit. Rifles were raised and bodies locked in close, ready to give their own lives to save their queen.

Protect her at all costs, Lira heard another voice whispering. Not in her com, but in what felt like her very soul.

It was the same voice she'd always heard since Nor took power, flickering into her mind throughout the day and night like a candle in the darkness. She latched on to the order, desperate to obey.

Protect your queen.

Figures emerged throughout the crowd, dressed in deepest bloodred—the color of Arachnid. Another shot rang out. The sea of people writhed and shoved and moved in too many directions at once, a wave rocking and rolling, ready to crash against the shore.

Enemy, Lira's gut screamed as she saw the black spiderweb design painted on their helmets. Where were they coming from? It seemed like they'd emerged from everywhere and nowhere all at once, holes in the universe that she couldn't trace.

She had to exterminate the enemy. She had to prove herself worthy of serving her queen, especially with her past affiliation with Andi weighing on her daily, shaming her.

Lira had to be better than her past.

This was her time.

Lira fought her way through to the center of the chaos, toward the stage where she'd last seen her queen. She could see Nor's personal guards now, forming a line of defense as redhelmeted enemies approached from all directions, but Lira saw not a glimpse of the queen or her crown.

Panic raced through her.

"Our orders are to remove all threats to the crown," Breck's voice said into her com. *"Whatever it takes."*

A man fell beside Lira, his head cracked and bleeding as he hit the pavement. He was Adhiran, his skin blue like hers. Like someone else she'd once known and loved—a twin who'd become a traitor. As he fell, Lira caught a full view of the stage through the gap in the crowd.

Her heart leaped as she saw the queen, alive and well. Nor was shoving back against Zahn, reaching for something…her lips forming a name.

Valen, she was saying. *Valen.*

"They're closing in," someone shouted. Gilly suddenly appeared beside Lira, her small frame moving like a warrior as she lifted her gun and fired twice, a smooth cadence that hit its target. One of Arachnid's soldiers fell midsprint, body convulsing before they dropped to the ground, trampled beneath rushing feet.

Their weapons only stunned, creating a short-term paralysis. Another order of the queen's, when she took up her reign. None were to die; only to fall. But the red-helmeted figures had no such constraints as they shot through the crowd, taking down anyone and everyone in their path.

The city, once beautiful and fully protected from war, was now a graveyard.

An enemy soldier sprinted past Lira. She lifted her rifle, breathing steadily as she centered him in her sights and fired. The stunner round took him down immediately. Beside her, Gilly shot another.

"Unaffected *scum!*" the child spit out.

The scent of electricity filled the air, mixed with the sour tang of blood as Lira and Gilly finally reached the stage. From this vantage point, Lira could see just how many fought for Nor; too many for Arachnid's soldiers to overcome. They would find a way to get her out, to get her to safety so they could clear the area without any danger of the queen getting hit.

Little by little, the circle of Nor's guards pressed toward the waiting transport ship, keeping the queen in the center, protected. Safe. Then another helmeted figure emerged from the crowd, firing off shots. Bodies dropped all around, and Nor screamed from somewhere inside the circle, the sound of a mother watching her children die. Lira felt that pain in her own chest.

So many deaths. So many, who'd finally seen the light, now fallen.

Breck fired three times. The stunner rounds hit the soldier in the neck. A convulsion—*one, two, three*—and the figure was down, still as stone.

"Tighten the circle!" Breck commanded, her voice echoing both inside Lira's com and out as the giantess stepped up alongside her. Gilly pressed in from her left. Together, the three of them joined the circle of soldiers guiding Nor to the transport. Another wave of red-helmeted enemies flooded the city streets, the moonlight dripping across their shoulders like blood.

Another fifty paces, and they would be at the ship. Ahead of them, Lira could see a young man waving his arms. Valen, his face desperate as he screamed his sister's name. The transport engine roared to life, steam spitting from its valves as it readied for takeoff.

Protect the queen. Lira heard that whispering, constant voice again, leaking its way into her mind.

She obeyed it.

She believed it.

"Faster!" Breck hissed.

Lira tripped over a fallen body. A large hand caught her by the elbow, lifting her back to her feet. "Keep moving, Lir. We're almost out of here," Breck said, grip tight as she guided her forward.

Protect the queen, the sweet song chimed again, and Lira stumbled once more as the back-and-forth of it all hit her with full force.

"LIRA! To your left!"

Her head felt like it weighed too much, like it was going to tumble from her shoulders, as she looked to the left. Then to the right.

A wave of crimson helmets rushed out of the shadows from all sides. More enemy reinforcements that had come from nowhere. The symbol of Arachnid was painted on all of them, hideous and horrible and *enemy, enemy*, as the group seemed to soar down the city streets. Lira's unit readied themselves, but now the tide had changed.

They were too few.

The enemy was too many.

Breck and Gilly lifted their rifles and started firing shots. Lira lifted her rifle, too, but it felt heavy and out of place in her hands. She positioned her finger over the trigger and sent out a whoosh of breath, for it was time for battle. *Protect the queen.*

"Shoot them, Lira!" Breck shouted, bumping into her with a broad shoulder.

She shot at the crimson figures closing in, too many of them still standing. Her unit reloaded, but there were too many enemies, and they were still too far from the transport. The queen was in the center of the soldiers, but the circle thinned out as a soldier was shot. The woman fell, hitting the ground with a wet smack. Her silver veins faded to a dim, dull gray in an instant.

Another fell to her left, nearly taking Gilly down with him.

"I'm sick of these stunners!" Gilly screamed. "We need real guns!" She fired, taking out two enemies, one after the other. Breck spun and hit three more. They closed the circle tighter, but they'd moved too quickly. They hadn't seen the one enemy soldier slip into their ranks.

Lira whirled, realizing with horror that it was already too late as the enemy lifted his weapon to fire. But at the last second, Valen appeared, shoving the enemy with all his might.

The enemy's gun angled right as the bullet left the chamber with an earsplitting crack.

Blood sprayed her face, painting her vision in red as Zahn

fell, pulling her down with him. Lira screamed in agony and fear, trying to rise, trying to see, trying to *fight*. But the crowd closed in around her, pinning her in place, and a single thought thundered through her mind, drowning out everything else.

She had failed her queen.

CHAPTER 18

ANDI

Klaren Solis, a woman the galaxy had long thought dead, was somehow standing before her, fully alive and well.

Scars covered half of Klaren's face, and her tongue was missing—hence the droid that spoke for her—but the other side, Andi noticed, looked like an older version of Nor. That same smooth brown skin, eyes burnished in gold, hair dark and slightly curled. And that pride in her gaze; the way she kept her chin tilted ever so slightly toward the stars, always.

"You deserve to die for bringing the Solis siblings into this world," Andi ground out. She had yet to unleash her vengeance on Nor and Valen, so their mother was the next best thing.

Andi reached for her swords, but they weren't there—she'd forgotten that the damned things were outside in Soyina's care.

She cursed and stepped forward to use her fists instead, but Dex held her back.

"No, Andi. She has compulsion. There's no telling what she might force you to do."

But the woman only stood motionless, watching them with sad eyes.

"Would you truly strike me down for the crimes of the children I bore?" Klaren asked through the droid, sending her a look full of disappointment. Andi felt her face flush, though whether it was from embarrassment or anger, she couldn't quite tell. "That is the least of the crimes I have committed over the course of my life. And I have long since paid for them, if such a thing is even possible."

Klaren touched the scarred side of her face gently, her eyes distant for a moment before she turned her gaze back to Andi. "In any case, I mean you no harm. My gift was stolen from me the day Cyprian cut out my tongue."

This was a trap. It *had* to be a trap. They'd come all this way, wrecking the *Marauder* and losing Lon in the process, only to fall into the hands of Nor and Valen's mother.

"What do you want from us?" Dex demanded. "Whose side are you truly on?"

"Mirabel's," Klaren said.

Andi's head spun as she tried to make sense of that declaration. "*Nor's* Mirabel, or…the free Mirabel?"

This was Arachnid, after all. *Klaren* was Arachnid. They were one and the same. And Arachnid had threatened Nor on the feed. Andi and Dex had seen it for themselves, when they were back in the nebula. Still…

"And why should we believe anything you say?" Andi asked. "For all we know, you compelled your way in here, killed the true Arachnid and now you're planning to destroy the rest of the Underground, too. Perhaps Nor's soldiers are already on their way."

The droid's red eyes blinked from where it perched upon Klaren's shoulder. "How little you know, Androma Racella. If I wanted to destroy these people, I would have done so ages ago. And as I said before, my compulsion has long been silenced, thanks to your predecessor."

Andi was about to ask what the woman meant, but Klaren continued on too quickly.

"If your hope is to kill me, then do it. I've longed for the grave all these years, though my mission is still not complete. But know you will never save your crew if you harm me. Of course, that hardly matters now, for they are only a small, insignificant portion of the galaxy that will soon fall to a fate far worse than death, should my children succeed in their plan."

"What plan?" Dex asked.

Andi looked back and forth between Klaren and him, unsure if she should allow them to continue talking. What if Klaren was lying to them even now? They had no way of knowing whether they were being compelled or not.

"My daughter and son are close to opening the Void," Klaren said, turning her gaze on Andi again. "And when they do, the future will be grim. If there will even be a future for people like us. But together, we can stop them. So if you wish to save your friends, I will help you—in exchange for your allegiance to me in this war."

"The Void? What are you even talking about?" Andi asked. She was sick of being confused, and she needed answers before she'd consider any kind of alliance with Klaren. "Cyprian killed you. The records say he got rid of you the day he destroyed Xen Ptera."

Klaren's eyes were somber as she nodded. "He tried. But we have little time to share tales." She sighed, and then that robotic voice said, "There is another world out there, beyond this one, called Exonia. And if Nor and Valen succeed in completing Nexus, they will use it to access the nuclear arsenals across

Mirabel. They'll then use those weapons to blast open the Void, just beyond your home planet, and bring Exonia forth."

Alfie's words from earlier came back to Andi suddenly. If Valen and Nor weren't from Mirabel, then of course their mother wasn't, either.

It made sense. Yet still, Andi found Klaren's tale hard to believe.

Klaren knelt before them, picked up a bit of charcoal and ran it across the floor, a deep black circle stark against the blue cave floor. "Exonia exists alongside Mirabel. It is a world that has watched ours for eons, waiting in vain for a savior to open the doorway. Exonia is my true home. Or it once was, anyway."

"And that means your children…" Dex trailed off, mistrust in his eyes. "They're from Exonia, too?"

"Their blood is half-Exonian, yes," Klaren said. "That is how they inherited the compulsion ability I once had. But even at my full strength, my power was weaker than theirs. I require my tongue, my real voice, to compel the minds of others. Cyprian Cortas took that from me—and he took my children, so they would remain separated. They were less of a threat to him that way. But before he cast me out, I was able to pass a message to my daughter, Nor, through a mental bond we shared. I told her about her true lineage, and that she had a brother."

Despair filled Klaren's eyes as she added, "And I told her that Exonia was in need of a savior like her, to allow them entry."

"Why do they need a savior?" Andi asked.

"Exonia is a dying world," Klaren explained. Slowly, she began to shed her heavy red armor, unbuckling it piece by piece to reveal her small frame beneath. "I came here long ago, with one other, in hopes of becoming that savior. I wanted the glory for myself, and yet, when I came to Mirabel, I fell in love. This is a world of purest light, so different from the vast Exonian darkness I had always known." She lifted her hands, which were scarred and yet somehow delicate. "In this world, you have bodies. You have *freedom*. The Exonians are not so blessed."

"You don't have...bodies?" Dex asked, wide-eyed. There were plenty of races in Mirabel, but nothing quite so unique as that.

"No," Klaren said. "Instead, we have abilities, gifted from the Godstars themselves. A few of us, called the Yielded, were once the strongest of our kind. We were given bodies, ones that took centuries to create, so that we could make the journey to Mirabel and find a way for our people to someday join us here. There's a small doorway in the Void, a tiny tear that allows us entrance, but our elders feared that if all the Exonian people tried to come through at once, the Mirabellians would see us as an invading force, and respond accordingly."

"So you came over," Andi said. She still didn't fully trust the woman, but if there was any truth to her tale, they needed to know everything Klaren could tell them. "To be that person? To open the Void?"

Klaren nodded. Her little droid scuttled across her shoulder, concealed for a moment by the smoke from the fire. "We were supposed to come over as a group, the Yielded and I. But I have never been one to place my trust in any other." She swallowed hard. "I killed them all, in one fell swoop. I should not have done it. But there is no changing the past. They live among the Godstars now."

A dangerous woman, no doubt. And yet she was spilling the truths of her past as if she truly regretted them.

Klaren continued. "I arrived, with only my adviser, in hopes of using my compulsion to sway the system leaders of Mirabel, to persuade them to allow the Exonians peaceful migration into this galaxy."

"But you're supposedly working against your children?" Dex scoffed. "You said you need to stop them from finishing what you started, but if that was your life goal, if *you* started this in the first place... What changed? And how can we be sure you aren't simply trying to help them now by destroying the Underground—the only people who are standing up against the Solis siblings?"

Klaren's face folded into a frown. "The tale is a long one, full of pain and regret."

"We all have pain," Andi said with a growl. "Why the hell should we care about yours?"

Dex placed a calming hand on her wrist. Andi almost yanked away from him, but he sent her a meaningful glance before looking back at Klaren with careful eyes, nodding slowly for her to carry on.

"When I first arrived in Mirabel, I managed to compel my way into the heart of the Xen Pterran king," Klaren began. "Adonis was a good man. Kind. I couldn't help falling in love with him, and because he loved his planet so deeply, I grew to love Xen Ptera, too. To love all of Mirabel. And then…" Her eyes softened, turned wistful. "I got pregnant with Nor, and I loved her above everything else. In my happiness, I began to forget my mission—I lost myself in the life I'd made here."

She looked at the fire, eyes distant as the flames flickered back in them. "But as everyone now knows, the full might of Arcardius eventually came to Xen Ptera. The war was bloody, and brutal… Our people were dying by the thousands. So I gave myself over to Cyprian in order to save them, to save Nor. With the aid of my compulsion, he agreed to a cease-fire. But I never saw my husband or my daughter again. I left Nor in the care of Darai, so that she might someday learn the truth about herself and her abilities."

"The adviser you came here with?" Dex asked.

Klaren nodded. "During my time on Arcardius, I compelled Cyprian to love me. To this day, I find myself wondering whether my control over him was ever real, or if he was always seething below the surface of my compulsion, desperate to break free and end my life. Still, I became pregnant with his child, during those years I spent on Arcardius."

"Valen," Andi said, as the realization hit her fully.

Klaren nodded, looking so much like Nor in that moment that it sent tendrils of unease crawling down Andi's skin.

"Eventually, Cyprian discovered a way to overcome my compulsion. I still don't know how he did it, but...he managed to trick me. I begged him to return me to Xen Ptera, knowing that my chances of opening the Void were gone, once he knew the truth about me. And I no longer wanted to—not really. I loved Mirabel too much." Tears began to fill Klaren's eyes. "But after we flew to Xen Ptera, as we hovered above the planet...he cut out my tongue. He destroyed Xen Ptera. And then he cast me out, ripping me away from Valen and Nor forever."

Andi had heard the story, about the great explosion that rained down from the sky when Cyprian gave the order to destroy the Olen System's capital planet for good. But she'd never known Klaren was aboard his ship that day. She couldn't imagine how devastating it must have been to watch—even if Klaren hadn't been born on Xen Ptera, it was clear that she had embraced it as her home.

"In that moment, I hated everything Cyprian stood for," Klaren admitted, and Andi couldn't find it within herself to blame the former Xen Pterran queen one bit. "I wanted to destroy him. I had hoped that if Nor heard my message, if she knew about the mission I'd failed to complete...then perhaps she could finish it for me. Perhaps she could do something good for Mirabel. Take over, with Valen at her side, and become the leader I was never able to be. She could rule both worlds together, as one.

"I haven't been able to connect with her since," Klaren explained. "When Cyprian cut me off from my compulsion, I lost my ability to create that mental link between us. And she was so young, and untrained... I didn't know if she'd received the message. I didn't even know if she would survive the attack. And I never knew…" She looked down, brushing away the tears that streaked down her cheeks. "I never knew what terror she would bring to Mirabel. That she would reign with an iron fist, so like Cyprian. Or that she would use Valen's compulsion, far stronger than her own, to ensnare the minds of so many."

"Well, her entire planet was virtually destroyed, and she was forced to grow up in the rubble," Dex pointed out. "So perhaps it's not that surprising."

"Seriously, Dextro?" Andi snapped.

"I'm not saying what she's done is *right*," Dex said defensively. "It's just that…revenge is a powerful motivator. It makes people do the wildest things, even give all of themselves, to see it through to the end."

"Perhaps," Klaren admitted, "but I fear that she may also have been unduly influenced by Darai all these years."

"Your old adviser?" Andi asked, trying to keep track of all the new information the woman had revealed thus far.

Klaren nodded. "Yes. After Cyprian exiled me, I crash-landed on Solera." She gestured to her face. "That's how I wound up with these scars. For a time, I thought Darai might find a way to track me down, but he never came, and I didn't have the resources to make the journey back to Xen Ptera myself." Her expression darkened. "I sent him several messages, which he never responded to. Then I learned that Nor had survived, that she had assumed the throne after her father's death, with the aid of a distant relative. An uncle, by the name of Darai.

"I never should have left her in his grasp." The voice of Klaren's droid was quiet, barely audible. "I trusted him once, but after having years to reflect on his behavior… I don't believe that Darai ever really cared about *me*, but rather, my power alone. He was weak when I first met him back in Exonia. He was…something strange, a dark sort of being I came across. A Yielded who'd been stripped of his power for a reason he always claimed was unjust."

"But you somehow found it within yourself to trust him anyway?" Andi asked incredulously. "Even knowing that?"

Klaren bowed her head. "I was young and careless, and I cared more for my own ambitions than the well-being of our people. And now I'm afraid that my children—and this entire galaxy—will pay the price for my youthful mistakes. Unless you help me find a way to stop all this, before it's too late."

"Would it be so terrible if the Exonians came here?" Dex asked tentatively. "There are plenty of habitable places in Mirabel that are only sparsely populated. Maybe there's a way to negotiate with Valen and Nor. If we allowed the Exonians entry, perhaps they could lift the compulsion in exchange? Set the Mirabellians free?"

"It's not that simple," she said. "You remember what I told you—that the Exonians don't have bodies of their own?"

Dread crept up Andi's spine as she nodded. She had a feeling she wasn't going to like where this was going.

"If the Exonians come through the Void, they will need to… occupy the bodies that are already here," Klaren said, the droid's voice slow and deliberate. "Our own world is very different from this one, more compatible to our natural forms. It is a place of water and darkness, but here, in the air and sunlight…we would require a host body in order to survive."

"So you're parasites," Andi spit out.

Klaren flushed. "In a manner of speaking, yes. That's why Valen and Nor require absolute control over the minds of this galaxy—they need the Mirabellians to serve as willing hosts for the Exonians when they cross over."

The look of horror on Dex's face mirrored exactly what Andi was feeling.

"Exactly what kind of monsters are your children?" she cried. "How could they want to do something like this? They'd essentially be wiping out an entire galaxy of people—their *own* people, no less—to make room for some parasites from another world?"

Klaren raised her hands in supplication. "I don't think they truly understand what will happen when they open the Void," she insisted. "From the information I've managed to gather over the years… I don't believe Darai has told them the full truth about our people. Nor sees herself as a savior—she thinks that she's fulfilling the destiny I failed long ago, and that she can save my people from death and ruination. And while that's true, Darai has failed to tell her what the cost will be. And Valen…" Klaren looked away. "After the way Cyprian treated him all these years, I'm not surprised that he's embraced the idea of having a real family at last—and of finally having some power of his own."

"That still doesn't give them the right to take over the minds of everyone in Mirabel," Andi protested. She took a deep breath, trying to keep her emotions in check. She had no love for the capital planets of Mirabel, had only felt *wanted* by the people who wished to put her behind bars. Sometimes, she dreamed of the worst people in the galaxy—the people like her parents and Cyprian—getting what they deserved. Given a taste of a life on the run, a life always spent looking over one's shoulder, for fear of their own darkness catching up to them.

But this? This was something else entirely. She felt physically sick just thinking of the news Klaren had shared. Thinking of Lira, and Breck, and Gilly, their bodies stolen along with their minds. Forever prisoner to something *other* from Exonia. If it was true…then she wouldn't stand for it.

She wouldn't even let Nor and Valen get close.

"Look, I get it, they're your children. You want to believe the best about them," Andi said. "But my crew is back on Arcardius, trapped under your son's compulsion, doing your daughter's bidding, and now you're telling me that soon their bodies are going to be stolen, too?" The very thought filled her with rage. "I don't care what Nor and Valen do or don't know. I'm going to kill them myself, before it's too late. With or without your help."

Andi spun on a heel, heading for the tunnel back to the undercity, yanking Dex along behind her.

"Killing them won't do anyone any good," Klaren called after her. When Andi hesitated, she added, "Only the one who starts the compulsion can end it—and only by their choice."

The news of that nearly brought Andi to her knees.

"Then there's no hope?" she whispered. "No hope of saving anyone?"

She saw her crew's faces in her mind. Lira's soft smile, Breck's laughing face, Gilly's bright and mischievous eyes. But she also saw others. Countless others, who would *never* taste freedom again. Innocent lives, people spread all across the galaxy who were simply doing their best to thrive day in and day out.

"There is a way," Klaren said. "And strangely enough, we have Cyprian to thank for it."

Dex crossed his arms, brows rising into his hairline. "What way?"

"Nor and Valen cannot open the Void without access to all of Mirabel's nuclear arsenals," Klaren said. "Each planet has one, created during the Cataclysm. Cyprian spearheaded the effort during the years I lived on Averia with him. When we were together, I was constantly at his side, in meetings, at meals, where the leaders whispered of their plans behind the scenes. The weapons network can only be accessed by each planet's leader. But because they are all dead...only their successor has that power now."

"So Nor has the power," Andi said. "How does that help us? You said that as soon as Nexus is complete, she'll use those weapons to blast open the Void."

"Not quite," Klaren corrected. "Only a *rightful* heir, chosen by at least one of the previous system leaders, can gain control of the weapons network. There were countless fail-safes built into the system to ensure this."

Beside Andi, Dex began to shift uneasily on his feet. Andi shot him a quick glance, and he stilled, but kept his eyes averted from hers.

"So Cyprian's successor has power now," Klaren explained. "If Nor is able to get her hands on his successor, and bring them over to her side…then Exonia will be unleashed." Her expression turned pleading once more. "I am fighting to undo what I began long ago, Androma," Klaren said, her droid's voice soft now behind the light of the dying fire. "Because it isn't always about power. Sometimes it's about preserving the things that make living truly worth it."

Her words hung in the air between them like a promise— one Andi wasn't sure she wanted to believe.

And yet…a part of her *did* believe it.

"You said you wanted my help," Andi said. "Why me?"

"Andi," Dex started, reaching for her hand. His voice was almost pained—as if he already knew what Klaren was going to say. But how could he?

Klaren met Andi's gaze with those eyes, so much like her daughter's, rimmed in gold. "We've uncovered the identity of Cyprian's heir, just as Nor likely has, too."

"Who?" Andi asked, dumbfounded. "And what does that have to do with me?"

"You don't know? Isn't it obvious by now?" Klaren asked, holding out her hands. They, too, had scars across the palms. Burn scars that reminded Andi of the ones held together beneath her cuffs. "*You* are the General of Arcardius, Androma. Before his death, Cyprian chose *you.*"

Andi almost laughed. This was a joke—all of it some sick, ridiculous joke.

But the look in Klaren's eyes wasn't teasing. And Dex…

"Andi," he whispered, turning to face her, his voice pleading.

"Andi, you have to understand. I didn't want to tell you before, when you were still recovering… There was never really a good time to bring it up—"

"You *knew*?" Andi blurted out, betrayal coursing through her. "But how—"

Footsteps sounded out from the tunnel, racing toward them as Soyina ran into the cavernous room. "Apologies, Arachnid," she said, panting from the exertion. "I have news of the attack on Arcardius. Everything went according to plan—our message was sent to Nor, loud and clear. The Academy grounds are now a pile of rubble."

Andi whirled to face Klaren, so many thoughts racing in her mind at once, her heart threatening to leap from her chest. "You attacked Veronus? But there are innocent people there! Thousands of them, trapped beneath Nor's control!"

"Sometimes we must sacrifice the few to save the many," Klaren said.

"Like hell we do!" Dex shouted. "Andi makes those choices now. Arcardius is *her* planet, and if you want us to work with you—"

"You don't speak for me!" Andi snarled at him. "And it isn't my damned planet. I want nothing to do with Cyprian's twisted legacy. *Nothing.*"

Soyina chuckled from the shadows. "I take it our general isn't pleased about her new title?"

Andi's vision turned red as she glared at all three of them. "You all knew. *Everyone* knew, this entire time."

"Andi…" Dex started.

"Enough!" she hissed. She looked at Klaren next, pointing with a steady finger. "I may not have asked for this, but as long as I'm in charge, you will not attack that planet, or any other planet in Mirabel, without my consent if you wish to have me join you."

To Soyina, Andi said, "And *you*…"

The woman blinked slowly back at her, a smile on her lips.

"You will give me back my Godstars-damned swords, so I can run you through with both of them."

"There she is," Soyina cooed. "The Bloody Baroness, turned General of Arcardius. I take it you're ready to play games now, Androma Racella? We are *very* pleased to have you on our side."

"I'm not on anyone's side," Andi snapped, her hands curled into fists. She turned back to Dex, making him swallow nervously. "You have some explaining to do, Dextro Arez. And you will explain it all over a drink, or else I'll use my swords on you, too."

His answering look was one of pure terror.

Slowly, as if she was trudging through quicksand, Andi left the cave. The weight of Klaren's words, her truths, clung to her back, each step heavier than the last.

She had always been good at outrunning her problems.

But this?

This was something Andi couldn't escape from.

CHAPTER 19

DEX

Dex knew that Andi was furious with him. She'd looked at him like she had daggers for eyes, and he was more than a little terrified by the idea of being alone with her right now.

He'd known this moment was coming; had hoped to find a way to tell her what Cyprian had done in a way that was slightly less...shocking. But after what they'd just heard, her new status— and her anger at him—was the least of their worries.

So he followed her from the cave, leaving Klaren behind.

First, because he couldn't stand being with Klaren and Soyina a moment longer. And second, because he knew Andi was heading toward exactly what they both needed right now.

A stiff drink.

The whole situation was made worse by the cheers of the people out in the undercity, as news of the attack on Arcardius spread through the space like a wildfire. Dex knew that such a strike, a true show of the power the free-minded still had, was a viable option to scare Nor into submission.

But how many innocents had died on the Academy grounds?

And how many more would fall, before this war was over?

After retrieving her swords from Klaren's guards and strapping them safely upon her back, Andi began walking through the undercity, toward the heavy door that would lead them back to the surface.

"We're leaving," she said over her shoulder.

"Andi, we can't," Dex said, a ripple of alarm coursing through him. "This is the only place we're actually safe."

She looked back at him with a look of fury written across her face. "Are we?" she asked darkly.

"Well, we can't leave Havoc," Dex said, trying a different sort of argument, even though he knew Soyina was more than happy to spend time watching the demon cat. "You said so yourself earlier. Gilly will kill us both."

She didn't buy it, resuming her brisk pace until they finally reached the exit. She turned the crank, the old metal squealing as the door yawned wide.

"I know you're there," Andi growled to the empty tunnel. "If you try to stop us, I swear to the Godstars, I will gut you."

Eryn appeared out of thin air, leaning against the doorway as if she'd just stepped forward from another dimension. She smiled broadly, sweeping the metallic strands of her hair behind her ear. "It would be an honor to die by the Bloody Baroness's blades," Eryn replied, "but Soyina has requested my presence in the bathhouse after my shift, and I've never been one to miss out on a healthy prank with high odds of death, dismemberment or drowning."

Dex blinked. "You may be just as wicked as Soyina."

Eryn grinned even wider. "*More* wicked," she said with a wink. She turned to Andi then, her expression turning stoic. "Arachnid is a good leader. I'm not one to persuade anyone, but…" She lifted a hand, turning it this way and that as it flickered in and out of view, visible and invisible from one shifting motion to the next. "I bend light. I know it well, like an old friend. And even though Arachnid's actions reveal mostly darkness…" Her hand reappeared again. "There is also a great deal of light inside."

She flipped a golden Krev toward Dex. He caught it on reflex, then sent her a quizzical look. "What's this for?"

"I'll have to track you, by order of Arachnid," Eryn said apologetically. "But I'll stay just out of earshot, I swear it. And if you want to leave, and never come back… I won't stop you. But please, enjoy some drinks on me before you make your choice."

"Thanks," Dex said gratefully, inclining his head to her. He and Andi weren't exactly swimming in Krevs these days.

Then he followed Andi back up the tunnel, walking behind her in silence until it spit them out into the frigid atmosphere of the ice pub high above.

It was busier than it had been before, the tables and couches now packed with patrons eager to down a mug or two or three. The purple flames still flickered merrily in the ice-block fireplace, a droid rekindling the flames with some sort of purple liquid that turned to flame the moment it touched the rest. Two miniature fighting droids battled on a nearby table, surrounded by a laughing group of young men and women placing bets on which would win. A few feet away, a couple of Solerans sat at the bar, icicles on their lashes and brows, a peculiar sight as they played a game of Fleet. Dex felt a pang of sadness at the sight as he remembered the last time he'd played—with Gilly and Breck, aboard the *Marauder*.

It was too normal here, too happy.

Then Dex remembered there was an invisible girl following in their tracks, an underground city determined to fight Nor beneath their feet…and the General of Arcardius at his side. Couple that with the fact that Mirabel was neighbor to a world that had been watching them for countless years, waiting for their chance to invade…

Dex suddenly found himself grateful as hell for the golden Krev sitting in his pocket.

Andi slumped down at the bar, placing her elbows on the solid chunk of ice. She let out a deep sigh. "Why are we still here, Dex?"

"Because the world's gone to hell," Dex said with a shrug. "And because I'm afraid if we don't get some normalcy, our heads will explode."

"Normalcy?" Andi asked wearily. "I don't even know what that is anymore."

"You being pissed at me is normal," Dex said. "And you are pissed, aren't you?"

"Apparently you've known I was the General of Arcardius for weeks, and you chose not to tell me. So, yeah. I'm a little pissed, Dextro."

"Well," Dex said, as several fur-covered patrons filed past them, hoping for a chance at grabbing a fresh drink, "then I am encouraged that some things, at least, never change."

She blinked at him like he'd just told her he was the new king of Adhira.

"Why did you hide it from me?" she asked quietly.

"We were a little busy," Dex said. "You know, crash-landing on Solera, nearly being eaten by an ice dragon…"

"Losing Lon," Andi whispered, her face a mask of anguish.

He nodded. "He was a brave Sentinel. And…he knew, Andi. His last words to me…" Dex ran a hand through his hair, that memory heavy upon him. "He told me to tell you the truth. Do you remember?"

"Of course I do," she snapped. "I asked you about it afterward. So why didn't you?"

Dex was slightly afraid now. There were a lot of places in Craatia where he could hide. Once, he'd gotten lost inside a

Soleran bathhouse for days—though that had sort of been on purpose. He could try that again, or better yet, take his chances out in the tundra. He'd never been a fan of the cold, but maybe this time, he'd be better off.

"I'm waiting," Andi said impatiently.

Dex sighed. There was no way out of this conversation. Even if he tried to run, Andi would find him. Hell, with all the rage she was carrying, she might dismember him, limb from limb, if he even dared to display such cowardice.

So he ordered drinks for both of them, steaming mugs of blue Marnv that probably would have knocked him on his ass, were it not for his champion drinking habits.

He watched Andi down hers in three sips, then did the same himself and ordered two more, desperate for something to lighten the tension of the day. They'd learned so much. Too much.

The bartender droid refilled their mugs. Dex nodded in thanks, took another sip, then turned to look at Andi.

"I *was* going to tell you," he told her. "But I knew it would upset you, and I just couldn't seem to find the right moment."

"You've always loved your secrets," Andi said, slowly spinning her mug around on the bar top. Godstars, she knew how to make a man feel fear. There were a million different ways she could kill him with that mug—perhaps even more ways than his rampant imagination could dream up. The metal on her cheekbones glimmered with a flash of gold as the bartender droid whizzed past, filling mugs for thirsty patrons.

But Dex saw a shift happen then. He still saw the fury in her, but beneath that, there was a sadness in her stormy eyes. And something else Dex couldn't quite place.

"When did it happen?" she asked. "Tell me the details—now that Klaren Solis isn't listening in."

It was so strange it was almost laughable, that statement.

"It happened on the *Marauder*," Dex began. "The night Cyprian died."

She turned suddenly, giving him a suspicious glance. "Valen stabbed him, just like he did me. How is it that he had the ability to somehow make me General of Arcardius while he was bleeding out on my ship?"

Dex cleared his throat uncomfortably. "Well, uh…" He gave her a sheepish look and prayed she didn't run him through with her swords. "I might have helped him with that, a bit."

"You *what*?" Andi snarled. She reached behind her for the hilts of her swords, just as he'd feared. Dex scrambled to seize her wrists and scanned the pub around them frantically, making sure no one was looking in their direction.

"I know you're monumentally pissed at me right now, Andi," he murmured, his heart hammering, "but we can't make a scene in here. If Klaren was able to find out what Cyprian did, then Nor probably has, too. She may already have people hunting for us."

Andi glared at him a moment longer, then yanked herself out of his grasp and grabbed her mug of Marnv. She took a sip, swirling the strong liquid around her tongue. "You don't get to make choices like that for me, Dex. For *anyone*."

"I know, and I'm sorry," Dex said earnestly. "But I honestly didn't know what he had planned when he asked for my help. He was dying, right before my eyes, and he didn't tell me what he was doing until it was too late for me to stop him."

Andi took another healthy swig of her drink, still looking unconvinced.

Dex shook his head, trying to figure out a way to fix things between them. "He chose *you*, Andi. It was his dying command."

Andi slammed her mug down on the bar, sloshing some of the blue liquid onto the icy surface. "Cyprian Cortas was among the hundreds, perhaps thousands, of people in this galaxy who wish me dead," she hissed at him. "I'd even be so bold to place him as the one person who wanted it most. And yet you expect me to believe that his dying act was to hand over control of his precious planet to *me*?"

"I hardly believed it myself when he told me," Dex admitted. "But the system leaders are free to choose whoever they wish to be their successor. And his wish was to have you."

He ran his knuckles over a carving on the edge of the frozen bar top. Initials, likely those of lovers who weren't quarreling in this way. It was the kind of hopelessly romantic thing Dex and Andi would never do. Their lives had never been normal enough, and likely never would be. But he wished for it, sometimes. A chance to be together, away from the chaos of their real lives.

"Why me?" Andi wondered.

The anger was gone from her voice, replaced by disbelief. As if she'd been told a loved one had died, and didn't want it to be true.

Dex shrugged. "The short answer? Because you were the only Arcardian-born citizen on that ship."

Andi huffed a laugh into her mug.

"But I think it was more than that," he said, daring to reach for her hand, now that she didn't look as if she would gut him for it. "Yes, Cyprian may have had *very* dark feelings toward you. But I also think he believed you had the strength to handle the responsibility. He told me his entire story, Andi. About Valen, and Nor, and their mother. He talked about the things Klaren could do—the things that all of them can do. The compulsion was strong in Klaren, and weaker in Nor, but somehow it was too strong in Valen, just like Klaren said."

Dex swallowed hard. "And once he saw them together in that ballroom, once he realized that Nor and Valen were planning to use their powers to rule... I think Cyprian knew that the terrors soon to come would be so great, that maybe you were the only person strong enough to give Arcardius—and apparently, now all of Mirabel—a fighting chance."

"The Bloody Baroness," Andi said darkly. "The most wanted space pirate in Mirabel, now General of Arcardius. Keeper of the keys to some great arsenal of nuclear weapons."

"No," Dex said, gripping her hand more tightly. She flinched, almost imperceptibly, but didn't pull away. "Not the Baroness. Cyprian chose *you*. Andromia Racella. The girl who used to love Arcardius with every fiber of her being. Enough to give her life to its cause."

"That girl is dead, and it's not like Cyprian had much of a choice in his successor," Andi said sadly, pulling her hand away from his. Her cuffs clinked against each other as she slid her hands into her lap. "I don't want the title. It's worthless, anyway. Mirabel is destined to fall, and all of us with it."

"This isn't like you, Andi," Dex told her. "Where's your fighting spirit?"

Andi glared at him. "Gone, for the time being." Then her expression morphed into one of dread. "What if the girls are dead, Dex?" she asked, her voice full of pain. "What if they died in that attack on the Academy?"

"They're not," he said swiftly. "They're too damned stubborn to die. And you're too stubborn to give up searching for them." He gave her a grim smile. "Besides, now you know that you have a *real* bargaining chip, far better than the one we pulled from Alfie. This is our chance to get what we need to rescue the girls."

"What am I supposed to do? Fly to Arcardius, march into Nor's estate and demand she hand them over?" Andi shook her head. "Their bodies would be free, yes, but their minds won't be. Not until Valen gives up control."

Dex thought of what Klaren had told them—that even if they killed Valen, he would have had to relinquish his control on their minds in order to actually release them from his power. "I hate that sorry bastard," Dex said with a sigh.

Andi nodded. "I should have killed him long ago."

She played with the handle of her mug, her breath forming small puffs of white in the chilly air of the ice pub. "You're right," she said suddenly. "This is my chance—to use my title as a way to get information. Klaren said she has sources. Eyes all over the place. If she wants me to join her, then she owes me at least that."

"And a ship," Dex said, thinking of the *Marauder*, half-buried out on the tundra. Andi had always cared so much about that damned ship. But now he realized it was the crew within it that she'd cared for more. Without them, the ship was simply an empty, lifeless thing.

"And a ship," Andi echoed. She sighed again. "I didn't ask for this."

"I know," Dex said gently. "I really am sorry, Andi. So very sorry."

"I know you are. And I get why you didn't tell me," she acknowledged, staring at her empty cup. "But now that I know... I'm going to find a way to take out Nor."

"And until you do?" Dex asked, lifting a hand for the bartender droid to return. It was busy with patrons lining up, leaning over as they spoke in hushed tones about the Arcardian attack. A holoscreen in the corner of the pub showed Nor's earlier propaganda message, still playing on a loop. Dex wanted to throw the screen into the fire.

Andi met his eyes. "The way I see it, we have two choices."

"We could stay," Dex suggested hopefully. "Just for a while. Until we figure out what to do, figure out if we truly trust Klaren enough to see what help she requires from your..." He looked around, lowering his voice. "...new esteemed status in Mirabel."

"Or we could leave. Go out on our own. And likely die trying to save the girls from an enemy we know little about." She glanced around as well, dropping her tone to a murmur. "Klaren is the best chance we have to learn how to defeat Valen and Nor.

And how to free the girls' minds, if sneaking onto Arcardius and killing them both isn't an option."

"So we're staying?" Dex asked.

Andi closed her eyes, then nodded slowly, as if she couldn't believe she was agreeing. "We're staying. To rest. Recharge. Eat some decent food for once. And then we're going back to Klaren, and we're going to settle on a deal." She blew out a breath of frustration. "She's right about one thing, at least."

Dex had never thought he would hear those words come from her mouth. "Come again?"

"If her story is true…and as much as I hate to admit it, Dex, I believe her."

He nodded. "Unfortunately, I do, too."

"There's still a lot we don't know, and I don't trust her. But Klaren's right—this is so much bigger than just rescuing the girls," Andi admitted. "And if I can find a way to free their minds…then I'll have also found a way to free the rest of Mirabel's, too."

Andi's face took on a thoughtful expression. "Lira was the next in line to be Queen of Adhira. Did you know that?"

Dex nodded. He and Lon had spoken about Lon's regrets, in the hours aboard the *Marauder* while the two of them waited for Andi to wake. Lon believed he was the reason Lira had left Adhira, and Dex had sensed that the Sentinel placed some of the blame on himself for Lira's mind being trapped.

The galaxy ran on power—either the desire to have it, or the drive to run from it.

"She never wanted it. That power," Andi said. "It's why she ran away. But I know her heart, no matter how much her mind may have changed beneath the compulsion. And I know Lira would never turn her back on the galaxy. If she had the power, if she were in my situation…she would take up the crown, and use it to destroy her enemies, in the name of protecting the place she loves most. Breck and Gilly, too."

Dex laughed at that. "Gilly would likely use her power for evil."

"No," Andi said with a sad smile. "She's good. Deep down, they're all good, Dex. They're the best three women I've ever known. And if they were here, they'd have me marching right back down that tunnel and demanding Klaren send me on a mission at once."

"Then let's do it," Dex said, standing up from his ice stool. "Let's go back down there to do exactly that."

But Andi didn't move from her seat. "Not now."

Her eyes took on a look Dex had seen many times before. A scheming look. One he had learned to approach carefully, and with good reason.

Andi lifted a hand. "Bartender? Another round." She glanced over at Dex. "For now, Dex...we drink."

"I can't argue with that," he said, and swallowed his glass in one gulp.

CHAPTER 20
NOR

Nor couldn't breathe.

She gasped for air, but nothing filled her lungs.

Slowly, ever so slowly, the chaos around her began to fade, as her guards sought out the remaining attackers. The red-helmeted shooter was dragged away, limp in their arms.

Nor knew she hadn't been shot, felt the truth of it deep down. Her body was fine.

But Zahn...

"Nor," he murmured.

Her vision began to clear, and Nor realized the weight on her chest was from him, his muscular body lying facedown across her middle. But his voice sounded all wrong, full of pain and weakness, and something Nor couldn't quite place. It was as if he were already far away.

"Oh, Godstars," one of the soldiers said—Nor couldn't tell who it was. "Get the medical droids *now*."

All she could think about was Zahn—and the wet warmth slowly leaching into her gown from his body above hers. She struggled to sit up, to see what was wrong with him, but she was trapped, unable to move.

Darai appeared above her, his face wavering as if he were behind a veil of fog. Nor realized she was crying, tears blurring her vision as the guards gently hoisted Zahn's limp body off hers.

"Is he alright?" Nor sobbed, reaching for Zahn as the soldiers laid him on the ground next to her. Then she saw Valen, standing just beside Darai, his face pale and his lips parted as he stared, unmoving, at Zahn. Nor felt as if the world were moving in slow motion as her gaze fell to her hands, drawn to the bright red blood upon her skin.

Zahn's blood.

Nor felt numb as she drew herself up beside him on hands and knees. The city faded away, and the smoke, though heavy in her lungs, was nothing compared to the coldness she felt now as Zahn looked up at her, his eyes glazed with pain.

His whole body was shaking.

Nor removed her cloak, pressing it against the bullet wound in his chest with trembling hands. Blood immediately seeped through the fabric—too much blood.

She couldn't stop the bleeding, no matter how hard she tried.

"Medical droids!" Darai was shouting. "Where the *hell* are they?"

Hands found Nor's shoulders then, holding her tight. "I'm sorry," Valen said from behind her. Nor remembered seeing him, for just a moment, his face blurring in the crowd before the gunshot had gone off. "I'm so sorry, Nor. I tried to stop him. I tried…"

His words fell away.

Nor couldn't pull her gaze from Zahn's face as he lay on the ruined street beneath her, blood trailing from his body in a steady stream.

"You're fine," she found herself saying through tears. She reached down and grabbed his hand, but his grip was weak in hers. "You're going to be fine."

"Nhatilya," Zahn breathed out. "I…"

"Don't," she sobbed. Her tears fell upon his face, making tracks in the dirt and dust.

A trickle of blood slipped from his lips as he coughed, a wet rasp that rattled from his throat. "I love you," Zahn whispered. She could see him trying to reach for her, but his arms lifted only a few inches before falling back to the ground. "My queen…"

So quiet now, his voice. His words were scarcely heard among the screaming crowd, the chaos welling up all around them.

"And you're going to be my king," Nor said, swallowing back her tears. "We're getting you out of here."

A soldier appeared, a black cross stitched across his chest and a med droid at his side. He looked down at Zahn, then over at Darai. He shook his head without a word.

Not real, Nor's subconscious whispered.

"Hang on," she said to Zahn. "*Please*, don't leave me here without you."

"I…love you," he murmured again.

Zahn's chest rattled as he gasped for air. Then his eyes went dim, and his hand went slack in hers. Someone screamed, a mournful wail that had all the soldiers around her pulling back. Nor realized the scream had ripped from her own throat.

"Get her to the transport ship, *now*," Darai commanded.

She was vaguely aware of hands hauling her to her feet, pulling her away from Zahn.

"NO!" Nor screamed, desperation coursing through her as she fought to stay with him.

But the soldiers were already lifting his body, taking it away, a sea of darkness converging on him as someone took Nor's cloak and drew it over his handsome face. He could have been sleeping, the way he'd looked so many times when Nor rolled over in their bed to find him beside her each morning.

"NO!" she screamed again. "Don't touch him! Don't you dare touch him!"

But the person holding her back was too strong. A distant part of her mind recognized her captor as Breck, the giantess who had been standing guard as she'd issued her demands to Androma.

Androma, Arachnid…none of it mattered in this moment.

"Nor," another voice said. Valen was before her, blood on his own face, his expression full of pain.

"Make them stop," she begged him through sobs. "Compel them, right now. Make them bring him back."

Valen had tears running down his own cheeks as he took her hand. "I'm so sorry, Nor. He's…he's gone."

Then someone was guiding her away, her gait heavy as lead as she walked, one foot in front of the other, toward the waiting transport ship. She couldn't breathe with this emptiness in her chest, as if someone had stolen her heart right out of it.

"Come on," Valen said. He was limping along beside her, wheezing as he continued to hold her hand in his. Darai flanked her other side, shoving onlookers away.

Gradually, the crowd began to part, the smoke still casting a haze across the streets. Nor was led onto the waiting ship and strapped into a seat. She stared blankly ahead as the transport rumbled beneath her and took flight.

"She's in shock," Darai's voice said, again from so far away.

"Hurry," Valen urged. "We have to get her away from here." He coughed, and as Nor's vision waned, she caught a glimpse of his face, his nostrils dripping fresh blood.

She retreated deep into her mind as the transport soared toward Averia, the seat beside her cold and empty.

Nor Solis sat with her back against the cool stones of the tower, her forehead pressed against her knees. She was fifteen years old, and tomorrow, at her coronation, the people of Xen Ptera would see her not as a princess, but bow to her instead as their queen.

She'd hoped to find silence here, instead of the howling winds. They knocked at the tower windows, beckoning her to stand and peer down at her dying world.

"Save me," Xen Ptera whispered with the wind.

"I'm trying," Nor whispered back. She knew she had to, if she wanted to move forward with her mother's mission. But she remained in her spot on the floor, avoiding the view of her crumbling planet for just a bit longer.

A thunk sounded out from the doorway and the spiraling steps beyond.

Nor sighed. It was probably her uncle Darai, with yet more coronation plans for her to approve. "I said I wanted to be alone."

But the door creaked open, and Zahn Volknapp stepped into the circular tower. Nor blinked at him in surprise.

"Nobody really wants to be alone," Zahn said. "At least…I don't think so."

"And that makes you right?" Nor asked. Still, she felt a smile spreading across her face.

Zahn shrugged and settled down beside her, his shoulder warm against hers. He'd grown strong, this boy who'd pulled her from the rubble three years ago. No longer a boy, but a young man.

And lately, when Nor looked at him…she felt things she hadn't before.

A flutter in her chest. Heat that spread across her cheeks.

His arms had turned from lanky to muscular. His jaw had broadened, stubble forming along it. His hands, once soft and boyish, had become hardened with calluses. They'd grazed hers more than a few times in recent days. Small, accidental touches that didn't seem quite so.

"You're going to make a great queen, you know," Zahn told her. "But I think, if what we used to read in those insufferable fairy tales is true, you'll need a handsome guard at your side."

Nor stared down at her golden prosthetic. She'd never felt the need to hide any part of herself from Zahn. He accepted her as she was, just as she accepted him.

"My uncle would probably agree," Nor said, rolling her eyes at the thought of Darai.

He was a good mentor, and had trained her well in her gift. But he was always tired. He was always too…ancient. Nor couldn't settle on any other word to describe the man. And he wasn't her blood, not fully. Nor always felt something lacking when he was around.

She wanted a real family to call her own.

"Do you think I'll ever find him?" Nor asked suddenly.

She glanced sideways at Zahn as the wind slammed against the glass, dousing it with acid rain.

"Who?" Zahn asked.

His face had turned sharper, these days. Harder lines and angles, and his lips were much fuller than before. Nor found herself staring at them until Zahn met her gaze.

She felt suddenly too warm.

"My family," Nor said, and that very thought stole the warmth away, turned her as cold as the world outside the tower. "My brother."

He was out there, alive, and he was hers.

Nor had sworn to find him the moment her mother sent her that final message from the skies—and with it, a mental image of the young man her brother would someday be, living on a distant, glorious planet. Arcardius.

Valen Cortas was his name.

"What I think," Zahn said, "is that you can do whatever you set your mind to. You've proved that to me a thousand times, Princess."

"Not a princess for much longer," Nor reminded him.

She wanted to be queen, so desperately. But tonight, of all nights, the very thought made Nor's insides turn. She had to be the best Xen Ptera had ever seen. She had to make sure that in everything she did, she succeeded. Defied all the odds.

Deep breaths, *Nor told herself.* In, out and back again.

"So about that handsome guard," Zahn said, clearing his throat. "Is there a position open?"

Nor actually burst out laughing.

"It's not a joke," he said, though he did so with a smile. He nudged her with his shoulder. "I'm serious, Nor."

She lifted a brow. "Do you have any handsome guards in mind? As far as I know, there aren't many around."

For this entire building, for all of its attendants and workers and brilliant minds, lacked the vibrancy of youth and beauty. And even though Nor knew from the start that she was never meant to have a normal childhood, it was still nice to sit beside Zahn in this tower, hiding away from Darai's lessons and frowns, talking about simpler things.

Zahn's smile widened. Nor realized he was leaning in closer, that the space between them was smaller than it had ever been before.

"Well, I was thinking…me," Zahn murmured.

In that moment, Nor realized her heartbeat was too loud. That he could probably hear it slamming against her chest from the inside.

"I guess…" Nor trailed off as she leaned in closer, too. "I guess I could find room for you as one of my guards."

"So you agree?" Zahn asked. She could feel his breath on her cheeks. Her lips. "You think I'm handsome?"

A gentle laugh escaped Nor.

Yes, *she thought.* Yes, *she* did *think he was handsome. In this moment, he was the most beautiful person she'd ever seen, and he was looking back at her like his thoughts mirrored her own.*

She didn't forget about the coronation. She didn't forget about the screaming of the wind beyond the tower, or the desperation of her starving people, or the lifelong mission laid out before her.

But for just a moment, as Nor leaned in and bridged the gap between her lips and Zahn's, as she felt the warmth of him, the realness of it all as he wrapped her in his arms...

Her worries got a little bit lighter.

Nor came back to herself as the transport rumbled, its landing gear lowering as they neared Averia. Out of habit, she reached for Zahn beside her, seeking the comfort of his embrace.

But he was gone.

Gone, lost to the eternal darkness of death.

And he was never coming back.

CHAPTER 21
VALEN

The ride to Averia was one born from the pits of hell itself.

Nor sat across from Valen, slumped in her seat as shock overcame her. Her mind was a veritable storm—Valen could feel it, swirling with dark clouds through their mental doorway.

He wanted to comfort her. Godstars, if only he could.

But the guilt he felt inside…it was too much for him to bear, to *dare* even try.

For he had failed. It was his fault Zahn was dead.

"Zahn," Nor whispered, her forehead in her hands.

She kept whispering his name, over and over. As if saying it could hold him to this earth, even when his spirit was already gone. Beside her, Darai was silent for once, the old man at a loss for words.

Compel the crowd to calm, he'd said during the attack. *Compel them, boy!*

He'd tried. Valen had *tried*, harder than he ever had before. But his body...his mind...

He couldn't explain the terrible weakness that had overcome him, the exhaustion that had been slowly eating away at his body this past month, the effort of the compulsion too much for one man to handle.

During the attack, Darai had pulled him away, shoving Valen toward the transport ship, toward safety. But above the weakness, above the pounding in Valen's head, the *pain* as he'd tried to get his power to swell and control the crowd, he'd felt...fear.

The fear of having to continue in this life without Nor.

His mind had been a place of horror and despair, a place he couldn't calm, no matter how badly he'd wished he could. And in those fleeting moments, with panic racing through him as shots rang out across the city, Valen had failed his sister.

As they soared away from the chaos, the streets ran rainbow with the blood of Nor's supporters, who hailed from all across Mirabel. Their silver veins, gone dim. Their adoration, forever lost.

The cyborg pilot flew the ship at top speed, her voice the only sound in the transport as she spoke to the landing crew, ensuring a med team would be there upon arrival to take care of the remaining passengers.

Nor's body was fine. Valen was sure of it, because he'd seen the entire attack, having ripped himself away from Darai. He'd used all of his waning strength to stumble back to her. He'd seen the moment the enemy soldier slipped through the ranks of the guards and leveled a gun right at Nor.

Valen had acted on instinct. He'd lunged, palms spread before him, and, at the last second, shoved the soldier with every ounce of strength left in him. The soldier had fired.

And the bullet, meant for Nor…had hit Zahn in the chest instead.

It was his fault that Zahn was dead.

His fault that Nor was now alone.

The transport slowed, Averia coming into view, the white walls of the floating gravarock estate glittering in the moonlight as it hung in the sky.

"I'm so sorry, Nor," Valen finally said. His throat felt raw, the words useless. "I'm so sorry."

His words seemed to pull Nor out of her stupor. Her eyes, red-rimmed, were swollen from tears as she looked at him. "I want every soldier who failed me to be hung from the estate walls."

Silence reigned for several long moments, with nothing but the sound of the transport's engine to break the quiet.

"That is a rash decision, my queen," Darai said carefully. His eyes flicked back and forth between the two siblings, and Valen nodded his head in agreement.

Did she know what he'd done?

No, he thought. How could she?

Nor's eyes flicked upward to glare at Darai. Her tears were gone now. Only fury remained in their place. "Do not speak to me about rash," she hissed. "I want to know what happened. I want to know why—"

"The princeling couldn't have known," Darai interjected suddenly, calmly.

Valen's heart felt like it froze in his chest.

"What?" Nor asked quietly.

Please, Valen thought, desperately wishing Darai could hear him. But the old man had no such power. No ability to hear his mental messages.

"Valen was just trying to protect you, my dear. I saw the whole valiant act." He placed a cold hand on Valen's shoulder. "Were it not for his actions, pushing the enemy soldier away…

the shot would very likely have landed in *your* chest instead of Zahn's."

Valen couldn't breathe as the truth was revealed.

For a moment, Nor looked like she hadn't even heard Darai. Valen wondered if their uncle had really spoken the truth aloud, or perhaps it had only been Valen's exhausted mind playing tricks on him as the guilt ate away at his insides.

But then Darai nodded as the transport landed, a hiss of steam slipping past the windows as the engines began to cool down. "Valen *saved* you, Nor." He glanced at Valen and smiled widely. "He saved your life, doing what he did."

"You," Nor whispered, her expression turning to stone as she turned, slowly, to look at Valen.

A dark tendril of shadowy dread crept over him at the sound of that single word.

"*You* pushed the soldier who shot Zahn?"

Valen's lips parted. "I…" His words failed him. "He would have killed you, Nor." He looked to Darai, desperate for help, but the old man was already gone from his seat as the transport door opened, commanding the waiting guards to prepare the way for the queen.

"I didn't know…" Valen swallowed. "You have to believe me, Nor. I had no idea that the bullet was going to hit Zahn instead."

But his sister just sat motionless, as if so overcome with shock at Darai's news that she was unable to move.

Through the open transport doorway, Valen saw a floating gurney soar past, directed by a med droid.

Cold metal.

An empty bed, meant for a body that wasn't going to rise again.

Nor's eyes fell upon it. Her lips moved soundlessly, forming Zahn's name.

"You killed him," she said suddenly. Her eyes flitted back to Valen, then to the doorway again as the droid and Darai moved past. The gurney wasn't empty any longer. Zahn's body lay upon it, covered no longer by Nor's bloody cloak, but by a white sheet, forming a ghostly outline over him.

Nor stared at them as they faded from view.

"You killed Zahn," she said again.

"I didn't," Valen whispered. "Oh, Godstars, Nor, I was trying to save you. I could feel them, Nor. Each time one of our people was shot, and they died. I could feel it like someone was carving them from my mind, from my soul. I ran back to find you, and I saw the soldier preparing to shoot, and I did what anyone would have done—"

"You killed Zahn," she repeated.

Valen reached across the space and gripped Nor's wrist. "Please, Nor."

She jolted upright, ripping her hand away. "Don't you dare touch me!"

"*Please*," Valen said. "It was an accident… It was *war*."

"Then you should have compelled the crowd to protect me. Let them all fall, before Zahn or I were harmed."

"I saved your life," Valen begged. He willed her to see reason—that if it hadn't been Zahn, it would have been *her* on that gurney.

"No," Nor said, standing slowly. She walked down the transport ramp, where Darai was waiting, hand held out to help her. She refused it, shouldering past him.

"Nor!" Valen shouted after her. He stood, but his head was swimming, and the transport ramp felt like a rocking sea as Valen stumbled down it.

"Leave her, princeling," Darai said, but Valen ignored the adviser, nearly tripping over his own feet as he grabbed his sister's hand.

Nor spun, yanking it out of his grip, the motion so strong that Valen lost his balance and crashed to his knees on the hard ground of the docking bay. She towered over him, tears pouring down her cheeks, her gold eyes as cold as the dead.

"You did not save me, Valen," she said. "You just stole from me the only person I have ever loved."

The words hit him like a dagger to the chest.

"You don't mean that," Valen whispered. "Nor, please. I'm your brother. I love you." A sob escaped him against his will. "I'm sorry. Please, please forgive me."

"Sorry won't bring him back," Nor said flatly.

Then she turned and walked away, leaving him alone on the docking bay floor.

Valen wasn't sure how long he stayed there for, trapped in anguish. It could have been mere moments, or hours. Years, perhaps.

Darai appeared before him, offering him a pale hand. "You did well, reacting so quickly during the attack," he said reassuringly. "She will come around in time, and see that."

Valen took his hand, letting the old man help him to his feet. Then he groaned as pain lanced through his skull. His nostrils were dripping blood again, a slow leak that spread the taste of metal across his lips and tongue.

"Still," Darai mused. "Your compulsion failed us all during the frenzy. Perhaps you aren't as strong as I thought you were, if you're already crumbling under the pressure of this mission." He passed Valen a handkerchief. "I suggest you escape to your mind for a while, princeling. Clean yourself up, and do whatever you can to compel the galaxy to calmness after today's bloody display. Because when the queen is done mourning…she will pick herself back up. And she will need your power to complete the mission. Of that, I am certain."

Valen blinked at him, Darai's words leaving him cold and hopeless. "I've always hated you, Uncle," he said tiredly. "I wish it had been *you* on the other side of that bullet. Not Zahn."

He could scarcely see through the specks rapidly filling his vision. He needed to lie down. To sleep, and find solace in the darkness.

So he turned away from a suddenly silent Darai, calling forth one of the med droids who still waited patiently on the edge of the docking bay. The little droid wheeled over a floating chair, and Valen fell into it, weariness clinging to him like a second skin as he wiped the blood from beneath his nostrils.

CHAPTER 22
ANDI

Andi's vision was swimming when a familiar face walked into the pub. From across the dim room, she could see swirling tattoos gliding across the newcomer's skin, which briefly made her wonder if she'd had one drink too many.

Soyina nudged aside a few patrons who blocked her way as she approached. The icy look one Soleran man shot her was colder than his pallor, but Soyina just gave him a wink before sidling up beside an oblivious Dex, jarring him with a wicked slap on the back.

"Enjoying yourselves, it seems," she commented, leaning against Dex with one arm slung around his shoulder.

Dex gave her an impish grin. "*Enjoying* may be pushing it after everything we've been through."

Soyina shrugged, shifting her gaze to Andi. "You two coherent enough for a debrief on the attack?"

Andi might have been tipsy—or a little bit more than that—but her mind was still sharp enough to perk up at her words. She sat up a little straighter, blinking a bit to clear her vision.

Soyina idly played with a strand of Dex's hair, smiling flirtatiously. Andi felt a twinge of annoyance, but pushed it down. Dex wasn't hers—especially since she couldn't figure out if she was still mad at him or not.

Nevertheless, she found herself glaring at Soyina. Thinking of how to painfully break the woman's fingers.

As if he could hear her thoughts, Dex adjusted in his seat, making Soyina stand upright. The woman smirked, looking between them before pulling over a chair from a nearby table. She flipped it around and rested her arms on its backrest as she sat down.

"Well?" Andi prompted, brimming with curiosity.

"We definitely sent a message, but… Nor and Valen are still alive. They escaped in the chaos."

"Were they at least hurt? Preferably in a life-threatening way?" Andi asked, irritated. If she'd been there, both siblings would have a bullet between their brows. They'd taken her family—she wasn't going to play nice. Even if Valen was Kalee's brother, he'd betrayed her memory and the Cortas family in every possible way.

"We know someone got hit, but it's as yet unclear who it was. I know this isn't the news you wanted to hear," she said, sounding surprisingly apologetic. "Quite frankly, it isn't what we wanted to hear, either. We lost good fighters in that attack." Her expression turned distant as she added, "Just remember, you're not the only one with loved ones at risk."

Soyina, usually so snarky and cryptic, was anything but as she said those last few words. Andi couldn't deny that she was right—everybody in the Underground was affected by Zenith in some way, even if it didn't actually taint their veins. Affected just like she and Dex were.

"So what's next?" Dex asked.

Soyina blinked a few times. "Time to put you both to bed," she said, as if they were small children who had stayed up past their bedtime.

Andi didn't hate that plan one bit. She knew her head was heavy not only from the drinks, but also from utter exhaustion. They had been on the move nonstop since leaving the nebula. They'd suffered through loss, injury and Klaren's revelations, all without having a wink of rest.

It was a miracle they were still upright.

Actually, by the look of Dex, he was slumped a bit too forward to be considered awake.

"Lead the way," Andi told her, stifling a yawn herself.

With a nod, Soyina led them back into the undercity, leading them to a new sector Andi and Dex hadn't seen earlier. Rows of doors lined a narrow corridor.

"Welcome to your luxurious room," Soyina said, gesturing to a door marked with the number fourteen.

As they stepped inside, Andi noted it was far from a five-star hotel room, which was fine by her. The interior was largely bare, save for a bunk bed lining the left wall and a small desk and chair pressed against the right.

"I'll be back for you two tomorrow morning," Soyina told them. "Bathroom is down the hall and to the right. Don't use the third stall, though."

"Why?" Andi asked curiously.

"Just don't. Trust me."

Andi hardly remembered climbing into the top bunk last night, because once her head hit the thin pillow, she was out like a light. Dex, on the other hand, had somehow managed to fall asleep leaning against the doorway and didn't wake up even as she ushered him into bed.

Blearily, her gaze drifted to the clock mounted on the wall across the small room. Her eyes widened as they focused on the time. It was well past morning and dipping into the afternoon. Andi couldn't remember the last time she'd slept so late. Usually she was the first to wake and the last to go to sleep.

Though technically, right now she *was* the first to wake. She could hear Dex snoring away in the bed below hers.

Andi hopped off the bunk and landed softly on the stone floor below. Dex was still in the exact same position she'd left him in last night: face plastered against his pillow, legs hanging slightly over the edge of the bed. The only difference was the drool dripping from the corner of his mouth and pooling on the gray sheet below.

And, to her great surprise, Havoc was curled up in his arms, purring happily.

"That's a sight I never thought I'd see," Andi muttered. She poked Dex's cheek.

He didn't move an inch, so she prodded him again. Still nothing, so she shook his shoulder, but he just kept snoring. Havoc opened one eye, but mercifully didn't attack.

"Damn," Andi muttered. Usually Dex could be woken up by someone breathing too loudly. It looked like she'd need to resort to more extreme measures if they were to leave the room at all today.

She leaned in and flicked Havoc's horned head, then darted out of his range as the creature scurried from Dex's grasp, leaping over the edge of the bunk and out of sight. Then Andi grabbed the edge of the flimsy mattress and pulled. With a satisfying *thump*, Dex and his mattress fell to the floor, making him jolt upright. He reached for his gun, and Andi threw her hands up in defense. "Whoa there. Easy now."

Dex blinked a few times before giving her a slow smile. "Easy is boring. I like it har—"

"I'm going to stop you there," Andi said quickly, cringing at his dirty delirium. "Time to get up. We've slept nearly the whole day away."

Her stomach growled, making Andi wonder where they might dig up some food. After a night of drinking, the long sleep had fortunately managed to offset the potential for a killer headache, but she was dying to eat anything and everything.

"What's that?" Dex asked, pointing toward the door. A small piece of paper had been slid under the crack. Andi grabbed it and turned it over. The note was short and direct.

When you wake up, follow the signs to the dining hall.
Ask a guard to com me and I'll meet you there.
—Soyina

"Want food?" Andi asked after reading the letter aloud.

Dex jumped up, teetering a moment. "Desperately."

The dining hall wasn't far from the now-deserted barracks. Everyone was milling through the other corridors, going about their business before the day ended, and the dining hall was almost empty, other than a few patrons drinking coffee in the corner.

Rows and rows of tables lined the room from front to back. Every square inch was used, leaving only narrow walkways between the tables. On the left side of the room was a buffet-style food arrangement. It didn't look like there was much food left from the midday meal, but Andi didn't care. She'd eat mud at this point.

But before she dug in—unlike Dex, who was already piling beans onto his plate—she asked the steely-looking guard at the door to com Soyina. When he gave her a stiff nod in reply, she turned to the food table and started loading her plate with a bit of everything.

Crispy golden potatoes, green beans dripping in oil, a slab of some kind of purple meat—its animal origins were a mystery—and a smattering of thick gravy to top it all off. Andi was actually quite shocked by the spread of food before her. She'd anticipated dry, military-type rations, not food fit for a queen.

"Bet you didn't expect this, did you, Baroness?" Soyina asked as she entered the hall.

Andi quirked a brow. "Not one bit," she acknowledged honestly.

"We hit the jackpot last week when we captured a ship full of supplies that was en route to Arcardius from Adhira," Soyina explained. "Usually our dining options are a bit more limited."

"We're certainly not complaining," Andi remarked dryly, gesturing toward Dex, who was shoveling food into his mouth at an alarming rate.

The two women made their way over to his table. "Slow down, Dextro. You're going to wind up cramping or throwing it all up," Andi said as she sat down on the bench across from him. Soyina took a seat to her right, plopping a sack on the table before her.

Dex only gave her a wink in response. Andi rolled her eyes.

Soyina pushed the sack toward them. "Clothes and toiletries for you lot."

Andi thanked her, putting the bag on the ground by her feet. She couldn't wait to strip off her suit, take a shower and get dressed in fresh clothes. But first, food.

The moment the warm potatoes touched her tongue, she understood why Dex was shoveling the food down so fast. It was exquisitely prepared. The potatoes were perfectly crispy on the outside, soft on the inside, almost melting in her mouth. She stifled a moan as she chewed and dug in with enthusiasm.

"Klaren wants to speak with you two after you eat," Soyina said after a few minutes of their contented silence.

"Mhmm," Andi mumbled, mouth full of juicy meat. She'd expected as much.

"What about?" Dex asked, pushing his empty plate away and eyeing the buffet table, as if considering a second trip.

Soyina shrugged. "She didn't tell me much, but I believe she wants to discuss how you can be of use to the Underground."

Andi swallowed. "If the Underground wants to take advantage of our skills—and my new title—then it will have to be an equal trade."

Dex nodded. "We may be fighting the same enemy, but we have to rescue our crew first."

Hearing that *our* and knowing he was just as determined to save Lira, Gilly and Breck made Andi's heart warm. She met his eyes and mouthed, "Thank you." He smiled in return.

Soyina nodded, plucking a potato from Andi's plate.

She ignored Andi's glare. "I understand that you want to save them—we all want to save someone. Or kill someone, depending on who you ask. Am I right, Baroness?"

Andi didn't answer, so Soyina winked and continued. "But in order to save them, we need to pave a path. If you help us pave that path, I can't make any promises, but I bet Klaren would be more than happy to help our dear general."

Andi ate her last forkful of food, pushing her empty plate toward Soyina. "Then let's not keep her waiting."

CHAPTER 23
NOR

Time felt frozen as Nor sat by the fireplace in her quarters, staring into the flames.

Days ago, she'd done this very same thing, the weight of too many worlds pressing down upon her shoulders. The fire had failed to warm her then, but at least Zahn had been there to do so.

And now, despite the constant tending of the fire…she knew it wouldn't warm her, wouldn't erase the chill from her bones. She feared nothing ever would again.

BANG.

Nor flinched, remembering the sound of the gunshot.

BANG.

She would never forget the horrific, muffled cry that had come from Zahn, the blood that had sprayed as the bullet hit him square in the chest and he toppled against her, falling to the city streets.

A queen was not supposed to feel such weakness.

And yet here Nor sat, feeling as if she were weakness incarnate.

Her heart, gone. Her kingdom, frozen, as she awaited the arrival of Androma Racella.

And her brother, her greatest ally in Mirabel, was the cause of Zahn's death.

Nor closed her eyes, leaning her head back against the cushions. Grief was a tricky thing, a rocky sea she had been forced to navigate many times before. She'd learned to turn grief into something different. To twist the sadness into hatred, a burning desire for revenge against whoever had caused the feeling in the first place.

But how could she hate her brother?

The doorway between their minds was as cold as her bones. Empty of Valen's presence, as if he were too afraid to even approach it.

I saved you, he'd whispered, as he fell to his knees before her in that loading dock.

And he had. That, Nor knew, was a fact she couldn't ignore. Valen had made a snap decision to save his queen, as any of her subjects would have.

Yet a part of her wished he hadn't. For what was life without Zahn?

It was all she'd ever known. Zahn at her side, Zahn guarding her back, Zahn curled up beside her in their bed…

A knock on her door pulled Nor from her thoughts.

She didn't answer, willing whoever it was to leave her alone in her misery, but the door opened anyway, a sliver of light from the hallway accompanying the new arrival.

"My dear niece," Darai said softly, shutting the door behind him as he swept inside. "I cannot bear to see you in such pain."

Nor sighed deeply. "I didn't give you permission to enter. I said I wanted no visitors, and that includes you."

But Darai simply frowned, looking about the room. "It's dark as pitch in here."

"I don't want the light," Nor said.

She wanted darkness, embraced it.

An atmosphere to mirror the emptiness she felt inside.

Her uncle tsked in response, gingerly taking a seat beside her on the couch. "The Exonians would disagree with that statement. Such darkness, always. They long for the light."

"Then it's a good thing I'm not in Exonia right now," Nor said coldly. "What do you want, Darai?"

"I came to check on my niece, who is grieving."

She froze at those words. The sudden softness in his voice.

It wasn't often that Darai blurred the lines between uncle and adviser. But when he chose so, Nor knew it was best to just let him be. He was her family, even if they weren't bound by blood, and one allowed family certain freedoms on occasion— even queens.

She also didn't have the energy to convince herself otherwise right now.

"Zahn was a good man," Darai said, placing his hands in his lap. "A good soldier, too, but an even better man."

"Don't speak of him as if he's gone," Nor whispered, and suddenly she was crying again. "Not yet."

Darai reached out, slowly, and took her hand. The gesture was awkward; something he hadn't done since Nor was a child, when Darai had sat for hours at her bedside, bargaining with the Godstars to bring her back to health after the destruction of Xen Ptera.

"Did you know," he ventured, "that your mother made me promise her two things when you were born?"

Nor shook her head.

"The first was that I would always look out for you, that I would guide you and advise you and teach you the ways of Exonia, and about your true lineage, until the end of my days." He squeezed her hand, reminding her briefly of their true mission.

Her purpose, at least, still remained, though the task seemed more daunting than ever without Zahn.

"The second was that I would never lie to you," Darai said. He reached out, gently, and lifted her chin with his hand, guiding her gaze toward his. "You are still the queen, my dear. And a queen cannot crumble. Not even beneath the weight of grief."

Nor blinked back her tears, staring into her uncle's eyes, realizing she never really had before. Not since she was a girl, and he was first teaching her how to use her compulsion. Reminding her that though her body would be weak while she healed, her mind was still strong.

"You will not sulk in this room any longer," Darai said matter-of-factly.

Nor blinked. "Sulking? I'm *mourning*, Uncle. That's hardly the same thing."

He shook his head, still holding her gaze. His eyes were Exonian gold, so very close to the same shade as Nor's. "Zahn will not be forgotten. We'll honor him, when this war is over. We'll give him a warrior's funeral and adorn the entire estate in gold."

Nor shook her head, tears coming again as she thought of letting him go, *truly*. She didn't want to think of that now. "We can't—"

"We *must*." Darai said it like a command, his voice hard. Very few times, he'd spoken so openly to her. He saved such moments for when it mattered most. And tonight, as he watched her, holding her hand tight, as if he was begging her to come out of her stupor of grief... Nor realized that maybe she needed her uncle's harshness. And maybe she wasn't fully alone in this.

"Tonight, my dear, you need to put your mind on something else," he told her. "You need a reminder of what's at stake. Zahn was at your side during that attack, not because he had to be, but because he wanted to be. He believed in you and your mission. He believed in you ruling Mirabel *and* Exonia, the rightful queen of both. Do not let his death be in vain."

Nor nodded, holding on to his words.

They pained her, for they revealed the truth.

Zahn was dead.

And he wasn't ever coming back.

"How?" Nor breathed. "How do I go on?"

"By putting your mission ahead of your heart," Darai said. "It's what your mother would have done. It's exactly what she *did*, when she left you on Xen Ptera and flew to Arcardius at Cyprian's side." He smiled gently at her. "That's the real reason why I came to speak to you. Because I fear that your heart is going to get in the way of your mission. And if I allow that, Nor, then I will have failed just as your mother failed."

Those golden eyes shimmered in the firelight. "You're strong, Nor. You always have been. You've ruled over a dying planet, giving hope to your people when they needed it most. And in the face of adversity, you cleverly united with Valen and used his power to rise up. And I know you will not stop, not even after this. You will complete your mission, and I will help you do it. Together, we'll complete what Klaren started, so that Zahn's death will be a most worthy sacrifice. And that, I believe, is one of the greatest gifts he could ever have given you."

Nor's tears began to slow. She took a deep breath, letting his words fill her with…something. *Anything* but the grief she felt. And for a moment, she believed she could rise. That she could get off this couch, and make something of herself again.

But then she felt the absence in her mind.

The empty doorway, where Valen's warm presence normally resided.

"Valen," Nor said, pulling her gaze from Darai. "What am I supposed to do about him?"

She was desperate for an answer. For Darai to simply decide for her, because the pain she felt, when she thought of his actions…

What little was left of her heart split down the middle.

"I both hate him and love him at once," she said as she glanced at the fire again, the flames looking angrier than before.

Darai swept his hands down the front of his dark robes. "That is the very issue I came to discuss. I fear that the bond between the two of you will never be repaired. Not fully."

Nor kept replaying the events of the attack in her mind. "He killed Zahn," she said softly. "Not by choice…but he set into motion what was the killing blow."

Darai nodded. "He did what he had to do to save you. For that, I am eternally grateful… And that is why it pains me to say this, Nor. It pains me deeply." He huffed out a breath. "In Exonia, we believe that only life can pay for life. That when one person wrongs another, someone must pay the price."

"As you've said," Nor remembered. It was the reason why she'd wanted Cyprian dead. Why she would have brought him back only to kill him again a hundred thousand times, to pay for all the Xen Pterrans who'd perished during the Cataclysm, including her own father.

"And since I have always upheld the Exonian ways—and helped you to uphold them, too, as your mother made me promise—then I fear the only way we can solve this issue is to do what we have always done. To hold fast to our beliefs."

Nor wasn't sure where Darai was going with this. But her insides began to feel prickly.

"I do not advise such a decision lightly, but… Valen must pay for Zahn's death," Darai said. "It's the only way you will ever be able to truly forgive him and move on with your mission as queen of both Mirabel and Exonia."

Nor blinked, not quite believing her uncle's words. "I…I'm afraid I don't understand."

They'd built this kingdom upon Valen's compulsion. His

power was unbelievably strong, far stronger than any Darai said he'd seen before, during his upbringing in Exonia. It was because of Valen's power that they were even on Arcardius now.

"You wish to punish Valen?" Nor asked incredulously.

"Not punish." Her uncle pursed his lips together, considering his words. "Would you help me stand, my dear?"

Nor nodded and assisted her uncle as he got to his feet, breathing heavily. They walked over to the fire together and watched the flames flicker in silence. There were stars carved on the back wall of the fireplace, intricate little designs made by a steady hand.

"Your brother's power is like a flame, burning bright," Darai said, gesturing toward the fire. "The brightest I've ever seen. A true marvel, Valen is. But when we arrived here, and we began to spread his compulsion across the galaxy…"

He reached for the ornate key embedded in the wall beside the fireplace. He twisted it counterclockwise, pulling back on the gas that kept the fire burning bright. The flames quickly dimmed, dousing the room in near-darkness. "He is weakening before our very eyes," Darai told her quietly. "With every mind he compels, every person he adds to his mental fortress… his body is fading, Nor. I know you've seen it, too."

Nor thought of the blood trailing from Valen's nostrils. His rapidly declining weight. The way his hair, once full, had gone lank and greasy. And when she couldn't find him, when he wasn't in his mind castle, he was often asleep. Resting, so he'd be able to function the rest of the time.

"It will not be long before he breaks under the strain," Darai said.

Nor closed her eyes, swallowing back another round of tears. She still loved Valen, even with the death of Zahn on his hands. "How long?"

"A matter of weeks, I believe," Darai said.

Nor gasped, horror filling her. "Truly?"

Her uncle nodded sadly, his eyes downcast.

"But Aclisia is working around the clock to come up with a way to put his compulsion into the Nexus satellite," she said. "And once we can do that, the satellite itself will carry the brunt of the weight, and Valen's mind will be free. His body will be able to heal. That was always the plan."

Darai looked at her again, those lips pursed as if he were holding back a secret.

"Nor... You must believe my words," he said, looking into her eyes. "I have...held certain fears to myself lately, until I could be certain."

"Certain of *what*?" Nor asked.

Her uncle frowned. "Valen will likely not survive long enough for Aclisia to connect his compulsion to Nexus. Already he is almost too weak to stand—today, he could not walk, after you parted. He is now in the medical wing, being assessed, but... Nor, my dear, it's inevitable. Your brother will soon die. I have seen such things, long ago, in Exonia. And when he does...all will be lost."

"So then what can we do?" Nor asked desperately. "What are you saying?"

That horrible numbness, the emptiness, was creeping over her again. It ran through her, cold and bitter and all too familiar, after the events of the past day.

Her uncle's gaze held hers, golden as the sun. "We need his mind, Nor."

"But what does that mean?"

"We must plug his mind, his very essence, into the satellite. It's the only way."

Nor took a step back, horrified at the very idea. But Darai held fast to her hand, as if he'd known what her reaction would be. As if he'd suddenly gained a strength he didn't have before.

"It is the *Exonian* way," he said.

And Nor's chest ached.

Because she was horrified, still.

But she knew, without a doubt, the moment he'd uttered the words that they were true.

"I have kept the two promises I made your mother," Darai said quietly, that strength suddenly gone as fast as it had come. "I have always guided you in the way of the light, and I have *never* lied to you. So I will not lie to you now, and say there's a different solution."

Nor nodded, stepping back to give herself space to breathe as she took it all in. "How?" she asked. "How would it be done?"

"We would wait until the satellite construction is complete," Darai explained carefully. He, of all people, knew the delicacy of the situation. How it was killing Nor on the inside to even *hear* this plan. "I don't feel we should tell him, so as not to ruin his final days. When it is time, we can…ease him into it. Aclisia is fashioning a throne, of sorts—a place where Valen will sit, and his body will be nurtured, plugged into a series of tubes and wires meant to keep it alive for eternity."

Nor could see it all too clearly in her mind.

It made her sick.

But as her uncle spoke, she also understood the necessity of the plan. She heard the pain in his voice—he knew, just as much as she did, that Valen would be the ultimate sacrifice to free Exonia.

"We will also plug his mind into that device," Darai explained. "We will essentially upload his consciousness, and all that Valen is and does, into the satellite. He will feel no pain. He will simply become the Nexus, and the Nexus will become him, and then the galaxy will forever be beneath his compulsion. He will never lose control. You will reign, and your future children will reign, and Mirabel and Exonia will forever be yours."

Nor was breathless. She found herself sinking back onto the couch, Darai still clutching her arm, but this time he was the one supporting her.

He watched her intently. "I wish there was another option, my dear. But there is none." Darai nodded firmly. "Say the word, and I will give Aclisia a direct order to speed up her side work in completing the device."

It was too much.

All of this was happening far too quickly for Nor to process.

"He is dying, Nor," Darai pressed. "And when he is gone, all hope of saving the Exonians will be gone, too." He patted her hand, the way he once had, long ago. "A life for a life. You will be able to forgive Valen when he becomes a sacrifice, the same as Zahn. It will be a gift to him, that forgiveness from you. And he will die not as a failure, but as a savior. A worthy end, for a Solis."

The truth out, Nor and Darai sat in silence. After a time, she cleared her throat and spoke. "I will think on it."

"My dear…" Darai sighed, shaking his head at her.

"No." Nor glanced back at the flames, still low and dying out. It pained her greatly to even consider his plan. And yet the pain of having lost Zahn, the rift between her and Valen, forever to remain because of his hand in Zahn's death…and his health, already declining, his obvious fate…

The choice was all too clear.

Still, she would not make it now. "I will give you an answer soon, Uncle. I promise."

He nodded without words, as if he didn't trust himself to contain his disappointment. Or perhaps he was lost in his own pain over the choice they would have to make, as she was.

"There is still the matter of Arachnid to discuss," he said, changing the subject. "The attack was great, the casualties many. We must make a move while you decide what to do about Valen's fate. We have also had no word from Andromina Racella. Of course, we cannot be sure she saw the announcement, but surely she has heard news of the attack. Perhaps we should consider sending a second message, from within these walls, to let Arachnid know you will not falter, and to let Androma know you will carry out your threat if she doesn't comply."

Nor nodded. "Did her crew survive the attack?"

"They did. Smart soldiers, able to defend themselves. I believe the Godstars protected them as well, knowing what the future holds."

"Bring them to me," Nor said. "We will send out another message. If she didn't believe the last…this one, she won't ignore."

Darai inclined his head to her, then left Nor to her thoughts.

There was much to consider. But for now, she turned the flames of the fire back up to a full roar. Then she lay down, curling up beside the hearth, and allowed herself, finally, to drift off to sleep.

CHAPTER 24
VALEN

Memories were fickle things, for they often warped or revealed different sides of themselves with the passing of time.

Valen felt the reality of this, perhaps more keenly than he ever had, as he beheld the door leading to his sister Kalee's old bedroom. He could almost hear her voice echoing in the room beyond; could almost *see* Kalee's face, her eyes bright with life and laughter.

Nor had once looked at him like that, too. And now she might never do so again.

His other sister had changed a great many things about this estate since taking over, and Valen had been glad for it. When they'd first arrived, they'd torn through the halls of Averia together, ordering servants and droids to remove everything that reminded them of the Cortas family. Later that night, they stood together in the wide, green courtyard, watching Valen's past burn to ashes in a towering pile. So high, they'd stacked those mementos, that those who looked up from below on the city streets could see the trail of smoke spiraling into the cloudless sky.

It was a reminder that everything old was now made new. That the ways of General Cortas, and the old Mirabel, were now behind them.

He'd loved seeing the changes. Loved seeing the past melt away.

But Valen hadn't been able to bear the thought of anyone touching Kalee's things. She had been the one bright spot in his otherwise lonely childhood, and her memory had given him the strength he'd needed to survive in Lunamere. Knowing that she would have wanted him to live, to walk in the sunlight again, had been what kept him going in that constant darkness.

"Stop here," Valen said to the droid guiding his chair along. He was still too weak to walk, even after spending most of the evening in the medical wing of the estate, being assessed.

His body was failing him, in ways that utterly mystified the doctors and med droids.

But Valen knew the truth.

It was his power, and the strain it placed on him, that was doing this to him. He'd felt that strain ever since the minds in his fortress had grown three layers of cells thick. As it expanded, day by day, the strain only got worse.

Now he could scarcely think, scarcely keep himself together unless he was in that very fortress. The world beyond his mind was a place of pain and exhaustion, but inside, the fortress walls were like a safe harbor. Or a drug that kept pulling him back for more. Sometimes Valen wasn't entirely sure which was more accurate.

Back in the med wing, he'd been pumped with fluids and given a decent meal, most of which Valen could hardly keep down. And now here he sat, in this wheeled chair, on the threshold of one of the two places in Averia that he had never allowed Nor to touch.

"I have been instructed to stay by your side," the med droid said in its robotic voice.

"Instructed by who?"

"Master Darai," the droid told him.

Valen sighed. "Of course." The old man was inescapable, even when he placed someone else in his stead. "I'll just be a few moments."

The droid's expressionless face did not move. It simply stood there, waiting patiently like an obnoxiously loyal dog.

Valen turned back to the heavy oak door, his fingertips running across the tiny lines gouged on the door frame. Little by little, they stretched higher and higher, closely spaced at first, then further widening until they finally stopped near Valen's shoulder.

Those marks had kept track of Kalee, as she grew.

As Valen stared at them, he couldn't help but think of another set of tallies, carved across the sharp sides of two bloody twin swords. He wondered what Androma Racella was doing right now; whether she'd seen Nor's message, and started her journey toward Arcardius.

Valen knew Andi. She had her faults—too many to count—but she was fiercely loyal. She'd come.

It was only a matter of time.

With a sigh, Valen opened the door and wheeled himself inside Kalee's old room.

It felt like a dwelling for Kalee's ghost. The lamps were off, but the night sky cast its own light, fully visible now through a wall of windows. Many of the rooms in Averia were designed this way, the better to see the beauty of the manicured grounds beyond. It would be dawn, soon.

As he surveyed the space, Valen saw Kalee as a memory, fully formed and perfect.

She stood before her wall of windows, wearing a gown of all white, dancing as the sky shed moonlight on her ringlet curls.

A flash of bright light.

A screech that sounded like metal colliding against rock.

Then Androma Racella appeared in the room, bathed in Kalee's blood. Her hands dripped with it. Her eyes, silver as the stars, were cold enough to balance out the crackling heat of her electric blades.

Valen hissed between his teeth, and shoved all thoughts of Kalee and Androma away.

This room was empty. Absent of any life at all. It was Valen himself, and his cursed past, that brought back the ghosts.

He remembered Andi telling him once that the dead taunted her. The memory of Zahn taunted Valen now, too. The snap decision. That final, fateful push and shove, and the gunshot going off. Nor's panicked scream, as she realized Zahn had been shot.

Valen's own horror as he realized he'd been the one who caused it.

Why could the bullet not have gone elsewhere? Into the building, or another enemy, or even one of Androma's crew, standing close by Nor's side?

Would Nor ever forgive him? She *had* to. They were a team, the Solis siblings—his power, and her plan. Valen wasn't sure what he would do if she didn't.

White sheets covered all of Kalee's belongings. They looked ghostly in the light of the moons, even more so with the frost coating the windowpanes. He wheeled himself across the room, staggered to a standing position and tore the sheets from Kalee's four-poster bed. Dust rained down from above, landing on his shoulders like flakes of snow.

Beneath it, her old bed was untouched, and his chest ached at the sight of it.

His hand hovered over the plush, intricately designed blue

quilt. Threads of purple woven in with the blue, signifying the two moons of Arcardius.

In his mind, Valen saw Kalee as she once was, lying on her stomach on the bed, her socks unevenly pushed down around her ankles, a book outspread before her as she skimmed over the pages.

If she were still alive, she would have heard him entering this room. She would have glanced up at him, her eyes rolling as Valen gave her some message from their father about training, about duty, about…

All of the things Valen had never cared to learn.

How funny, now, that he was practically a prince. And how far, yet again, he had fallen.

And Nor might never forgive him for what he'd done.

The doorway between their minds was closed. Thick obsidinite bars covered it, so that Valen couldn't even reach through and knock if he'd wanted to.

And he *did* want to.

The guilt was a monster, writhing within him. But so was the feeling of loss. Abandonment. And with that…anger.

He'd saved her. Again and again, Valen would hold fast to the truth that he had *saved* his sister by pushing that enemy with the gun aside.

But you killed me in the process, a ghostly voice whispered to Valen, and he swore it sounded like Zahn's.

Valen sank down on the bed in despair.

They only had a short time left, before the satellite was complete. And once Androma came, their mission could finally unfold.

Nor might not ever forgive Valen on her own, but perhaps, if he kept working, if he was loyal to his breaking point…perhaps he would still remain a part of something.

For he could not bear the idea of being cast out, left to navigate this life alone again.

He sighed, sinking back against Kalee's mountain of pillows, wondering how many times she'd felt the weight of their father's world on her chest as she lay in this very spot.

He closed his eyes. Within his mind, his power waited. It sang his name.

With a twist of his brow, he focused, breathing deeply in and out, pushing aside the pain, the exhaustion, the fear that he would never be good enough for anyone, maybe not even himself—and especially not Nor anymore.

One moment, he was lying in Kalee's bed.

The next...

Valen set foot inside the confines of his mind.

Valen's boots crunched across those old bones as he walked past the demons he'd slain, toward the fortress doors.

They opened at his touch, and as they swung forward, he caught a glimpse of the Solis sigil on their front. How much comfort, how much *pride*, that sigil had once given Valen. But now he felt cold just looking at it.

As if he didn't belong.

He tried, once more, to call out to Nor.

"I'm sorry," he said. "Sister, please forgive me."

His words carried up the hillside, past the valley full of bones, up to the doorway that connected his mind to Nor's.

They echoed back to him, shut out and unheard by her.

With a sigh, he turned away and entered his castle. He walked aimlessly past cell after cell, peeking inside, ensuring that the minds held within were still loyal to Nor. That they didn't fear Arachnid, didn't harbor any doubts in their queen.

With each doorway, he normally felt lighter, like his footsteps were walking on air.

But tonight, Valen found himself slowing. Weakening with every step.

"Rest," he told himself. "I just need to rest."

He stumbled toward the castle wall, the cold obsidinite stones grazing against his arm. As he leaned against it for support, catching his breath, something caught his eye.

A crack in the stone floor.

It was small. A tiny fault line, that anyone else would have passed by without noticing, were they not the creator of this place.

Valen knelt, running his fingertips across the crack. Cold seeped out from it, causing him to shiver.

But he could fix this.

Close your eyes and will it to be so, Darai had once taught him, when Valen was learning how to build this very fortress. He'd fashioned row after row of cells, staining them black, filling them with minds, placing torches beside each and willing those flames to life, too.

He'd become a king here. A king who needed no crown to reign supreme.

But today, when he tried to will that crack back into non-existence, it disappeared for only a moment—and another quickly appeared in its place.

"Strange," Valen murmured to himself.

With great effort, he drew himself back to his feet. His chest ached with ragged breaths, and as he took step after step toward the exit, a trail of bloody droplets followed in his wake.

Drip.

A drop of blood from his nose, staining the stones.

Drip.

Another, beside a second crack in the floor as Valen neared the doors.

Drip.

He heaved those doors open again, grunting at their sudden weight, heavier than they had ever felt before.

Valen did not make it to the top of the hillside. His legs gave out beneath him, that weakness from the real world inexplicably manifesting here, in the landscape he had created with his power. He tried to stop the tears from coming, but it was already too late.

And so, alone in his mind, Valen curled up in his cloak beside the dead and sobbed.

CHAPTER 25
LIRA

Lira took the lead as the three girls filed into the room, their footsteps seeming all too loud. This receiving room was meant for smaller gatherings, but the decor still held enough grandeur to marvel at. Pristine, grooved walls soared upward, at least three stories high, before meeting the gold crown molding bordering the ceiling, and a few tasteful couches and chairs were scattered throughout the space.

Thus far, the room was empty, save for the three of them. None of them had any idea why they'd been summoned here, and Lira couldn't help feeling a twinge of unease. She'd obey any command given by her queen, no matter where it took her, but how could she serve properly with no information?

She'd failed Nor during the attack, and had not been able to ease her mind since.

"Are we in trouble?" Gilly asked in a small voice. Lira wished she could provide a reassuring answer, but she, too, was wondering the same thing. They had been in the barracks, getting ready for breakfast, when the queen's personal guards arrived to escort them away for some unknown reason.

Zahn, the queen's head of security, had died in Arachnid's attack. A flicker of worry echoed through her as Lira wondered whether the queen would blame them for his death. Lira knew that she blamed herself, at least in part—they should have found a way to do better. But no matter how hard they tried to protect everyone, it never seemed to be enough.

Breck just looked at her with a question in her eyes. Before she could put voice to it, however, a door on the right wall opened, and Queen Nor emerged from it.

The three girls instantly dropped to their knees.

"You may stand."

They stood without hesitation, like dolls on a string and the queen, their puppet master. Lira assessed her carefully while keeping her head dutifully bowed. Queen Nor wore a plain black dress that fell to her ankles, and her hair was tangled, her usual elegant updo an utter mess. In all the times Lira had seen her, never had the queen looked so unkempt. And her eyes were so tired, so sad.

Lira couldn't blame her.

She held her breath as Nor shifted her gaze to each of them, holding on to her silence. Lira wished she would just speak already, even if it was to punish them. She deserved punishment for failing the queen—perhaps she even deserved death.

"If you think I called you here to punish you, you're wrong." All three girls let out a breath. "But that doesn't mean everything is alright."

Lira nodded. "Please accept our condolences, my queen, for those who were lost in the attack."

Nor stiffened, and Lira froze, hoping she hadn't said something wrong. Then the queen acknowledged her sentiment with a slight tilt of her head, and Lira relaxed slightly.

Nor tucked a stray strand of dark hair behind her ear before speaking. "We cannot let the resistance continue to thwart our efforts. So we are going to bring their most precious member under our control."

"Andi," Gilly breathed.

Nor gave her a sly grin. "Correct. That is why I called you here. We need to find another way to draw Androma to us."

"But how do we do that when she knows we are loyal to you?" Lira asked, brow raised.

Their queen stepped up to her, arm outstretched. She placed one long, nimble finger under Lira's blue chin. Nor smiled again, but this time, it was menacing.

"We will have to do something she cannot ignore."

"What do you have in mind?" Breck asked from beside Lira, arms crossed.

Nor dropped her arm and stepped back, scanning each of them. Her eyes were sharp, even through her pain. So strong. So powerful.

Lira would do anything for this woman.

Anything.

Nor smiled sweetly. "I am going to kill one of you."

CHAPTER 26
DEX

"You coming in?" Soyina asked, raising a tattooed brow at Dex. They had made their way through the maze of caverns to Klaren's office, which now stood before them behind closed doors. Apparently that initial meeting in the cave business had just been for theatrics after all.

Andi straightened up, swords strapped over her back as if she were preparing for battle. Dex would have very much preferred to be on full alert like her, but such a task was proving itself difficult, as he was currently nursing a wicked hangover.

"Strange," Soyina said, looking at Andi and then back at Dex. "You used to be able to handle your Griss a little better, Arez. Getting soft in your old age?"

Dex not-so-casually scratched his nose with his middle finger. "Just let us into the spider's lair, Soyina."

"As you wish," she said cryptically, opening the iron door for them and striding away.

"You look like you've just barely survived a war," Andi murmured, coming up beside him, playing with her messy braid.

Dex shrugged. "Technically, I have," he said quietly. "I survived a crash landing, an ice dragon attack and, scariest of all, the new General of Arcardius. And let me tell you, she's positively terrifying."

Andi hummed. "Always glad to keep you on your toes. But I'm warning you now—if you keep anything from me again, I'll throw you into a deep, dark dungeon."

"A dungeon? I hope it's the fun kind." Dex winked.

"Very fun." Andi smiled, running a finger across his chest. "I find immense pleasure in your pain."

A shiver of apprehension ran up his spine. "You scare me sometimes," Dex said honestly.

"Good. Now come on."

Together they slipped inside.

Klaren was waiting for them, armorless this time, but still perched near a crackling fire. She held a piece of black rock in her fist and didn't look up as they entered, busily carving the floor with more of those strange patterns that littered the tunnel to the Underground.

"The Godstars look different, from Exonia," the droid, perched upon her thin shoulder, said for her.

Dex looked down at his own skin, covered with the constellation tattoos that represented them. When he looked up, his eyes met Klaren's, and he was struck by just how much the woman looked like Nor.

Beautiful golden eyes and dark hair, but missing that half-secretive smile, likely buried beneath a lifetime's worth of guilt. Dex couldn't blame her. She'd fallen in love with the galaxy that she was once supposed to steal for her own people, and now she was paying the price for it.

Andi stepped up to the fire, her boots close to being licked by the flames.

"The Godstars gift us our power," Klaren explained. "I may not be near them, not in the way I once was, back in Exonia. But I still worship them, and strive to uphold their ways."

She muttered something else, running her hands across the drawings on the floor before setting down her piece of black rock. "You've had time to consider my offer, General."

To Andi's credit, she didn't flinch at the mention of her new title. She simply stared down at Klaren with all the predatory focus of a lioness, about to consume her prey.

Or perhaps play with it before dealing the killing blow.

Havoc had done the same to him, just this morning.

"I have," Andi said. "And yet you still haven't told me what exactly it is that you require from me."

"I require nothing from you but your cooperation," Klaren said. "But the plan I have is not one you are likely to come back from."

Andi barked out a laugh. "I've come back from plenty of impossible plans."

"As I've heard," Klaren acknowledged with a nod.

"Tell me about the weapons network, and what my part in shutting it down would be."

Klaren considered this. "You'd have to manually gain control of the weapons system, using your own DNA. That was what Cyprian used to assign you as his successor in the system, was it not?"

Dex nodded. "I watched the process. He needed Andi's handprint, too, but it wasn't just that. I think he took a scan of her internal DNA."

Klaren continued. "The system will know her by that signature, and will respond accordingly. There is a hub on each capital planet that controls it. My team believes the one on Arcardius is in the general's old estate."

"He kept everything in his office," Andi said. "His alcohol, and his war plans."

Dex didn't like the sound of this.

Not one Godstars-damned bit.

"In that case, you would have to go in and shut it all down. Destroy it from the inside. There is a self-destruct mode for all the planetary weapons, but it must be triggered manually and in person."

"Of course it must," Dex said with a sigh. He glared at Klaren. "There's no other way?"

"I didn't create the system," Klaren said apologetically. "I can't change how it operates."

"Then we'll leave now," Andi said decisively. "We can't afford to let this go on. We'll shut it down, and stop Nor from being able to open the Void."

Klaren shook her head. "If you wish to help me, if you wish to free your old crew and save Mirabel…then you must be patient. You must remain here, until we're able to turn the tide of this war. Until we have more intel, and more of an idea of *how* to—"

Her words trailed off as footsteps pounded down the hallway.

Dex turned in time to see Soyina burst through the door, a male soldier at her side. Soleran, by the look of him, as if his very skin were made of diamonds.

"You need to see this," Soyina said, marching toward Klaren, all her usual bravado gone, replaced by a soldier's hard expression. The Soleran man followed behind, a holoscreen in his hands. "Show them. Quickly!"

He set it down beside the fire, tapping it with a crystalline fingertip so that a holo of the feeds appeared before them, blocking out some of the flames.

Andi sucked in a breath, and Dex's eyes widened, shock coursing through him as he took in the scene.

Nor stood in General Cortas's old office. Dex had been there once before, when Cyprian broke the news that he would be withholding Dex's payment for intercepting Andi and her crew, until they all attended the Ucatoria Ball as guards.

He'd never gotten those damned Krevs.

With Nor were three figures that Dex had come to know very well.

"This message is for Androma Racella," Nor said.

She looked so very real, that hideously wicked smile on her lips as Lira, Breck and Gilly knelt before her. They looked right into the camera, staring straight into Andi's eyes.

"They're alive," Andi whispered beside Dex. She fell to her knees, kneeling before the girls, as if they were truly here with her in Klaren's office. She reached out a hand, as if she could reach through the holo and touch them.

"It has come to my attention that you believe you are the true General of Arcardius," Nor announced, glaring into the camera as she stood with her chin high and spoke her demands. "That you believe I am not the rightful ruler of Mirabel. My patience now grows thin, since you did not respond to my initial message."

"What message?" Andi growled, looking up at Klaren and Soyina. "What is she talking about?"

"There was a demand," Soyina said quietly. "Just before the attack. For you to journey to Arcardius and give yourself up, in exchange for your crew."

"And you didn't think to share that with me?" Andi cried.

Before they could respond, Nor continued, her image flickering for a moment. "My people are searching for you, Androma. They will find you, and bring you to me, dead or alive. You cannot run, and you cannot hide."

"She lies." Klaren spoke up from her droid. "She knows the truth about the weapons network. She will want you alive."

Dex couldn't look away from Andi, as she kept her gaze frozen on her crew.

"But I will allow you three more days to deliver yourself to my estate. If you do not arrive…" Nor held out her hands, gesturing to the girls kneeling in front of her. "Then your crew will not survive."

A shadowy man, robed in black, appeared on the edge of the image. He placed a golden blade in Nor's hands.

"What is he doing?" Andi whispered.

It was torture for her, Dex knew, to sit here and watch her crew, unable to help them.

The three of them remained motionless before Nor. Mere statues as she spoke above them. They didn't move even as she began to circle them, that blade held in her hand.

Gilly, so small, her red hair still braided, as if she hadn't changed one bit. Beside her, Lira and Breck were dressed in the uniforms of Xen Ptera. Otherwise, they looked the same, Lira like a regal bird, Breck a warrior who could tear down any enemy without so much as breaking a sweat.

And all three of them watched Nor, with that blade held out, as if they were staring at a godstar come down from the heavens.

"Who is your queen?" Nor asked the girls.

"You are," they said in unison.

Andi pressed a hand to her mouth, covering her gasp. "No," she said. "They would never bow to her."

"The compulsion is strong," Klaren explained.

Dex's heart thumped against his ribs. A coldness moved through him as he stared at the blade in Nor's hand.

"This is your first warning, Androma," Nor said, turning to look at the camera again, rouged lips curved in a feral smile. "Come unarmed to my estate, in three days' time, or another will fall."

"Another?" Dex asked, confused.

It happened so quickly.

Nor lifted the blade, turning her back to the camera as she swung toward the girl kneeling on the right.

Lira.

"NO!" Andi shouted.

Dex had only a moment to see Lira fall, her body crumpling to the floor of the office before the holo shut off.

Then only the flames remained, flickering happily as Andi screamed.

CHAPTER 27
ANDI

The slash of that blade…

The sound of Lira's body hitting the floor…

Andi stood, turning to face Klaren as her entire body shook with rage.

Lira.

Her friend's face peered up at her from her mind. Lira, so loyal and strong and brave. Lira, who always put the crew before herself. Lira, who had dared to run from a crown so she could instead follow her dreams.

"Andi," Dex breathed from behind her. But she didn't want to listen to the pain in his voice, the pity as he tried to comfort her. She barely felt him as he placed his hands upon her arms, his own body shaking, too.

For what they had just seen…

"It wasn't real," Andi said. She refused to believe it.

Still, for now, she was no longer Andi. She was the Bloody Baroness again, her body like a taut coil ready to spring. It was the only way to escape the pain, the fear, the desire to crumple into a pile of tears right here and now in this office. So she shoved the feelings down deep, replacing them with the only emotion that had never let her down.

Rage.

"We leave now," Andi announced.

Silence filled the room.

"Come again?" Klaren asked.

"We leave *now* for Arcardius," Andi snapped. "You wanted my cooperation. You wanted a general. Now you have both. Get me a damned ship and a crew."

"You can't just go right now!" Klaren protested, her droid's eyes flashing with each word. "You'll walk right into what is clearly a trap."

"My pilot, Lira," Andi started. "My *friend* was just…" Her words fell away as Dex squeezed her arms. She took a deep breath, shoving that pain back down as it tried to bubble back up in the form of tears.

The Bloody Baroness did not cry.

"I don't care if it's a trap," Andi said decisively. "You want the General of Arcardius, well, I'm the damned general. I'm going to Arcardius, I'm shutting down that weapons system and I'll shove a blade through Nor's throat in the process."

"I can't allow that," Klaren said. "Not like this."

"You have no ownership over me, Arachnid," Andi hissed. "A ship. *Now.*"

"In time, yes. But now that we know for certain Nor is aware of your general status, we must be smart. We must take some time to make a move, consider all of our options—"

"I don't have any time to waste!" Andi yelled. In her mind,

she saw Lira falling. She saw Breck and Gilly, gazing up at Nor as if they truly loved her, as if she were their one true queen.

In one motion, Andi drew her blades, swinging them until the electricity crackled on and they hovered mere inches from Klaren's throat. "I am leaving. *Now*. Whether you like it or not."

"Enough," Dex said.

His hands had left her arms, and now he was suddenly standing before Andi. Suddenly those blades were pointed not at Klaren, but at *him*. Directly above his throat.

"Move," Andi snarled.

Dex shook his head, his eyes wide and pleading. "Andi, please. I want her dead, too. I want Nor's head on a spike for what she just did…"

"It wasn't real," Andi said through gritted teeth.

"I don't want it to be real, either," Dex said, those blades still hovering over his throat. "I want to make her pay. I want the girls to be free. I want… I want all of this to have never happened, Andi. But it did. It *is* happening. And you have the power to stop it. But not like this. You go there, you rush to Arcardius, and Nor will be waiting. She'll trap you, use you to control the weapons system and all will be lost."

Every muscle in Andi's body was screaming.

She wanted to swing those blades.

She wanted Nor before her, kneeling as she made the queen's head roll.

"We'll get our revenge," Dex assured her. He looked to Klaren, who had stepped aside now and was watching them with widened eyes. True fear was written on her face. "But we can't go like this. You've never gone into a mission without a plan. Without a crew."

"I have a crew," Andi growled. "They're next to face Nor's blade if I don't go."

"And you will go," Dex said. "But—"

"But not without a ship," Klaren cut in. "I am sorry for your loss, General. Deeply sorry. But such are the ways of this war. And if we wish to win it, then I cannot allow you to embark on a mission that will surely end in the loss of our only true weapon against Nor and Valen. You will not take a ship. You will not take a crew. I will do whatever it takes to stop you, and I can promise you, General…you *will* fail if you try."

Soyina cleared her throat. "Perhaps we should give the general some time to consider, Arachnid. Perhaps we should reconvene in an hour or two, in light of recent events?"

"Reconvene?" Andi snapped back. "Why reconvene when you've already made up your minds not to let me go?"

"We will not hand you over in order to save two, when you could save the *many*," Klaren said. "So for now, you will remain here, beneath my care and protection."

"I am not yours to protect," Andi said.

"You are within my Underground, and therefore, you will abide by my rules."

"Rules?" Andi barked out another laugh. "You can't keep me here."

"You are one woman. I have hundreds who will stand in your way. I don't care how deadly or desperate you are, General. No one is leaving this place today."

Andi looked to Dex. "You're with them on this?"

He held out his hands, looking hopeless. "No, Andi. I'm with *you*, and that means keeping you from walking right into what is clearly your own death. And for what? You show up there, Andi, you hand yourself over, and they *still* win. Your crew will still be prisoners to the compulsion. They won't be free. Not truly. They'll use you to blast off those weapons and…" His eyes had actual tears in them now. "Godstars, Androma, I'm *begging* you right now… Please, just wait. There has to be another way."

Seeing Dex's anguish, Andi's anger slowly began to dissipate. Now all that was left was sorrow.

For she knew that they were right. She knew, yet again, that she was powerless to save her crew.

Andi turned off her swords, the electricity fizzling out. Dex let out a deep sigh as she placed them back into their sheaths.

"Thank you," he said. "Now—"

But Andi turned away.

She could listen no longer, when the image of Lira's body still haunted her, the cracked mask of the Baroness not enough to hold it at bay.

She found herself walking away from the group. Ignoring them calling after her as she stepped, one foot in front of the other, into the darkness.

For now, it seemed, the darkness was her greatest friend.

CHAPTER 28
NOR

"Well done, my soldier," Nor said.

She smiled at the Adhiran girl lying on the ground, arms splayed on either side of her body like a fallen bird.

Beside her, the other two members of Androma's crew stood, grins on their faces as they watched Nor.

"She'll come for us now," Gilly said, glancing down. "Lira was always her favorite."

"And when she does come, she won't be alone," Breck responded. She looked at Lira's body, too, as if she were contemplating an interesting portrait.

For a moment, Nor was almost convinced that the Adhiran truly *was* dead.

But then she rose, just as she had in that ballroom during

Ucatoria, a smirk on her face as she looked at her queen. "Was it convincing?"

"Very," Gilly answered. "Andi's probably losing her shit."

"Language," Breck hissed. She lowered her voice, eyes widening. "We're in front of the *queen*."

"It's alright," Nor said.

It struck her then, as she watched the crew, that they truly were a sisterhood. All of them, like extensions of the others. Nor had never had any female friends before—someone to lean on, someone to share the world with.

She'd had far better with Zahn.

Anger swept through her, followed by a surge of grief, and she found that she could not look upon this crew—this *family*—any longer.

It would be such a shame when she actually had to kill one of them to prove a point to Androma. For if she didn't come, the blade wouldn't be dull.

It would be sharp enough to sever one of their heads.

"You've earned your rest for the day," Darai said to the crew, standing from his place in the corner of the room. He took the false blade from Nor, placing it into his robes before looking back to the girls. "Head to the barracks. Tell no one of our plan. We'll summon you if we have need of you again."

The girls bowed to Nor before they left, all three of them looking as if they could take flight from the joy of serving their queen.

Nor hated their happiness.

The room was silent for only a moment after they left. Then Darai turned, hands clasped together as he looked at Nor. "Have you given any thought to my proposition, Majesty?"

Nor took a seat, her body weary. But she found that every inch of her itched with the need to move. To do *something*, for the longer she sat, the more the pain of losing Zahn haunted her.

"I don't know, Darai," she said. "I haven't considered all of my options."

That's a lie, her mind whispered. For she'd thought of nothing but the plan since Darai had planted the seed in her brain, needing it to ease her mourning.

What would the Godstars wish? What would her mother have done?

"You must choose soon," Darai reminded her. "The clock is going to continue running down, and when it does, your brother *will* fall. You alone have the power to choose whether he falls in vain, or falls as a sacrifice to the salvation of Exonia."

The door burst open, and Nor glanced up. A sickening sense of guilt rushed through her as Valen entered.

She didn't know what she'd expected to feel at the sight of her brother. Fury, perhaps, over what he'd done. Hatred, even, some sort of wound that couldn't ever be healed.

But instead, she was struck with grief as he entered the room. Each of his steps, burdened.

Each breath, labored, as if he'd just completed a race. But Nor knew he hadn't. He'd declined even further since she'd last seen him yesterday. His fine clothes hung from his frame as if they were rags, and bruise-like shadows darkened the skin beneath his eyes. Darai met her gaze from across the room, nodding almost imperceptibly as he watched her take in the sight of her brother.

Valen was dying.

But how much time did he have left?

Nor cleared her throat, looking past Valen's shoulder, as if she didn't care that he was here. As if the sight of him didn't bruise her heart or make her feel a thousand conflicting emotions at once. "What are you doing here, Valen?"

"I came to try to fix things," Valen said. He looked over at Darai, who stood with his arms crossed, a frown on his face. "Can we speak? Alone?"

Nor was about to agree, but Darai held up a hand. "I think it would be unwise to allow the two of you to be alone together. In light of…recent events."

Nor didn't argue. She didn't have the energy to.

"I'm so sorry, Nor," Valen said in a rush. "I've been in my mind all night, trying to find Androma. Trying to do something, *anything*, to please you. Do you truly think I meant harm to come to Zahn? Do you honestly believe, after everything we've been through together, after everything we've done to get to this point, that I would try to hurt you in such a way?"

There were actual tears running down his shallow cheeks, sliding across the protruding bones. "I love you, Nor. You're the only family I have left. The only family I've ever needed. And it kills me inside…" He took a deep, shuddering breath. "It kills me, to know that I had a part in taking Zahn from you."

Nor couldn't speak. Because the anger was gone, replaced by an onslaught of emotions she didn't want to face.

"I want you to know something, though," Valen said, taking her silence as a chance to fill the awkward space with more words. "I wouldn't take it back. Not for one second. It kills me, what happened to Zahn, and I will forever carry the burden of it. And someday, the Godstars will punish me for what I did, but it would be far, far worse if that bullet had found its way to you. So I will bear the pain. Because you were Zahn's queen, and you are my queen, and Mirabel and Exonia would be *nothing* without you."

Tears were in Nor's eyes now, too.

"Valen…" she started. "I…"

She wanted to forgive him. She wanted to tell him it was okay, that everything between them could be healed. But then Darai moved behind Valen, pacing across the room. He met her gaze, his eyes hardening. He shook his head, almost imperceptibly.

Nor thought about his plan again. This time, however, she was disgusted by it. If Darai was certain Valen was to die, then she would do whatever it took to stop it. Or at least delay it, for as long as she could.

"Will you forgive me?" Valen asked. "I'm begging you, Nor. Forgive me, and turn your focus back to the mission. We started this together. I'd like to end it together, too."

She wanted to. Godstars, she truly did.

And she was about to tell him, when Valen coughed.

He lifted a hand to his mouth, to cover it.

But Nor saw the blood that trickled down his chin.

"Valen, you're—"

Her brother doubled over, coughing so hard he couldn't breathe. Nor rushed over to him, realizing with horror that there was a puddle of blood on the ground, pooling from his lips.

"Medics!" Nor shouted as he collapsed to the floor. "Darai, get help!"

The adviser rushed from the room, and Nor knelt before Valen, her hands on either side of his face. "Breathe, Valen." She willed her compulsion into him, but his eyes were wild as he retched and gasped for air. "Breathe!"

A medical droid and one of the estate's doctors, a Tenebran woman whose body was modded to look like metal, entered. "Move aside, Majesty," she said sternly, though not with any lack of respect.

Her med droid, with its clawlike arms wired for strength, lifted Valen's body onto the floating stretcher. His coughing had slowed, but he still gasped for air, his chest rattling as if it were full of fluid.

"Nor," he gasped.

His eyes met hers, wild as a cornered animal.

But she had no words to soothe him as the doctor ordered him from the room, already hooking machines up to his chest and waving a diagnostic wand across his middle, a holo floating above to show her the problems it discovered within his dying body. The droid directed the floating stretcher from the office, and Valen was gone.

The silence that followed was almost painful.

Nor felt as if she'd just seen Zahn dying all over again. The memory of his face…it morphed into Valen, and she saw the two of them, side by side in a grave.

A hand touched Nor's elbow.

She flinched, thrown back into the present, where she realized she was still kneeling on her office floor, her breathing haggard as she tried to hold herself together.

"I know it pains you to see him this way, even with what he has done," Darai said to her, as he held out a hand. "But the boy must be used to power Nexus, before it is too late."

"I can't," Nor choked out. "I can't lose them both."

She wanted to hate Valen, because hating him would mean not having to deal with the loss of him once he was gone.

But she couldn't. He was her *brother*, and he'd saved her, just as he'd said. And he would save her again, even if it killed him inside. Even if it killed a piece of her heart.

Because he always put their mission first, as she'd made him swear to. He'd done what the most loyal servant would do. He'd allowed Zahn to die…so that she could live.

"You must let go of your love and focus on our goal," Darai insisted. As he looked into her eyes, Nor found that she could not pull herself from his gaze. Those Exonian eyes were golden, as golden as the sun, and she'd looked into them since she was a child. She'd trusted them. She'd never been betrayed or let down by them.

"The answer is obvious," he continued. "Your brother's body is failing him, but his mind is still strong. His mind is desperate to escape that failing body, to be given a chance to truly stretch and reach the height of its abilities. We can give him that. And we *must*, before it's too late."

Nor's heart felt broken in two.

And her head…her head felt all wrong, as if she were staring through a layer of fog and into darkness.

"He's dying," she said. "Truly dying?"

Darai nodded. "Time is running out. The satellite is nearly complete. And when it is, we must plug Valen into it. We must allow him to follow his fate."

"But maybe Aclisia…" Nor trailed off. "If she had just a few more days…she could perhaps find a way to…"

"No," Darai said. "You're not listening, my dear. There is no time. You know what must be done, Nor. You just don't want to admit it to yourself, because you fear it."

"I'm not afraid," Nor said.

But she was. She *was*.

Darai gazed at her, so insistent as he helped her stand. "He is too weak. He is already almost gone. A true queen would see that, Nor. She would also see that in his weakness, he is perhaps even more useful than he ever has been. You must decide. You must give me the order, before death comes to steal him away. Before Exonia falters, because of your fear to use him."

She almost said it.

She almost gave the order.

But something inside of her screamed *not yet*.

Nor pulled her hand from Darai's grasp, glancing away from his gaze. "You overstep, Uncle."

He frowned, his jaw working as he likely sought the right words. "I am only doing my duty, my queen."

"You will give me time," Nor said. "That is your order."

Then she left the room, her cloak trailing behind her as she headed toward the medical wing of the estate. She would not decide what to do with Valen.

Not yet.

And certainly not today.

CHAPTER 29
VALEN

He was back in Lunamere again, lying facedown on the cold obsidinite while the guards slashed their light-whips over his back.

He smelled the singeing of his own flesh, the metallic tang of his blood.

He heard his own muffled cry, the crackling of the whip over and over again.

"Please," Valen begged. "Make it stop."

The crackling turned to a soft beeping. Valen opened his eyes to find a world not doused in darkness, but drenched in light, the white walls and ceiling of Averia's medical wing all around him.

And Nor, fast asleep in a chair at the edge of his bed.

In the few years that Valen had known Nor, *truly* known her, he had never seen her as she was now, utterly unguarded as she slept. His half sister was a private woman, stubborn enough to force back her tears until she could hide herself away. Her happiness manifested mostly in small smiles when they were together. Sometimes, she laughed in triumph. When Valen had finally allowed her inside of his mind, she'd grinned like she'd just captured a planet in her outstretched hands. Above all, Nor displayed her fury, her determination and her pride, like a set of badges proudly pinned to her chest.

But never...*never* had Valen seen her so exhausted. So empty.

"Nor," Valen said hoarsely, as he tried to lift himself up on his pillows. His arms were weak, but he managed.

Her eyes fluttered open, panicked at first as she gasped, reaching for the sparkling necklace at her throat, then calming as she looked around and reality seemed to settle in.

A pang of guilt hit Valen. Zahn had given her that necklace.

"You slept," Valen said. "Good. You needed the rest."

They felt like the only words he could say. Stupid, empty words. But he'd spilled his heart already in her office. Before... He tried to remember what had happened then.

He grimaced as it all came flooding back. He'd nearly coughed up his own lungs, feeling like he was drowning in his own blood. He'd seen Nor's face hovering over his, and then darkness. The kind he thought he might never come back from.

The beeping Valen had heard earlier still played in the background, emanating from monitors checking his vitals. The med droid that had carried him stood motionless in the corner of the room, likely ready to spring into action should Valen need any care.

"You slept, too," Nor said. No crown, no extravagant gown. Her eyes were rimmed in red, and she looked at him like Valen imagined anyone would look at a dying person. Like every glance might be their last.

But he wasn't dying. Valen was *strong*. Darai had always told him that, and Nor had, too. He was simply pushing himself too hard, too far. But was there any other choice?

No, Valen thought. There wasn't, not when the satellite was nearly done, and Androma was likely well on her way to Arcardius to hand over her access to the weapons network.

"How do you feel?" Nor asked.

"Like I nearly died back there," Valen said with a shrug. He was still weak, and his breathing was labored, but he actually felt better than he had in days.

"The medical staff has assured me you're being well taken care of," Nor said, looking around the room. At the monitors behind him, at the white walls, at the pillowcase as she ran her fingertips across a loose thread. Valen realized she was looking at anything *but* him.

"Nor," he said. "What I told you before, in your office—"

"I know," she said. "I want to forgive you, Valen. And to be honest, I didn't think I would ever be able to. I'm still not sure that I can. You saved me, but you stole him away from me."

"But I didn't," Valen said. "I didn't shoot that gun, Nor."

She closed her eyes. "I know." A deep sigh, as she opened them again. "After you collapsed in my office, I realized something. I want to forgive you, Valen."

"So forgive me," he pleaded. "Let's go back to what we once had. Let's focus on our mission. Together."

Nor held up a hand. "I *want* to. I'm not there yet, but I'm telling you that the desire to at least exists. It will take time. And... and difficult choices."

Valen raised a brow. "I've always been loyal to you, Nor," he said. "Since day one, I was yours to command."

The work he'd done to get the people to worship his sister went deep. And his own heart... It was tethered to her, just as his mind was.

He was nothing without Nor. His first family was dead, and his second now treated him like he was made of glass, something that needed to be protected. But later, when their plan came to fruition, and Exonia was opened wide?

He'd have a third family. Perhaps the one he'd always belonged to without knowing.

Nor shifted her weight beside him, and Valen realized he'd been lost in his thoughts again.

"I feel like I want to keep going, but I'm not sure that I can," Valen admitted. "I made one mistake, Nor, one mistake that was really only *half* a mistake, because it ended up saving you… and yet you're ready to throw me away. Cast me out. And what's terrible is that part of me thinks that you should."

"No," Nor said, looking up at him, eyes reddening. "That's not what I want. You're a vital part of this mission, Valen. So vital it isn't even an option to go on without you."

She trailed off, her lips quivering as she held back tears. Valen knew he wasn't the main cause of them, and yet the fact that he'd had some hand in them nearly tore him apart.

Family wasn't supposed to destroy. Family was supposed to build, to support, *always*.

"I'm not good enough for you or Exonia," Valen said quietly.

Nor shook her head vehemently. "You are. You have no idea just how good you are."

But then she looked away again, refusing to meet his gaze. As if just watching him pained her inside.

"How do we go on?" Valen asked. "How do we move past this?"

She wiped a hand across her eyes as the tears finally fell. "We make a choice," Nor said.

"A choice?" Valen asked.

Nor nodded. "We choose to go on, even when it hurts us. Even when it may tear us apart." She reached out and took his hand, squeezing it once before Valen felt her enter his mind.

"Get some rest, little brother," she said through their mental doorway. Valen was shocked to feel it open again, to feel that

connection between them. It wasn't forgiveness—not fully, not yet. He could still see her battling within herself, still feel the tension coming off her.

But he would take this small step forward today, and wait for another one tomorrow.

Nor helped him lean back, adjusting his pillows before she turned to leave. She gazed at him, eyes heavy with sadness, as she stopped at the door. "The mission is what matters," she said firmly. "And we'll do it together, every step of the way."

Then she left him alone with his thoughts.

Exhaustion called to Valen, and he wanted, desperately, to sleep. Now was as good a time as any. But before he could float away to his dreams, the door to his room opened again, and Darai stepped inside, clad in heavy gray robes.

Valen frowned at the sight of the old adviser.

"I've been instructed to rest," he said, "by the queen herself. You can come back later."

Darai ignored him as he usually did, taking the chair Nor was in moments ago. "You look terrible," he said.

Valen huffed out a laugh. "I could say the same about you."

"I believe you have, many times before."

"That's because it's true," Valen snapped.

Darai's eyes looked about the room, taking in the machines as if he were disgusted by them. He crossed his arms, leaning back comfortably in the chair as he focused his gaze again on Valen. "Your power is killing you, boy."

Valen felt like he'd just been punched in the face.

He opened his mouth to speak, but no words came out.

"I always knew you were too strong for your own good. From the moment I met you, I sensed it. Such raw strength, such an ability…it cannot be contained for long inside a Mira-bellian body. It was meant for a full Exonian. Someone like your mother, who failed to realize that the mission must come before all other things. Even family. Even love." Darai smiled cruelly.

"Those are the things that make us weak. Klaren's power, the power you inherited? It was wasted on her, and we cannot allow it to be wasted on you."

Darai and Valen had no lost love between them. The two had always spoken boldly to one another, Valen usually with more acid in his words than Darai. But this? This was an entirely new level of boldness, one that Valen knew the adviser wouldn't show if Nor were here.

"My sister wouldn't stand for you speaking to me in such a way," Valen said.

He wanted so badly to rise from his bed and leave the room. But he was too weak. His limbs, despite having rested, still felt like they were full of lead. And each breath still came with effort, as if a weight was sitting upon his lungs.

Darai shook his head. "Your sister is doing the one thing I warned her never to do. She put her love for Zahn in front of her focus on the mission. She's lost track of it now."

"She's mourning," Valen said defensively. "Zahn was half of her heart."

Darai nodded, worrying his hands together, the strange scars on his skin catching Valen's eye. Whatever he'd been through in his earlier years in Exonia...the man must have survived a unique version of hell to have gotten those. And the ones on his face were far deeper.

"What are you even here for?" Valen asked. "Did you just come to advise me about my own failures? If so, I'm not interested."

Darai shook his head, leaning forward in his chair. "Quite the opposite. I came here to tell you the truth. To open your eyes to the reality of what's to come, Valen." His eyes took on a strange gleam. "I've waited in this galaxy for far too many years. Your mother failed to free Exonia, and your sister has nearly failed me, too, falling prey to love. She loved Xen Ptera too much. She loved Zahn too much. And now she loves *you* too much. I warned her not to form a bond with you, that you would be, in many ways, greater than she ever could be, and such greatness cannot be contained. That's why, thanks to your part bringing about Zahn's death, the love Nor once had for you is gone. Fractured beyond repair."

Valen felt like he was spinning, listening to the old man's words.

"Nor is going to forgive me," he stammered. "She just told me so."

"She came here to ease her own conscience," Darai scoffed. "Because she has been given a choice to make, in order to save the mission."

Valen remembered Nor's words from earlier, about difficult choices. "What choice?"

Darai smiled smugly at him. "Your sister is going to betray you, Valen."

"What?" Valen blurted out. The very idea of it was utterly ridiculous, and something Nor would never do.

But Darai continued, his expression eager as he leaned forward, reaching out to grip Valen's arm. "Yes, princeling. Your body is dying, an unfortunate side effect of such a display of power, such a stretching of your compulsion across the galaxy. Of course, I knew that would happen all along," he said dismissively, while Valen stared at him in horror. "No one can live forever, stretched in such a way. So, thanks to my plan, Nor is going to take your mind and wire it into Nexus before you die. Your body will falter, held in endless limbo by the satellite's life-support system. But your mind, and your power...that will remain forever. Cast out across the galaxy, so that we can rule until the end of the end."

Terrifying words.

And ones that Valen refused to believe, as shock raced through him, holding him in place.

"Guards," he called out. "Guards!"

But his voice was too weak. And before Valen could reach for the panel beside his bed, to request a nurse, something seized him. His body froze, as if it was no longer beneath his control.

He cried out as a jolt of pain shot through him. A pain that Valen vaguely remembered feeling once before, the very first time Nor had entered his mind.

"What...what are you doing?" Valen asked frantically.

Because it was *Darai* touching his mind now. Darai, a man who had no power, a man who had simply hovered in the shadows all along.

"It has been far too long," Darai whispered. Then he closed his eyes, and suddenly Valen's eyes closed, too.

He tried to open them, but he felt like a hand was clasped over them. A mental hand was in his mind, too, squeezing, gripping tight, pulling all control from Valen. He groaned as the pain worked its way through his skull, like a parasite digging deep, inch by inch.

"Powerful, yes," Darai said, his voice speaking into Valen's mind. *"But you are no match for a true Yielded of Exonia."*

Valen screamed as he felt himself ripped away from his own body. As he entered the familiar domain of his own mind, his fortress in the distance. Something carried him across the sky, over the valley of the dead, the cold wind slapping him across the face as he soared toward the castle.

He was thrown inside, into one of the turrets, where his head cracked against the black obsidinite stones.

Pain lanced through his skull, and the last thing Valen saw, before the darkness swallowed him whole, was Darai.

Standing over him, watching with those otherworldly Exonian eyes.

CHAPTER 30
ANDI

Andi wasn't sure where she was going.

She simply needed to move, to get away from that room, that crackling fire where she'd watched Lira die.

Not dead, Andi told herself. She refused to believe it.

And yet with each step she took, winding her way through the undercity, the truth began to sink in more and more.

Lon was gone, having sacrificed himself so Andi could get to Lira and set her free. So that she could rescue the girls, and together, they could all *live*.

But if Lira was gone, too, then Andi had failed him. Lon had died in vain, and Lira, her beautiful Adhiran pilot, so full of talent and passion and loyalty and dreams…

Lira was gone.

Tears filled Andi's vision as she walked, blurring her path.

She let them fall, lifting her hand to her ear to touch the place where her com still remained.

If only she could reach the girls, she might be able to discover if Lira was truly gone. She might find them all together, alive and well and free.

But she knew that was another lie, another impossible dream. She'd seen them bowing to Nor, looking as if they praised her with every breath. It wasn't really *them* on that holo, Andi knew.

But would they ever be themselves again?

Andi walked faster, desperate to find someplace to be alone in her misery.

She had no ship. No crew.

And Dex had chosen Klaren's side, stopping Andi from accepting Nor's offer. She'd give herself over in a heartbeat if it meant that Breck and Gilly, who still lived, could walk free.

As she walked, Andi passed by a set of siblings, a brother and a sister, forging armor by a crackling fire, their dark ringlet curls glimmering in the firelight as they hammered the bulletproof armor to their own cadence.

"I dare the queen's silver bullets to get through this," the girl said, using heavily gloved hands to dip the armor into a bucket of fresh Soleran water.

"I'd like to see her try," the boy challenged, pounding his own set of armor with a wicked grin.

Looking at them reminded Andi of Lon and Lira, and it shattered her heart.

Lira would have loved the sounds, the smells, the feel of this entire place.

Here, beneath the surface of the world, every man, woman and child, no matter their age, no matter where they hailed from, had come together as one. They'd created an army of the galaxy's outcasts, of those who had nowhere else to turn.

Unity wasn't easy to come by in Mirabel. People were always fighting on different sides. They had their own beliefs, often warring against each other's. Even Nor, who had united the galaxy, had only done so by force. By using a wicked sort of magic to compel people to get along, to be united in the cause of worshipping her.

But here?

Here, the ways of the old world had been stripped away. Gone were the differences in class and race and religion. Everyone had joined together because they believed in a world where they would have a choice in how to live their lives.

Free will was a cause far more powerful than any other.

"Last call for the Lights!" someone shouted.

Andi walked on autopilot, following in the direction of where everyone else seemed to be heading. A small group had formed at the edge of the main cavern, passing a few at a time into a small tunnel she'd never noticed before.

Andi was about to enter herself when a hand caught hers. She spun, a flash of heat driving through her, but it was only Dex.

"What do you want, Dextro?" Andi asked.

His lips parted as he looked into her teary eyes. "You shouldn't be alone. No one should, after…after that."

"Just say it, Dex," Andi said. "Lira is dead."

He blinked back at her, unable to find the right words.

Andi turned, and Dex followed.

The tunnel eventually spit them out into a space large enough for a decent crowd. Others had gathered with blankets and mugs, nestled in quiet corners around the dark space. They all faced a massive wall of thick ice that stood like a barrier to another world, aglow with a cool, oceanic blue light.

Andi chose an empty spot by the back of the cavern. Dex sat down first, leaning in his casual way against the rock wall, and Andi settled beside him, close enough that she could feel the heat of his body.

She hated him for not choosing her side.

Hated him more for being right.

But his presence was an unexpected comfort nonetheless.

"I never thought it would come to this," Andi whispered.

"I know," Dex said, squeezing her hand. "I'm so sorry, Andi."

For a time, they simply sat, watching the others enter the space and choose their respective seats on the ground. Conversations were muted, soft enough that Andi began to wonder if this was a sacred place.

"Why are you so willing to walk into danger?" Dex asked suddenly.

Andi leaned her head back against the rocky wall. Dex offered her his shoulder instead. She hated the thought of leaning against him, of being like any other couple, when they were so clearly *not*. But as she shifted closer to him, accepting his comfort, she knew that Dex was simply another part of her story. He'd stuck with her through battles and blades, and they both had the scars to show for it.

So why wouldn't he choose her side now?

"You know, I never wanted to be a space pirate," Andi said. She could feel Dex's soft breathing as his shoulder rose and fell beneath her. "I just never wanted to be someone else's lackey. Running around the galaxy, doing their bidding. So I did it, originally, to survive. But it wasn't until I met the girls that I fell in love with taking care of them. Being their captain. And it didn't matter what I had to do to see them sleep soundly at night, to give them a home with me on the *Marauder*."

She glanced sideways at him, so close she could see the deep scar on his neck that she'd once given him.

"That hasn't changed, Dex. No matter where it leads me, no matter what I have to do… I'll protect my girls, at all costs. Even if it means losing my life in the process."

Dex closed his eyes suddenly, pinching them tight as if she'd just stabbed him in the chest all over again, as she'd done all those years ago. "Do you not care about *your* freedom, Androma? Do you not care about your own life?"

"Not without my crew," Andi answered at once.

"Don't you want to know what I think about all of this?" Dex asked, eyes flicking open to fall on hers.

No, she wanted to say. But the word failed her.

"I think," Dex said, not pulling away from her gaze, "that you love your crew so fiercely, and with such loyalty, that sometimes you forget about yourself."

"I…" Andi's words trailed away.

Because he was right again.

"You've been running from death for so long, but now you want to turn around and sprint right back toward it," he said angrily. "You have no idea what Nor is going to do to you when you land on Arcardius. She could kill you, Andi, or hell, with what she and Valen are capable of, I don't know what horrors she might unleash on you. After all that you've been through, and all that's been done to you in return, you finally have a chance to fade away from it all. To stay here. To be safe beneath Klaren's protection, until the time is right, and then she'll have an army of soldiers to keep you safe as she tries to pull the galaxy out from under Nor. Let her fight this battle. Not you. We could wait this all out, allow things to settle, live our lives the way we always hoped we could. You deserve to be free. You deserve to be at peace."

"What you're speaking of is a coward's plan," Andi growled. "I will *never* be at peace, Dextro. Not without them."

"Just imagine that future, for even a moment," Dex pleaded with her. "Walk away from this. Give yourself a chance at freedom."

"There is no freedom, for any of us. Not if what Klaren says is true, if the Solis siblings open that Void. If I can help…if I can be a part of stopping that—"

"Do you even care about the galaxy, or is this still all about the girls?" Dex demanded.

He glanced away, his jaw tight. She couldn't give him the answer he wanted, and she knew she was hurting him, but in this moment, she couldn't help it. She was tired of keeping secrets, tired of holding back words that desperately needed to be said.

When Dex looked back at her, his face was full of such sadness that Andi wanted to look away, but he reached up and cupped her face softly in his hands. "I always believed we had a future together, you and me. I always believed it would be us against the world."

For years, she'd longed to hear words like that from a man. And Dex had given them to her, time and again, since they had repaired their broken hearts back on Arcardius. Since they had forgiven each other's sins. But tonight, his words filled her with a sadness so deep she could scarcely breathe.

"You're asking me to choose," Andi said. There came that familiar burn in the back of her throat, that hideous wetness threatening to slip from the corners of her eyes. "Please don't make me choose. We could escape. We could go to Arcardius, together. You could help me, Dex. We could free the girls and get out of there as a crew."

"But their minds, Andi. They won't be *them*, even if we could get them out of there!"

"At least they'll be alive," she said.

"But is that truly living?"

He swallowed, looking like he, too, was going to cry. Dex did *not* cry. He shook his head slightly, hair falling into his eyes. "The galaxy's being threatened, and you're one of the only people who can help stop it. And I just know there's a way, Andi— there *has* to be a way to get around this. To free the girls *and* save Mirabel, without putting you in unnecessary danger."

"There's no time to find that way," Andi insisted. "You know it's true. They're going to die, Dex, just like Lira. She won't hesitate to kill them to get to me. And it will be my fault."

Dex shook his head. "How could any of this be your fault?"

"Nor killed her because of *me*," Andi sobbed. "I have to go. For Breck and Gilly. I have to, Dex. I can't lose them all."

"I know," he said. "But, Andi, I'm afraid you're going to die no matter which path you choose. And I'm afraid you're completely okay with that."

She didn't know what to say. So she backed away from him, settling against the cold cavern wall.

As she stared forward, a new silence seemed to fall over the crowd. And the wall of ice, still barely aglow, began to transform.

It was a slight change at first, like the time before the rising of the sun. The blue, once a gentle glow that spanned the entire surface of the wall, took on a deeper hue. As if something was coming closer.

Then a tendril of thick, fiery red light appeared on the other side of the ice, soaring from one side of the wall to the other, then darting away, fading as it went. Andi's breath caught in her throat as she watched, utterly transfixed by the sight. Another appeared, this time as yellow as the fields on Uulveca, bright as a burning sun.

"They're not lights," Dex marveled, pointing at the wall of ice as Andi watched, wide-eyed, the moving display. "They're massive needlefish. That ice wall is holding back an underground lake that's been here for centuries."

The fish danced, appearing like ribbons of light, flashing in colors so brilliant that it reminded Andi of the fish inside the Adhiran mountain of Rhymore, where she'd once fought and trained with her girls. It was in Rhymore where Andi had discovered how great a source of strength the girls were for her. But she was a source of strength for them, too. Each one of them, including her, creating a sort of glue that held everything together.

A family.

And somewhere along the way, Dex had come back into her life, into her heart. He'd carved out a space just big enough for him.

Could she love them all—her crew *and* Dex? Could she open herself up to the threat of pain that would come when she inevitably lost him, too?

People didn't stick around in Andi's life. So she'd gotten used to running.

The problem with Dex was that he was too damned stubborn to stop chasing after her. Even when she'd driven a knife into his chest and begged him to quit.

Andi looked up as a school of smaller, more brilliant needlefish arrived, their outlines like bursts of fireworks on display. The entire cavern flashed and lit up with their colors, and the crowd watched in reverence as they spun and danced in the water beyond.

"If you go to Arcardius, I'm going with you," Dex said suddenly, taking Andi's hand.

She turned to him, a question in her gray eyes. "I have no plan. I have no guarantee that I'll survive this. That *we'll* survive this."

His grip was warm and so familiar. "I know that. But I learned, ages ago, that when you put your mind to something, no one can tear you away from it. So if you're going...then I'm going, too. We'll free the girls, and then we'll find a way to shut down that weapons network from the inside. Just like Klaren said."

"I can't ask that of you," Andi said. "If you want to run, find somewhere safe..." But she knew there was nowhere safe. Not anymore.

His eyes were fierce and determined as he said, "*You* are my safety. Andi, we're two of the most unlovable people in this galaxy. And yet somehow we found each other."

She wanted to laugh at that, at the sincerity and pure *Dex*ness of that statement. But he kept going.

"I intend to see to it that you live through this mission. So that when all is said and done, after we burn that mind-robbing witch and her brother to the ground, I can finally give you the life I've always wanted to give you. The adventures I always promised you."

"I don't need you to give me anything," Andi said. "I can happily take it for myself."

"You're right," Dex said. "You don't. But I'd like to try anyway."

"Okay," Andi whispered. "How about we start with—"

He pulled her to him, pressing his lips against hers.

They hadn't touched, hadn't been close, in so long. But she found herself turning molten in his arms, found herself desperate for more of him as she wrapped her fingers in his hair and every part of her became a flame.

"I love you, Androma Racella," Dex whispered against her lips. "I love you, and there's not a damn thing you can do to change my mind."

It was painful to say it. Terrifying. But Andi took the chance. For when tomorrow came, she wasn't sure what would be left of her.

"I love you, too, Dextro Arez."

They'd seen the darkest, most shadowed places of each other's hearts. And yet here in this cavern, the world aglow around them as they kissed, all Andi felt was light.

CHAPTER 31
DEX

Dex felt great for a guy who might die tomorrow.

Knowing that Andi loved him meant that he would die happy. His whole body hummed knowing that, after so much time and through immense pain, he and Andi would always make their way back together. Not as the people they once were, but better.

He only wished he could take away the pain that he'd seen in Andi's eyes since the moment of Lira's execution. But pain like this needed to be felt, hard as it was to see it coursing through her. He could kill Nor for what she did, but he wouldn't. That was Andi's job.

"So what's the plan?" Dex whispered into her ear as they turned down an empty hallway.

She stopped at a door and waved him over. "Through here is an entrance to the ships," Andi whispered. "We'll slip through and hijack one of them. From there, we'll make things up as we go. I know Averia like the back of my hand. We'll find the girls and get out."

Dex wasn't a stickler for precise mission planning; he usually liked leaving room for improvisation. But right now, they didn't have any room to make mistakes. Sadly, they didn't have time to make a solid plan. It was now or never.

He reached out and grabbed her hand, smoothing his thumb over her calluses. "Okay. We'll make up the rest as we go."

Andi smiled, but it didn't reach her eyes. "Follow me."

"To hell and back," Dex agreed as Andi opened the door. She disappeared inside for a moment. He heard a muffled cry, then a *thump*, followed by the sound of groans. Andi stuck her head back out.

"All clear."

Dex slipped through the door and emerged in a cavernous room full of hundreds of crates, stepping past two unconscious bodies.

"Sorry, friends," Dex murmured to them.

The crates stretched across the dimly lit space, creating small walkways between stacks. The room looked like a warehouse where the Underground stored equipment for the ships. A few loose tubes dangled from one crate, while another was bursting with wires.

Andi was already a few paces ahead, scanning each aisle before moving on. Once clear, she gestured for him to follow.

It didn't take long to cross the room. The ceiling was much higher than the room was wide. A door met them on the other side, this one armed with a keypad.

"Got the code?" Dex asked, eyeing the numbers.

Andi quirked a pale brow. "I may be good, but I'm not *that* good."

She was right. When would she have had time to swipe access codes, since this whole plan had been configured in a blink of an eye?

"So what are we—" Dex stopped as Andi slipped a knife from her belt and slid the tip across the seam of the keypad. The front section popped off, revealing a mess of wiring, not unlike the crate he'd just passed.

She twiddled the colored strands between her fingers, following each wire to its source before picking the yellow one. She sliced it in half, and the door popped open.

Andi pumped her fist into the air as Dex whistled, impressed.

"We had similar keypads in Averia," she told him. "I used to do this all the time to get into places I wasn't allowed."

"Naughty," Dex teased.

Andi rolled her eyes. "Come on. We have to be quick."

This time, Dex went first. Inside was an entire hangar of ships ripe for the taking, spread out like a display before them. There were older models scattered in with the new, all of them painted with the Solis crest on their sides and beneath their wings. To the left, Dex's eye caught an old Ripper, a sleek white ship designed for the Solerans that he knew usually sounded, quite literally, like it was shredding the skies in which it soared. It had its bumps and bruises, and a wing that looked patched, but he'd never seen one before in person. Beside it was a newer model of a Scuttler, a ship that was razor-thin and lightweight, known for crumpling like a tin can if it was crashed, but marveled at for its capability to outsoar any ship even half its size.

Throughout the hangar, workers of all shapes and sizes marched around, droids and humans alike, busy as they hauled gear from ship to ship. Some of the ships were being torn apart entirely, reinforced with bits of metal from a massive pile at the end of the hangar. A graveyard of old ship parts, it seemed. Water dripped down from the top of the cavernous space, landing with a constant *plink, plink, plink* atop the ships.

"I miss my ship," Andi murmured from beside him. Dex

shuddered to think of what the *Marauder* looked like right now, out there, lifeless on the ice.

"You mean *my* ship," he joked, trying to lighten her mood, even by just a fraction. She had enough heartbreak to handle as it was—no need to add more atop the pile, just to have it topple when she needed to keep it together the most.

"Act like we're meant to be here," Dex said, switching back to the mission. Sometimes hiding in plain sight was the best disguise.

Andi gave him a nod, and together they strolled into the hangar. A couple of engineers in green jumpsuits passed, and Dex gave them a casual nod, which one returned.

"Which ship do we grab?" Dex asked under his breath once the engineers were out of earshot.

"I say we go for the Sneaker in the back corner," Andi suggested.

Dex followed her gaze and pinpointed a small ship across the way. To say it had seen better days was an understatement, and that was Dex being generous about its looks. The silver hull was marred with meteor dents and its nose had been scorched so badly, it was now charred a solid black.

But if it got them to Arcardius, he wasn't going to complain. Still, Dex let his gaze linger longingly on the Ripper once more before heading toward their chosen ship.

"Going somewhere?" a familiar, metallic voice said behind them. Dex and Andi both stopped in their tracks.

"Arachnid," Andi hissed.

Dex's heart leaped, and he rested his hand near his gun. "Act casual," he said quietly, but even while saying it, he knew the suggestion was futile. Nothing about this situation could be called casual.

Klaren came to stand in front of them, eyes hard. Dex sighed. Out of everyone who could've stopped them, it just had to be her.

"I'm not here to stop you," Klaren said, her hands held up defensively. "I'm here to go with you."

"Sure you are," Andi said, a mocking tone in her voice. "Because you seemed so willing to let me go when we spoke earlier."

"I've done a lot of thinking since you stormed out of my office," Klaren admitted. "We've tried to alter the outcome of all this by physical means, by pitting soldier against soldier. But if I know Nor and Darai, they won't be fazed by that—they'll just use our actions to inspire their followers even more."

"So what are you going to do?" Dex asked.

"I am going to try and reason with them," she said simply, as if they were merely discussing a fight between two toddlers.

Andi scoffed. "Like that will change their minds."

"I only need to change Nor's mind," Klaren insisted. "Darai has been influencing it for far too long, but I think I can convince her to listen to reason. In any case, they'll eventually figure out a way to access the nuclear arsenal, with or without you, Andi. You being out of their reach has just delayed the inevitable. And even if I ask you to stay, I know you'll still try to figure out a way to rescue your girls."

If there were any left to save.

"Fine," Andi agreed. "So what's the plan?"

"We get on that ship," Klaren said, pointing at a slick Tracker ship to their left, "and meet your crew."

Dex had loved ships all his life.

When he was younger, he'd never wanted anything but small models of the many ships in Tenebris's fleet—and later, from the unique fleets of planets beyond his own. He'd pored over books about them, studying the way each beast had the capability to take to the black skies. Reveling in the way they could cart a person from one world to another in a matter of days, and do so in style.

He'd always admired them, been curious about them, even

humored the idea of pursuing a career in piloting, before his life as a Guardian came into play.

His love for sleek ships only grew when he acquired the *Marauder*. Which was why, when Andi took it, he'd felt as if he'd lost the two most important things in his life—Andi being the first, of course, but the ship was definitely a close second. So many memories lingered in the halls of the *Marauder*, and not having it now, for such a monumental job, felt wrong.

Still…the Tracker was beautiful.

"This. Is. Heaven," Dex said, slapping his hands together. He leaned back his head and howled like a wolf, then trotted farther into the Tracker. It was brand spanking new and full of gadgets Dex had never seen before.

"She's a beauty, huh?" Soyina said, sliding down the ladder to his right. She landed lightly, like a cat. "She's the newest vessel of her class."

"How?" Andi asked in awe.

Soyina shrugged and waved a hand. "You'd be surprised to know how much loot we've managed to steal for our cause. I guess you could call us pirates. Better watch out, Baroness. The Underground is coming for your brand."

Andi rolled her eyes.

Klaren, who had already climbed the staircase at the back of the cargo bay, waved them up before disappearing from view. The three of them followed, but once at the top, they were met with a solid wall.

Dex furrowed his brows, running a hand against the cold metal. "Where did she—"

"Just watch," Soyina said, interrupting him. She swiped one finger against the wall, and it seemingly evaporated before his eyes, revealing a control room beyond.

"I'll drink to that," he said with an approving nod.

Andi waved her hand through where the wall once stood. "What was that?"

"Soluble nanotech. First of its kind," Klaren answered from across the now-visible room. She sat in the elevated captain's chair, lines of screens stretching out before her like a computerized army. A table stood in the center of the room, with a map of Mirabel projecting from it.

"So what's your plan for getting us onto Arcardius without getting caught?" Andi asked.

Before Klaren could respond, another voice piped up. "That would be me, the answer to all your problems."

Dex nearly leaped out of his skin as Eryn materialized before him.

"Where did you come from?" Andi breathed.

Eryn smiled, climbing atop the table, making the map twinkle out. She pulled her knees to her chest. "I've been following you almost all day."

Oh, Godstars, was she there when he and Andi...?

Dex pushed the thought aside. Eryn grinned at him with all her teeth, as if she could read his mind.

"And how are you going to solve all our problems, exactly?" Andi asked, propping a hand on her hip.

"I'm going to hide the ship." As she spoke, Eryn placed both hands on the metal hull, closing her eyes and tilting her head at just enough of an angle to still show off her smile. Then she hopped off the table and went to the front of the ship, placing her hands against the controls.

"Come, come." Andi and Dex sidled up next to her.

"Watch the outside of the ship." She closed her eyes, and they watched as the front of the ship began to flicker, gradually fading from view. Then, as soon as it disappeared, the cloaking lifted as Eryn raised her hands again.

"They won't even know we're there until we start kicking some ass." She smirked.

"Enough showing off. Get over here, people," Soyina said from the table.

All five of them gathered around. Klaren spoke first.

"We've received new intelligence that the satellite is going to be launching sooner than expected, due to Valen's declining health," she told them. "That's another reason for me agreeing to this preemptive internal strike. If we can end this with just the few of us, countless lives will be saved. But if we fail, I've given orders for the Underground to move ahead with our original plan."

Dex and Andi exchanged a look. "Which is…?" he asked.

"War."

CHAPTER 32
VALEN

Valen awoke to a hideous throbbing in his temples.

It was cold, *so cold*, when he opened his eyes to a darkness as deep as the night.

He tried to lift his hands, but they were stuck. Pressed tightly together behind his back, as if someone had taken a cord and bound him.

"Hello?" he whispered.

He couldn't see his legs when he looked down, couldn't make out his torso or the chair he could feel himself sitting in. But Valen knew that he was inside his mind castle, could feel it when he closed his eyes.

What had Darai done?

How could he have had such power—the ability to lock Valen up inside his own mind—and Valen had never even sensed it?

He tried to think back on the past moments they'd shared, tried to remember *something* that would have given the Exonian away…but the memories were distant. Already fading, as if tugged away from him on a spectral wind.

Valen closed his eyes, trying to regain control of himself. He was in his mind, safe in his fortress. And yet the chill of the air was so deep that it stung with each breath he took. His head kept pounding, like the angry beat of a drum.

This was *his* domain. He could control it. Will it to obey him, for he was the creator. And once he got out, he would find Darai and solve this once and for all.

Nor is going to betray you, Darai had said.

Valen couldn't let himself believe it. Not now.

He imagined the darkness lifting, the light of a burning torch as his guide.

There, to his left. A torch flickered into existence, the light a brilliant glow that chased the darkness away. He craned his neck as far around as it could go, trying to look behind him. Nothing but walls, endless and without an exit door or window.

He rocked back and forth, trying to loosen his bindings, but they remained as tight as ever. No matter what he did, the castle refused to bend any further to his will. The bonds refused to fall free. The obsidinite walls remained intact, neither crumbling when he imagined it, nor splitting apart to create a door to the other side when he begged it to do so.

Had he finally lost his power?

He began to wonder if Darai hadn't been lying. If perhaps Valen was already trapped inside Nexus, and would spend forever inside his mind, locked in a castle of his own making.

Valen screamed, rage coursing through him. Panic took over. This was *wrong*, terribly wrong…

"LET ME OUT!"

He thought he was screaming to no one, until a figure made

entirely of shadow stepped through the obsidinite walls and into the room.

"Valen, Valen," it said. "When will you learn? There is so much more for you than this."

The figure spread its arms wide, black coils of shadow undulating around it like chains.

"Darai?" Valen asked, the word forming clouds in the cold air.

Darai laughed, the shadows shaking and hissing.

"I tried, Valen. I truly did try to keep it a secret until the time was right. But it seems your foolish sister cannot make the choice she needs to."

"Keep what a secret?" Valen asked.

Darai stepped closer, the cold intensifying as his hands touched Valen's temples.

Valen screamed as his mind went black.

A ruined canvas, and a painter that did not belong.

"Your mind must be opened," Darai whispered, "so that you can see whose side you really wish to be on. I tried to bring you to my end of things, in the beginning. Don't you remember when I visited you in Lunamere? Before your sister ever did."

But Valen was lost to the pain. Lost to the shadows. And as he screamed, the darkness reached inside and dragged its claws across his mind.

"All this time, I needed you to grow stronger. To hone your skills, so that you could rise up and give your sister the power she needed. Then, finally, once your body failed and I got you out of the way... I would become the king Exonia needs."

"You will never be king," Valen said through gritted teeth.

Darai's power rolled through his mind. Such pain. Such fire.

Suddenly, a scene came to life before Valen, and he saw Exonia.

He saw his *home*, but it was a place of darkness, an endless sea that spread on forever. The only light came from a dark tower in the distance, and below it, the conduit. A swirling abyss of colors that was the other side of the Void.

Soon it would be opened.

Soon it would allow the Exonians through.

"Look at them," Darai's voice said gleefully, as Valen stared in horror at the other world. "Look at your people."

The Exonians had no bodies.

It was a sea of shadows, writhing beneath the surface, endlessly hungry. Eager to devour, to take up a place in a body. They had never had bodies, could not walk freely the way the Mirabellians did, and they were forced to stare through the conduit forever, seeing the Mirabellians in all their mobility. Their lives, walking among the many planets and worlds.

The Exonians hissed and snapped their shadow-jaws.

"When they come through to this world, Valen," Darai told him, "they will take the bodies that are already waiting here. They will become a perfect army, to head out and conquer other places. Other worlds beyond this. With your power, with your might...imagine what I will accomplish."

No, Valen wanted to say.

But fear had stolen his voice.

The Exonians were supposed to be *peaceful*. That was the truth Valen had always been told, that Nor had believed, too. The Exonians were living in a dying world. They were meant to come to Mirabel, and survive alongside the people who existed here. Nor would rule over them, in a world without war. A world fully given over to peace.

She'd gone about it in the way she had to, and the wicked things she'd done would be worth it in the end, when Exonia and Mirabel became one.

But this?

This was a monstrosity.

This would be murder, of an entire galaxy full of people.

"You can't do this," Valen sputtered. "And you won't. Nor

will never agree to continue with the plan. You said she'll betray me? She won't do it. She would *never* bind me to that satellite. Exonia will stay locked away in its dark prison forever."

With a surge of rage, he shoved against his uncle's power.

Shoved with everything he had.

The walls trembled around them, and Valen screamed, pain lancing through him. But he would not quit, even though he felt himself fading as he pushed, desperate to escape Darai's power.

Yet Darai only laughed, chuckling as if he were a giant holding back a child from swinging tiny fists at him. "You're right," he said. "Nor loves you too much, the foolish girl. She would never bind you to the satellite—not unless you chose to do it yourself. So you'll go to her, and tell her you're dying. That much, Valen, is true. Right now, while your body lies in that hospital wing, you're dying."

"I'm not," Valen said.

But he knew it was a lie. A hope that was already crumbling.

"You'll tell Nor you want to be a worthy sacrifice, a loyal soldier," Darai instructed. "And that if you are to die, you would rather hand over your body to the cause, and let us keep it alive while your mind stays attached to the mission." He patted Valen's shoulder with a sigh. "Such a strong princeling. But not strong enough to fight my abilities."

"Why are you doing this?" Valen begged. "If you have compulsion, why not use it yourself, and leave me and my sister out of it all?"

He was nearly lost to his pain, unable to fight any longer.

"Because the foolish Godstars wounded me," Darai snapped. "They stole my power and tried to destroy my Yielded body, too, when they thought me too dark for a place in their world. But I escaped. I ran, along with a kernel of my power. I've tended to it for years, waiting for it to grow. Years, in this miserable galaxy, I have bided my time, waiting to unleash what is left of my power. It isn't enough to rule on my own, and soon, it will fade. But your compulsion will be uploaded to the Nexus long before then."

"No," Valen gasped. "Nor will see the lie. She'll never do that to me."

"But she will," Darai said with a shrug. "Because you will convince her to. Did you know, Valen, that I made you shove that soldier toward Zahn? I compelled you to do so. My plan played itself out well, weakening Nor's heart. Creating a rift between the two of you, to help guide her into going along with my plan."

Horror surged through Valen. "You did that?"

He hadn't even felt the compulsion, and yet somehow, Darai had been the cause of Zahn's death. Not Valen. *Darai.*

"Come along, boy," Darai said. "I'm growing tired of this game. Nor awaits us."

The view before Valen changed in a flash. He was no longer in his mind castle, but back in his body, lying in his hospital bed. Only he no longer had control of it.

"Get up," Darai said, those golden eyes shimmering.

Valen stood, aware of how weak he was. But also aware of a deeper, horrific power propelling him forward.

A power that he was helpless to fight.

Nor was surprised to see them when they arrived.

"Valen!" She stood, pulling a cloak over her shoulders as she crossed the room to his side, pausing quickly to look at Darai. "He should be resting. Why did you bring him here?"

"Apologies, Majesty," Darai said, and Valen felt sick as the adviser's tone changed, as his face crumbled to that weakened state he'd always shown them, so different from the monster Valen had just met in his mind.

How many times had Valen missed the truth about Darai?

How many times had Valen sensed the old man's compulsion, but thought nothing of it?

"The boy is weak," Darai said as he kept his grip on Valen's arm, helping to support his body. "I tried to change his mind, but he insisted. He wishes to speak with you, said it was urgent."

With every step Valen took, he begged Nor to see him resisting.

He begged her to understand that he was *not* a part of this, that he was a puppet, and Darai was the master pulling his strings.

But she only helped guide Valen toward the couch across the room, settling him against the cushions.

"I tried to find you in the medical wing, Majesty," Darai said, sitting down across from Valen in a chair. "I just received word that Nexus is complete, and I came to alert you of it, but found Valen instead. The doctors informed me that his time is short, so I thought it best to bring him up to speed on our plan."

"What?" Nor asked, raising her voice. She looked to Valen with widening eyes. "You told him?"

Darai inclined his head. "I know it is unforgivable of me to have overstepped. But we are running out of time, and the opportunity will be gone from us if we do not decide immediately. I thought it would ease your pain if we told Valen, and if he was given the chance to decide for himself."

Nor was silent, as if she couldn't believe Darai's words.

He's lying! Valen screamed from his mind, sending the message as far as he could, pushing it toward their mental doorway. *I'm still here, Nor! You have to hear me!*

But the message rebounded back to him, unheard.

Dread swirled through Valen as Nor looked from Darai to him and back again.

She believed Darai. Oh, Godstars, she believed him, and Valen would never get free.

"Tell her, Valen," Darai said, his voice so sickeningly false that Valen wanted to scream, to cringe and scurry far away. "Tell your sister what you told me."

Valen closed his eyes, trying to fight the Exonian. But his

mind was like a reed, bending in the wind. Darai was too strong, his mental grip icy as he held fast, unrelenting.

"I'm dying, Nor," Valen said. His lips moved against his will. The words were not his, but Darai's, compelling him with such ease that Valen felt like he was in a dream. "Every day I draw closer to death. I don't want to die in vain. I want to die an honorable man. As a sacrifice for my true home."

"Don't say that," Nor begged him. She turned to him, taking his hand.

Valen could *feel* it, the sincerity in that grip. He tried to squeeze her hand back, to squeeze so tightly that perhaps it would tell her something was wrong. But his hand felt as if it belonged to another. He looked down at it, unable to control his fingers.

"I have to say it," Valen heard himself say. "It would be the greatest gift I could ever give, Nor, to the woman who gave me a purpose in life. You saved me from the darkness when you found me, when you helped me learn of my power. You gave me a true life, and though it has been short, it has been full of beauty."

Lies, Valen screamed. *Please, Nor, you have to hear me! You have to see the truth! It's not me speaking! I don't want this!*

The message, again, did not reach her.

Sweat began to bead on Valen's temples as he fought back against Darai's compulsion, but Nor likely saw it as a side effect of his condition.

"Darai has promised me there will be no pain," his lips said, the words still not his own. "He says that when you plug me in, it will feel like I've gone into a peaceful sleep. But instead of death, instead of eternal darkness, I'll be there in the satellite, sending out the truth to the galaxy. Ensuring that Exonia will have a home, and the two galaxies will always live in peace, because of *your* rule. And after you're gone, I will remain, keeping that peace. Keeping everyone in the truth and the light. Your children's children will reign, and I will ensure it is so."

Nor was crying now, as Valen spoke.

As if he was saying something beautiful, instead of spouting the words of a monster.

"You can't possibly want this," Nor said, still holding his hand. "Can you?"

His body shook as he pulled himself back into his mind, toward the mental doorway that connected him to Nor. If he could just send her a message…if he could just get one word through the gap, then perhaps she would see. Perhaps he could warn her about Darai, about the truth of the Exonians that Nor didn't know.

But when he reached the doorway, he found, with horror, that it was covered with thick obsidinite bars.

No! Valen screamed, pounding mental fists against the bars. *Nor! I'm still here! Please, Nor, you have to hear me!*

The bars turned to a swirling darkness, thick black smoke that burned to the touch. Valen screamed as the smoke wrapped around his wrists, yanking him away from the locked door.

A valiant effort, Darai's voice hissed in Valen's mind. *But a futile one.*

Then Valen was thrown from his own mind, hurled back into the world where he sat with Nor still holding his hands.

She was right there, right in front of him, but she couldn't hear him scream.

He was a prisoner to Darai.

CHAPTER 33
NOR

"Please, Nor," Valen said. "You said you wanted to forgive me for what happened with Zahn. If that's true, then allow me to do this. It's my dying wish."

Tears rolled down Nor's cheeks as her brother spoke. She looked to her uncle, eyes pleading. "Is there truly no other way?"

This couldn't be the only answer.

She'd already forgiven him, had forgiven him the moment he'd collapsed in her office, when she'd feared they would lose him. He was all she had left, and he was asking her to let him go. Like a soldier, ready to walk onto the front lines of a war he knew he wouldn't come back from.

"There is not," Darai said gently. "The boy knows it, too. And he is brave for still wishing to do it."

Nor looked back at Valen.

He sat before her, so weak, yet so sure.

Still, something didn't feel right. Nor sank into her mind, reaching for the mental doorway between them, and found it shut tight. She'd closed it herself, locked it up during their argument after the attack in the city…but she'd opened it again, back in the hospital wing. Perhaps he'd closed it once more, wanting them to have some space before they spoke so intimately again?

Nor was about to knock on the door, to try to open it, when Valen spoke, more insistently this time. He gripped her hand tighter, with a strength he hadn't shown moments before.

"We have no time to waste." He coughed into his sleeve, leaving behind a few flecks of blood. Darai stood and offered him a bit of cloth. Valen nodded his thanks, wiping his mouth clean. "I'm sorry, Nor. But this is our duty to Exonia. It's time."

She swallowed and chewed on her lip. So quickly, the tide of this war had turned. So quickly, she'd gone from feeling as if she had no choice, to Valen suddenly deciding for her.

"You're sure you know what this means?" she asked. "You know that once you enter that satellite, once you go forward with being uploaded…you'll never be able to take it back."

Valen nodded, his eyes downcast. "I'm fully aware, Nor. Darai has answered all of my questions. I'm ready. I want this. And I know you want it, too."

It was all happening so fast.

Nor turned back to Darai, to ask him a final time, to *command* him to find another option. But then the door to her office swung open, and Nor's head analyst rushed in.

"Majesty!" The woman's silver veins were bright as she bowed.

Nor stood at the same time as Darai. "What is it?" she asked.

"We've received a message from Arachnid," the analyst said, panting slightly. "He has AndSroma Racella in custody. And he's en route to Arcardius, this very moment, to offer her up as a token of peace. He requests that the girl's remaining crew be there, ready to hand over as a trade, as well as the body of her pilot, so she can be buried. He's also asked for a cease-fire—if we stop the attacks on his people, he'll stop the attacks on ours."

Nor felt like the ground was about to fall out from beneath her.

"Are you certain?" Nor asked, her heart hammering.

The analyst nodded, face bright with excitement at the happy news. "We're certain, Majesty. What would you have me do? Arachnid is waiting for a response."

Nor looked to Darai, who nodded his encouragement. "The time is nearly here, my dear. Perhaps the spider has finally realized he is vastly outnumbered. He has come to his senses."

Valen smiled weakly at her from the couch. "Tell him we accept. Give him the girls—we don't need them. And we'll head to Nexus immediately, to begin preparations."

"But of all people, Arachnid arrives with Androma in tow?" It felt like a trick.

"Perhaps they had formed an alliance, which Arachnid is now using to his utmost advantage. A wise decision, if he wishes to save himself," Darai suggested. "We'll have all of our soldiers at hand. An army ready to capture them both."

"You would make a false deal?" Nor asked.

Darai nodded. "*You* would do so, my dear. As you have before, when you sent Valen to Arcardius masquerading as an innocent, helpless boy to pave the way for you." He looked to the analyst. "Arachnid is coming, but with how many ships?"

"Only one," the analyst said. "One ship. We will meet them in the skies and escort them here to Averia."

Darai looked to Nor, taking her hand, eyes meeting hers. He smiled warmly, and she felt peace fill her from within at his touch, at his gaze. Peace with the plan. It was nearly all over.

She wanted this. She wanted to move to action, before it was too late.

Nor glanced back at her brother, struck by a sudden thought. "What use could Arachnid possibly have for Androma's crew?"

"I imagine Androma probably asked for their freedom in exchange for surrendering herself peacefully," Valen said. "She was always selfless when it came to them."

A burst of energy filled Nor, followed by the need to get up and move as Darai squeezed her hand once more. "Then send our response," she said to the analyst, again filled with that sudden burst of courage, that strange need to *move*. "And arrange for the girls to be there when Arachnid arrives with Androma. Arrange for a full guard, too. Zero opportunities for the Bloody Baroness to escape. I want her in my grasp, so we can transfer the power from her to me immediately. You will be there as well, to ensure everything goes as smoothly as possible. And once Arachnid gives us Androma, we must seize him, too. The man can't be trusted. We'd be fools not to take them both together."

"He will resist," Darai said.

"And if he does, kill him," Nor said boldly. "In fact, kill him even if he doesn't resist. He's too dangerous to be left alive."

The analyst nodded, then raced from the room to carry out her orders. Nor turned back to the others, a new energy pulsing in her veins.

This was it. The moment she'd been working toward for so many years.

"A fortuitous ending to our day," Darai said, smiling. "We must go at once, and begin the process of uploading Valen."

Nor's smile fell from her face. She'd forgotten, momentarily, about Valen's choice.

She looked to him a final time, her heart still racing. Was this it, then? Was this to be the way things ended between them?

"Don't think of it as an end," Valen said suddenly. Quietly. As if he'd been reading her mind. He lifted a hand to her, and she went to his side to help him stand. He was so weak. So frail, compared to how he'd once been, when they'd first met on Xen Ptera, when they'd truly become the brother and sister they'd always had, but never known.

"Think of this as a new beginning," Valen said. "A new life, Nor, for countless others. I'm ready. I'm willing. And I can't wait to see how beautiful it is, when Exonia finally walks free."

He kissed her cheek then, and squeezed her hand once more.

"It's time," he whispered, backing away with a small smile on his face. "I'm ready, sister."

Darai stood, joining them. "You're very brave, princeling. Brave and loyal to your core."

For a moment, Nor thought she heard the echo of her brother's voice, calling out to her from within. But then Valen grimaced, as if he were in pain, and she reached out to support him.

"No more time to waste, Nor," he said weakly. "Come on."

So Nor forced back her tears and took his arm. Together, they left the office, ready to complete their mission as one.

CHAPTER 34
DEX

Dex had never been a man capable of staying in one place for too long. It always made him feel like the rest of the galaxy had ceased to exist, like the world outside of wherever he was stationed was simply gone.

It was always good to be back among the stars. To head out on another mission.

And even today, with the threat of what was to come looming on the horizon, Dex felt like he could breathe a little bit easier, staring out at the stars as they streaked by, the ship soaring through hyperspace.

This ship wasn't the same as the *Marauder*, by any means. Though full of incredible tech, it was smaller in its common areas, with far less room to stretch out and find some silence. But Dex had somehow found himself blessedly alone for a moment, seated in one of the lookout chairs below the main deck, and the hum of the ship's engines was slowly lulling him to sleep— a sound that Dex hadn't realized how much he'd missed while they were on Solera.

The flight away from the Underground was breathtaking. They'd soared up through a massive tunnel carved by soldiers of old before the Cataclysm, dug so far it stretched beyond the dome of Craatia above. They'd burst through a cavernous, ancient space adorned with one of Solera's few waterfalls that wasn't frozen over—a steamy, near-boiling cascade at the western edge of the Wastes.

No one had tried to stop them as they'd soared away, up through the atmosphere and into the blessed black skies.

Dex yawned, leaning deeper into his seat.

The new crew would work together well enough, especially with Eryn's talents at their disposal. But he missed Breck and Gilly and Lira, and their perfect cadence with each other, almost as if they were Guardians of a different kind. They were warriors, Gilly perhaps the most terrifying of them all, despite her small stature.

"Hiding?"

Andi's hands slid onto Dex's shoulders. He eased into her touch. "Mulling over our impending deaths," he said.

She huffed out a laugh as she slid into the seat to his right, dressed in her usual black, her hair braided back to reveal the silver implants across her cheekbones. She belonged here, too, in the stars, heading toward another mission. Dex could see it in the way she moved, the way she held herself—she was in her element again.

"We thrive in the face of death, Dex," Andi said, crossing her legs, the tips of her boots kicked up against the viewport. "I thought you knew that. Once a captain, always a captain."

"Or a general," Dex said dryly. "We're really messed up, Andi. How did it come to this?"

She shrugged. "The galaxy wanted nothing to do with us. So we had to wreak a little havoc in return."

"Speaking of Havoc," Dex said, looking over his shoulder. Andi had insisted the creature be brought along, for when they rescued Gilly. She'd said some part of her hoped that Gilly would remember the bloodthirsty little beast. That even if the compulsion held, her love for Havoc might have remained. Dex had agreed, if only because he loved Andi—and because he'd arranged for Soyina to be the one to deliver the creature to their new ship.

He reached across the space between himself and Andi now, grabbing her hand, lacing their fingers together. "Do you truly think we'll survive this?"

Andi's eyes found the streaks of starlight as she spoke. "I'm really hoping so."

"But you're not certain."

She smiled sadly. "Life isn't about certainty, Dex. It's about taking risks, and hoping that they'll pay off. No one ever lived by playing it safe. I wasn't going to stay down there, hiding out, while my crew's lives were in danger. Watching the clock run down, hour after hour, until Nor swung that second blade. We had to leave that place, at one time or another. Nor just fast-forwarded the clock. Got us into motion sooner than we'd planned for."

"I know," he said. If he'd been in the same situation, he wouldn't have been able to sit idly by, either. He squeezed her hand. "I'll be by your side the whole way. And Eryn will keep us all hidden until the moment is right."

"And I won't hand myself over until they agree to release Breck's and Gilly's minds from the virus," Andi said. "They will walk free, and then you'll help get me out of there. We'll get into the mansion, shut down the weapons system…and that will be the end of it all."

"For now," Dex said. "There's still the matter of freeing the minds of millions of other people."

"Yeah," Andi said with a sigh. "That, too. But that's Klaren's job. She said she had it covered. Not all battles are ours to face, Dex. We didn't break this galaxy. In many ways, Klaren did. Let her help put it back together again."

"And we believe her?"

Andi finally looked at Dex. "Do we have any other choice?"

He stood, pulling her up with him so that they could see the stars more clearly. "Do you remember when we first danced together?"

"Dex," she groaned. "Now is not the time."

"Now is the perfect time," he insisted.

Because he suddenly felt like he was seeing her for the very last time. Her stormy eyes, her cautious smile, her fearlessness as she stood in the face of adversity and refused to blink or look away.

Dex reached out and took her braid gently in his hands, unwinding it so that her hair fell around her face. "So beautiful," he said softly.

She smiled at him, wrapped in the starlight shining behind her. Dex stepped forward, sweeping her into his arms. When he spun her, she laughed, eyes annoyed at first as she stopped again before him, as if he were only playing a joke.

But when she saw the expression on his face, she stopped.

"What's wrong?"

Dex shook his head. "I just want to remember this. I want to remember you, every part."

"We're going to survive this, Dex," she said, so much certainty in her eyes.

"I know," he said. And in this moment, he wanted to believe it. He leaned forward, guiding her toward the viewport to kiss her.

But at the last second she spun, pressing him up against the viewport instead, her palms splayed against the glass on either side of his face, as if she were touching the stars.

"Godstars, Androma," he breathed. "I don't know how I got so lucky to love you."

She smiled. "I don't think luck has anything to do with it."

Then she kissed him like she never had before. Deeply, and fiercely, until their breaths were one and their heartbeats were like one cadence beating in time. Dex's hands found their way beneath her shirt. Her hands were moving across his body, too, searching. Her tongue found his, and he gasped for a breath as she...

"So this is how you strategize for battle," a voice said.

Dex and Andi broke apart, him cursing, her looking like she wanted to tear Soyina's head off.

"We're closing in on the Phelexos System, so Arachnid wants to chat," the woman said. She smiled knowingly at Dex and Andi. "Take a moment to collect yourselves. Now isn't really the time for...this."

"Now is always the time," Dex said.

Soyina blinked at him. "Now that I think about it...ahh, yes." She snapped her tattooed fingers. "I think I remember you saying those *exact* words to me, moments before I chained your naked body to a toilet during our short try at love."

"There's a toilet on board," Dex growled. "Why don't you go shove your head into it, Soyina? Or better yet—"

He cursed again when Andi slapped him across the back of the skull. "We'll be there in a minute," she said to Soyina.

But the moment the woman left, Andi turned back toward Dex, a wicked smile on her face as she pushed him against the glass once more.

Arcardius hung in the sky ahead, a tiny orb growing larger by the second as they closed in on it, no longer in hyperspace. The sky around them was filled with stars again, winking happily in the sky.

It all looked the same as it had on their last visit to Arcardius. Dex supposed he shouldn't be surprised, but after everything that had happened in the past few weeks, it seemed odd. Nothing was normal anymore. He had always lived a life full of adventure, and the mundaneness of everyday life had seemed so foreign and dull to him before. But now he craved the idea of it.

But in order to find out what normal was really like, he'd have to finish this mission.

Klaren and the others sat in their respective seats in the bridge, looking out the viewport as Andi and Dex arrived. Klaren was back in her full Arachnid armor, to hide her identity from Nor.

"The transmission was received, and we've gotten one in return," her droid said, eyes flashing bright red. "She wants us to land on the estate, below the Nexus satellite. She's expecting only two of us—Androma and me."

"And no one will see me, Soyina or Dex," Eryn said, reciting their plan once more.

"Not until Andi is about to be handed over," Dex added, crossing his arms.

Andi nodded, braid back in place, expression stony as she readied herself for battle. "There will be a fight," she said. "I'm certain Nor won't let me go easily. She'll do whatever it takes."

"But she will also have to keep you alive," Klaren reminded her. "The system won't accept commands from a dead leader. If you die, the system will shut down, and Nor won't ever gain control that way. So she'll ensure you're kept safe."

"Which means the rest of you will be targets," Andi said, looking to Dex.

"Not quite so easy to take us down, though," Eryn said. She marched over to the corner of the bridge, to the storage bins welded against the curved wall of the ship. Dex grinned as she hefted up a set of armor, the very same that they'd seen being made in the Underground. "I packed a little something for our journey."

Three sets. Enough for Dex, Eryn and Soyina.

Klaren had the armor of Arachnid to protect her, and Andi likely wouldn't be shot at. *Likely* didn't ease Dex's mind at all, but even if she was shot at, they knew now that she was immune. Nor wouldn't be able to bring her over to their side—not in that way, anyway.

"We're closing in," Soyina said from the pilot's seat. "Our team rigged the ship's internal computer to combat their tech. No heat-seeking systems will work, so they won't know anyone else is on board. But you've got to move quick once we land, Eryn. Be ready to shield us from view. When that loading ramp opens, the three of us will have to be silent and get off the ship before the cooling system shuts off. Otherwise they're likely to hear us moving down the ramp."

Eryn nodded, hands clasped together. "You won't be seen."

"And in the event that all hell breaks loose?" Dex asked.

Andi answered that one. "Hell has already broken loose. We don't have any backups. If it goes badly, we get back in the ship, we get out…and we don't return again."

Dex heard the lie in her voice. She wasn't going to leave that planet. Not without the girls. Which meant he wasn't leaving, either.

"One-shot mission," Eryn said. "Not great odds."

Dex shrugged, because though he was scared as hell, he realized it was too late to care or turn back. "Andi enjoys missions with little to no chance of success. So this kind of thing isn't new for us."

"To not great odds," Soyina said, lifting a pretend glass in the air. Then she angled the ship toward Arcardius, ready to take them down to the devil's lair.

Dex took back what he said about everything looking normal, because the moment they soared into Arcardius's atmosphere, they were met by a sea of black ships.

"Rovers," Soyina said, bringing their ship in to hover in the sky just beside Averia's floating mountain. "The same ones Nor has had seeking out the Unaffecteds across Mirabel all this time. Nasty little ships."

The Rovers were small, but loaded with tech. The Solis crest was painted on their sides and underbellies, a menacing reminder of what they were soon to face. Dex wondered how many of the crews inside were there of their own accord, or if everyone was under the influence of Valen's compulsion now.

"Looks like they're here to guide us in," Andi said, leaning forward in her seat. She looked back over her shoulder at Klaren. "You haven't seen your children in years. Are you sure you're ready for this?"

"I'm ready." Klaren's droid spoke from its perch on her shoulder. "I should have come to face them both a long time ago."

Their ship rumbled as the Rovers locked it in place with a magnetic field. Then they were sinking down to the floating mountain where Nor's estate awaited them.

There was no going back now. They broke through the layer of clouds, and the estate finally came into view, white and sprawling and exactly as Dex remembered it.

Only now, it had a new addition.

As the ships sank toward the estate grounds, Andi cursed. "It's massive," she whispered.

In front of them stood the largest satellite Dex had ever seen— planet-side, at least. It was a giant metal circle, more than double the size of the mansion. At the structure's center was a circular pod. Dex could only wonder what was inside.

A smug smile pulled at his lips.

Normally satellites were built in orbit, but this one was rooted firmly to the ground. Since Andi still had control of their systems, they hadn't been able to launch the pieces they needed into space. And if everything went according to their plan, Nexus would never even reach the atmosphere.

"There," Klaren said from the front captain's chair. "I see them."

The enemy lay in wait below, a line of soldiers moving steadily from the estate toward the rendezvous point. Klaren turned, standing up in her massive armor. "Eryn? Hide the lot of you, before it's too late. We'll exit the moment we touch the ground."

"Of course, Arachnid," Eryn said, but she had already faded from view. Her cool, invisible touch landed on Dex's wrist. He yelped, but silenced himself when the other three women looked at him.

"Scared, Dex?" Andi asked with a smug smile. But he could see the anticipation behind it, her eyes roving over that group of soldiers, searching for any sign of Breck and Gilly.

He shrugged and tried to lighten the tension, the way he always had on jobs. "It was just a sneeze."

She rolled her eyes, likely trying to do the same thing he was. "Of course."

"Alright." Eryn's invisible voice spoke up from Dex's left. "Away we go."

It suddenly felt like cold, icy water was slowly being poured over Dex's head, spreading across his shoulders, stretching down to his limbs. He looked down, mesmerized, as his body began to fade. Inch by inch, he seemed to slip from existence, until he was no longer there at all.

"Incredible," Andi breathed, looking at the place where Dex still stood.

Then the ship landed with a gentle *thud* on the estate grounds, and Dex reached out, grabbing Andi's hand for a moment.

"I'll be by your side the whole time," he said. "I dare them to try and take you."

"I'd like to see them try myself," Andi said back. She turned to Arachnid, who lifted a set of magnacuffs. Andi nodded, holding out her hands. The cuffs were fake, the magnets inside rendered useless by Soyina, the woman's wicked enjoyment of science proving useful yet again, but they looked convincing enough, and the sight of her in them made Dex's chest ache.

He would do whatever it took, no matter the cost, to see that she remained free after this mission.

"Ready," Andi said.

Klaren placed a heavy, gloved hand on Andi's shoulder. Her droid clicked its claws against her armor as she pressed the button to lower the loading ramp. "Let's go see my children."

The loading ramp lowered with a hiss, the cooling systems spreading steam across the front, and then they were moving. Dex felt like a ghost as he walked, feeling his own footsteps and Eryn's and Soyina's on either side of him, but seeing nothing at all to reveal they were there. They moved quickly, following close behind Andi and Klaren, so as not to allow the steam to reveal that there were five bodies, instead of just the two that Nor had demanded on her return message to the ship.

The steam cleared as Dex's boots touched Arcardian soil. It was cold, the wind whipping angrily, the very same as it would have been on Tenebris this time of year.

The winter solstice, a time meant for happiness.

Instead, Dex felt like he was walking toward his own grave.

He saw the line of soldiers first, clad in Solis black as they moved like a trail of darkness across the estate grounds. Each of them was polished to perfection, chins angled high, weapons in their fists. Those weapons, Dex knew, were likely loaded with the Zenith virus. But were other bullets mixed in as well—not to transform the target's mind, but to kill?

He kept his eyes on Andi's back. To her credit, she walked with the pride of the Baroness, instead of the broken steps of a prisoner. Arachnid was nearly three times her size in that New Vedan armor, but beneath, Klaren was actually smaller than Andi.

What would Nor and Valen think when that helmet came

off? When they saw their mother, a woman the entire galaxy had long thought dead?

They passed beneath the shadow of the massive satellite, the wind biting colder now, without the sun to warm them. Nexus rose high above them, perched on its side as if it were ready to fall and crush them. As if it were a living thing, waiting to end the ways of Mirabel for good.

"Where is Nor?" Eryn whispered from beside him as Andi and Arachnid stopped in the shadow of the satellite.

The line of enemy soldiers also came to a halt, a mere twenty paces away. Dex could feel the tension radiating from Andi as the soldiers parted, pointing their rifles to the sky in one sleek motion, like a salute.

Queen Nor walked out from behind her guards and into view, a night-black cloak of velvet billowing behind her as the wind caught it, making it look as if she were emerging from a cloud of darkness. A golden crown perched atop her ringlet curls. Valen strode beside her, wearing a cloak of bloodred. It hung from his body, which was so emaciated that he now looked even worse than he had when Dex and Andi first pulled him from the depths of Lunamere.

Dex clenched his jaw. What in the hell had gone on here, in the weeks they'd been away?

The adviser came next, an elderly man covered in thick, angry scars. He, too, wore a cloak, and as the wind died down for a moment, and it cascaded to the ground behind him, Dex saw three more figures trailing in the queen's wake.

Gilly, Breck...and *Lira*, following just behind, her beautiful blue eyes proud, her chin angled high as it had ever been.

All *three* girls.

Andi let out an almost imperceptible gasp. Dex didn't think she would have been able to hide it even if she'd tried. For he'd seen Lira die, too, saw the flash of the blade and heard her body thumping to the floor.

Yet here she was, alive and well, standing beside the queen with Breck and Gilly, their faces expressionless as they stared ahead.

Andi's body was taut, her fists clenched, tension palpable in every part of her body. Dex could practically feel her fury as she looked at Nor and Valen.

"So you lied," Klaren said. The words from her droid carried across the space between the two groups like a gunshot. She slowly shook her helmeted head from side to side. "I suppose I would have done the same. And it was what brought the Bloody Baroness to me, after all, whom I now give to you as a peace offering."

Nor was terrifyingly beautiful as she stood before them, one gloved hand clasped over her golden prosthetic. She inclined her head slightly in a mocking salute. "Arachnid. Strange, how you spoke so boldly about stopping me, only to appear before me now, defenseless, and handing over my adversary." She smiled, those rouged lips the very same Dex had seen in his nightmares ever since Ucatoria. "One would have to assume you're here either to attack me or to surrender."

Klaren's droid clicked its claws into her armor, that robotic voice speaking loud. "I will not be surrendering today, but as I said, I am offering you Androma Racella in exchange for peace between us."

"My entire reign is about peace," Nor explained, holding her arms wide. "Everything I have done has been for the greater good."

"Enslaving the minds of millions," Klaren snapped, "is *not* something I would consider to be for the greater good."

"And slaughtering hundreds in your petty attacks across Mirabel?" Nor raised a brow and tsked. "Some savior you are."

"I did not come for an argument," Klaren said. Dex could almost hear the woman's frustration, even in the robotic voice of her droid. "I came to give you what you seek, and in return, my demand is that you stop any further trapping of minds. Anyone you discover to be Unaffected, you will refrain from enslaving to your cause. And you will allow any Unaffecteds currently in hiding to flee to a safe zone, where they can live out their lives freely."

Nor threw back her head and laughed. "Is that all, Arachnid?"

"I also ask that you release the minds of these three prisoners," Klaren said, lifting an armored hand toward Breck, Gilly and Lira, "and let them walk free. I will bring them onto my ship, and I will soar away from here. You will not stop me, and you will not send Rovers after me. Consider this a cease-fire."

"A cease-fire," Nor said, nodding as the wind blew and her cloak billowed out behind her again. "I do not honor cease-fires."

Klaren froze. "You are alive because of a cease-fire, Nor Solis. There was once a Xen Pterran queen who gave herself over to the enemy in order to honor one."

"Don't speak of my mother," Nor said. There was no change in her expression, but her tone was different. Tighter. "The dead are of no use to me, and neither are their failures."

But Klaren barreled on without a hitch, without any visible reaction to hearing such words spoken about her. "Do you accept my terms?"

"On one condition," Nor said, glancing only briefly toward her adviser, who had stepped closer to her, watching Arachnid with prying eyes. "You will personally come forward and make the exchange. And you will reveal your identity to me."

An interesting offer.

Dex didn't trust it one bit. There was no way Nor Solis would allow her enemy to walk free. They'd planned for this, considered that it would happen…yet his body still broke out in a cold sweat, that strange sensation of his heartbeat in his ears as Klaren took Andi by the arm.

"Free them first," she said. "I will honor my deal with the girl."

With a sigh, Nor lifted a hand. "Of course. Free them, Valen."

Valen walked over to Andi's crew, each step labored, as if he were in pain.

His cheeks were shallow, the bones protruding from his skin, his eyes sunken. Dex had seen people in such a state before, long ago when he'd visited A'Exal, a gas planet whose citizens were plagued with horrific side effects from exposure to the atmosphere. Valen looked like the very worst-afflicted of those poor people—on the verge of death.

And yet he still moved forward, his face revealing no pain, as he stopped before the girls.

Valen held up his hands. For a moment, they shook. His whole body trembled, and his eyes seemed to roll back into his head. But then the shaking ceased, his body stilled and his eyes opened once again.

For a moment, nothing seemed to happen. There was no sound but the wind, howling as it whipped through the space between the two groups.

Then, one by one, each of the girls slumped to the ground.

Andi took a step forward, but Dex placed his invisible hand on her shoulder. "Not yet," he whispered, a mere breath in her ear.

As quickly as they'd fallen, the girls began to rouse, as if coming out of a deep sleep. It was much the same as it had been when the dead rose during the Ucatoria Ball—only this time, when the girls woke...

Dex saw it in their eyes.

They were themselves again.

CHAPTER 35
LIRA

When Lira was younger, she'd once gone to the ocean with her family.

She remembered being transfixed by the peaks of frothing waves, curling and dipping until they crested and met the angry, churning surface below. Again and again, they did this powerful dance, making her fearful to swim in their wake, afraid of being swept away.

But then Lon dipped beneath the surging water, gliding under the surface before emerging with a bright smile on his face. Seeing her twin do it with such ease gave her the confidence to follow his lead.

So she dived, breaking through the water like a bullet.

Her body had hummed at the contact.

Every inkling of doubt she'd had on land evaporated, and

when she surfaced, she felt a clarity unlike anything she'd ever felt. Like a slate wiped clean.

Lira was experiencing the same feeling now.

It was as if her mind had suddenly been swept clean after being stuffed with gauze. With each blink, her brain cleared more and more.

One moment, she was serving her queen, and the next, she wasn't. Just like that, as if a tethered spring had been snapped, her mind was her own again.

Lira gasped, her knees buckling as her gaze collided with Andi's just a few yards away.

"Andi?" Gilly whispered, her green eyes wide. Breck, too, looked as if she had seen a ghost, her hand plastered against her mouth.

Even from this distance, she could see tears spring into Andi's eyes.

And though they stood surrounded by the enemy, Lira knew that they were finally home.

CHAPTER 36
ANDI

They were back.

Tears poured down Andi's face, and she didn't even try to stop them from flowing. So long, she'd dreamed of this moment, holding back the fear that they would never return to the world again, not as they'd once been.

And yet here the girls were, crossing the gap from Nor's side over to hers.

She wished, desperately, that she could remove her cuffs, wrap her arms around her crew, her *family*, and feel at home again.

But instead she simply stood there, joy enveloping her heart as the girls reached her side.

"You came for us," Lira whispered, practically falling against Andi as she wrapped her arms around her. Gilly came next, and then Breck, and for a moment it was just the four of them again, not standing before an enemy queen, but standing free, in the bridge of the *Marauder*, surrounded by the shining stars.

"I'm so sorry, Andi," Breck said, and there were tears rolling down her cheeks, too. "For everything we did. For everything we thought." She was sobbing, hardly able to catch her breath as she squeezed the girls tighter. "She made us believe we hated you. Made us believe that we were wrong to have ever been on your side."

"It doesn't matter," Andi said, shaking her head. "None of that matters. It wasn't you."

Gilly pulled away from the hug first, sneaking out from beneath Breck's embrace to turn and glance back at Nor and Valen.

"I want her dead for what she did to us," Gilly said. She shook, whether from holding back tears or the joy of newfound freedom or the long overdue rage spreading across her face, Andi couldn't tell. But when Gilly looked back up at her, that beautiful, tiny gunner who had always been so fearless…

She was afraid.

Afraid of the queen.

And it made Andi's heart ache all the more for what she was about to do.

"It's time," Klaren said. The droid's voice was jarring, like a jagged blade about to sever the joy that Andi felt, seeing her girls walk free. "Are you ready?"

Lira's smile, so beautiful, so *alive*, crumbled. "Ready for what?" She looked past Andi then, to the empty space and the cold, waiting ship. "Where are Dex and Lon?"

Andi couldn't tell her. She couldn't.

Not now.

She felt that invisible hand again, squeezing her wrist from behind. Dex. Gentle, silent support in this moment.

Andi pushed her fear down, forced it to settle beside the newly blooming sorrow. For none of them knew. Not the girls, and especially not Dex. She gently pulled her cuffed wrists away from Dex, feeling the solid weight of the blade hidden beneath her sleeve, and she thanked the Godstars that he had not asked about it.

"We made a deal," Andi said, inclining her head toward the girls, and wishing she could see Dex's face one last time.

"No," Lira breathed. "You can't go, Andi."

"No!" Breck echoed. She had her arm around Gilly's shoulders, squeezing the child to her side. "We're not letting you walk into Nor's hands. She won't ever let you go."

"She was willing to kill us all just to get to you," Gilly cried.

"It's okay," Andi said, her voice breaking. But she held back her remaining tears, refusing to let them fall. She would not let her crew see her cry in this moment, would never be able to stomach that being their final memory of her.

She looked to Klaren, who took her by the arm and began moving forward.

Gilly reached out, trying to grab her sleeve, but Andi looked to Breck.

"Trust me," she said.

Breck held Gilly back, though there were new tears in her eyes now, too. Lira grabbed Breck's other hand, and together, the three of them stood, watching their captain walk away.

So little time, they'd had to reunite.

They could have seen the entire galaxy together. All of it, not just the darkest parts, but the places that shone the brightest, too. Good memories, without drawing blood or running. They could have chased after something good. Something right.

It nearly broke her to turn away from her crew, but Andi allowed Klaren to guide her away from them. They'd made it only a few paces when that invisible hand gripped her elbow again, pulling them to a stop.

"What are you *doing*?" Dex's voice hissed.

Klaren froze, glancing down from within her crimson helmet.

"You have to take the girls, Dex," Andi said, angling her head toward Klaren so that, to anyone on Nor's side, it would look like it was the two of them who were speaking. "You have to take them and fly away from here, as fast and as far as you can."

"What?"

His voice was pure shock. She could imagine his face, those eyes narrowing as he tried to make sense of what she'd just said. But she only saw the outline of her girls in the background, the waiting ship, the edge of the floating mountain that led off into the Arcardian sky.

Another disembodied voice came from a few steps behind where Andi imagined Dex was standing. Eryn's voice, this time. "Dex, I can't keep you invisible much longer. You're moving too far out of reach. You have to come back this way."

But he wasn't listening.

Andi could still feel his grip on her elbow, holding tight. "Andi, this isn't what we discussed. You're not going over there. We're supposed to distract the soldiers. Then you're taking the girls and shutting down the system."

She'd told him that, yes.

But it hadn't been the truth.

"I'm sorry," she said. "I love you, Dex. You have to trust me. Go back. Take the girls and get out of here."

"Dex," Eryn's voice hissed. "Come *back*. Now. I can't hold it!"

But he didn't move, refusing to let her go.

Klaren took a step forward, pulling Andi with her.

"Dex!" Eryn hissed. Then she cursed, and Andi looked down and realized, with horror, that he was materializing before her again.

There was Dex's tattooed hand, gripping her elbow.

And then there he was, with Eryn and Soyina behind him, becoming solid again, as if they'd just stepped forth from a separate dimension.

"What is this?" Nor's adviser shouted. "GUARDS!"

Klaren whirled as Nor's soldiers lifted their rifles.

Andi saw it all happen as if she were in someone else's body. Nor lifting a hand, shouting a command at her soldiers. The rifles swinging, aiming *past* Andi and Arachnid, toward Dex and Eryn and Soyina, who had suddenly reappeared, as well.

And aiming at Breck, Gilly and Lira.

"No!" Andi shouted.

The first shot was fired.

Not by Nor's soldiers, but by Soyina.

A soldier clad in black dropped to the ground.

Then Dex was shooting, too, his gun held before him with steady hands.

"SEIZE THEM!" Nor shouted. "Kill the others!"

Her soldiers rushed for them, guns at the ready. Andi heard shots fired, saw soldiers dropping. Someone cried out from behind her, and she couldn't tell if it was her crew or Dex or Eryn or Soyina, but her mind was screaming, pleading for her to stop it.

Klaren's armored body slammed on top of hers, blocking a shot as it nearly hit Andi from the side.

"Not the girl!" Nor was screaming. "Hit everyone but the girl! Take them down!"

Arachnid's armor was too heavy. "Get off!" Andi shouted, but Klaren was like a boulder atop her, protecting the one person who could stop this entire war.

But Andi didn't care about the damn war.

Mirabel be damned, her family was in danger.

She had no weapons, no swords, no gun. Fear raced through her, not for her own life, but for all the people that she loved, standing behind her in the line of fire.

"Get me a gun!" Breck's voice shouted, and Andi couldn't see. *She couldn't see a damned thing* around Klaren. She ripped her wrists free of the cuffs, screamed as she put all her strength into pushing the massive armored form off her, the plan be damned…

"Enough!" the droid on Klaren's shoulder shouted, so loud that it broke through the chaos.

Andi gasped as Klaren lifted her body off her own, gulping down air. She watched as Klaren turned toward the queen and reached for her helmet. Steam spilled out from the sides as she removed it, and the soldiers paused as Nor lifted a hand and told them to hold their fire.

Her eyes widened as she took in Arachnid's true identity, her lips parting as if she wasn't sure whether to cry or to scream. Beside her, the adviser's eyes turned to narrow slits.

"You wanted to know who I was," Klaren Solis said, staring her children down. Her droid's voice carried out across the grounds as Nor stood there, frozen in disbelief at the sight of her mother. "Well, here I am, Nor. Back from the dead. And it's time you and I had a talk."

CHAPTER 37
NOR

It was impossible.

"But you're dead," Darai sputtered. His face was a mask of disbelief.

Nor just stared in shock, feeling like she was absent from her own body as her mother stepped closer.

It wasn't her, it *couldn't* be her...and yet every fiber of Nor's being screamed that it was.

The woman laughed. The sound was unlike the one from Nor's memories, coming not from Klaren's mouth, but from the spiderlike droid upon her shoulder. But the way her eyes crinkled and her face turned upward...it was like a ghostly replication of her mother's laugh.

Nor had never forgotten that expression, in all the years they'd been apart. Yet it was somehow different, the look in her mother's eyes not one of joy, but almost sorrow. Her face also wasn't as Nor remembered it—not fully. Half of it was scarred, as if she'd lived through a great crash or been pulled from a bloody battle.

But those golden eyes, so like her own, so like Darai's and Valen's, were impossible to miss, even from twenty paces away.

"Cyprian tried to kill me, yes," Klaren said, her dark hair swaying with the wind and falling across the scarred side of her face. "But I survived. You should know better than most, Darai, that Exonians are not so easy to kill."

"What sort of trick is this?" Darai demanded, stepping up beside Nor. He took her hand in his, as if he wished to pull her away from Klaren's gaze.

Klaren's eyes, their Exonian color burning bright, swept past Darai, narrowing as they looked at his hand on Nor's. She tilted her head slightly.

"Still up to your usual tricks, I see," Klaren said.

"You're a fool, Klaren," Darai hissed. "An utter fool to have come here today."

Klaren ignored him as her eyes flicked back to Nor's face.

There was so much emotion in that gaze.

Nor felt like she was torn in two beneath it. Half a child, desperate to run to her mother, who after all these years had simply come back to life. But the other half seethed with hatred. With a burning desire to march across the space and demand an explanation.

For her mother, her own Exonian flesh and blood, was Arachnid. Her enemy.

They were one and the same.

"What is the meaning of this?" Nor asked. Confusion swarmed through her as she tried to make sense of this reveal. She looked to her soldiers, who continued to stand at the ready. A few had fallen in the cross fire, but plenty still remained. "No one moves," Nor commanded. "If they take a step, you are to fire at will."

"There is so much you don't know," Klaren said, drawing Nor's attention back. "So much that he has done to you, child."

"She is a *queen*," Darai snarled from beside her, his grip on Nor's hand intensifying as he spoke. "You call her child again, and you will fall."

"Enough," Nor said to Darai. "This isn't your battle, Uncle."

His jaw shook with the effort not to speak.

Nor looked back to her mother. She had only the evidence of what had transpired with Arachnid to lean on—and the evidence said that Klaren was Arachnid, her *enemy*, who had come to Arcardius and waged war, who had gotten Zahn killed, who had threatened to drive the killing blade into her own chest.

Nor had feared Arachnid.

But without the helmet on, that threat now seemed diminished. Klaren's true size was revealed, and she was much smaller than Nor remembered, for she'd been only a girl when she last saw her mother. Less of the regal, beautiful queen she'd once been, now more of a woman who'd been forced to find a way to survive—who had likely done terrible things to make it so.

"You were once loyal to Exonia," Nor said, harnessing that angry part of herself, pushing the chill of the day away. "How could you betray our people like this?" Her mind swarmed with the sudden and intense surge of rage, the very same that had come over Nor all her life, had driven her decisions, had made her the queen she was today.

"Don't listen to her, Majesty," Darai said. "She is a traitor to you, and a traitor to Exonia!"

Yes, Nor thought.

It made Nor's blood boil as she thought of how this woman had simply disappeared from her life. Gone in an instant, leaving nothing but a message and a mission, half-complete, only to return now, years later, on the wrong side.

"Why have you come to me today, acting as if we are enemies?" Nor demanded. "Was it not you who told me to complete the mission you started?" Nor would never forget those final, parting words her mother had sent down to her from the sky while Nor burned, crushed by the rubble of their old Xen Pterran palace.

"Exonia is not what you believe it to be," Klaren said. "I have little time to explain everything to you, but you must know, Nor. I was wrong before."

"She lies," Darai hissed. "Take her hostage! You have the upper hand. You have Androma Racella in your grasp! Now is the time to strike and end this war."

"You take Androma Racella, and you will *never* hear the truth," Klaren said, placing her armored hand upon Androma's shoulder and squeezing tight. "You mark my words on that, daughter."

Nor felt like she was losing control.

She saw it happening, felt it within herself. She tried to rein it back in, to regain her equilibrium. Her mother had come to talk. If that was what she wanted, then Nor would play her little game. It would buy her time to come up with a new plan.

"It's been years, Klaren," Nor said. "You have had *years* to come to me, to show me that you were alive and well. That last message you sent to me was about saving our home. *Our* home, the very place that birthed you, that gave you your power. You told me about Valen's existence, and how we could work together to finish what you failed to do. And we've nearly done it, together."

Nor looked at Valen, who had yet to say a word.

He'd never known their mother, never had a relationship with her the way Nor had. He'd been just an infant when Cyprian had cast her out in that final battle of the Cataclysm.

Still, she'd expected some response from him in light of seeing his mother for the very first time. But Valen only stood at Nor's other side, staring ahead, blood seeping from his nostrils as he swayed, looking ready to fall.

Valen, Nor called. But the door between their minds was still closed.

He'd made his decision. He'd shut her out, and he was ready to enter the satellite. To sacrifice himself.

Perhaps he was accepting that all fully now. Perhaps he was in shock that he was seeing his real mother for the first time now, at the end of his time.

Either a blessing from the Godstars, or a curse.

Nor wasn't sure which.

"Whatever Darai has told you is a lie," Klaren said. She'd released her grip on Androma, who now stood only a step away, watching with hardened eyes. The Tenebran Guardian hovered just behind her, and the three members of her crew were frozen in place, pinned down by the rifles Nor's soldiers still pointed at them.

"Exonia is not what you believe it to be," her mother insisted. "It's a world of darkness, a world that seeks to come into Mirabel and destroy it, to suck all life from it until nothing but a gaping hole remains. Then its people will move on to the next galaxy, and the next, until all creation is destroyed. Darai never wanted you to know that. He seeks to become king, to push you aside once you've opened the Void and help the Exonians destroy all that's here and is still to come."

Darai scoffed. "Nor, I have been your adviser, your only family, since you were abandoned by this woman when you needed her most. I helped to heal you and guide you and I have taught you everything you know, including how to use your compulsion. I helped train your brother, too, and I helped place that crown upon your head. Why would I try to trick you? This woman is full of lies."

"This woman," Klaren countered, "is trying to stop you from allowing Exonia to take over Mirabel and all the lives that have been established here."

"You're wrong," Nor said, shaking her head. It couldn't be

true. "If you believe that's our mission, then you are the real fool here. We're trying to save our people. The Zenith virus, and Valen's union with the satellite, will allow us to establish control and peace as Exonia assimilates with Mirabel. When we open the Void, we'll be saving our home. We'll ensure peace, Klaren. Mirabel and Exonia, together at last. Just like you always hoped for."

What had changed, after all these years? What had been done to her mother, to make her doubt the truth?

A tendril of unease slid down Nor's spine, making her skin itch.

Could Klaren be speaking the truth? Could Darai have been lying to her all this time?

Nor didn't want to believe it. For if what Klaren was saying was true…her entire life would have been a lie.

"He's using you, Nor," Klaren said, turning her gaze to Darai, whose grip had become so strong that Nor's hand was beginning to go numb. "Can you not feel it? Can you not sense what he's doing, even now? He used me, too, for years and years. I didn't realize it until later, until I felt the lingering stain of his compulsion in my mind. *Trust Darai. Follow Darai. Give your life up for the mission.* Those thoughts didn't leave my mind until weeks after we parted, and by then I was too busy compelling Cyprian to spare the people of Xen Ptera. Darai and I came to Mirabel together because *he* convinced me to do so. *He* convinced me to slaughter the other Yielded, not because he believed I was the strongest, but because he probably saw the destructive ambition in me. He believed that he could someday overthrow me, once I did all the hard work for him. But when I failed, and Cyprian cast me out, and I spent *years* fighting for my survival as a Mirabellian, powerless without my tongue… I saw the truth. I fell in love with this galaxy, and I realized I could not stand to see it fall."

Tears were streaming down Klaren's face now. "I tried to

reach out to Darai, but he didn't come to my call. He abandoned me, left me for dead, for all he cared, Nor. And he'll do the same to you."

"Seize her," Darai said, spittle flying from his lips as his face twisted in rage. "Before she destroys everything we've worked so hard for. She's trying to get into your mind, Nor. Her compulsion was always strong. She's using it on you now."

Klaren held out her hands, taking a step forward. The guards snapped into position to shoot.

"Hold!" Nor said, lifting a hand.

"Can't you see it, Nor?" Klaren asked. "Your brother is already gone. My boy...my brave, strong boy, taken prisoner in his mind by this monster."

Shock filled her as Nor turned to Valen once more. She didn't want to believe Klaren's words. How could she, when this woman was standing on the opposite side? But that doorway between Valen's and Nor's minds was still sealed shut. And now she swore she could sense darkness leaching from beneath it. As if a stain had begun to spread, overtaking the doorway until it looked entirely made of shadow.

Nor tried once more to reach through it. She knocked, but no answer came. The sound was sucked in by the darkness, unheard.

Doubt began to form in her mind, little cracks that she was starting to see through. All the times Darai had overstepped, had pushed her hard in a direction of his own choosing...had that been his compulsion at work? He'd guided her away from love and into power. He'd hated it when she fell for Zahn, and warned her against feeling love again when she'd found Valen.

Love makes us weak, Darai had said.

He'd never loved Nor. He'd only been there to whisper in her ear, to ensure that she did not falter in her steps. But wasn't that what he was meant to do? An extra mind to support hers. Another Exonian, hell-bent on the mission to free their home.

She'd never sensed power from Darai, for he said he had none left—that he had lost it long before he'd journeyed to Mirabel with Klaren. But perhaps that was part of his plan.

"Darai is a fallen Yielded," Klaren explained. The wind howled, trying to cover her words, but Nor hung on to them, taking a step forward. Leaning closer as she tried to determine the truth. "His power was ripped from him by the Godstars themselves when he tried to overthrow them. He's been biding his time, waiting for the chance to strike, holding on to that shred of his remaining power to become king. And I fear that it's already too late, Nor. For that, I am sorry. I was afraid of him, and once I saw that you had risen to power, and he was standing by your side when your speeches aired across the feeds... I feared the worst."

Her mother held out a hand. "Come to my side. Have your soldiers put down their weapons. We can speak, and I will share every truth I know. Together, we can find a different way. It's not too late to release the minds of these people. To start over, and rule over Mirabel as its rightful queen. Not by imprisoning your people, but by winning their trust and their love."

"*Enough!*" Darai shouted. "You were always too stubborn for your own good, Klaren. And you gave that tendency to your daughter, too. So many times, she's shown a weakness I could not ignore."

Nor turned to him, shocked at his boldness. "Darai. You speak out of turn."

"I speak the truth," he said, and his whole body was shaking, as if he was trying and failing to hold his fury in. "I have stayed silent for far too long. Kill her, Nor. Kill this traitor to the crown. We have work to do."

"Let go of her mind, Darai," Klaren warned. "You will not succeed."

"I'm afraid I can't do that," Darai said coldly.

Nor tried to pull her hand away, but he was unrelenting.

And that anger was back again. Hideous, like a venomous

snake that hissed from within. She could feel it uncoiling in her mind, ready to strike. So suddenly, it had come over her.

"Command your soldiers to shoot her, and be done with it," Darai told Nor.

But Klaren reached down and pressed a button on her armor, revealing a gun inside a hidden compartment. When she lifted it, Nor expected her to aim at Darai.

But she aimed the gun at Androma's head instead, pressing the barrel against the girl's pale temple.

"No!" the Tenebran Guardian behind them shouted.

"If she dies, the Void will never be opened," Klaren said. "As General of Arcardius, you need her to access the weapons network, Darai. Without the nuclear arsenal, your plan is doomed to fail. But I'll keep her alive if you set my children free. Send them to my side. Give them back their minds."

"It's too late," Darai snarled. "You failed me, Klaren. Not once, but twice. And I am not foolish enough to buy into this. You won't harm the girl, because you are in league with her. Because you need that weapons network to fight back against me, too. I saw it the moment you landed, and I planned ahead." He looked to Valen. "Command the guards to shoot Androma's crew."

"Valen, no. You do not take orders from Darai," Nor protested.

But her brother wasn't listening. He swayed on his feet, blood dripping from his nostrils as he closed his eyes.

Behind him, the soldiers aimed their rifles as they felt his command in their minds.

"No!" Androma called out this time. She lifted her hands over her head in surrender, the magnacuffs coming loose. False ones, then. "*No.* I will go with you. Leave them out of this. Just take me. Take me and be done with it."

Darai smiled. "So typical, these Mirabellians who love so deeply." He held out a hand. "Come forth, Androma. Come forth and hand over your title."

Androma stepped forward, eyes blazing. Behind her, her crew cried out, begging her to stop. But she didn't look back as she crossed the space, joining Nor's side.

"My crew walks free," Androma said, fire in her eyes as a guard came forward and locked her wrists in real magnacuffs, sealing them tight. "Swear it."

Darai nodded. "A deal is a deal."

Fear trickled into Nor's mind, trying to pick away at the anger. What was happening? She'd just stood idly by. She'd just watched, without saying a word. She had what she wanted, but why did that suddenly feel so wrong?

"Darai," Nor started. "You need to remember your place."

"I have remembered it," he said. "And now you will remember it, too."

Nor screamed as another mind slammed into her consciousness like a searing blade, turning her vision black. She fell to her knees, hands clapped over her temples as she tried to claw out the pain.

"Enough," Darai said. "Silence, Nor."

Her scream faded, as if it had simply dried up in her throat.

I have always had to take matters into my own hands, Darai's voice hissed inside Nor's mind, an unwelcome, poisonous presence. Her legs shook, her body trembling with the effort to shove him out. *Command the guards to seize you. Hand yourself over to me.*

A terrible coldness had overtaken Nor. It spread, inch by inch, through her system, until she was encased in ice. "Guards," Nor heard her own voice saying. She wanted to scream, wanted to take it back, but she was helpless. "Darai is now in command."

She had no way to stop it as she heard her mother's robotic voice cry out across the field. "Nor! Fight back! Fight against this! You have my blood in your veins. You can resist him!"

She tried, with all of her strength. But she'd never had compulsion like Valen, never had power even close to his, and now, Nor could tell that he had been taken, too. And if *he* had fallen to Darai, with all of that strength he possessed…then there was no hope, not even a shred of it, for her.

Her own guards seized her, pulling her away from Darai so that she stood beside Valen.

"Take him to the satellite," Darai commanded. "You should be the one to upload him, Nor. Imagine how poetic that will be." He looked at Androma. "You, too, my dear. We will need your access to destroy this world."

Nor's hand reached out and took Valen by the arm, her fingers wrapping around his thin frame.

No, her mind screamed. *Stop this, Nor. Fight back!*

But she had no fight left. Her legs moved as if they were someone else's. She couldn't even try to stop them. Slowly, Nor and Valen moved toward the satellite, and Nor knew, she *knew*, that Valen was gone. That he had been for a while now, that he'd never wanted to give himself over to the cause. She'd sensed something was wrong in her office, when he'd told her what he wanted to do, but something had told her to brush it off, to accept what Valen wanted, to put the mission and his sacrifice first.

It had been Darai all along. This wasn't a willing sacrifice.

It was murder.

And if what Klaren said was true…then Exonia was going to destroy Mirabel. She'd been fighting for the wrong side all these years.

"Go ahead." Darai ushered them forward with a hand. Ten armed soldiers joined them, rifles aimed at Androma, the only one not beneath Darai's compulsion. "Take them inside. Begin the uploading. Aclisia is already there waiting for you, and your trusted analyst will transfer the power from Androma, too. I've done all the hard work, Nor. Now you get to have all the fun."

It would be the end of everything Nor had ever known and loved.

A gunshot went off behind her, but her legs kept moving,

obeying Darai's command as she directed Valen into the looming shadow of Nexus, the group of soldiers flanking Androma.

"No!" Klaren's robotic voice screamed as they walked away. Another shot.

Keep walking, Darai's voice commanded Nor. *Do not look back.*

Her neck would not turn to reveal to her what was happening behind them. She simply walked, a prisoner without chains as she hauled her brother toward the satellite that would become his grave.

CHAPTER 38
DEX

Well, this isn't ideal, Dex thought as a dozen angry soldiers surged toward them like a rogue wave.

He and Klaren were just pebbles against their tide. But even pebbles didn't always budge in the surf.

Dex pulled his second gun free from its leg holster. Against Nor's heavily armed soldiers, he felt seriously outgunned, but surely he made up for that in training and strategy. He doubted any of these mind-controlled troops were Guardians.

Footsteps sounded behind them.

Shit.

Lira, Breck, Gilly and Soyina sidled up next to him.

"I told you to leave," he seethed. They each shot him a glare.

"Well, we didn't," Breck said, pulling out her own gun. "Deal with it."

Annoyance shot through him. He didn't want casualties that could be avoided. "Stop being difficult. Get out of here while you can."

"Do you really think we're going to leave Andi behind?" Lira demanded.

Dex would've rolled his eyes if they weren't narrowing in on the soldiers that were almost on top of them.

"Of course not, but she wants you safe. So go!" He shouted the last part as the first soldier lunged at him. Dex dipped away, narrowly missing the butt of a gun to his brow.

Klaren blasted a shot to his head and the man collapsed in a heap. The remaining soldiers paused for a moment, staring at their fallen comrade.

"You take the guys on the right. I got the left," he said to Klaren.

"Who do we take?" Breck asked.

He couldn't shake them, and right now, they didn't have time to argue. "Breck and Gilly, cover Klaren. Lira, Soyina—you're with me."

The girls moved into position. "What are you waiting for?" Dex taunted, and the soldiers continued their procession forward. One took a shot at him, and if it weren't for the electric shield that suddenly materialized in front of him, he would've been a goner.

"Thanks," he said to Klaren as she stepped back, retracting the barrier back into her crimson armor. If he survived this fight, he wouldn't mind adding those gadgets to his personal armory.

Dex blasted a round at the closest soldier. The man flew backward, as if being yanked by strings, before colliding with two of his comrades. Dex immediately focused on his next target, failing to notice the group of three soldiers coming up behind him.

A splitting pain radiated through his back and he tumbled to the ground.

Quick as he could, Dex tried to scramble up, only to be met

with the muzzle of a gun hitting him square in the jaw. Blood flooded into his mouth, the metallic taste making him gag.

The man smiled at him with yellow, rotten teeth.

"Good night, traitor."

He was dea—

The man crumpled to the ground, followed shortly after by his two lackeys. Dex jumped to his feet, but couldn't spot his savior in the chaos of battle. Smoke rolled across the estate grounds, concealing bodies as they fell. All the others were busy grappling in their own fights.

"Soyina was right. You truly are slow sometimes." He jumped at the sound of a female voice behind him. He turned just in time to see Eryn appear before him.

"Of course," he breathed.

"Bet you're glad to see me." She smirked, pushing her shining strands of hair out of her eyes. "Or not see me."

"You have no idea," Dex said, his heart pounding erratically in his chest. "Come on. We have to get to the satellite."

"I'll clear a path through the remaining guards."

He nodded, turning to Klaren, who was fighting with an electric baton. She dipped and twirled the weapon in fluid, deadly arcs before bringing it down on her opponents. She lunged and twisted with ease, showcasing moves Dex only wished he knew. With a swift downward kick, she brought one man to his knees and knocked his helmet off.

He was young, too young. But age didn't matter in the game of war, and Klaren delivered his death blow, singeing the surrounding skin until it turned black.

Dex shifted his attention back to the battle, which was almost won. Only a few soldiers remained. As he watched, Soyina blasted one from a few yards away, and Lira had another in a choke hold, holding the woman there until her body went limp. Dex knew she wasn't dead—that wasn't Lira's way of doing things. But among the scattered bodies, the dead and the living were difficult to distinguish.

Dex turned to follow the path Eryn was mowing down between the remaining soldiers. They dropped like flies, completely helpless against the invisible force.

"Time to go!" he yelled.

Somehow, they'd all made it out with their lives intact, though he couldn't say the same for their opponents. But he couldn't dwell on death when they still had so much left to do.

Dex was suddenly, fiercely glad Andi's crew had stayed to fight, despite his attempts to make them leave. These women had the power to bring the world to its knees, yet here they were, saving it.

CHAPTER 39
VALEN

The interior of the satellite was silent.

It was a strange disconnect from the battle waging beyond its walls as Nor guided Valen inside, Androma and the soldiers following. The door to Nexus slid shut behind them with an ominous *bang*, effectively trapping them inside.

"Welcome!" Darai said, stepping past them. His voice echoed as he held his arms wide, like a proud architect revealing his very first creation to the world. "A beautiful specimen, unlike anything I've ever seen. Imagine how good it will feel when she's finally cast into the sky."

Inside his mind, Valen continued to struggle for freedom.

Fight back, he thought. He'd commanded the minds of millions. He'd turned an entire galaxy to his sister's side, even gotten Androma's crew, fiercely loyal, to turn their backs on their captain.

But now he couldn't even compel himself to break free of Darai's mental chains.

"Look at it, Valen," Darai said, reaching out and scraping a jagged fingernail across Valen's cheek. He couldn't even flinch away from that touch, though he despised it so. "See how wonderful it is, your new home for eternity."

"Please," Nor ground out between gritted teeth as she stood beside him. "Don't do this, Darai. There must be another way."

He must have allowed her more freedom than Valen had, for there were tears streaming down her cheeks as she looked around the satellite. And though she couldn't move her arms or legs on her own, Nor's head turned to focus on Valen as she begged. "Let us go, Uncle. You can have the power. Take it. Just let us all go."

Darai clicked his tongue, shaking his head. "I'm afraid I can't do that, my dear. We've come too far to turn back now. Exonia awaits us, and we cannot disappoint our homeland."

He marched deeper into the satellite, motioning for them to follow. And follow they did, as if they were truly caught in a current of his power, being towed along.

"I'm so sorry, Valen," Nor said. "I'm so sorry I never saw it, or felt it in him."

He wanted to answer her. He wanted to say that he was sorry, too. That they had both made mistakes, both been fooled by the one man they thought they could trust in this galaxy.

But all Valen could do was take in the sight of the place that was to be his eternal grave.

The interior of Nexus was just as Valen had imagined, much like the hollowed inside of a metallic egg. Curved silver walls arched toward the sky, as far as Valen could see, lined with lights and metallic panels that hummed with life as the satellite booted up, ready to be launched into space. The Exonian godstar symbols glowed across the interior, as if the entire satellite were a shrine to the other world.

Valen saw it for what it truly was now, his head filled with visions of the truth.

A world full of monsters, swirling with eternal darkness.

A world that would destroy Mirabel, and with it, all light and life, Darai leading the charge toward the end of all things.

"I don't suppose I can change your mind," Andi said, as the guards hauled her forward after Darai. Her voice was so strong, so calm in this moment. "You don't seem like a man who is easily threatened."

Valen regretted every betrayal he'd committed against her now. For she would likely die as well when Darai was done with her, after he'd taken away her title and her power over the weapons network.

Darai didn't answer, and so Valen continued to take in the full scope of the space.

Jutting out from the panels overhead were massive tubes flowing with what looked like liquid starlight. The Zenith virus, full of Valen's DNA, full of his compulsion power that Aclisia had so flawlessly replicated. He followed those tubes with his eyes, numb to the horror of what was to come. They trailed from the walls like the very veins of the satellite, twisting until they formed one thick cord that led down to the center of the space, where a metal pod, much like the med bay healing pods he'd seen on starships, sat waiting.

The pod door was ajar, a light inside revealing the throne Darai had spoken of.

It would be his prison for all eternity, a coffin that would never be buried beneath the ground, but instead, cast out into the stars.

And there Valen would forever remain.

"It's beautiful, isn't it?" a voice asked. Aclisia and Darai came out from behind the pod, Aclisia's two heads focused on the group. The left head smiled from ear to ear, while the right head spoke excitedly. "You've come just in time. We've completed our work, and now we'll finally see the fruits of our labor!"

"Such a performer, always," Aclisia's left head said to her right. Both heads turned and smiled again toward Valen, their teeth sharp as a shark's. "Come along, Prince. You are to be our very greatest achievement!"

Both hands reached out toward him.

"No," Darai said. "Nor is going to do it herself."

Valen felt it then, the horror returning to him as Nor turned, tears pouring down her cheeks as she grasped Valen by his wrists. Her grip was fiercely strong, the nails of her hand digging into his skin, her golden prosthetic as cold as ice against his other wrist.

"I can't stop it," she whispered, pulling him toward the open pod. "I never should have listened to him, Valen. You were right all along. You were the only one who ever sensed his wrongness, and I ignored you."

"Get the general into position," Darai instructed.

Beside the pod stood a panel on a thin podium. The soldiers guided Androma over to it, flanking her on all sides. She didn't resist, almost as if she were being compelled by a power similar to the one commanding Valen now. But he knew she was immune to the virus, had known it since she and Dex resisted the attack at Ucatoria.

Perhaps it was her own resolve driving her to follow Darai, for Valen knew she did not fear death. He'd seen her find her way out of worse situations before.

Perhaps she had her own plan, as she always did.

Valen wished, desperately, that he could speak to her, that he could see into her mind to discover whether she was thinking of a way out of this.

"Valen first," Darai said, gesturing to the pod.

"Please," Nor begged him. "I'll do anything. *Anything* to

change your mind. Do you truly have no love for all we've built together, Uncle? We can still change things. We can still rule in this galaxy ourselves. We have the power. Isn't that enough?"

Darai just threw back his head and laughed, the sound so wicked it sent chills skittering across his skin.

Valen had never heard that laughter before, did not know that Darai could feel such joy.

But as his uncle's gaze fell upon Nor, Valen realized it wasn't joy. It was an evil sort of hysteria, a thick, oppressive darkness oozing from the old Exonian.

"I am no uncle of yours," Darai said mockingly. "Pathetic, how you saw me as family all this time. Family has no meaning in Exonia—only power does. And there can never be enough of it. Now stop groveling, Nor, and put your brother where he belongs. The princeling needs a throne, don't you think?"

Fight him, Valen thought to Nor. *Please, fight back against him. You have compulsion. You have the strength of our mother in your veins!*

But Nor's hands shoved Valen into the pod, settling him onto the cold, metal throne. "I forgive you—for Zahn, for everything," she sobbed. "It was never any fault of yours. I see that now."

Thank you, sister, he thought. But he knew she couldn't hear him, so he hoped she saw it in his eyes.

From inside the pod, he could see the tubes and wires that were to connect him to Nexus. Over his head, a dome-like helmet hung near the ceiling of the pod. Soon it would lower, and it would connect to his brain, stealing his mind from him, just as Darai had explained earlier when he first captured Valen with his power.

How long before that power ran out? Darai said he'd been hoarding his complusion for years, saving it up for this very moment.

How much time did they have before the Exonian was no longer able to hold them?

Not enough time, Valen thought. For everything had already fallen into place, and the plan was nearly complete for the old man.

"A nice fit," Aclisia said, grinning down at Valen as she stepped past Nor and began to work on the pod, fingertips flying across the network of glowing panels inside to begin the process. The pod hummed with life as straps snaked tight across his chest, closing over his wrists, his ankles.

Sweat beaded down Valen's temples as he tried, with all of his might, to push against the dark power surging within.

"There will be pain," Aclisia's right head said somewhat apologetically as she tapped in a command.

"Oh, yes," the other head said. "Though it's best not to scream or fight it."

Another thing Darai had lied about, then.

"He won't fight," Darai said. "He has no strength left in him."

The helmet began to lower until it hovered just over Valen's skull, and he felt the sharpness of needles above his hairline, ready to be injected into him, like nails driven deep into a board.

"Don't do this," Nor pleaded to Darai. "I'll give you the crown. You can have it. Just let Valen go."

Valen had a clear view of her now. She was beautiful, even with the tears streaming down her face. They made her gold eyes, the color of her lost crown, stand out all the more. She was the family he'd always dreamed of having, and he found himself wondering what could have been, had they lived a normal life, been given the chance to get to know each other without kingdoms and crowns, without compulsion.

Without Exonia.

It struck Valen then, what he'd done to the entirety of Mirabel. He wondered if they'd felt any pain, the very same he felt now, when he'd stolen their minds. He wondered if they had gone down fighting, as he was, or if they'd simply ceased to exist.

The Godstars had seen his sins, and now they were punishing him for them.

"You'll be executed publicly when this is done," Darai said to Nor as he stepped back and watched Aclisia work, arms crossed over his chest. "Valen will be launched into the sky, his compulsion sending out the message that I am now king. They will worship me and me alone."

"Initiating the first sequence," Aclisia said.

The first needle began to slide into Valen's skull.

He tried to scream, but no sound came out.

"By then, I will have used Andromo to gain control of the weapons network. The Void will be blasted open, creating a hole between the two worlds, and when the Exonians come through…they will be mine. Through Valen, I'll command them to do my bidding. Little by little, we'll make our way to other worlds, other galaxies. We'll take over every living soul we can find. All will bow in fear at the sound of my name, and the very Godstars will quake from their thrones in the sky."

Valen's eyes moved to Andromo. She stood so quietly, so calmly, amid the ten guards watching her. Their rifles were aimed at her chest, her head. She would not be able to get away from them, not even with her strength.

But she hadn't even tried.

Her eyes met Valen's for a moment. There was horror in them, for what she was seeing. Perhaps for how he looked, so weak as his body failed him. Perhaps horror for what he'd done, the secrets he'd kept from her, despite the friendship she'd thought they were building aboard the *Marauder*, despite the forgiveness he'd said he'd given her, for her hand in Kalee's death.

But there was something else, too.

The look of a soldier standing before a firing squad. Facing death…but not fearing it.

"You are a monster," Nor was saying. So strange, to see her wrapped up in the arms of compulsion. To see her standing free, when he knew that on the inside, she was just as trapped as he was.

"And you are going to die," Darai said, turning to face her as the second needle slipped into Valen's skull.

He screamed audibly this time, but Darai ignored the sound as he spoke to Nor. "The entire galaxy will hate you, and *oh*, how they will call for your death. Your head will be mounted above Averia's doors for all to see."

No, Valen thought.

Where was his power?

How had it been crushed so quickly, so easily?

He dived back into his mind, seeking it out. Begging it to reveal itself, for a tiny bit of it to have remained, as Darai's power had when the Godstars ripped it from him.

Still, there was nothing. Only a castle that was slowly cracking as a fault line crept across the black stones, as Darai broke through it piece by piece.

"Take me, then," Nor said. "I will go in his place."

Darai howled with laughter. "Your pathetic power would be of no use to me, Nor. I'm surprised by how much you believed my praises toward you all these years. You were never as powerful as Klaren, and never even close to what Valen is now."

He reached into the pod and touched Valen's cheek again. "Exonia bred true in you, my boy," Darai marveled.

A third needle pierced Valen's skin.

He could no longer feel the pain, for he had become it. He saw red fill his vision as blood trickled into his eyes from above. Cold was beginning to take over his body, freezing him inch by inch. He knew death would try to come soon, as Darai promised, but the pod would keep him alive. Barely, so that he would never be able to fight back as his power was used forever.

Andi's eyes were locked on Valen, her hands clenched into fists, wrists bound in their cuffs. Yet still, she did not move, did not even try to fight the soldiers that guarded her. They may as well have not been there at all.

Would she truly give over her title so easily?

"The entire galaxy will watch as I remove your head from your neck," Darai said to Nor. "But on the bright side, you'll finally be reunited with Zahn on the other side."

She could not die. Not his sister, not his family. Rage filled Valen at the thought, bubbling up from his very soul. He had to fight. He had to save Nor, if it was the very last thing he did in this life.

Another needle, this time injected into his arm. His blood turned cold as something filled his veins.

"The upload is beginning, sir," Aclisia said. "And we're beginning cryosis."

Valen felt it happen. A shift from within.

Deep in his mind, something rumbled. Valen slipped back inside, desperately seeking his power, but the doors to his castle were locked, the Solis symbol changed to something else.

The godstar of death, split in two.

It was cold here now, and flecks of snow drifted from the sky as his castle began to fall.

A single obsidinite stone slipped from its place atop one of the turrets. It careened to the ground, tumbling edge over edge until it landed with a soft *thunk* atop the dead grass, beside a pile of bones. Snow piled over it.

Another stone fell.

Then another, until it was like a black rain, quickly covered over by frozen white.

Darai's laughter filled Valen's head, and he was pulled out of his mind, back into the pod where he looked out at Nor, who had fallen to her knees, tears running down her cheeks as she watched him. Was this truly the end for him?

Then a commotion from beyond drew Darai's attention away.

The sound of gunfire, growing closer. "Useless soldiers," he growled.

In that moment, Valen thought he saw Androma flinch. It was almost imperceptible, but he saw it. The shimmer of something silver beneath her magnacuffs, sticking out from beneath the edge of her sleeve.

Her eyes found Valen's again, and she nodded, only once, before Darai turned back to look at the group. "Faster!" he said. "The battle is nearly done."

Valen wasn't sure who was winning, but he knew the end was coming, no matter who came through that satellite door.

"The uploading and cryosis both take time," Aclisia said, both heads focused on Valen as more blood slowly trickled into his vision. "We need five minutes, my King."

Darai's voice was acid. "We may not have five minutes. Make it three."

"We cannot speed the process up," Aclisia said. "Though you could begin the transfer of power now, if you're insistent on saving time."

Darai glared at her, then signaled to the guards holding Andi hostage. "Bring the general to me. We'll transfer her power, and then I want her body dumped over the edge of the estate. Let her fall from the sky to the city below."

It was then that Androma moved.

So fast Valen would have missed it, had he not been watching her, feeling certain that she was about to do something to alter Darai's plans.

Her wrists were still cuffed, but she'd slid a knife from beneath her sleeve, whirling so that the guard gripping her arm screamed as his wrist popped. Almost instantly, she dug the knife deep into the neck of the guard to her left.

He gasped, reaching up as blood welled through his fingertips.

Then he fell, the other guards turning to level their guns at

Andi in retaliation just as the door to the satellite burst open. Smoke filled the entryway, accompanied by the sound of gunfire.

"Don't shoot her!" Darai commanded the guards as Andi began to fight, turning into the Bloody Baroness that Valen remembered, that he had been waiting to see return. "We need her alive, you fools! Turn your weapons to the others!"

But then the smoke cleared from the doorway, and Valen's heart surged with a final bit of hope as Arachnid and Andi's crew stepped inside.

CHAPTER 40
ANDI

It had been some time since Andi had been in a real fight.

She embraced the chance, lunging at another guard with her small hidden blade. It didn't matter the size, so long as the blade struck true. The guard dropped beneath her attack, blood spraying as he fell, staining the metallic exterior of the pod.

Andi dropped to the ground, wrists still cuffed as a guard swung the butt of his rifle toward her head. He missed, narrowly avoiding hitting Darai instead.

Another guard leveled his rifle at her, finger poised over the trigger.

"I said *don't shoot!*" Darai howled. "Get the others, but leave the general to me!"

He had Nor in front of him, shielding his body with hers, the coward.

Andi turned her gaze to the old man, spinning the small blade around in her fingertips until the tip pointed at him. *"You,"* she snarled as she strode forward. "You are not going to take my title. You deserve to die for what you've done."

"Go ahead—try to kill me," Darai said, glaring at her from behind Nor's frozen form. "You won't succeed."

He closed his eyes as if he were concentrating, a rather strange reaction to being faced with an enemy and a sharpened blade. Andi realized, too late, what he was about to do, as Nor's frozen form suddenly lunged forward, her body moving like a trained fighter's. She swung her leg upward, then down to arch over Andi's shoulder, just over the spot where Valen had stabbed her during Ucatoria. The hit struck hard and true.

Andi fell to the ground, pain lancing through her as she rolled with her hands pressed to her chest, magnacuffs gouging against her skin. The old wound screamed with phantom pain as she rolled to her feet, blade still held carefully in her grip.

Andi circled, sidestepping Nor.

"You cannot defeat me," Nor said, but Andi knew the words weren't hers. They came from her lips, but they belonged to the puppetmaster she was unwittingly protecting. Her eyes rolled back into her head, revealing only the whites as she lifted her hands, curled them into fists and smiled. It looked exactly like the grin on the old man's face as he stood beside the pod, eyes closed, motionless. All the while, the two-headed scientist continued her work on Valen.

The moment it was completed, the moment he was uploaded, the satellite would be cast into the sky. And then all Darai would need to complete his mission was Andi's General access, to unlock the weapons network.

"Let go of her mind," Andi growled. "Release Valen and Nor from your power."

"I'm afraid I can't do that," Nor said back, speaking Darai's words. "You have one more chance, Androma, to hand over your title and stop this fight."

"And why would I do that?" Andi asked.

Nor smiled. "Because your crew is about to die trying to get to their dear captain. Every last one of them."

The door to the satellite filled with enemy reinforcements.

They were clad in the crimson, bulletproof armor of the New Vedans, similar to what Klaren wore, but lighter in weight, helmets covering their faces. They filed into the massive satellite, one after the other, at least fifty in number. They far outweighed Andi's small crew.

"Line up!" Breck shouted from the other side of the rounded space.

Andi saw her crew, fearless as ever, get into their formation, side by side, Dex along with them. Her girls, so beautiful in their freedom, were still here. Why hadn't they left yet?

But Andi knew. Their hearts were just as loyal as hers.

She wouldn't have left without them, either. It made her ache even more, for what she would likely have to do.

"Fire!" Breck shouted.

A spray of bullets hit the soldiers, but they rebounded off their armor, useless.

The soldiers turned their rifles to the crew, and Klaren screamed, lifting her arms up as the soldiers fired. A crimson shield of electricity flared to life, holding back the spray of bullets. They pinged to the ground in a silver rain.

Breck moved to stand behind Klaren, supporting her as the soldiers shot again. The shield crackled, but held strong. Lira and Gilly were behind it, safe, Dex at their side.

But for how long?

"They will fall," Nor said as she lunged at Andi again. Andi careened to the right, slicing out with her blade, but Nor dodged it. "That shield will not last forever, Androma. And when it fizzles out, I will make sure that you watch me destroy them all one by one. So come forward, and give me your title. You're only wasting time in a battle you cannot win."

"Never," Andi swore. "I will *never* willingly give you that access."

She'd hoped, *oh*, she had hoped, that her crew would have been able to fight their way out of this. That they had been able to get to Valen, to kill him before the upload began.

But the plan had failed, had gotten out of hand.

Nor laughed, diving toward her again. Andi slashed out with her knife and sliced Nor's wrist, a wicked cut that went deep, but the woman didn't even flinch, didn't even seem to feel the pain as she paced, circling, ready to attack again at Darai's command.

My children must live, for the galaxy to be free, Klaren had said to Andi, in their private moments together aboard the ship on their journey here. While the new crew and Dex had slept, they'd met in secret. They'd spoken of their plans to save Mirabel, together, in the midst of a hopeless war. They'd come up with a second plan, should the first fail.

For they *would* lose.

Andi and Klaren had known it from the start.

Still, she'd hoped there would be another way.

Behind Nor, Andi could see her crew still fighting. The world seemed to move in slow motion as Breck lifted her rifle, shooting past Klaren's armored body and the electric shield that spanned from one edge of the satellite to the other, looking for a weak spot in the line of enemy soldiers. Dex knelt, shooting from a low point beside Gilly. Lira paced, waiting for her chance to move forward and swing with her fists.

More bullets sprayed against Klaren's shield.

One broke through, slammed against the back of the satellite's paneled wall.

"Oh, dear," Nor said, laughing. "So close to the end, for your crew."

Breck fired, and one of Darai's soldiers fell. She'd found a break in his armor, locked onto it, the brave gunner. Andi saw Gilly and Dex perk up, following suit as they aimed for the same spot Breck had found on other soldiers.

A few of the enemy soldiers rushed forward, sprinting toward the solid shield wall. The moment they touched it, their bodies collapsed, seizing until they went still.

For a moment, Andi felt hope, but it was quickly crushed. The enemy numbers were too many. The satellite had become a dam, ready to break. Soon, the Godstars would choose a side to win and a side to fall. It would be determined the moment Klaren's shield shattered...and Andi knew which side would lose.

It was nearly time.

She'd held off for as long as she could.

"Release Valen and Nor," Andi said again. "Release the minds of everyone in Mirabel, or I will kill him."

"You can't get to him, child," Nor said with a laugh, her eyes still white as bone, still rolled back in her head.

Andi swung the small blade, but Nor was too quick.

She whirled, almost knocking it from Andi's grasp with her foot.

They circled, lunging at each other.

They were matched, move for move.

Andi had to find a way to reach him, free him from the pod before it was too late.

"The clock is ticking," Nor said. Behind her, the two-headed scientist clapped her hands, and inside the pod, Valen was practically aglow as his veins filled with cold fluid. His mouth hung open in a silent scream.

"You know that one soldier's shield won't last long against the onslaught, and there's no way out of here with my soldiers guarding the exit. When Klaren's armor fails..." Nor smiled. "Everyone you love will die."

Andi chanced one more glance back at her crew.

The shield was breaking down, little by little.

Nearly thirty soldiers still remained. And even if they fell, Darai would just send more. Her crew would never make it out of here alive.

Nor landed a kick against Andi's jaw. It didn't crack, but pain spread through her face, bringing tears to her eyes.

Across the satellite, Klaren's eyes met Andi's.

There was so much emotion in that golden gaze.

Andi nodded at her, stepping closer to the pod where Valen was held, guiding Nor's attacks in that direction. Darai remained motionless beyond her, controlling Nor's every move in his mind.

"Give up, Androma," Nor said, smiling wide as Darai continued to speak through her. "It's already too late."

The gunfire continued. Klaren's shield was close to breaking. So, so close, for every bullet that hit, red light spread across it in glowing fracture lines.

"It's not too late," Andi said.

She thought of Klaren's words, her promise that she would ensure her crew was well cared for, once all was said and done.

Andi lifted her blade, watching as Klaren's shield wavered.

Another bullet got through.

"No!" Klaren cried out as Eryn fell, her body flickering in and out of existence as she hit the ground, reaching a hand toward her leader.

Another bullet nearly hit Lira, but Breck turned her body, taking the shot in the back, the bullet pinging against her bullet-proof skin.

It was now or never.

Andi wondered how it would feel when she fell. She thought of the weapons network, and how it would sense her death. How it would self-destruct without a chosen successor.

If Andi died, and didn't choose a successor, no one would have the power. In her mind, that was how it should be.

Her crew would have no captain. But Mirabel would be safe,

the Void impossible to open for a time, long enough for Klaren to discover a way to release her children from Darai's power.

"Fly true," Andi whispered to herself.

She closed her eyes as she pressed the tip of the blade above her heart.

CHAPTER 41
VALEN

He was nearly gone now.

Valen felt his very life freezing up as his veins filled with the cryo liquid.

As his mind, little by little, was pulled away from him, up-loaded into the inner workings of the Nexus satellite.

Inside his mind, the valley of bones was covered with snow that looked like ashes.

His castle had fallen. Only a few stones still remained.

He found himself falling in and out of awareness. Half of him was seated in the pod, watching the battle wage on, Nor being used as Darai's puppet as Androma fought against her, Nor's body moving in ways it never had before. The other half remained seated in the snow, trapped inside his mind.

At one point, the snow began to fall backward, drifting up toward the sky.

Each flake contained a memory of Valen's.

One flitted past his gaze. In it, he saw himself as a child, playing with Kalee in the courtyard of Averia. She'd played the part of queen, Valen, the king.

"Someday, we'll lead this planet side by side, Val," Kalee's small, young voice said. Her smile faded from view as the memory floated upward and away.

Then gone.

The sound of gunfire drew Valen back to the world, into his body. He watched as Andi sliced Nor's arm. Blood dripped from the wound, but they still fought, Nor trying to get control of Andi, to take her to the scanner where she would pass her title on to Darai.

He fell back into his mind, watching his memories drift into the sky.

Another flake floated past Valen's vision. In it, he saw his father's face looming over him as he screamed at Valen, calling him worthless. Telling him that he would never be good enough, that he was ashamed Valen carried his blood.

That memory, Valen did not care to hold on to. He smiled as it flew away.

Again, he slipped back into the world.

He saw Androma lift her blade.

Saw her turn it on herself and knew what she was going to do. Only the bravest, the most selfless leader would do such a thing, to turn the tide of the war. To save millions.

But it would only calm things for a time. It would not end the war, for the moment Valen's body was in full cryo, the moment he was uploaded into the satellite, the threat would remain forever. Even if Androma had managed to kill him, the minds of Mirabel would have remained trapped beneath his compulsion. Only the compeller could release them, by choice.

And his death would prevent that from ever happening.

They'd remain in that state, worshipping the thoughts Valen had placed in their minds, growing useless without new directives from their compeller. He could not release them, not while Darai had him leashed like a helpless dog.

It was almost too late. Valen sensed the uploading nearing its completion, as his mind began to feel light. Empty. And Darai's power continued to surge through him, still barring Valen's ability to fight back.

But as that blade touched Andi's chest, just over the space where Valen had once tried to kill her with his own blade…

Something inside him whispered his name.

It was not Darai's voice.

It was lighter. Softer.

A delicate voice that called to him. Valen sank into his mind, back into the world that was covered in ashen white, the rubble of his castle a pile at the base of the valley.

"Valen," the voice called.

It sounded like Kalee.

Even in his mind, he could scarcely move. But some part of him still surged forward, following the sound of Kalee's voice. It led him to the rubble of his castle, where his power had once thrived.

"Valen."

The sound was growing dimmer by the second.

He reached out, touching the obsidinite stones.

So cold. His palms ached, bleeding as he began to dig. Tears of blood slipped down his face as he pulled stone after stone aside, searching.

He found it at the very bottom.

A little orb of light, a tiny kernel of it, no larger than a small seed.

Valen reached out with shaking, bleeding hands and scooped it up.

The orb was warm, a welcome feeling to shake off the chill of death. He held it to his chest, letting it soothe him, and as he pressed it close, he found that it gave him strength.

Fight back, Valen, the voice called from the orb.

It was his power.

It was his very soul, all that remained.

Darai must have overlooked it. Perhaps the Godstars were on Valen's side after all. Perhaps they'd seen his regret for what he'd done to Mirabel.

Perhaps they'd led him back to his power, after all this time.

He could right his wrongs. He could do something, *anything*, to fix what he'd broken.

With great effort, Valen pushed himself from his mind, back into his dying body.

He saw Androma, nearly ready to press the blade too deep. Blood welled from her skin already, staining her shirt beneath the blade.

"Don't," he ground out, using that kernel of his power to speak against Darai's will. "Andi, stop."

The old man hadn't noticed yet. Hadn't felt Valen breaking through, as he willed his soldiers to keep fighting Andi's crew.

"Stop," Valen said again, and by the Godstars' mercy, she heard him.

Her eyes flitted toward his, the blade pausing over her heart. She moved closer to him, a careful step within earshot.

"What are you doing?" Nor was saying to her, speaking Darai's words. "Stop that at once! Put down the blade!"

"Kill me instead," Valen said, praying that she could hear him. "Kill me, Andi. I'm releasing the minds. Do it, before it's too late. I don't have…much time."

He saw her turn, the motion swift as she held out the blade.

Not a second of hesitation as she slid it across his throat. Valen felt the blood begin to drain from him, and he smiled.

"NO!" Darai screamed just as Valen sank into his mind, using those remaining moments of life to undo what he'd started so long ago.

It was cold, *so cold* inside his mind, where he sat atop the rubble of his castle once more. He moved the final stones aside and clawed at the frozen ground, digging a hole large enough for that kernel of his power to fit. He dropped it inside the small hole as he gasped for air. Blood fell upon it, staining the ground around that tiny bit of power.

The kernel soaked it up.

And then it began to grow.

And as it grew, Valen felt his power returning to him. A final push as his mind tried to hang on to life, even while his body was already gone, his last breaths wheezing from his lungs.

"I release you," he whispered to no one.

But he saw, little by little, the stones begin to quake.

Each one of them, a mind in Mirabel stuck beneath his compulsion no longer.

With a smile, Valen lay back on the cold ground to sleep.

Peace, he thought, as he closed his eyes and let himself slip away. *At long last.*

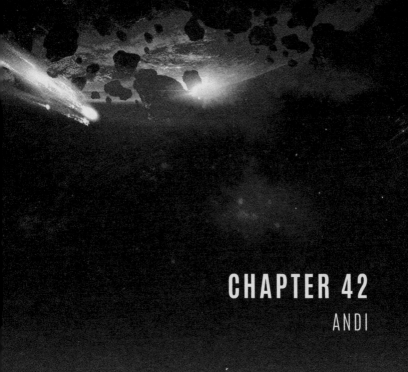

CHAPTER 42
ANDI

The blade was wet with Valen's blood.

The soldiers began to surge toward her, but as Valen took his last, weak breath, they suddenly stopped.

As one, the entire group collapsed, their bodies and weapons hitting the satellite's metallic floor with *thunk* after *thunk*. Nor fell, too, in a graceless heap beside Valen's pod.

And then the satellite was silent.

The only sound was Darai as he opened his eyes and stumbled forward, watching the scene play out before him. "What have you done?" he breathed.

He glanced at Valen's body, the red gash across his throat signifying that he was, indeed, gone.

His eyes were wild as he looked back at Andi. "You *fool!*" he snarled. "You're going to—"

"Enough, Darai."

Andi turned to see Klaren standing over her shoulder, still in that armor, alive and well. She smiled and reached out to take the knife from Andi's hand, fingertips closing over the handle, still warm with her son's blood. "You're growing old, Darai. It's time you rested. Don't you agree?"

He sputtered to form words, but they never left his lips.

Because Klaren swung, that wet blade arcing through the air as she slammed it into the side of his neck.

His blood was golden as the sun.

Darai gasped for air, clawing at the blade, but his hands trembled as that golden lifeblood left him. Slowly, the rage in his eyes dulled, and then his body fell to the ground, unmoving.

Klaren stared at him for a moment, then deliberately stepped across his back, his bones crunching beneath the weight of her armor. As if to ensure that he was, in fact, dead.

"You did well," she said to Andi. "I wasn't sure that you would be able to stomach the sacrifice, but… I'm impressed."

Groans filled the room as the soldiers began to stir. Andi tensed, waiting for them to attack. But instead, they blinked wearily, as if waking from a long sleep. Slowly, they seemed to come back to themselves.

Some cried out as they saw their fallen comrades. Others began to walk about absentmindedly, reuniting with their friends, calling out for their loved ones. A group of them simply sat and wept, staring down at their hands as they remembered what they'd done, as they remembered the darkness they'd felt beneath the compulsion.

Finally, they were free.

Klaren knelt before Nor, reaching out to rouse her gently. The fallen queen opened her eyes, focusing them on her mother, hope in her gaze. Then she looked to Valen, lifeless in the pod, his body still encased, his eyes still open and unseeing.

"No," she gasped, turning to Andi with a murderous expression.

Andi held out her hands, ready to defend her choice, but Klaren spoke instead. "It was a mercy, Nor," she said, her robotic voice as gentle as could be. "Your brother was long gone, lost to Darai's power. And now...he set the galaxy free."

Tears poured from Nor's eyes as she stood, reaching out for Valen. Klaren helped her undo his bindings. Andi turned, giving them their space, just in time to see her crew approach.

Gilly came first, a blur of red hair as she leaped at Andi, wrapping her tiny arms around Andi's middle. Breck followed, slapping her across the shoulder as she pulled both of them in for a hug.

Lira was the last to approach, her blue eyes holding Andi's as if she'd seen what Andi had been about to do. As if she knew, and was not impressed by what her captain had almost done.

"I had to, Lir," Andi said. "There was no other choice."

"I know." Her pilot smiled sadly. "But we must thank the Godstars that they found a way around that choice, and made a new one for you."

Andi realized, suddenly, that she hadn't yet told Lira about Lon. But her friend seemed to sense that, too. "Did my brother die well?" she asked.

There was pain in her words, but also something more. Adhirans had always had a different way of looking at death, knowing that though a body was gone, the spirit carried on.

"He saved us," Andi said, watching as Lira's scaled cheek slowly began to glow, then dim again as she took a deep breath. "He died a hero, Lir."

Lira nodded, then reached out and squeezed Andi's hand gently.

Dex arrived next, bleeding, but alive. And more handsome than Andi had ever seen him, a soldier who'd survived a brutal war and grown stronger because of it. He looked past their group as Klaren and Nor placed Valen's limp body on the floor.

"They have no leader now," Dex said, but there was no pity in his eyes as he looked at Valen.

"He asked me to kill him," Andi said. "He wanted it, Dex. Almost like he thought it could right his wrongs."

Dex shrugged. "Does that really erase what he did, though?"

"He may have been under Darai's compulsion the entire time," Andi said. "We'll never know for sure, but maybe he never had a choice. Maybe he never wanted any of this."

Andi wondered if the last true Valen she'd known was the one who'd hated her after Kalee had died. She didn't know if the forgiveness he'd given her, back on Adhira, was truly real or not.

But now wasn't the time to focus on that.

"It doesn't matter," Lira said. "He's gone now. And we have to start anew. These soldiers will be calling for blood soon, when they realize Nor is still alive."

"If you're going to punish her properly," Breck said, her face twisted in anger, "you'll need to keep her alive. It won't be long before they turn on her."

They were right, of course.

But Andi was tired. So tired.

Dex wrapped his arm around Andi's shoulder, pulling her close. "You're the general, love. It's your decision here, what we do next."

"What if I don't want to decide?" Andi asked.

But there were no other leaders left in Mirabel…except one.

Klaren Solis knelt beside Nor, helping her wrap Valen in Nor's cloak. Andi got a final glimpse of his face as they pulled the fabric over his head to cover his eyes. He'd saved the world, but he'd also broken it. So Andi wasn't sure what awaited him on the other side.

"Well?" Gilly asked. "What are we supposed to do now?"

"We destroy the satellite," Andi said, for that decision was obvious.

"And then?"

She sighed. She'd never wanted this. The title of general, the mission to save the galaxy. Mirabel had never loved her. It had seen her, in all of her faults, and called her unworthy.

But when she turned to look at her crew, watching her with such trusting eyes...

There was good in Mirabel. If Klaren, an Exonian, had learned to love it, then perhaps Andi could, too. Or at least she could until she found someone else to whom she could pass along the title.

She kept her gaze on Klaren's back, knowing that it would be so easy to give the responsibility over to her. Klaren would make a fine general, and she could take all the weight of it from Andi's hands. Klaren would gladly take it, for she'd been a queen of Xen Ptera, once, and she'd led the Underground. She was used to ruling, but Andi could see that, deep down, Klaren still loved power.

Still craved it, perhaps as much as Nor.

She'd have to find a way to deal with the two of them. To establish new leaders of the planetary systems, and together, they'd create an entirely new set of fail-safes for the nuclear arsenal. It was staggering to even ponder on such things. To even consider that Andi—a space pirate, and the Bloody Baroness—would have a hand in that.

"Cap?" Gilly asked.

Andi turned back to look at her crew.

Loyal. Honest. Brave.

All of them, waiting on her word.

"It's actually General now, Gil," Andi said, surprised by how the word seemed to feel different now as she said it. Frightening, yes. But it wasn't a role she stepped into alone. She took in all their faces, one by one. Lira. Breck. Gilly. Dex. A family that had faced the very worst and stayed together through it all.

"We're going to do what we've always done," Andi said. "We're going to take it one step at a time. Together."

She had no idea how to run a planet, but she had a team at her side, and together, they would find a way to restart things. To find the right people to put into place.

"But first…" Dex said, turning so that they faced the exit to the satellite. "We're going to blow this thing to bits."

The sun had set, the two moons just beginning to glow in the Arcardian sky.

"Can I do the honors, *please*?" Gilly asked, running past Andi toward the exit, out into the waiting night. The soldiers were already exiting the satellite, walking in a haze as the compulsion wore away and freedom sank back in. It would take time for everyone to regain themselves. To settle back into their own minds.

So many lives had been lost.

Far too many to count.

Still, Andi found herself smiling softly as she watched Gilly rush away. "Breck, make sure she doesn't do anything stupid."

"On it," Breck said, following after Gilly's shadow. "Though I can't make any promises."

Lira looked at Andi and Dex and raised a hairless brow. "They say the estate has a very nice Griss cellar. It was Lon's favorite. In Adhira, we drink for the dead. And I believe there are many souls that need to be honored tonight."

"Go ahead," Andi said with a solemn nod. "We'll catch up soon."

Then she and Dex stepped out into the night. The wind was cold, giving Andi a sudden burst of energy. Soldiers filed out across the estate grounds, ready to head back to their homes, to find the ones they loved.

Klaren and Nor stood waiting in the shadows of the satellite. Klaren nodded knowingly at Andi, as if she sensed that Andi did not trust her fully. As if she sensed that her daughter would have to pay for her crimes. As if she knew that she likely would, too, and was not afraid to face whatever that punishment may be.

"Griss," Dex said. "It's what every fine general would drink after a brutal war."

Andi sighed, taking his hand in hers, squeezing tight. "I don't have time for a drink, Dex. There's work to be done."

He kissed her lightly, smelling of gunpowder and lead. "To-morrow, General."

"Tomorrow?" Andi asked.

He nodded. "Come on, Androma. The galaxy can wait."

She let him lead her away, one step at a time.

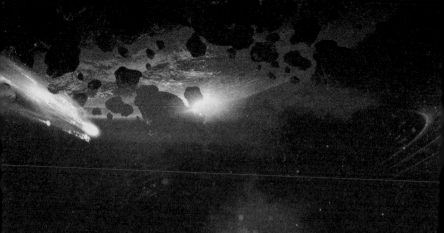

EPILOGUE

SEVERAL MONTHS LATER

Space was silent.

No sound could touch its depths, and even light had to fight to shine in the darkness. Some people, even if given the chance, would never leave their home worlds. Never explore the dramatic swirls of nebulas or witness the explosion of a dying star.

Life in space wasn't for everyone, which was why it was perfect for Andi.

Once, she'd hidden within its dark clutches to shield herself from the past. But no longer would she fear her worst demons. She had fought the fight to win back her soul. And here, above the worlds that were scattered across the expanse, there was peace.

Now she was free.

Andi leaned into Dex, allowing his warmth to engulf her.

"What do you think happened to them?" he said into her hair. "Klaren and Nor?"

Once the satellite had been dismantled, they'd buried Valen, as Andi had guessed they would. A funeral no one attended.

But Andi had slipped into the back of Kalee's garden, where it had been held, and whispered her goodbyes. It wasn't truly forgiveness, but it was better to let go of the hatred. After all, Valen had died a hero in the end.

Klaren and Nor had been sent into exile for their crimes, with trackers installed beneath their skin to keep them in check. They hadn't been heard from since, and Andi hadn't been able to bring herself to personally keep tabs on them, leaving the task to Averia's security team.

"I don't know," Andi said honestly. "But I doubt they'll be coming back."

Nor may have been fighting for the wrong side, but Andi truly believed it hadn't been with malicious intent. She'd loved her people, and even after everything that had transpired, the new leaders of Mirabel had granted the Olen System clemency. Its inhabitants were allowed to dwell anywhere across the galaxy, as long as they didn't return to Xen Ptera.

Not that any of them would willingly return to the barren rock that had brought them so much pain.

The door to the *Marauder*'s lounge opened and the girls walked in. Alfie trailed behind, with Havoc gnawing on the lower leg of his new body. It was almost identical to his old one, with a chrome-plated exterior and exposed mechanical gears whirling in his skull. Havoc's frothy drool dripped down Alfie's leg, pooling onto the floor, but the AI didn't seem to care.

In Andi's short stint as general, she'd ensured that her ship was recovered from the Soleran Wastes. She'd used the best that Arcardius could offer to repair and resupply the *Marauder*, and now it was filled with the people she loved most once again.

Andi and Dex joined the girls at the porthole across the room. "Ready?" she asked Lira.

Her friend gave her a sad smile. "As I'll ever be."

"Memory, turn off the lights," Breck said, and the ship went dark.

Lira turned to face the four of them, eyes twinkling with unshed tears. The only light in the room came from between her fingers.

"On Adhira, when a loved one dies, we send them off with an *Orvana*." She opened her cupped hands to reveal a glowing blue flower. "The Godstars give us life, and it is our duty to live it to the fullest, to light the way for others. But when that light twinkles out, it doesn't merely disappear. It moves to the skies." Andi noticed Lira's scales turning a deep purple. "In our religion, when death takes us, our soul becomes a newborn star. The Godstars made us, and now it is our turn to join them once again."

A tear slipped down Lira's cheek.

"Lon walked his whole life following the light of the Godstars. He was full of hope and wonder, of love and wisdom." She stroked a petal, and it burst with light. "He was a light that shone brighter than all the rest. So for that, I honor you with this *Orvana*."

Lira turned and opened the airlock, placing the flower inside the compartment and then sealing it shut. "I love you, big brother."

Then she placed her hand on the unlatching lever, and with one swift downward pull, the compartment opened and the flower shot out into the stars, its blue light shining bright.

Andi came up behind Lira and enveloped her in a hug. Breck and Gilly joined them, followed by Dex.

They stood like that, watching the flower grow farther and farther away. But even in their sadness, Andi was certain of one thing.

They were a family.

And this was the most content Andi had ever felt.

"Fly true," she whispered.

"Now what?" Gilly asked, shoveling a hunk of cheese into her mouth.

"Red," Breck warned. "Close your mouth when you chew."

Gilly opened her mouth wide and gave Breck a cheeky wink. Lira tried, and failed, to suppress a snicker.

They were in the bridge once more, Lira in her pilot's chair, Andi in her captain's seat and the others scattered across the room.

Dex leaned against the console, twiddling a knife. "I got word from an old Guardian pal that there's a big ransom for a Fiora Kaii. She's been snatching up displaced Xen Pterrans and selling them into unpaid servitude."

Andi had made a name for herself in this galaxy by pirating goods and living outside the law. But maybe it was time to switch sides—not entirely, of course, for she'd given up her General status, handing it over to the one person who terrified her most.

Soyina.

The new general had done well, in the months after the attack. She'd rebuilt the capital city and turned Arcardius back to its military state, while Andi and Dex had helped to appoint leaders across the other planetary systems. Soyina, much to her credit, made a strangely refreshing general, albeit a terrifying one.

And now Andi was free. She knew she was meant for other things, and while the darkness in her was still great, she'd since decided to use it for good.

And if she could make a pretty penny and throw killers and criminals into the deepest pits of Tenebris, then hell. Sign the Marauders up.

Andi quirked a brow. "Ladies, what do you think?"

Breck and Gilly pounded fists. Breck had once rescued Gilly

from slavers, so Andi knew they would be more than ready to fight. "We're in."

"Me, too," Lira said with a wicked smile.

Dex shrugged. "Wherever you go, I'll follow. Captain."

Andi grinned. "Then let's go kick some slaver ass."

★ ★ ★ ★ ★

ACKNOWLEDGMENTS

SASHA ALSBERG

Whether you have made it to the acknowledgments from reading *Nexus*, or are just flipping to the end: Hi! Thanks for being here! Wow, what an adventure this has been.

Lindsay, you are first, because… DUH! You and I have been on this crazy journey together for over three years, and although this chapter is coming to an end, I'm excited for the future—which probably consists of horses and rainbows.

To my boss queen agents, Joanna Volpe and Devin Ross. I cannot put into words how thankful I am to have you both by my side.

Thank you to the entire New Leaf team—Kathleen Ortiz, Mia Roman, Pouya Shahbazian, Hilary Pecheone and Abigail Donoghue—and to Peter Knapp and Park & Fine Literary and Media.

To Lauren Smulski—thank you for believing in us, these rag-tag characters and this galactic world. Also to the fabulous team over at Inkyard Press and Harlequin Canada, as well as Sarah Goodey, Lucy Richardson and the whole team at HarperCollins UK. Forever grateful.

To my entire family and beyond: Dad, Mom, Marisa, Jennifer, Nicole, Stephanie, Marina, Aunt Marcia, Aunt Nancy, Sam Wood, Wanda Wood, Jeff Wood x2, Danielle Wood and Alberto Dagostino. And let us not forget my little beasties, Fraser and Fiona.

To my friends and author buddies: Gabby Gendek, JD Netto, Francina Simone, Laura Steven, Ben Alderson, Taran Matharu, Natasha Polis, Jackie Sawitz, Tobie Easton, Nicole Andrews, Carmen Seda, my BookTube pals (you know who you are!), Alexandra Cristo, Roshani Chokshi, Adam Silvera… Okay, I need to stop here, or else this will go on for pages.

To my online family: Without you, none of this would be possible. XOXO

Oh—and to Scotland. Yes, the country. Don't judge me.

ACKNOWLEDGMENTS

LINDSAY CUMMINGS

It's bittersweet to close out another series, but I have to say... Wow, what a journey everything surrounding The Androma Saga has been.

It's stretched me in more ways than I ever could have imagined, as *Nexus* went through *several* drafts to reach its current state—all in the midst of pregnancy and becoming a mom for the very first time. What a year.

There are many people who helped support me and lift me up during this journey, and I'm always afraid I will forget some of the countless brave hearts who helped guide me along the way. Here we go:

First and foremost, as always, I want to thank God. It's not through my strength, but yours. I am second, you are first, and I am so grateful that you help me see beyond myself.

To my husband, Josh—you are my best friend and my partner in all things. I love you, I love you, I love you.

To my baby boy, Zion. Little Z, you'll never have any idea how much you've done for me—just how far you've pushed me to do better, *be* better, and yet also be wholly myself as I journey into motherhood (and writing books from home, with you in the background, is definitely an adventure, to say the least).

To my parents and sister, I love y'all. You're the best fan club a girl could ever ask for.

To my in-laws and many brothers-in-law, I love you all. Thank you for being in my court.

To my agent, Peter Knapp, I don't think I can ever express to you how grateful I am for our partnership, your steady mind and your guidance. You're the best of the best, and nobody will ever be able to convince me otherwise.

To the team at Park & Fine Media and at New Leaf, thank you for your tireless efforts in championing this duology.

To my church family, my lifegroup family and the other members of the church band: Thank you for loving me just as I am.

To the Duck Danglers (it's a real club, I swear), thanks for helping me keep my cool when the days are long and frustrating.

To Honey: Woman, you're a miracle worker for giving me days to write in silence.

To Harlequin/Inkyard Press and our editor, Lauren Smulski, and everyone who has had a hand in pushing this series to new heights: Thank you. You've made this so much more fun every step of the way!

To every reader, bookseller, teacher, librarian, bloggers, YouTubers and all others involved in the publishing world who have supported this series—our loyal Marauders, THANK YOU.

And lastly, to my coauthor, Sasha Alsberg: Wow, what a wild ride it's been. It started with a simple Twitter poll, and it ended up taking us and our story around the world. It hasn't always been easy, but the work was worth it. We made the dream happen, and I'm so, so grateful for it *all*. ♥

ONE PLACE. MANY STORIES

Bold, innovative and
empowering publishing.

FOLLOW US ON:

@HQStories